SONGS OF HEALING

SONGS OF HEALING

THE DICRANDIA CHRONICLES BOOK 1

R. L. S. HOFF

The Pencil Princess Workshop
Arvada, Colorado

ISBN-13: 978-1-7350742-3-8

Cover design by Maria Spada

Printed in the United States of America

CHAPTER 1

I never should have checked my messages before taking a free afternoon. I scowled at the note from Lady McGivern. "To sum up, your entire proposal is slip-shod, thoughtless, and overbudget, but what should I expect from the illegitimate fifteen-year-old daughter of a decrepit political dynasty?"

Stupid woman. My proposal wasn't that bad, the Peace Party had plenty of life, and I wasn't illegitimate. The whole country had seen the blood tests, not that it was any of their business. I took a couple of deep breaths and set my phone on "do-not-disturb." Even that didn't make me feel better, so I folded the device into the teen fashion magazine my mom had (erroneously) thought I might want to read and put both into the seat pocket in front of me. I hoped neither my guard nor my driver was watching me closely at that particular moment.

Neither of them said anything to me about the phone either then or when they dropped me off at the back entrance to the private half of Peace Park. I let myself in the huge wrought-iron gates, turned around, and waved. I watched the limo pull away, to make sure it left.

Then, since I'd come straight from school, I rushed to the first clearing with a decent-sized boulder, shucked off my school flats, and changed into hiking boots. Until I reached the castle-side gate of the park, two miles from where I stood, I would be alone—no servants, no guards. People somewhere tracked my movements on their map-screens and monitored me whenever I was in range of a camera, and I couldn't leave the walled-in forest, but this was as close to private time as I ever got. I flung my arms out wide and breathed deep, soaking in the smell of new flowers and recent rain.

On my own for the first time in a month, I laughed and spun in a circle until I was so dizzy I tumbled to the ground, hard enough to scrape my hands.

Sure, it was childish. Who cared? There was no one nearby to see, to tell me to act my age, or to freak about the blood trickling from my palms. I stared at the red liquid for a moment before wiping it on my skirt. Yes, I knew skirts were a bad idea in the woods, but I'd already worn pants to school three days in a row and mother insisted I swap out a skirt at least one day of every four. "No, you can't break the rule for your afternoon off," she'd said that morning. "If you didn't want to wear a skirt in the park, you should have thought about that yesterday."

Anyway, there I was, in the woods, in a now blood-stained, knee-length skirt that I couldn't change. (I couldn't imagine the trouble I'd be in if one of the park cameras caught me in my underwear.) Blood welled up on my right palm again. Enough of that already. I scanned the area to make certain nothing and no one was watching and hunched so that if any unseen cameras covered this spot, they wouldn't be able to see my hands. Then I sang a tune my mom's mom had taught me back when I was still a kid. As I sang, the scrapes on my palms grew scabby and itchy, then shiny, then whole. I stopped singing and stared at my hands. No sign remained of my fall except a bit of dirt on one palm.

No matter how many times I did this, it still felt weird. Magic. It wasn't supposed to be real. Only maniacs and babies believed in fairy tales.

So, how could I explain my hands?

I couldn't, so I brushed off the dirt and sauntered down the path, determined to enjoy my afternoon of freedom. Last year's soggy leaves deadened the sound of my footfalls. A chickadee trilled. Breezes carried the scent of pine mixed with lilac to my nose. Tension I hadn't realized I was carrying rolled off my shoulders.

Crack! Was that a gunshot? Someone cried out. They were hurt. Badly hurt, by the sound of it. I ran toward the sound, though I knew it was dangerous, stupid even. I could have been heading into a trap. But somehow, that didn't matter. Something deep inside me compelled me to help. What if I got there too late? I sped up, sure of the direction, though I didn't know how I knew. An invisible line pulled me toward the park border, and I couldn't help following, even when it led through a mess of rhododendrons and raspberry bushes that left red welts on my skin. The compulsion ended when I reached a clearing beneath a great oak tree that grew against the wall.

I knew the compulsion had brought me to the right place when I saw a boy in a tattered and mud-spattered Regency North uniform sprawled face down on the ground. Waves of pain emanated from him, breaking across me like surf.

"Are you OK?" I asked. What a stupid question. Of course, he wasn't OK.

The boy lifted his head, and I caught a flash of brilliant blue eyes. "Prince Philip," I whispered. What was the War Prince doing in Peace Park—my park?

His eyelids flickered. "Of all the rotten luck," he said before sinking back down.

I stepped forward, wincing as the waves of pain intensified. "What's wrong?"

"What a great idea. I'll tell you exactly where I'm injured, so you know where to stomp."

Ouch. That hurt even more than the pain rolling off him. I wasn't that kind of person, was I? Though, how would he know? He only ever saw me in Joint Council meetings and other official functions where I was his opposition. But that was politics. This was real life. I moved closer, within about a pace of him, even though the pain coming from him worsened. "How about we leave the stomping for a day when you're back up to your fighting weight, Your Highness? Where are your guards?"

"Where are yours?"

"I'm in my own park! I can have people here in ten minutes, though." I swung my backpack off my shoulders and dug for my panic button. Before I could reach it, Prince Philip rose on one knee, lunged toward me, and grabbed my wrist. Then the full extent of his injuries crashed into me. On my own face and ribs, I felt the bruises from his; my chest stung with welts I knew laced his. Worse than all the rest was a horrid crunching pain in the leg he wasn't using. I almost fell with the agony of it.

"Don't call anyone," he said, but I had trouble focusing on the words.

I'd felt others' pain before. Any time I got close to someone who was injured or sick, I felt it. This was more painful than anything I'd felt since my grandma died. I closed my eyes, trying to block out the sensations, but they got stronger. Now I could see the ragged, unaligned femur and torn muscles around it. Blackness swam before my eyes. "Let me go."

"Only if you promise not to tell anyone."

I grit my teeth to keep from crying out. "Please let me go get help. You've got a broken leg. You need a hospital."

The prince dropped my hand, and the pain lessened, though I could still feel it.

He asked, "How do you know about my leg? That didn't happen until I fell out of the tree. Joe and the others you encouraged to jump me had already left."

Joe? Did he mean Joe Psalting, his best friend? I wasn't working with that drugged-out jerk, and I couldn't imagine anyone else in my family working with him either. Joe had to be insane, intoxicated, or both to beat up the War Prince and then leave him in Peace Park. He could get both royal families mad at him doing something like that. "Your Highness," I said as gently as I could, "I didn't encourage anyone—and certainly not Joe Psalting—to injure you. I may not like you, but this . . . this is inexcusable."

The prince groaned, and new waves of pain attacked me.

"Please let me go get some help."

"Kid, if you want to help, call Lord Burns. He'll help without asking too many questions."

Kid? I was fifteen, only two years younger than he was. I was about to get into it, but another wave of pain hit, and I decided the argument could wait. "I'd call, but I left my phone in the car. Do you have yours?"

"You think I'd still be here if I had my phone?"

Well, yes, since he'd fallen out of the tree about five minutes ago, but that didn't seem like an argument worth getting into either. "So, what are we going to do? I suppose I could run back to the gate. There's an emergency phone there."

"Forget it. That's no better than your panic button."

"I have a code I could use to call someone other than emergency services."

"Who would you call? I can't have any more Peace people seeing me like this. No. Go away and forget you ever saw me, kid. I'll think of something."

Yeah, like that was going to happen. The prince might be a jerk, but if he died out here, I would never be able to live with myself. Besides, there would be an inquiry, and I'm sure someone would figure out I'd been here. "There is something . . . but you have to promise you won't say anything about what happens here today. To anyone."

"You think I want people to know about this?"

"Promise me."

"If you'll promise the same."

"Deal." I held out my hand to him. He raised himself up and gripped it. His pain slammed into me again, and for a moment, I had trouble concentrating. Then I focused on the leg and started to sing.

My fingers tingled. The pain intensified, and I could see torn flesh and broken bone in gory detail on the inside of my eyelids. I concentrated on that image, bringing the bone into alignment, pulling torn parts together. I heard a soft click, and the prince's hand pulled out of mine.

I opened my eyes. "I wasn't done."

"What did you do?" The prince rubbed his leg, and then scrambled to his feet. "What the Infernal Heights did you do?"

I no longer felt so much pain, but bone-weariness had sunk into my soul. I pushed myself to stand straight, so the prince didn't loom over me. "I'm not sure. I . . . I sing. And sometimes . . ."

"Magic. Like in one of the old legends."

"Well, yeah."

"Impossible."

"I know." I breathed out slowly, catching my breath and trying to read his reaction. Now that he knew, could he keep it to himself? But he had something to tell, whether I finished the job or not. I stepped toward him. "If you'll let me touch you again, I can finish."

"Doesn't it get tiring?"

"Excuse me?"

"In Bengeldon and Windersong—you know, the old tales—when people did too much singing, they always got worn out. Occasionally even croaked."

He was worried about me? I was tired, all right, but I'd felt worse. Lots worse. I laughed. "Your Highness, Bengeldon and Windersong are myths."

"Myths? Kid, you sang my leg from excruciating to better than normal. You were probably right before about it being broken, but it sure doesn't feel like it is now. Unless you secretly hit me with a painkiller . . ."

"Don't call me kid. I have a title."

"Excuse me, Your Highness." He bowed, deeply enough for me to feel like he was mocking me. "Princess Sarah, I deeply appreciate your help, and I can't say that I'd be heartbroken if you decided to martyr yourself, but if you peg out while we're together in Peace Park, that'll make the mess I'm in right now feel like eating pie at a provincial fair."

I wanted to pull out my hair. He was always a better debater than I was, and I didn't know how to make him see I was fine. I'd done more than this in an afternoon before, and it wasn't that big a deal.

Well, maybe not more than this, but I'd certainly healed as much that time my horse stepped in a prairie dog hole when we were visiting Westerville. And I'd already fixed the biggest problem—the leg. I could do more without danger to myself. But how could I convince him? I didn't want him going home looking like he did now—someone would see, and that wouldn't be good for either of us. "You have a point, Your Highness."

"Yes, I do."

How could he be so full of himself? "And I'd agree with you, except I don't feel all that tired yet. I have some idea of my limits. Besides, what are you going to do, walk out the back gate looking like you're dressed for a pantomime on grave-sweeping day? No way can you get all the way to the other side of town without someone seeing you."

"I don't have a choice. Even if you fixed everything wrong with me, There's still the mess on my clothes. Unless you can magically clean and repair them, too."

No, I couldn't do that. Not that I knew of, anyway. "I could . . ."

"What?"

"I don't know. Maybe it's a bad idea, but I have a place with running water and some spare clothes. My cousin Andy always leaves a set there."

"I'm not going into the Peace Palace."

Because we had so many choices. I sighed. "I said my place, not my parents' place. Come or not, it's up to you. But if you decide to risk the streets in your current state, don't mention me when people ask you what happened." I turned and headed out of the clearing, as if I didn't care whether he came along.

After a long moment, when I heard him follow, I let out the breath I'd been holding.

I skirted the rhododendron and raspberries as much as I could, then retraced the route I'd taken to find him. It was easy to see the broken bushes and deep footprints. I frowned at them. I didn't usually leave such destruction in my wake going through the woods.

Soon I found a trail and picked up the pace. I didn't know how much time we had before security people, or worse, reporters showed up, but it wouldn't do for either group to find me with Prince Philip. I moved even faster.

His Insufferableness matched my stride without complaint or even apparent strain. I was grudgingly impressed. Most people either fell back or started whining when I led them through the woods.

Fifteen minutes later, the prince still wasn't having any trouble with my pace—and he was in pain. I could feel it now and then, slapping into me across the space between us.

We had nearly reached the heart of my private world before I fully considered the consequences of bringing him here. I slowed, suddenly unwilling to crest the last hill.

"Everything OK?" he asked.

"I don't bring a lot of people here."

"Well, I'm not really here."

I laughed nervously. "You might not talk, but you'll still remember. It's too late to do anything else, though." I paused, sighed, and then led him over the rise. There it was—a tiny stone cottage nestled against the far side of a little ravine. A curving path edged with herbs and star flowers led from its front door to a glistening pool. On our left, a tinkling fall of water fell over the face of a shallow cave into that same pool.

"Wow," the prince said.

That's exactly what I thought every time I stood in this spot. I glanced at the prince, but couldn't read his expression, so I plunged downward to a sandy path that circled the pool to the waterfall and then dropped down three flat steps into the cave behind it. I reached out my right hand, so that the water could pass through my fingers. The prince laughed. He had a surprisingly nice, warm laugh.

Moments later, we were at the cottage door. I swung it open and stared at the small trestle table in front of me, where six dolls sat, posed for dinner. I wanted to sink through the cottage's front stoop. My face heated. "Looks like I didn't clean up after the last time my baby cousins were here." I stepped forward and swept up the nearest doll.

The prince put a hand on my arm. "I promised I wouldn't tell anyone about our afternoon. Any of it. Even if I hadn't promised, I wouldn't tell this. I have limits, kid."

And now he was back to calling me kid, though I supposed I deserved it this time, seeing how I got caught still playing with doll babies. Still, he seemed sincere about not telling anyone. Was it possible he got as tired as I did of people thinking he was heartless?

Slowly I put the doll back and pointed toward a little door in the corner. "Washroom's there. I'll get the clothes."

He ducked in and started the water. "You know, this is a nice place. I wish I had something like it."

I laughed. "My family thinks it's childish."

"So, let them think. It's keeping you sane, isn't it?"

"I'll get those clothes," I repeated instead of answering.

Upstairs in the cottage, I had to stoop. I wasn't short enough to stand in the child-sized rooms anymore. It only took a moment to find Andy's duffel bag where I'd stuffed it in a cupboard under a doll changing table. I dragged it out, peeked inside, then sat, hugging it to my chest. What was I doing with the War Prince in my dollhouse? And how was I supposed to handle him being nice? Our families didn't work that way. Never had.

"Find anything?" his voice came up from below. "I'll need at least a new shirt. This one's past hope."

"Yeah." I got up and crawled to the stairs. He stood at the bottom, his face wet and shiny. He held a bloody washcloth to his nose. I tossed him the duffel.

He scrounged inside, pulling out a t-shirt, some sweats, and a pair of sneakers, which he turned over. "Too small." He put the sneakers and sweats back in the bag. "Do you have masking tape?"

"Art supplies are behind the cornflower tea pot."

He rummaged through my art box, tossing items onto the table as I came down the stairs. Crayons, glitter, smiley stickers. I cringed every time he pulled out something new. If he'd thought I was a kid before, what would he think now? Fortunately, he didn't comment on any of it until he found the masking tape.

"Got it," he said, disappearing into the washroom again. I heard him bumping into things, and then more water running.

When he came out, he was shirtless. Even without the angry red stripes, his chest would have been an arresting sight. Taut, well-muscled. I forced my gaze away, to examine the tear in his pants. To my surprise, I could hardly see it. "I'm impressed," I said, not sure whether I meant his mending job or his torso.

He smiled in a way that made my face heat up again. "Mom taught me to do emergency repairs years ago. She sure gets mad when I come home messed up."

That sounded like my mom. I giggled, sounding silly and nervous. What was with me? I had to get myself under control. I took a moment to focus, then said, "I assume you want me to fix up your face?"

"And anything else that will be visible."

I nodded and walked around the table so that I could get close enough to touch him. I couldn't stop thinking about his eyes—and his bare chest. What was it about him that made me react so strongly? I'd seen guys without their shirts before. All the same, my fingers shook as I brought them to his face. My song sounded ragged, but the nose healed. Then I touched the puffy bruise around his left eye, and I forgot everything but the pain. My hand steadied as I sang healing into the abused tissue.

There was more to do, but I was tiring. "Give me a second." I leaned against the wall.

"Do we need to stop?"

Never admit weakness in front of War Royalty. Father's voice echoed in my head.

"I'm OK," I said.

"Are you sure? I could get by now." He sounded warm—maybe even concerned about me. My father would tell me not to believe it. Besides, the job wasn't done.

"Your lip is still cracked. I'll be fine if I rest for a moment."

"It's your funeral." He started pacing—three steps away from me, three steps back. On his fourth return, he stopped and asked, "Why are you helping me?"

"You need help."

"Sure, but you could have gone to a phone or pushed your panic button."

"You were right—that would have created a media frenzy."

"What do you care? It would have been good press for you."

"No, it would have been bad press for you. That's not the same thing. Besides, you were hurting. No-one I could call would have been able to fix that as quickly as I did."

"Again, what do you care?"

"Maybe it's stupid, but I can't leave someone in pain, not even my worst enemy." I pushed myself away from the wall. "I'm ready now. Let's finish this." My hands didn't tremble at all while I sang healing into his lip, chest and arms, but as I was finishing, I stumbled.

Prince Philip caught and steadied me. "Are you alright, kid?"

"Fine, but you might not be if you keep calling me kid. The name's Sarah." I pushed him away.

He chuckled. "You shouldn't threaten people when you can't stand up, Your Highness."

I glared at him. He grinned and stepped toward me. I backed up and stumbled again. This time when he caught me, he didn't let go. "I'm sorry I questioned your motives. It's been a bad day, and you . . . you're unexpected."

"Your Highness—"

"Call me Phil."

I smiled up at him.

"Hey, Sarah!" someone shouted. The door slammed open. My cousin Andy stood in the doorway, panting. His eyes darted from me to the prince.

I jumped back, away from Phil. "Andy! What are you doing here?" Why didn't Andy say anything?

"Cripes," Andy said.

I stepped farther back. "What's going on?"

"At least six wall-jumpers in the last half hour, and your guards can't reach you. I've never seen them so pissed. They're searching the woods. I thought you might be here—came to warn you. You have ten minutes, tops."

I nodded and glanced at Phil. He seemed frozen.

I grabbed the t-shirt and shoved it at him. "Put this on. Andy, you've got to get him out of here. Use the back gate."

"No good. *Star Snoop* is parked back there."

Star Snoop? Who tipped them off? Not that it mattered right now. "The East Street entrance then."

"That turnstile requires a pass for each person, and it's nigh on impossible to fool."

I strode to my shelves, took two carefully hoarded passes from a cedar handkerchief box, and tossed one to each boy. "Get out of here. And Andy, if anyone hears about this, I'll make your life miserable for the next thirty years."

The guys raced out the door. I felt like watching to be sure they disappeared quickly, but I didn't have time. I had to get the bloody washcloths out of the bathroom, Philip's old shirt hidden somewhere, the art box cleaned up . . .

When the straggle-haired freelance photographer found me five minutes later, the cottage showed no sign of my afternoon adventures. His camera flashed on me putting away the last of the doll tea party.

CHAPTER 2

I'd never seen my parents so angry.

I wondered how this would have gone if that reporter had caught me with Phil still in my dollhouse. I smiled.

"You think this is funny?" Dad's beard bristled, and his dark eyes flashed.

"Darling," Mom said, though her darker eyes also flashed. "Quietly. There are still reporters in the house."

"That's what we're talking about—reporters in the house! How are we supposed to deal with the crazy proposal War is bringing to Joint Council this weekend when we're doing damage control?"

Mom shook her head. "We'll figure it out. We always do. But, Sarah, that doesn't make what you did all right. Leaving your phone was dangerous. You could have been hurt."

"How could my phone have helped? I still had my panic button." It was working, too. I'd pushed it the second the reporter broke into my dollhouse, and guards caught him before he got out of the ravine. He'd already beamed his pictures out, though. School tomorrow would be a treat.

"If you'd had your phone, we could have warned you he was coming," Mom said.

"And ruined my only free afternoon this month."

"Your mother's right," Dad said, so quietly I shivered. "It was dangerous to stay in that man's path. You do know how your grandfather died, don't you?"

Ouch. He was hitting me with that? Of course, I knew about the assassination that killed my grandfather before I was born. Everybody knew about the assassination. "Dad, it was just a reporter."

"We didn't know that. And if he got a picture, he could have gotten a shot."

"But he didn't. I'm fine. And you know that's not the way assassinations work—they have to know where you are, not blunder around on a vague tip, hoping to bump into you, like that guy did today. I wouldn't have even been in the dollhouse if I hadn't needed to . . ." I cut myself off. I couldn't believe I'd almost spilled about Phil. That couldn't happen. But what could I say that wouldn't sound suspicious? I needed to think. Fast. Then I had it. It was even true—sort of. ". . . use the bathroom."

"You needed to use the bathroom?" Dad's eyebrows lifted nearly to his hairline.

"Yes. Use the bathroom," I repeated, "I assume you didn't want me going in the bushes?"

"And once you'd finished, you decided to have a doll tea party?"

"Well, the dolls were right there. I figured I might as well enjoy them. It's not like I expected to be interrupted." My face heated like it did every time I lied. Why did I have to start making things up?

"You *did* expect to be interrupted?" Dad said.

Well, of course, as soon as Andy showed up with his news about reporters. But I couldn't tell Mom and Dad that. "Not when I went to the dollhouse," I said, staring at my shoes. Direct eye contact right now would convince him I was lying, I was sure.

The room stilled. Mom stood, gazing at Dad, like she was posing for a magazine cover. Dad stared at the mosaic on the floor. It was a traditional thorn-and-rose pattern, maybe a couple of centuries old. Not engrossing enough for such an intense stare. Not half as interesting as the ancient tapestry on the wall behind Mom and Dad that showed some battle scene. Darrick Harbor, maybe? I wondered how it wound up in our palace instead of over in War. Was the tapestry older than the War palace? That would make it way old. Thinking of old, how old was I going to be by the time my parents started talking again?

Finally, Dad said something. "You never used to lie, Sarah."

"And you were on me about it all the time."

"Don't get snarky with me, young lady. You know I never meant for you to keep things from us."

Guilt twisted in my gut, but I couldn't tell them about the prince. I'd promised I wouldn't. "So, how long am I grounded for?"

Mom smiled at me. "Actually, your father and I have decided not to ground you this time."

"Seriously?"

Dad nodded, slowly. "That's right. Your mother and I have decided it's time you start cleaning up your own messes. Since your escapade hurts our chances of defeating War's ridiculous camp proposal in the Joint Council this year, the proposition is now your project."

"What? No."

"You have to get more involved in the legislative side sometime, sweetheart, and this is a nice easy project to start with."

I'd never killed a War proposition on my own before, but I'd seen Dad and Uncle Malcolm do it. It took intense attention for weeks. "I'm not sure I'm ready," I said, hoping there was some way out.

"Let's find out. I'll have the proposition's casebook and today's newspapers sent to your room."

"But, Da-ad—"

"You got yourself into this mess. You're going to get yourself out. Zelda, darling, is the group from Mega-Conglomerated Oil still waiting?"

"In the Southeast Sunroom, my heart. Lord Richter's entertaining them."

"Richter supports the Green Coalition!"

"But we couldn't send . . ."

I listened to their voices fade as they got farther and farther away. How could they have foisted this battle off onto me?

How I wished they'd grounded me instead.

Chapter 3

When I got to my tower, a white, three-ring binder almost three inches thick sat on my desk. Why did we still make hard copies of these things? Wouldn't it be easier and more environmentally sound to compile and send digitally? I made a note to myself to ask about it and sank into my desk chair. Best to get it over with.

I flipped open the binder and thumbed through the first few blank plastic-sleeved pages until I got to the title page, which listed the proposition's number, title, and sponsor—Walter Cagnew, the junior representative from Silvershire.

I'd never heard of him.

The proposition seemed familiar, though. In fact, I was sure I'd seen something similar, perhaps even identical, last year. And the year before that. And the year before that. The name of the proposition and the sponsor might change, but the proposition itself never did. It called for two-week camps for high school students in four Northwestern provinces. The young people would be taught to defend their homes from the occasional wild animal attacks and outlaw raids the area faced.

"What's wrong with that?" I'd once asked Uncle Malcolm, who wasn't really my uncle, but my parents' friend and the highest-ranking Peace official in the country after my father.

He'd smiled sadly. "If War wanted to help remote areas defend themselves, they'd suggest camps for parts of the western mountains and some coastal counties. Those areas have trouble with animals and outlaws, too. But War only wants to help the Northwest. We're pretty sure they just want to influence the voting in a swing area."

I should have known that. Unlike the coast, which always voted Peace, or the western mountains, which reliably voted War, the Northwest voted War or Peace depending on its mood. But if War got time to indoctrinate every kid about to vote in those provinces, they could probably change that. They'd certainly try. "So, we kill this one," I said.

"We kill it," Uncle Malcolm confirmed.

And we did—every year when it came up, we stopped it before it could even get a hearing in the full Congress. Before, I'd helped block the bill. Now, I had to do it on my own. I sighed. Since I'd helped before, it wouldn't be too hard, but I'd still have to read all the materials and do all the groundwork.

I drew the casebook closer to me and noticed it was a lot thicker than I remembered. The proposition was the same, and the arguments supporting it hadn't changed, but the evidence section was huge, full of police write-ups; newspaper reports; blog accounts and links to amateur videos. These detailed dozens and dozens of violent incidents in the Northwest this spring. Some terrorist had blown up a car next to a general store in a Westerberg village. I remembered seeing something about that on the news.

Another article told of a group of green-clad outlaws who had burnt down a dozen farms in Silvershire and begun to attack a village when the local militia surrounded them and captured all but one. I'd read about that before, too, but I hadn't seen this stuff about the escaped leader blasting people with light that sprang from his fingertips. What was this paper, *The Investigator*? No. It was a local paper linked to a reputable alliance of news organizations. Weird.

I shook my head and flipped the page. The stories went on and on. Looting here. Wolves immune to rifles there. Immune to rifles? Come on. More likely, the hunters weren't as good as they thought they were.

Even discounting the patently ridiculous stuff, I had to admit the Northwest had a problem—lots of injuries, lots of damage. Even an entire village destroyed. I rubbed my forehead. Was it this bad in previous years? I didn't think so, but I supposed I'd better check. I put in an archive request for the casebooks from similar propositions in the last five years. Then I pushed the casebook away. I needed to think about something else.

As if in answer to my need, someone knocked on the door. Surely that wasn't the other casebooks already?

When I opened the door, a freckled twenty-something in round glasses dumped a weighty stack of newspapers into my arms. He was a newish member of staff. George, if I remembered his name right. "Newspapers," he said, turning toward the stairway.

"Newspapers?"

"Your f-father said to deliver them."

"Oh. Right. Thank you."

Before I finished talking, George dashed down the stairs. I shook my head after him. New staff often took a while to get used to being around royals, but this one was taking longer than most. It wasn't a lack of ability. A few days before, I'd overheard him talking intelligently about Androlian poetry. But he stammered and disappeared quickly whenever he saw me.

I dumped the papers on my desk and forgot everything else.

"Princess's Petit Party," the *Daily Sun* joked over a six-by-eight picture of me setting the teapot on a shelf, a doll under my arm. "Royal Rebel!" screamed the *Evening Post* next to a picture of me being dragged into a van near the back gate of the park. I'd thought I was cooperating at the time, but the picture made it look like I was a criminal resisting arrest. No wonder my parents were upset.

I flipped back to the Daily Sun. My own mug stared back at me from the front page, challenging the world to care that I was having tea with dolls I was supposed to have outgrown years ago. Or that I wore hiking boots below my pleated navy skirt. And a ball cap over my stringy dark hair. And scratches on my knobby knees.

I took in a sharp breath. No wonder Phil had called me a kid. Did I really look like that?

I swung toward the mirror on the back of my closet door. It was me, all right. Why hadn't anyone ever told me I looked like such a goose? I yanked off my cap, but it didn't help much. My hair was still stringy, and my face seemed impossibly young. I squeezed back little tears. I hated to cry. Anger was better. But I hardly knew who to be angry with.

I was still standing in front of the mirror when I heard the next knock on my door.

"Supper will be served in twenty minutes, Your Highness," a muffled voice said.

I usually ignored the twenty-minute warning, waiting until the last possible second to jump into something dressy enough to pass muster at my parents' table. Since I was thinking about how I looked anyway, I decided to dress.

In my walk-in closet, a short, spangly, red dress lay on the clotheshorse. I liked red, but that dress always made my knees seem huge. I hung it back on its rack and thumbed through my other dresses. Most had the same problem as the red one. The pastel pink silk was longer, but I disliked the color, and I'd worn my dressy navy pantsuit six times in the last two weeks. The last time, my mother had told me it would be permanently removed from my closet if I wore it again before May.

I grimaced. There was nothing else there except a long, cream-colored, chiffon skirt. I'd brought it down from a box in the attic to use as a cloud in an impromptu play some friends and I staged one rainy afternoon. It must have gotten dumped in my laundry because a week later it had appeared on the dressy rack of my closet, cleaned, pressed and shimmering.

I pulled it out. The shimmers were little gold flecks in the creamy layers. I wondered if it would fit. What would I wear with it if it did? My shiny brownish-gold blouse? And pearls? I dug through my cubbyholes and boxes. I knew I had a slip somewhere.

"Five minutes, Your Highness," a voice said.

"Thank you," I shouted around the comb I held between my teeth as I pinned up my hair.

Finished, I inspected my reflection. Not too bad. The skirt billowed in soft puffs, hiding the scrawniness of my legs. For once I didn't look too thin. Just tall.

"One minute," the voice said with a hint of panic.

"Coming!" I laughed. It usually took me twice that long to make it to the dining room from my tower. I gathered up my skirt and ran. I couldn't afford to be late for supper.

CHAPTER 4

I halted my dead run a few feet before the double doors to the formal dining room. Hastily checking my hair in a mirrored panel, I pushed the doors open.

My mother, a few Peace Council members, and a couple of older gentlemen were standing around the table. Mother frowned at my breathlessness, but one of the older gentlemen stepped up to me, smiled, and held out his hand. When I gave him mine, instead of shaking it, he lifted it to his papery lips for a moment, and then closed his other hand on top of it. "It's a pleasure to meet you at last, Princess Sarah."

I managed not to grimace as I murmured, "Thank you," and gently drew my hand away. Who was this creep? He must have been important since he hadn't bothered to introduce himself. If I'd glanced at the notes my parents always sent up before dinner, I might have known. Too bad I'd forgotten. I resisted the urge to rub the spot the man's lips had touched.

Fortunately, a fanfare announced Dad's arrival, and I was able to escape the old guy without any further interaction. Everybody found their seats, and dinner began.

The elderly gentleman with the kissing hang-up was apparently Walter VanderHausen of Mega-Conglomerated Oil. The other older guy was his brother Henry. Both were non-stop talkers. They praised the Peace Palace grounds and the Peace Party's views on environmental regulations. I caught my dad's eye when I heard that but decided to say nothing when he frowned at me. Instead, I sat patiently, nodding at the continuous chit-chat. It was worse than a bad commercial.

When dinner finished, the adults moved to the drawing room for coffee and more talk. I was glad it was a school night, and I had an excuse to slip back upstairs. I said goodnight, forced a smile when Walter VanderHausen again kissed my hand, and exited slowly and gracefully. My antique skirt billowed around me. I liked the way it floated, making me feel like I was sailing serenely down a gentle river. I closed my eyes and two steps later, tripped over the edge of an area rug. My skirt got caught up in my next step, and I set all the crystal and silver knick-knacks on a nearby table rattling as I bumped it on my way to the floor.

"Are you all right, Princess Sarah?"

Of course, someone would see that. "Fine," I snapped.

"G-good. I'd b-better be going, then."

Too late, I realized it was George who had seen me. And I'd yelled at him. Bother. "George," I said before he was out of earshot.

He turned.

"Y-yes, Your Highness?" His ears were turning pink.

"I'm sorry. I didn't mean to speak so sharply. The truth is, I was walking along with my eyes closed, and when I tripped on the rug, I felt foolish. I shouldn't have taken it out on you."

George smiled. "I g-guess I'm lucky nobody was around t-to watch me growing up. Will there be anything else?"

"No. Thank you, George."

He bowed slightly and backed away.

Well, that went better than most conversations with him. I wondered if he'd ever feel comfortable working around me. I shook my head and continued toward my tower. This time I kept my eyes open.

Back in my room, the casebooks I'd ordered were piled on my desk. I flipped through the top one—a forest fire, a wolf pack near a village, a group of bandits, and a child's disappearance. There was nothing as serious as the stories in this year's casebook. What was the date? 10605, five years ago. I found the next one. More of the same. 10607 and 10608 were similar. Last year's casebook was slightly thicker with a few disturbing incidents just before the proposition was written, but nothing like this year's.

I pulled this year's book toward me. It was three times bigger than any previous one. The events it documented were more serious. Was this year that much worse? I swung to my computer and drummed my fingers on the desk while I waited for it to start up.

Eventually, I got online but wasn't sure where to search. The databases I usually used for school and work projects had articles from research journals and big-city papers. But those papers weren't carrying these stories. My parents made me read Bentralia's *Daily Sun* and the *Dreamvale Liberal Investigator* every day. On Sundays, I had to read the *Mendovia Times* and the *Evening Post*, too. Stories about rifle-immune wolves or guys who shot lightning from their fingers would have caught my eye. Unless they were in the lifestyle or entertainment sections. I didn't usually bother with lifestyle, and I avoided entertainment on principle—too many stories about my family.

After I put "attacks" into a general search engine, the machine whirred for a minute and then came back with nearly two million entries. The first one was about asthma. The next three concerned soccer.

With "wolf attacks," the first few pages of results included four urban legend sites and dozens of fringe sites that accused the government and media of conspiring to hide the evidence of werewolves. As the third-ranking member of the Peace Party, I knew whatever the government knew and was sure we didn't have any evidence of werewolves to hide. Unless you counted the articles in the casebook. Conspiracy sites certainly did. Of course, they also posted first-hand accounts of alien kidnappings and documentation about me performing miraculous feats in towns I'd never visited.

This was not helping. I pushed away from my computer, got up, and walked around the room. What was I trying to do? How would this help me defeat the stupid camp proposition?

I stopped in front of the clock. Eleven. Maybe I should leave the problem for morning.

I was hanging up my blouse when it hit me: My research wasn't going to help me defeat the proposition. It was going to help me decide whether I should.

I breathed in sharply. A cool breeze from a round window high above me tickled my shoulders, making me shiver.

I'd never disagreed with my father on politics before. When he told me to vote a certain way, I did it. Occasionally I asked why first, but I did it. But if unprecedented, inexplicable violence was spreading through the Northwest, it didn't matter what my dad said. I wouldn't fight this proposition. The Northwest needed it.

Standing up, I threw a shawl over my shoulders and went back to the computer. I had to find out the truth. This time, before searching, I thumbed through the casebooks. Most of the evidence came from small-town newspapers, but some were police reports and applications to the Peace Relief Fund. I jotted down some names, pulled up a map, and plotted this year's incidents in red, last year's in blue, incidents from two years ago in green, and ones from five years ago in purple. Then I went looking for evidence of more blue, green or purple dots.

However many small-town newspaper archives I scrolled through, or however many Peace Relief records I browsed, I couldn't find any events from previous years that weren't already on my map. I found half a dozen more from this year, though. By three in the morning, I was sure this year's problems were unique. I had to do something.

But what? Sure, the proposition could easily get through Joint Council if I didn't fight it. War had a majority there. Once through, though, it would flounder in the Peace-controlled main Congress. It would take months, clog up the system, and not pass in the end. After all, everyone would assume the proposal had passed Joint Council because I couldn't do my job. No one would believe I'd let it pass on purpose. As Prince Philip reminded me all afternoon, I was just a kid. Nobody ever took me seriously.

I smiled. Maybe it wasn't entirely bad that nobody took me seriously. I grabbed paper from my printer and scribbled a plan. Names, a schedule, bits of speeches, and pieces of law.

I was still scribbling when the morning gong woke the palace at five.

CHAPTER 5

The gong echoed through the passages up to my tower. I lifted my pen from my paper. All around me, balls of crumpled white and yellow paper lay scattered among sheets full of my black scrawl. If I left this mess out, someone was sure to sweep my plan into a waste-paper basket along with the false starts.

I stood, stretching lazily from side to side, then backward until my hands were flat on the floor. I couldn't believe I'd been up all night. Feeling loose, but strangely alert, I collapsed out of my backbend, stood back up, stepped over my papers, and padded toward my balcony. Pale light washed through the etched glass of the doors onto the never-used, ornate, flowered chairs my mother insisted I keep in my room for entertaining guests.

I frowned at the chairs. A place to meet guests was a decent idea, but I didn't like floral patterns or ornate wooden detailing. That was my mother's style, not mine.

I yanked open the balcony doors with more force than necessary.

Cool air hit my arms and midriff. It felt cleansing after my night's work. I walked out to the marble paling and leaned against the balustrade. Off to my left, two tiny figures were cranking open the kitchen gate with difficulty. It probably needed to be oiled. And why hadn't it been converted to electric power when the rest of the castle gates were?

Did I seem as small to the people on the ground as they did to me? Suddenly, remembering my green-shawled, hair-specked-with-paper state, I backed from the edge of the balcony and ran back inside.

Ten after. Plenty of time to get ready for school, clean up, and work some more on my project.

If I was going to pull off official meetings, I needed to seem more grown-up than usual. Digging under my bathroom counter, I located the conditioner my mom had suggested I try. It was in the back, behind a tub of unopened make-up, a box of unused hair accessories, two half-used bottles of bubble-blowing mixture, an assortment of untouched face cleansers, two brand new loofahs, and a perfume sampler someone had given me the previous New Year. I left everything where I'd dumped it while I showered. The floral scent of the conditioner was overwhelming, and I hoped it was worth it.

The part of my closet devoted to school uniforms was small and frustratingly full of plaid pleated skirts that stopped just above my knobby knees. Since my three pairs of school pants were dirty, that left my jumper, which made me look about ten years old, and a pair of crazy, full-legged silk pants I'd never worn. No one had worn that piece of the uniform in at least a decade. I'm sure mom only bought them because they were silk.

Since that day in the store, I'd never had them on. But today, I was in the mood for something different. At least these were pants. I pulled them on, chose a white shirt instead of the light blue one, and then remembered my best school flats were in yesterday's backpack. While putting on my second-best pair, I wondered where the security people dumped the bag after yesterday's fiasco—or if they'd even grabbed it from the dollhouse while they were hustling me out of there. Fortunately, I didn't have homework yesterday, so there was nothing critical I needed from the bag.

I examined myself in the mirror. All right if you didn't count the hair. It was still limp. I could run a comb through it, but since that was what I did every day, it probably wasn't enough. I went back to my desk and stared at the phone. Its digital display glowed 5:30 at me. My best friend Steph wouldn't be up for another fifteen minutes. Andy wouldn't get up for an hour and wouldn't be any help whether he was up or not. Gen was a new enough friend that I wasn't sure when she got up, and I wasn't sure her hair was enough like mine for her advice to be helpful.

I bit my lip. Finally, I picked up the receiver and dialed my mother's extension.

"Morning, darling." Mom yawned. "Did you sleep well?"

I froze. I couldn't tell her I hadn't slept at all. "Uh . . . um . . . well, I was a little worried about this project."

"Oh, sweetie. You know, if it's too hard for you, your dad and I could discuss it again."

"No, no. It's fine. Actually," I took a deep breath. "I was calling about something else." I took another deep breath. "How do you get hair to stop being limp?"

I could almost hear Mom straighten up. "Well, darling, it's simple. You'll want to mousse it, give it a good blow-dry, and then put in a little curl for fullness."

I yelped. "That could take hours! And I need to look good today."

"No problem. I'll send Estelle over."

"Estelle?"

"Certainly. We should have been getting your hair done professionally for years now, but your father said to wait until you asked."

"Oh!" I'd never imagined that the professional primping sessions I endured before formal state dinners and big media events would become a daily part of my life the second I expressed interest in my hair. I wished I'd awakened Steph.

"Are you still there, darling?" Mom asked.

"Yes."

"I've upset you, haven't I? Oh, honey, you don't have to do it if you don't want to. You sounded ready."

Ready? Would I ever be ready for daily sessions with a hairstylist? Why couldn't my life be reasonably normal?

"Sarah?"

I had to say something. Taking another deep breath, I managed to sound calm. "I was just a little shocked. But I need help with my hair. When should I expect Estelle?"

"I'll send her right over. I don't have anywhere to be until nine. And darling?"

"Yes?"

"We'll talk this weekend about how regularly you want help."

"Thanks, Mom." At least I wouldn't have to think about significant lifestyle adjustments for a couple of days.

✳✳✳

Estelle had been fussing with my hair for twenty minutes when Clare Dunham, my only female bodyguard, pushed open the bedroom door.

I smiled. "I forgot it was your first day on the school shift."

Clare didn't smile back. She was holding my backpack.

"Wow, Clare. Thanks. I was wondering how I'd get that back."

"You haven't got it back yet. I've got a few questions to ask you first."

"Estelle, are we almost done?" I asked.

"Absolutely." Estelle fluffed more and then left.

I glanced at my reflection. Not too bad. I was no beauty, like my mom, but I didn't look like a kid. I turned to Clare. "Questions about what?"

"Bloody clothes and washcloths in the dollhouse."

"Ah—those." I thought fast. It was probably best to tell as much of the truth as I could without giving the prince away. "Yesterday, I ran into a friend near the back gate. He'd been in a fight. I took him to the dollhouse to get cleaned up but shoved him off when I got wind of reporters coming. We couldn't afford to get caught together."

"Getting caught having a doll tea party was better?"

"Definitely."

"Do you see this young man often?"

I wasn't sure how to answer, so I talked slowly, thinking through each word. "Fairly often, but we're not generally alone together."

"You realize that arranging to meet young male friends alone in the woods will look bad when it's found out?"

"Of course. I'm not a moron. We didn't arrange to meet. I was hoping for an afternoon *alone*."

"And this friend just happened to be there?"

"Unlikely as it sounds, yes."

"You know I've signed an agreement not to discuss what you do with anyone, even your parents, right?" Clare said. "But to protect you, I should know if you've got a secret boyfriend who is in the habit of getting in fights."

I laughed. Prince Philip my boyfriend?

"It's not funny," Clare said. "If you can't be honest with me, they need to find you someone else for this job."

I stopped laughing. Clare was my favorite guard. Would telling her break my agreement with Phil? Maybe, but security people were usually good at keeping secrets.

I hoped I wasn't making a mistake. "Clare, the guy was Prince Philip. I helped him, but we're not dating." I chuckled. "Or even good friends. It won't happen again." And that was almost a pity. I liked meeting Phil for real. I wondered if he felt the same about me.

Clare gaped and dropped the backpack onto my vanity. "Are you out of your mind?"

"Probably, but I can't stop to worry about it. I have a massive political campaign to organize."

Clare shook her head and muttered something about "too much for fifteen," as she backed toward her post by the doorway.

I smiled and picked up the phone. I called Steph first.

"Honestly, Sarah. A doll tea party? Of all the wild and crazy things you could do on an afternoon off, you have a doll tea party?"

I imagined the twinkles in Steph's eyes. "There's a reason those half-holidays are supposed to be private."

"Yeah. Frankly, I can't believe anyone was willing to brave all the extra security for that. I mean, they got pictures and all, but it's not that big a story. I bet this news about Prince P. breaking up with his girlfriend will preempt you before lunch."

"Ph—the prince has—had a girlfriend?" I felt strangely hollow.

Steph laughed. "You sound shocked. Don't you ever read celebrity news?"

"You know I try not to."

"True. Well, the prince has a new girlfriend once every month or so. One of the many reasons why I'm not interested in dating him."

"He's asked?" I felt an unreasonable jolt of jealousy. Phil's interest in Steph shouldn't matter to me.

"Nah. Dad lets me know every time there's a break-up in hopes that I'll jump on the opportunity."

Oh. Of course, Lord Montressor would want his daughter to hook up with the War Prince. Steph's dad was fourth on the War Council. "I guess that makes sense."

"Not when I'm already dating someone."

That's right. Steph and Andy had been quietly going out for a couple of weeks. "So, you've told your parents about you and Andy?"

"Well, not exactly. But they know I'm interested in a guy on Regency North's baseball team."

"Steph, *the prince* is on Regency North's baseball team, too."

"Oh, right. Somehow I never see him when I'm watching Andy's games."

I laughed. "I don't see how you could miss him, the way they announce over there."

"Sarah, did you call me just after the crack of dawn to talk about the prince and baseball?"

"No, sorry. It's this project my parents are making me do as punishment for yesterday."

"Punishment? You didn't do anything wrong."

"I left my phone in the limo. When they tried to contact me about people climbing the fence, I wasn't available."

"And they're making you do some project? That's crazy. Can I help?"

"I hope so. It's more than I can handle on my own. But will your dad let you?"

"We're best friends," Steph said. "He needs to get over it. Tell me what you want me to do."

"Do you think you could set up a meeting for us with the proposition's sponsor, Walter Cagnew?"

"Sure. Oh, and Sarah?"

"Yeah?"

"Don't let anybody get to you today about the pictures. Maybe what you do for fun is weird, but there's nothing wrong with it."

"Thanks, Steph."

After we wound up the conversation, I checked the clock. Six-thirty. Another phone call or two, the mess on the floor to clean up, and homework to do. I had forty-five minutes. I thought I could make it.

As I picked up the phone again, there was a knock at the door.

"Breakfast. Fifteen-minute warning."

"Drat breakfast," I muttered. "Who's got the time?"

CHAPTER 6

It was harder than I expected to get Steph and myself excused from fourth period, so we could meet with Walter Cagnew.

The stern-eyed office secretary glanced at my carefully prepared note, and said, "Humph. You could at least be original. Prince Philip has tried this stunt four times already at Regency North. We've been warned." Then she shot the paper back at me and returned to typing.

I bit the inside of my cheek to hold back my angry words, pulled out my phone, and called my father.

He picked up after six rings. "Is something wrong?"

"Dad, sorry to bother you, but a friend and I are supposed to meet Walter Cagnew for lunch today about that proposal you have me working on, but the school won't let us out of fourth period."

"Walter Cagnew?"

"Sponsor of the proposal."

I heard paper shuffling, and then Dad said, "Oh, right. Surprised he's willing to talk to you. Can't you schedule it for after school?"

"I have three committee meetings today, and I'm not sure the lunch period is long enough."

"All right. I'll call the school office."

The line went dead, and the phone on the secretary's desk rang. I enjoyed the conversation, which from my side, sounded like, "Yes, Your Majesty," "Indeed, Your Majesty," "I'll see to it, Your Majesty."

But after the woman hung up, she glared at me. "Very smooth. I can see you think you're getting away with something. Well, you watch yourself, kiddo. I'll throw the book at any student playing hooky on my time, princess or no." She filled out little pink and blue slips. "If you or your friend is found anywhere you're not supposed to be, you can bet your buttons you'll both be cooling your heels in detention every night for the next three weeks."

"Yes, ma'am," I said.

"And don't give me any of your sass."

"No, ma'am." I grabbed the slips and almost got ahead of Clare in my hurry to flee the office.

A wave of giggles followed me as we sped down the main hallway. "Hey, Princess Sarah," someone shouted. "Can I come to your next tea party?"

I forced myself not to answer.

The second bell rang as I slid into my seat, and several people snickered. I wasn't sure whether it was the tea party pictures, my late arrival, or the unorthodox silk pants. Then, when I grabbed my trigonometry book instead of Dicrandian literature, the laughs really started.

Mrs. Anderson, a dumpy woman with a mass of brown curls pinned precariously atop her head, turned from the board and demanded, "Miss Watson, would you care to explain what's so funny?"

"Nothing, Mrs. Anderson," Julie Watson said, choking back a laugh. "I can't imagine what's got into me."

Several other girls laughed harder.

"Ladies! Quiet!" Mrs. Anderson said above the noise. "Class is beginning. Take out a sheet of paper and define the following words: Sylvan, melancholy . . ."

I pulled out a sheet of paper. All around me, giggles subsided, and paper rustled. Mrs. Anderson kept on giving vocabulary words. At the fifth one, she stopped next to Clare, who was sitting at the desk behind me.

"Why aren't you writing? Even if you're new here, you have to take quizzes."

Somebody giggled.

"Er, Mrs. Anderson?" I said. "I'm sorry, but Ms. Rivers isn't a student. She's my bodyguard."

The whole class was giggling now.

"Quiet!" Mrs. Anderson said. Her top layer of curls bounced angrily. Everyone laughed harder.

"I demand silence," Mrs. Anderson shouted into a crescendo of laughter.

I rubbed my temples. It was going to be a long day.

Biology was almost as bad as Literature, and Trigonometry was worse since Ms. Pelmar made sarcastic comments about my tea party and my clothes that encouraged my classmates' ridicule.

I was profoundly glad to see Gen leaning against the wall outside my Trigonometry classroom. At least I was until she waved her phone in my face and said, "Sarah, is this some kind of joke?"

"Is what some kind of joke?"

"This nonsense you sent me about werewolves and magic in the Northwest!"

"It's not—" I noticed half a dozen girls had stopped near enough to listen to our conversation. I tilted my head toward Julie Watson, the nearest, "Let's talk about this later."

Gen's eyes followed the direction my head was pointing. I could tell the moment she saw Julie because her eyes got wide. "Right. Um. When's good?"

I walked toward the front of the school where I'd be meeting Steph, and Gen followed along, as did a fair few of our listeners. "Can you ride along with me to my place after school? I've got a committee meeting, but I think I'd have time before that to introduce you to the head groom like I promised."

"Could I? I haven't been on a horse since I left Coredlian. I'll have to check with my mom first, but it shouldn't be a big deal. I'm not grounded or anything."

At the wide marble stairs that led to the double front doors of the school, I stopped. "Cool. Text me when you know, and if your mom's being a pain, we can figure out something else."

Gen gave me a thumbs up and walked off toward the B hallway, where she presumably had her next class. Most of our audience drifted off when she did, and the couple of girls that remained stayed in the entry hallway when I went out the doors. I was glad to lose them. I'd had enough giggling to last a month.

Steph met me in front of the school, coming from the direction of the gymnasium. Even with her honeyed curls soaking wet, she looked spectacular. "Nice amendment, Sarah, but how are you going to get it through Joint Council?" she asked when she got near.

"I'm hoping we can convince Cagnew to add it. If it's his, War might not pay too much attention to it."

"But to campaign for it later, you'll have to say you're in favor of the law. Surely that will tip them off."

I handed Steph my plan for Saturday as we got in the limo.

"You're going to pretend to be an airhead? Did you stage the tea party to make that more believable?"

"I wish."

Steph laughed. "Well, if we do this right, maybe people will think you did."

Wouldn't that be nice?

***

I could have mistaken Walter Cagnew for a college student. His khakis and polo were barely nice enough to meet the Plaza's dress code, and I couldn't picture his sleek black ponytail and feather earring on the Congress floor. But I knew he was the representative we were meeting by the nervous way he twisted his watchband, and when we approached, he knocked an umbrella stand off balance. Steph caught it with her left hand and held out her right for a handshake.

"I don't know if I should be here," Walter Cagnew said. "I couldn't reach Lord Burns this morning."

"Thank goodness," I said, "If you had, he'd have told you not to come, and we'd have no chance of passing this."

"Passing? You want to pass my proposition?"

The shock was enough to keep him quiet as a hostess ushered us back to a fussy private room, full of floral prints and fancy wainscoting that reminded me of my mother. But it had a screened patio overlooking a curve of the Rheme. I nodded toward it, and the hostess led us there, spread white linen over a glass-topped bamboo table, and settled us with menus and drinks.

Once she'd left, I explained how the difference between this year's casebook and previous ones had convinced me it was time Peace changed its position.

At the mention of earlier casebooks, Representative Cagnew twitched, his eyes widening. "Earlier casebooks?"

I stared at him. "Nobody told you that War's put out almost this exact proposal ten years running?"

"I know people have considered it, but Lord Burns never—"

"I'm sorry," I said. "I have a couple of the old casebooks with me." I slipped one out of my backpack and handed it to him. Behind me, a shadowy presence cleared its throat. I glanced back, surprised I hadn't seen the tall waiter enter.

Steph asked, "Why don't I order?"

"Thanks," I said, and Steph and the waiter left the patio, consulting together in low whispers.

When I turned back toward the table, Representative Cagnew was scowling at the proposition page from last year's book. "You say this has been presented ten years running?"

"To my knowledge. They might have offered it before, but I didn't have to sit in Joint Council until I learned to read."

"Can I ask what happened to the other proposals?"

"None but 10606 got out of Joint Council. That one mucked up things in Congress for a few months before they voted it down."

"Why?"

"Why did it muck things up?"

"No. Why did Congress vote it down?"

"Congress isn't going to pay for War propaganda schools in the largest undecided voting region in the country."

"They're not—we want to defend ourselves! We could add some Peace training. First aid would be handy right now."

"Actually, that was what I was going to recommend." I shoved a piece of paper across the table at him. "If you add this to your proposal, it'll stand a much better chance of passing Congress. Since it's your idea, you might not even have too much trouble with Joint Council."

"Joint Council is War-controlled. They'll vote for my proposition," Representative Cagnew said.

Steph slipped back into her chair. "They'll vote for your current proposition, but with the amendment? I don't know. I don't think my dad would go for it."

"I don't see why he wouldn't. We're not trying to set up War propaganda schools or whatever you called them."

Steph looked at me and shrugged. I forced my own shoulders to stay still. This was too important to dismiss lightly. If Uncle Malcolm was right about why War wanted this legislation (and Uncle Malcolm was almost always right when it came to political analysis), a first aid amendment would almost certainly derail the proposition before it could get to Congress. If that happened, there wouldn't be any assistance for the Northwest Provinces—not anytime soon, anyway.

I smiled at Representative Cagnew. "Maybe we're wrong. But if you decide to add the amendment, I wouldn't emphasize it when you talk to War Council members this week."

Representative Cagnew laughed. "When I talk to—Your Highness, you're the first Council member—War or Peace—who's been willing to meet with me about this."

Well, that made my life easier. If the War Council wasn't talking to Representative Cagnew, he couldn't alert them to my plans. But surely someone was monitoring him. "What about Lord Burns? It sounded like you talk with him."

"He hasn't been answering my phone calls lately. When I first contacted him about the violence in the Northwest, he seemed interested, but since I agreed to sponsor this proposal, he's been hard to reach."

That was a lousy way to treat a first-term representative. Lord Burns, like everybody else on Joint Council, knew this camp proposition had been shot down ten years in a row, but he still offered it to Cagnew as a realistic solution when Cagnew told about the increased violence in the Northwest. I wished I could believe the old curmudgeon was dodging Cagnew's calls because his conscience was troubling him, but more likely, the shrewd old counselor was busy and no longer had any use for Cagnew.

I would have to prepare Cagnew for the fight ahead myself. If I could win his trust. I wasn't sure where to start but thought I'd ask a few questions about what I hadn't understood in the casebook and recent news reports.

Representative Cagnew tensed up at first, but when he realized I was genuinely interested, not baiting him, he answered my questions as fully as he could. The more he spoke, the more I became convinced that something was terribly wrong in the Northwest this year.

Somewhere in the middle of lunch, Cagnew asked me about the best way to get his proposal passed, and long before we finished our peas and roast duck, he'd committed himself to putting in my amendment and keeping quiet about it.

When we left lunch, after shaking hands cordially all round, I smiled. One hurdle down. How many more would there be?

CHAPTER 7

Steph and Gen spent the night Friday to help me get ready for the Joint Council meeting. Gen researched, Steph served as a fashion consultant, and they both coached me on my speech. None of us slept until late, and nervousness had me up early pacing back and forth, reviewing my notes. Not that I expected to use all the details I'd memorized. I was hoping people wouldn't notice Cagnew's new amendment, and the proposal would slip through without a fight. It should work if we succeeded in distracting people and if everybody voted as expected. I tallied the votes again in my head.

Steph lifted her head from the couch. "Sarah, relax. When you crinkle your forehead like that, you look about thirty. And we want you to look young."

"Right." I scowled.

"No, no. That's worse." Steph rose gracefully from a tangle of blankets and walked over to me. Ok, now, smile."

I smiled.

"Not like that. Like you mean it."

I smiled again, but even I could tell the smile didn't reach my eyes.

Steph pulled me over to the mirror. "You've got to have some real feeling in there. Come on. Remind yourself of how excited you are to co-host the annual Royal Tea this year."

I groaned. The Royal Tea was the agenda item this morning that we thought I could use to distract from the Camp Defense proposal, but that didn't mean I was excited about it. "I hate the Royal Tea. I've been dreading co-hosting for years."

"There's got to be something about the tea that excites you," Gen said from her spot by my laptop. I wasn't sure she'd ever gone to sleep.

"It's a tortured waste of time, I tell you."

"You'll get to have a gorgeous new dress," Steph said.

I stuck out my tongue.

"And hang out all day with Queen Salome," Gen said. "She's supposed to be charming."

I tipped my head to one side. "If she didn't start off deciding to hate me."

"You'll get to see half the War Reps stripped to the waist for the game. It's their turn to play skins." Steph laughed.

The image of Philip stripped to the waist swam in front of my eyes. I flushed and tried to laugh it off. "Do you think Representative Cagnew will be on the team?" I asked to cover my confusion.

"Sarah!" Steph said. "He's at least ten years older than you."

I laughed. "They're all at least ten years older than me." Except Phil, of course. I took a deep breath. I was absolutely nuts. There was no way anything could happen between me and the War Prince.

My parents' eyes widened when I came downstairs. I couldn't blame them. It had to be disappointing to see me in this pleated plaid skirt and brass-buttoned red jacket. With my polished Mary-Janes and twin braids, I looked about ten.

Reporters crowded the rope line in front of the Joint Council building today, their news cameras looming larger (at least in my mind) than its crenellated columns. About twelve flashes popped, nearly blinding me. More than usual. The outfit must really have been doing the job.

"Break a leg," Steph said in my ear before heading to the staff room where she and Gen could watch the proceedings.

The Council table was nearly full when I arrived. King Randolph stood near the head, on the War side, earnestly talking with Lord Psalting. I wondered how much either of them knew about the fight their sons had been in this week. Nothing, so far as I could tell. But then again, would they let tensions between them show here? Maybe not. I glanced away.

Prince Philip's golden hair bobbed near the War refreshment table. My heart hitched, and I scanned the room for something safer for my eyes to land on. On the Peace side of the room, four lords had already found their seats, but Lord Richter stood at the foot of the table arguing with Lady McGivern and Lord Montressor from War.

I didn't want to talk to Steph's dad right now, so I turned to the Peace refreshment table to pick up a glass of water and almost bumped into Walter Cagnew.

"What is that you're wearing? Are you crazy?" he said.

I dropped my voice. "It's meant to be distracting. Glad you think it's working. By the way, you should be getting your coffee over there." I pointed toward where Prince Philip was collecting cookies. "This is the Peace table."

Representative Cagnew looked at the people around him, nodded brusquely, and said, "I hope you know what you're doing."

I nodded at him reassuringly, but my heart thumped in my throat. I so didn't know what I was doing.

While slipping into my chair, I nearly knocked over my water glass. Queen Salome glared at me. How could someone so cold be Phil's mom? Of course, I'd thought Phil was equally cold until I'd met him for real earlier that week. Maybe Queen Salome was as delightful as Gen had heard—in other contexts.

Soon the mediator called us all to order. The War side of the table was full—all eleven regular Council members were there, plus Walter Cagnew. Today, with Uncle Malcolm back home seeing to his mom, we had eight on the Peace side. The empty space to my right felt huge.

I had trouble paying attention during the opening ceremonies and reading of the minutes. I drummed my fingers on the table until Dad glared at me. Then I doodled on my notepad, creating an ever-expanding black spiral.

At nearly a quarter to ten, Queen Salome stood. I gripped my pen tightly, hoping no one else could hear my heart thundering. This was it.

"As you all know," Queen Salome said, "Our bi-partisan Royal Tea is approaching. I'm thrilled to have been chosen as this year's War hostess. Today, we need to appoint the other members of the host committee. Has the Peace Party prepared a nomination for co-host?"

"The Peace Party nominates as co-host, Princess Sarah Tressarian," Dad said.

"Princess Sarah?" said Lady McGivern, a tall dark woman who sat halfway down the war side of the table. "She's just a child."

"I'm fifteen-and-a-half," I said, putting as much petulance into my voice as I could muster without throwing up. "Mum and Dad have always promised me I could co-host the Royal Tea once I was fifteen." Threatened me that I'd have to was closer to the truth, but who cared about the details? I took a deep breath, "And I've been looking forward to working with Queen Salome. She's so sophisticated and fashionable."

On my left side, Mom gripped a water glass so hard that I could see her knuckles whiten. I glanced at her, but her face was unreadable. Still, I guessed my last comment hurt her. I hadn't meant to imply that Mom wasn't sophisticated and fashionable. I was about to say something to try and undo the damage when Queen Salome said, "I . . . goodness . . . I hardly know what to say."

"It's obvious the girl is too young," Lady McGivern said. "The Royal Tea would become a laughingstock."

"The princess isn't even done with doll-parties," said another War member—I didn't catch which one, though I didn't think it was Steph's dad.

"Hey, that's hardly fair!" shouted my cousin Andy's dad from his spot three left of my mom. I could always count on Uncle Maurice to take my side. "The Princess—"

"Made a complete fool of herself three days ago, and now you want her to help host the Royal Tea?" said Lord Times, another War member.

"We agreed to let Prince Philip host the annual New Year's ball days after he and three of his friends released frogs into all the Central Park toilets!" said Lady Smith, a tiny but ferocious Peace member who usually couldn't stand me.

Arguments broke out all across the table.

"Order! Order!" The mediator shouted, pounding his gavel on the table. No one paid any attention to him. It took ten minutes, and several threats of keeping everyone from lunch to get us all quieted.

And I started it up again with a, "Please, please, Queen Salome. You've no idea how much I'd love to work with you on this." I knew it was easy to get the Joint Council to argue instead of deal with real business, but never having deliberately tried to stir up trouble before, I had no idea how easy it would be.

The arguments broke out again, and this time, even the mediator's best attempts to calm us had no effect. After twenty minutes of shouting, pounding his gavel, and making threats that no one heard, he banged the emergency gong. It filled the whole room with a deep resonant tone that vibrated the furniture and seemed to rattle my bones.

When its echoes died away, there was silence. The mediator mopped his brow. "Thank you, Your Majesties, Your Highnesses, Lords and Ladies. I believe we must resolve this debate with a silent vote tally. He moved around the table, setting small squares of paper before each Joint Council member. "You have ten minutes to write 'aye' to approve Her Highness Sarah Tressarian's nomination to the post of co-host of this year's Royal

Tea or 'nay' to vote against said nomination. The clock starts now." The mediator turned the hand on a timer at the front of the room.

When I was younger, I'd had dreams of voting against my own nomination for this post, but I could hardly do that after I'd just begged for the job. It would raise too many questions. I sighed, and wrote "aye" on the paper, folded it in half, and set it on the collection tray in the middle of the table.

A couple of the War Council members took the full ten minutes to fill out their ballots, but after the mediator droned out the names and votes, I was unanimously appointed to the role. Down at the far end of the table, Representative Cagnew's brow drew together, as if he were puzzled by what had happened. I wished I could be closer to explain to him that while Joint Council debates were private, and as such, good places for members to get vitriol off their chests, votes were recorded, and nays might require potentially embarrassing public explanations. The Royal Tea wasn't worth the effort.

Then came time to nominate the other three members of the committee. Queen Salome nominated Lady McGivern, and all agreed. I nominated Stephanie Montressor.

"But Stephanie's a member of the War Party," Lady Smith said.

Lord Montressor scowled. Maybe he expected me to explode this myth. Instead, I said, as sweetly as I could, "What difference does her party make? It's a bi-partisan tea, isn't it?"

"But Queen Salome will be nominating only War party members," Lady Smith said.

"Really?" I said. "Surely Queen Salome isn't that petty."

Arguments broke out again, but this time Prince Philip didn't join in. He watched me intently. Maybe he didn't like me calling his mother petty. Maybe he'd figured out I was playing a game. I hoped he wasn't going to cause trouble.

This time, the mediator managed to calm us down before having to use the gong, and he invoked level three rules of order for the rest of the meeting. That meant no-one could speak without first being recognized. That suited me fine. Level three rules always slowed things down. By the time we finished the nominating process, it was past eleven o'clock.

The mediator called Representative Cagnew to the platform. As he moved toward the front, I asked to be recognized.

"What is it?" the harassed man said.

"Since we've only fifty minutes left, I would like to move for a quick vote with shortened table debate."

A place away on my right, my father jerked upright.

The mediator must have seen the movement because he asked, "Does the Peace Consul for this proposition agree?"

"I am the Peace Consul for this proposition," I said. Dad nodded, his lips pressed close together.

"What does the War Consul on this proposition have to say?"

Lord Burns looked at my dad and smiled broadly. "We'd be happy to accept those terms."

With that, the mediator nodded at Mr. Cagnew, who plowed in. He had charts and figures but was nervous and kept repeating himself. The speech dragged on without clarifying the issues.

When it was finally my turn to talk, I moved to the front, arranged my notes on the podium, and then glanced out over the room, trying not to give anything away as I caught each member's eyes as I'd been taught to do. Mom's dark eyes were puzzled. Phil's bright blues were way too interested. His father, fortunately, seemed barely awake. My father, on the other hand, frowned. Disappointed, maybe? I looked quickly away. My hands shook. I gripped the podium to hold them still, took a deep breath and started, speaking as persuasively as I could. Perhaps no one would take me seriously, but at least this once, they'd hear facts about the quantity and gravity of this year's violence. I gave my position as straight as I could while still downplaying Cagnew's first aid amendment.

I met everyone's eyes again as I finished. There were some good signs, but I couldn't read Phil's expression, and I could tell I'd be having a conversation with Dad as soon as I got home.

When I stopped speaking and took my seat, the room sat in silence for several full minutes. They were stunned, I supposed. Finally, the mediator seemed to remember his job. He stumbled to the podium. "Arguments for or against the bill?"

No one lifted a hand. The required thirty-second waiting period passed without a sound.

"Other comments?" The mediator asked.

Again the thirty-second waiting period passed. This was better than I'd hoped. Maybe the bill would pass through without a hitch.

"Then we will begin the vote," the mediator said. Starting at the War side of the lower end of the table, he called out each person's name. I held my breath, counting each vote as it was tallied. We needed eleven ayes for passage.

One.

Two.

Three.

Four.

Then a nay. But, Lord Walburn was a pacifist. I'd never expected him to vote for this.

Five.

Another Peace nay. I stifled a sigh.

Lady McGivern stared at me critically, and I held my breath. Finally, she said, "aye." Six. I let my breath out as slowly as I could.

Uncle Maurice voted aye. I smiled at him, as I counted seven in my head. Maybe this would work, especially since the next War Council member also voted aye. We were up to eight.

The next vote was a nay, but Steph's dad and Phil's mom both voted "aye." Ten. Only one more vote.

Mom voted against me, and it hurt, even though I hadn't expected anything else.

Then the next War Council member put us over the top, and I was so busy celebrating my win, I almost didn't hear the mediator ask for my vote. 'Aye, of course, aye," I said when I realized the man was waiting for me to answer. Lady McGivern laughed softly, but I didn't care. We'd won. The Northwest would get the help it needed.

'Prince Philip?" The mediator said.

There was a long pause. Phil glanced at me, flipped over the proposal, and said, "I think …" Then he stopped. He scanned the bill quickly from front to back. Then his eyes met mine. They were cold, angry. "I wondered what game you were playing. Put aside political maneuvering indeed. What do you call this little add-on?"

"Your Highness will please confine yourself to an answer of "aye" or "nay," the mediator said.

Phil wrinkled his forehead as if he didn't understand what had been said to him. A couple of people on my side of the table snickered, but everyone else was skimming the bill for what the prince had seen. Let them. I already had enough votes for passage.

"An answer, Your Highness?" the mediator prompted.

"An answer?" Phil said in a vague voice. Then, more firmly, "An answer. As second-ranking member of the War Council, I request a discontinuance of this vote and a recount as provided for under section 7.2 of the Joint Council Code."

A recount! Could he do that? Blast, he could! The vote wasn't finished yet. I vaguely remembered doing this once before.

The mediator blinked and brought out his black reference on Council Code. "Section 7.2—yes. This vote is officially discontinued. You, Princess Sarah, and Lord Burns have ten minutes to arrange the details of the recount." He indicated a private room behind him, centered, as the Council table was, between the Peace and War sides of the room. I got up and stumbled toward it. What now?

Phil reached the small room ahead of me.

"Do you want an immediate recount?" I asked.

"Why? So, you can have the pleasure of seeing a whole row of War Counselors reverse their decision after finally noticing that wisp of poison you snuck in?"

"Poison? It's first aid! And your man thought of it. He's sure you guys are in the business of defending people. Of course, he's only been a representative for a couple of months, so—"

"We are in the business of defending people."

"Then what's wrong with giving this proposition a shot at passing Congress?"

"Peace will never pass this, no matter what you attach to it."

"With the amendment and how much worse the violence is this year, I think I can convince enough people."

"Please. You get it through Congress, and I'll ask you to the Spring Fling."

I flushed. How I wished I weren't wearing braids and Mary Janes right now. And not just because it was harder to project confidence when I was dressed like this. But I was no baby. I stood straighter and looked him right in the eye. "You keep your people from changing their votes, and I'll go with you."

"Go with him where?" Lord Burns asked as he maneuvered himself and his walker through the doorway.

"Doesn't matter," Phil said. "It's a political bet she'll never make good on."

The old man pulled his glasses out of his shirt pocket, seated them on his nose, and stared at us over the top of them. "That's a dangerous game to be playing. Bad for both parties, I imagine, but you know your own business, no doubt."

"We do, actually," I said before recalling that I needed the man's help to set up reasonable terms for the recount.

Phil stepped in, smoothed things over, and gave me what I wanted— time to persuade people, but not so much time that the help would be too late for the Northwest. We'd hold the recount in Joint Council next week.

The rest of this week's meeting was a blur of formalities. After I filed out with the other members, Steph and Gen rejoined me. I gave them a weary smile. "I tried."

"You were good," Gen said. "It almost worked."

"Who'd have guessed Prince Philip knew you well enough to call your bluff?" Steph said.

I felt my face heating, and was glad when Gen asked, "What do we do now?"

"We take our argument to each member of Joint Council individually," I said. "It's going to be a long week.

CHAPTER 8

"Sarah, I told you to defeat Proposition 7342," Dad said. He stood at the sideboard of his study, pouring himself a glass of wine.

"I know you did, Dad, but I couldn't. These people need help. They may need a lot more than camps for young people, but the camps can get to them quickly if Congress passes the bill in the two weeks we've given it."

"Sarah, this proposal gives a permanent edge to War in the Northwest. We can't afford for that to happen."

"We can't afford to let four provinces get wiped out while we quibble about an aid package," I answered. "And I don't think it's going to give permanent advantage to War. There's equal time for Peace professionals, and I'm supporting this bill. When Silvershire, Westerberg, Livingston and Walksly get the aid they need, they'll know it didn't come out of a Castanay Council meeting."

Dad shook his head. "I can't support you on this, Sarah."

"Then I'll do it on my own. But at least read my report, will you? Really read it?" I thumped a small folder on the sideboard next to his wineglass.

Dad picked it up and thumbed through it. "You've given this a lot of thought, haven't you?"

I nodded.

"I'll read it."

"Thank you." That went better than I'd feared, but I wasn't done by a long shot.

***

When I got to my room, Steph handed me a crazy-long list of messages. Four newspapers, a TV show, my mother, three Peace Council members, Lord Burns, Walter Cagnew…

I ran my fingers through my hair. The braids had long since come unplaited. Where should I start? I got Steph calling the media outlets and setting up appointments with War Council members and had Gen setting up appointments with Peace Council members. They'd talk to her before they'd talk to Steph, even though Gen believed in War. Nobody asked about a high-school student's politics, but everybody knew Steph was Lord Montressor's daughter.

Meanwhile I called my mom. I hadn't made any headway in ten minutes of explaining that when I'd said Queen Salome was sophisticated and fashionable, I'd never meant to suggest that my own mother wasn't. So, I asked if I could have Estelle style my hair every day. I was sure I'd regret it later, but it was worth it to have Mom in a good mood again, right?

Steph and Gen were both on phones when I finished with my mom, so I took my cell into the closet for some privacy and dialed again. "Representative Cagnew?" I said when he answered. "Sarah Tressarian, here."

"You called back," he said.

"Of course. You think I'm going to try passing a bill without any help from its sponsor?"

"They're saying you pulled that stunt today to defeat the bill—that if we'd taken the recount right then, it would have gone down in flames."

"Why do you think we're taking the recount next week? Think about what happened today. We had enough votes for passage. All we needed was for Prince Philip, my dad and King Randolph to vote something— anything—and we were through. We were a hair off having this thing on the floor of Congress on Monday. Now it's going to be harder, that's all."

"How much harder?"

"Pretty ugly, actually, but Steph's making me appointments with War Council members, and another friend of mine is setting up meetings with Peace folk. Anyone who won't talk to me, Steph will set up with you, if that's OK. And we've got materials you can use. Smaller than the casebook, more convincing. Can you come over sometime this afternoon?"

"You've got materials for me to use?"

"I think you'll find them helpful." I hoped he'd take the hint. I didn't want to have to say his speech today had been awful.

There was silence on the other end of the line.

"Representative Cagnew? Are you still there?"

"Oh, I'm here all right. Just contemplating the legendary royal charm. I hadn't believed in it until I met you."

"Royal charm?" I laughed. "Everybody says I don't have it."

"Then they're fools. And I'm a fool, but I'm coming over. Where are you?"

"Oh, at the Peace Palace. Do you need directions or a car?"

"No, I think I can make it."

I smiled, closed the conversation and leaned back against the closet wall, resting my eyes. I wondered if there would be any way to get a walk in Peace Park this week.

My phone rang, saying it was my personal line. The number that popped up was local, but not one I recognized. It didn't say it was a scam, but it didn't identify the caller either. Curious. I swiped the phone on. "Hello?"

"Hello."

The voice was male and vaguely familiar, but definitely not Andy. "How did you get this number?"

The voice laughed. "Andy gave it to me. I'm afraid I let him imagine there was more going on between us Wednesday than really was. It was easy, you know, after what he saw."

"Phil!"

"Yes."

"Don't you have my business number?"

"This isn't business."

"Excuse me?"

"I wanted to apologize for this morning."

"You mean you're regretting your dare?" I asked, unreasonably disappointed.

"No, just that it was a dare and not an invitation."

I breathed in sharply.

"I'll do all I can to keep up my end of things. I don't suppose you can help me out with that?" he asked.

"I'll send over anything I think you can't use against me later."

"You don't trust me," he said.

"You don't trust me," I answered.

There was silence on the line for a long moment.

Then he said, "But I want to."

Did he say he wanted to trust me? "I want to trust you too," I whispered. "I can't stop thinking about you."

"If our parents find out…" Phil let the threat hang there.

"*When* they find out." Suddenly the dangers of this conversation occurred to me. "Where are you?"

"Public booth. You know, the relic they've left in the mall? My guards are watching from the ice-cream parlor. I've checked the phone for bugs."

That sounded safe enough. "All right then. I'll send the stuff."

"See you Saturday?"

I laughed. Joint Council meetings weren't the same as seeing him.

***

After a week of non-stop politics, I was exhausted and nearly desperate. I'd confirmed almost—but not quite—enough votes to get Cagnew's proposal through Joint Council.

I sat at the bar in Steph's kitchen, drinking orange juice. We'd attended four straight meetings since school ended—with Lady McGivern (who'd been going to vote no until Gen convinced her she shouldn't), Uncle Maurice (who'd hardly needed to be convinced), Lord Richter (who we'd buried in statistics until he agreed the Camp proposal was warranted this year), and Lord Walburn (who we'd talked to more out of courtesy than hope that he could be persuaded). Gen had to go home after the interview with Lord Richter, but Steph had stuck with me, and since her house was on the way home, I'd been happy to take her up on her offer of a snack.

It was good to kick off my shoes at the door, slurp orange juice, and run my hands through my hair. Estelle would be furious, but I didn't care. "Give me the numbers again," I said to Steph.

"Well, how'd it go with your mom?"

"She thinks it's precocious of me to be striking out on my own like this, but when it comes down to it, she's going to stand by her man."

"So that's a no."

"It's a no. What about your dad?"

"Are you kidding? But Walter got Sharp and Burns for sure today."

"Good." I couldn't remember when in the week we'd started calling him Walter, but Representative Cagnew sounded strange to me now. "Plus, we've got the Castanays."

"How'd you find that out?"

"I have my sources." In fact, Phil had called, but he didn't want me mentioning the call to anyone, even Steph. I understood him wanting to keep whatever it was we had between us secret but found it difficult not to be open with Steph. Or my parents.

"Be that way, then. You know I'll find out eventually."

She probably would. I couldn't decide if that was good or bad. "Back to the votes. With me, I'm counting nine."

"I thought Lord Psalting said he'd vote for it."

"OK, ten. We still need one more. Uncle Malcolm's going to fly in from the coast, but it's storming, and I don't want to count on that."

"What'll you do if we lose?"

"I don't know. I'm worried about the Northwest. There have been another three wolf attacks, and a couple of strange fires in the last week. Maybe I could convince Uncle Malcolm we need to sign special powers over to the War Party for the Northwest this spring. But even if it's for a limited time, that would weaken Peace. Not to mention that Dad would kick Uncle Malcolm off Joint Council. He's got one of the appointed seats."

"Then we can't lose this vote."

"Do you think Lord Castellan would talk to us again?"

"I'll call from my room. It echoes in here." Steph said and left the kitchen.

When she'd gone, a door off the kitchen opened, revealing a small office. Lord Montressor stepped out, his height and white mane giving him the air of a statesman despite his faded jeans and ancient Perlman sweatshirt.

I straightened up. "Lord Montressor! Steph ran to make a call. I'm sure she'll be back in a minute."

"I know where Steph went. My office isn't exactly soundproof." He smiled sheepishly and pointed to a little window over the door he'd emerged from. "I'm afraid I eavesdropped. I was reading when you came in and didn't realize you were here until you and Steph were already talking politics. I should have come out sooner, but between inertia and interest in the conversation…" He shrugged.

I went fishing for something to say and came up empty.

Lord Montressor pulled up a stool, put his elbows on the counter, and touched his fingers together. "You know, when you and Steph first became friends, I was sure you'd use her as a pawn in the political game that is your world. But she'd fallen under your charm, and only time would show her. It would be a bitter lesson, but she'd learn."

I started to protest, but Lord Montressor put up his hand.

"I've been around Dicrandian royals a long time. Both kinds. You've got true friends, but most of your acquaintances are people you need, nothing more. I thought, given my position, that Steph was probably one of these."

"Steph is my best friend!"

Lord Montressor shrugged. "When Steph told me last Thursday that she was helping you, I thought it was starting."

"But I…" I couldn't go on. Probably Steph's name had helped me meet Walter Cagnew. It might have helped with Lady McGivern. My face heated. "I hadn't even thought about that when I asked her." I felt horrified. "We're friends. I thought she'd want to work on this. I didn't even think about you—except I thought you might be upset."

Lord Montressor laughed, sounding a lot like Steph. "You guessed that, did you?"

I sighed. "My lord, I really am friends with your daughter. I don't want to use her—or anybody else for that matter."

"I think I'm beginning to see that. I'm sorry you haven't come by more. I might have worried about Steph less had I known you better."

Steph came back into the room. She glanced from her father to me.

"Dad? I didn't realize you were home."

"I know. I'm early. I've been having an interesting talk with your friend here."

"About our bill?" Steph asked.

"No about you," Lord Montressor said.

"Too bad." Steph turned to Sarah. "Lord Castellan's got a nephew's birthday party to attend. I tried to convince him to see us after the party or early tomorrow morning, but he says his mind is made up; he's voting no."

I slumped.

"Well," Lord Montressor said, "Perhaps you two can explain what's so important about this bill that Princess Sarah's thinking of crazy drastic measures to take if it fails."

"That's easy," Steph said, whipping out one of our glossy brochures. "It's a matter of life and death for…"

I left her to it. It had been a long week, and I had a lot of thinking to do.

✳✳✳

The next morning, Proposition 7342 passed the Joint Council by a vote of eleven to eight. The storm kept Uncle Malcolm from all but the end of the meeting, but Lord Montressor came through with a yes.

CHAPTER 9

I'd hoped that getting the camp proposal through Joint Council would make it easier to get the bill through Congress, but it didn't turn out that way. For one thing, Dad was still against the proposal, and he'd made his views widely known. For another, although the violence in the Northwest was getting worse by the day, big papers weren't covering much of it, so the news was relegated to local news sources, obscure online journals, a few scandal rags, and late night talk radio. I would have started to doubt the reality of it all myself if I hadn't started getting letters and email from people in the affected areas. Many had lost homes. A few had lost family.

I threw myself into meetings, sharing the stories and wishing I were a more experienced politician. As it was, I wasn't sure what I could promise these people.

All the while, I had a nagging sense that I was forgetting something important.

By four-thirty Wednesday, when I stepped out of a meeting with the five members of Bentralia's Water and Sewage committee, I was exhausted. Out of long-drilled habit, I kept my shoulders high and my head up, but I wasn't succeeding with the act, judging by the concerned tilt of Clare's eyebrows.

"I'm fine, really," I said while consulting the calendar on my phone. Miraculously, there was nothing planned for the next two hours. But at six-thirty I had a meeting on this side of town with an up-and-coming War congressman who had been unwilling to meet with Walter, Gen or Steph.

That didn't even give me enough time to go home and change into something comfortable before heading out again.

"Where to, Your Highness?" the driver asked.

I needed to rest. Where could I do that on this side of town? Then I had it. "Regency North High. Andy's got a baseball game today."

This wouldn't be the first time I'd gone to Regency North to watch one of Andy's games, but it was the first time in a long while that I'd done it alone. Ever since I'd met Steph, I'd watched with her.

That was nearly two years ago. I'd been shaking with nerves. Regency North was almost as much enemy territory as the War Palace complex, but both my parents had been too busy to come along. I'd promised Andy I'd watch him pitch his first high school game, though, so I'd marched up to the ticket window and asked for two tickets for the home-side box.

I'd known something was wrong when the freckled ticket seller had smirked and handed over the tickets with a far too polite, "Will that be all, Your Highness?"

I couldn't figure out what was wrong, though, so I'd taken the tickets, passed one back to my guard, and headed to my seat.

What was wrong, it turned out when I got to the press box, was that King Randolph was already there, his guards filling the place. Seconds after I opened the door, silence fell.

"Your Highness," King Randolph dropped into the stillness. "What a lovely surprise.".

I was tempted to turn around and go back the way I'd come. I'd never been alone in a room with this man before, not that you could call me alone now, what with five guards plus a lanky blonde teenager in the front, right-hand corner, away from the king's entourage. Still, my parents weren't around. They were the ones who always kept up the polite word wars when the two Dicrandian royal families met. Here I was on my own.

Much as I wanted to disappear, I knew that if I did, it would be all over the webiverse, and my folks wouldn't let me out in public by myself again for weeks. I forced myself to smile. "I've come to watch my cousin Andy pitch," I said. It's his first time."

"Ah!" King Randolph said with an icy smile. "So, it's your cousin Andrew who is the new pitcher my son keeps talking about." His tone of voice suggested he'd heard nothing good.

I clenched a fist but managed to keep my voice calm. "That's right. Prince Philip plays shortstop, doesn't he?" What a dumb thing to say. Everyone in the kingdom knew Prince Philip played shortstop. I felt I didn't even deserve the curt nod King Randolph gave me in response.

"Andy says he's fantastic. I'm sure it'll be a good game," I said, almost instantly regretting being so positive. *Never give War royalty compliments for free* was one of my father's mottoes. But perhaps I'd said the right thing. King Randolph's smile unthawed slightly as he said, "I certainly hope so. Unfortunately, I can't stay for the entire game. I have an appointment in an hour."

"That's too bad," I said, trying to sound like I meant it. Then I escaped to a seat next to the blonde.

"Hi, I'm Sarah," I said softly as I sat down.

The girl smiled, her green eyes lighting up. "I know," she said equally softly.

My face heated.

"I didn't mean to embarrass you," the girl added. "It's just kind of obvious."

"It was stupid of me," I said. "I forget that people know me even when I don't know them."

Laughter returned to the girl's eyes. "I imagine that's hard. I'm Steph." She held out a hand. "Stephanie Montressor."

"Nice to meet you, Steph," I said, grasping the outstretched hand.

"I think it's brave of you to walk in here like this," Steph said. "I probably would have gone over to the Away box with the other Peace folk even if the view is better here."

So that's what the ticket seller had thought funny. "Not brave, just stupid. I didn't know Peace folk usually sat in the Away box. I'm glad I'm here, though. I'll get to see Andy a lot better."

"He is worth watching. Pity we can't get him for the softball match at the Autumn Festival."

"You're thinking about that already?"

"I'm in charge of the War team this year. Today I'm scouting."

"Wow. You must be good at softball."

"So-so. My real game is soccer. But I'm good at organizing."

"Really? I'm terrible at it. For my last birthday, my parents bought me a special calendar app for my phone. It blips at me every hour to tell me what I'm supposed to be doing. It's cut down on my goof-ups."

"You have a calendar that tells you what to do? What a pain!"

"Not as much of a pain as what happens to me when I forget important meetings."

Steph laughed aloud this time, a tinkling golden laugh that made all the guards and King Randolph stare. That shut us up. We watched the game quietly until King Randolph left. I was glad to see that Andy pitched well. I hoped King Randolph noticed that my cousin could play.

Of course, Prince Philip could play too. Andy gushed about the prince's skills when no adults were around to hear. At least I wasn't seeing those skills in action at the moment. Andy struck out the next two batters to end the inning. I wanted to jump up and down and scream, but with King Randolph there, I merely punched my right fist into my left hand and softly said, "Yes!"

Not too long after that, King Randolph left, and I let loose, muttering encouragement to batters as they came to the plate. "Come on, Wilson, you can do it." As if they could hear me, they slugged away. The bases were loaded when Prince Philip came up to bat. "Come on, Castanay," I said under my breath.

Steph glanced at me. "You want him to do well?"

"Of course. I want Regency North to win!"

Steph looked at me strangely a minute, then laughed. "You're not at all what I expected, Sarah Tressarian."

Just then, Prince Philip sent a ball soaring over the back fence, and we both jumped out of our seats, whooping.

I vaguely remembered Regency North winning the game by six runs. What I remembered clearly was high-fiving Steph at the end of the game and asking impulsively, "Do you want to get some ice cream?"

Steph had stepped back for a second, then nodded. "Yes. Yes, I'd like that."

Since that afternoon, we'd been inseparable, and I felt strange standing at the ticket counter alone. "Two tickets for the home-side box," I said. Today the ticket seller didn't bat an eye.

Like the first time, King Randolph and his guards monopolized the box. They nearly hid a couple of reporters. "Good afternoon, Your Majesty," I said without too much of a quiver as the king turned to see who was coming this late into the game. "How are they doing?"

"Afternoon, Your Highness. Down by two."

"The Hawk's pitcher hit your cousin," a reporter added. "Hard."

"Is Andy OK?"

"Looks like a broken arm," King Randolph said. "They've called an ambulance. He's down under the bleachers waiting for—"

"Thanks," I said, turning and running down the bleacher stairs, Clare clattering behind me. In the grimy cement and metal maze below, I could hear Andy before I saw him.

"It's starting to feel better, I tell you. I can play. Besides, I've got three people to meet after the game. I'm fine."

Great. So, Steph had roped Andy into meeting people, now? He'd insisted he was too busy when I asked him. I rounded a corner and saw him struggling with a couple of guys dressed in Regency North uniforms.

"Andrew Delagardie Sanderson," I said. "You're not playing with a broken arm."

The guys with him looked up. One smiled and moved away.

"Sarah," Andy said. "I thought you were—"

"I had a break. Came to see you play. Good thing I did." I was at his side now, feeling his left arm. Waves of pain poured out of it, and I could envision the crack.

"I don't think it's broken, Sarah," Andy whined. "Just bruised."

"He can't lift the arm or move his fingers," the other player said, matter-of-factly.

That was Phil. Where was his—oh. A guy in a suit stood in a shadowy corner not far away. I snapped my mouth shut. Princesses don't show surprise, I reminded myself.

"I can," Andy said bringing my attention back to him. He could what? Oh—move the arm.

Sweating, Andy lifted the arm about two inches before letting it drop back down. A spasm crossed his face. "See, it isn't a break."

"Coach wants you to get it checked out anyway," Phil said.

"But with you and me both out, they'll cream us," Andy said.

"You're out?" I said to Phil.

"Twisted ankle." Philip smiled ruefully. "A base runner went out of his way to knock me over."

"Man, they play nasty," I said.

"Can't you do anything about it?" Phil asked.

"What's she supposed to do? Kiss it and make it better?"

"Something like that." I laughed nervously and glanced back at Clare. She was calm and watchful, trustworthy as always. Clare wouldn't tell anyone if I did something bizarre. I glanced at the guy in the suit.

"He won't say anything, "Phil said. "And I won't either."

That left Andy, and he wouldn't talk. He was more than half afraid of me already. I let my hand glide over his arm again, humming softly and closing my eyes against the sight of candy wrappers and nearly petrified popcorn cemented to the concrete by brown and orange goo. I concentrated, feeling Andy's bone growing back together. The arm was almost perfect when I stopped. I needed to leave something for the paramedics to look at. "You could probably use that arm now."

Andy stretched out his arm, wiggled his fingers. "How'd you do that?"

"With those nonsense songs Grandma taught us when we were kids. I don't know how; it just happens. And if you tell anyone, I'll give that picture of you in the fifth grade to Steph. Here, let's see that foot." I turned to Phil and squatted down.

He rolled down his right sock to reveal a swollen ankle. "Aah," he said, jerking backward as I reached toward him.

"I haven't touched you yet. Hold still." I reached out again, concentrating. This wasn't nearly as painful as his injuries a couple of weeks ago. I hummed softly.

It didn't take long to mostly fix the sprain.

"Thanks," Phil said.

"Don't mention it. Really." I got up and brushed off my slacks. "Shouldn't the real medical people show up soon?"

As if in answer to my question, a couple of paramedics came in from the parking lot.

"What've we got here?" the shorter, spiky-haired one said.

"Not much," Philip said. "We both got knocked pretty hard, and coach wanted us checked out before we go back into the game."

"I thought it sounded more serious than that," the man said. But as the two paramedics ran their tests, everything looked good.

"Well, guys, I'd say you've got nothing to worry about. I don't see any reason why you can't keep playing."

"The things we get called out for these days," the other one muttered as they left.

"Come on, Daniels," the first one answered. "It's the prince!"

"Let's go, Sanderson," Phil said. "We've got some paying back to do." Before heading back to the dugout, he gazed into my eyes and said softly, "Nice to see you as always, Your Highness."

They were gone. Exhausted, I turned back toward the bleachers.

"Let me get this straight," Clare said. "When you sing, people heal?"

"Yes."

"And you keep this a secret?"

"I get enough publicity being a princess. I don't need to be a freak, too."

"How badly messed up was Prince Philip when you found him last week?"

"I've promised not to talk about that," I said.

"Ah," Clare said, looking at me shrewdly.

Sometimes I wished Clare were a little less perceptive.

It was all I could do to hold myself properly upright as I climbed back to the home-side box. Fortunately, everyone was too surprised by Philip and Andy's sudden reappearance in the game to notice me.

My explanation that the paramedics hadn't found anything seriously wrong with either boy was met with suspicion, but when neither seemed to be in pain, the questions soon ended. I sat in a corner with some popcorn and enjoyed seeing Regency North make their way back to a tie before I had to go.

✳✳✳

That night, after all my meetings and homework were done, I slept fitfully, dreaming of piercing blue eyes. In the background, a rumbling voice, like far off thunder, was saying, "Nice to see you as always, Your Highness."

CHAPTER 10

However busy my schedule got, I still had to do my homework. I had a couple of spare hours after the Joint Council meeting, so I headed to the Royal Library to research Amanda Minkwell, the poet.

Since the royal archives were in the library, I stopped on the way and picked up a dozen red-tipped carnations to thank a librarian who had helped me research the camp proposal.

I'd have done roses, but I was getting worried about finances. Since I'd decided to support Cagnew's bill against my dad's wishes, I'd been using my own money to campaign. Between business meals, car service for five, printing costs, and transforming the balcony area of my tower, my funds were depleted. I'd have a bit left at the end of the week if spending stayed where it was, but what if something else unexpected came up? I rubbed my forehead.

"You worry too much," Clare said. "It sounds like you've already got the votes you need for passage, and that sad business on Copernati Peak that was in all the papers today…"

"I know." It was a sad business. Two children had been discovered, feet bleeding, running naked down the mountainside. They were too terrified to talk. A group of hunters had headed up the mountain and found the children's village intact, but all the people dead, huddled in a mass of twisted bodies behind the barred doors of the village meeting house. Their eyes were wide open, and horror filled the dead faces. One of the hunters snapped half a dozen pictures, and the terror was now splashed across the pages and screens of every news outlet in the country. *The Daily Sun*, which only a week and a half ago had felt my tea party more newsworthy than my statement about the camp proposal I was trying to push through Congress, now loudly demanded immediate governmental action. Congresspeople who had brushed me off when I tried to talk to them last week now rushed to pledge support for Cagnew's bill.

I sighed. What if the Northwest needed more potent assistance than the camps? I didn't have the resources for another campaign like this one, over my father's head.

"You're not mooning over you-know-who are you?" Clare asked.

I laughed. I'd completely forgotten Phil for the moment. "No, I'm thinking about the Northwest. The bill will pass, but what then? What if they need more?"

"You work harder at convincing your father."

"But what if—"

"What-ifs are bad for your health. Better to keep to the job at hand, I'd say. What is the job at hand, by the way? I thought you'd already researched the Northwest problem."

"A paper for literature class. Due Tuesday," I said glumly as we pulled up to the marble library steps. All the same, my mood was picking up. Something, triggered by what Clare had said, wriggled inside my brain, trying to come to the surface. *Gently*, I told myself. *If you don't push it, it'll come.*

What had Clare said? She'd mentioned sticking to the job at hand. No, that wasn't it. She'd also reminded me I'd already researched the Northwest problem. There! Had I already researched the problem? Sort of. But if I'd started with the problem of the violence in the Northwest instead of whether to pass the bill, I'd have researched differently—dug up similar problems in the past and consulted experts on the subject. (Of what? Fending off weird terror?)

I was still thinking about new research possibilities when I got to the archives and found myself face to face with Laura Travers, a librarian who had often helped me over the phone. From her voice, I'd imagined a young woman, with thick glasses. But Ms. Travers was at least fifty with snow-white hair and forget-me-not eyes. She wore a bright red cardigan and reminded me of grandmothers in books.

"Are these for me?" Ms. Travers asked in the same wispy voice I'd become used to over the phone. I tried not to look disconcerted.

"For your help the last couple of weeks. And I'm afraid I've got more work to do." I explained that I wanted historical accounts of violence similar to what we were seeing in the Northwest this spring. "Could you tell me how to get started?"

"Leave it with us, and we can have someone send you everything we've got in a business day, maybe two. We'll bill the time to your account for the camp bill."

"No good. Dad cut off the money to that account almost two weeks ago."

"Then how are you paying for the massive campaigning they say you're doing?"

"Personal account, but it's not bottomless, so I'd appreciate a few pointers to get me started on my own."

"Well, I'll be. If I were you, I'd petition Joint Council for your own business account. The paperwork is a pain in the rear, but how are you supposed to preserve independent judgment if you've got no cash?"

"Business account?"

"Yes. Congresspeople all get one, you know. Joint Council members' accounts are bigger. And royalty also get staff accounts."

"Staff accounts?" I wished I could think of something to say beyond parroting back Ms. Travers' words.

"Honey, haven't they taught you anything about the money side of your job?"

I shook my head, hoping my face didn't show how much I felt like I'd been buried under an avalanche of world-rocking information.

"Well, it's about time somebody did. You can't get anywhere without money."

"Thanks. I'll look into it. Do you think, in the meantime, you could help me?"

Ms. Travers could, but I quickly realized that doing the job well would take hours. Hours I didn't have. Ms. Travers suggested she herself could start on the problem in her spare time and turn over the work to one of my people if that suited me better.

"Ms. Travers, it's not fair for you to do this on your own time."

"You're doing it on your own money."

"Yes, but—"

"But nothing. When something's important, you do it with the means you've got available."

"Thank you so much."

"Don't mention it. You keep doing good work. If you keep this up, you'll turn out to be much more than our ordinarily good Dicrandian leader."

"I'm not doing anything special."

Ms. Travers smiled. Before she could say anything else, the phone on her desk rang.

"I'd better go," I said. "I'll be here after school Monday—or somebody will." Not that I had high hopes of finding "people" before Monday, but maybe Gen would be willing to help me out with this. She didn't like meetings much, and she wanted to do something.

Back in the main part of the library, I began my search for Amanda Minkwell, a topic that felt more unreal and disconnected from life all the time.

Unbidden, a memory leapt to mind. I must have been nine or ten at the time. My father and I had been walking down High Street in the rain, together under one umbrella. My father had seemed to sag. Across the street, a young boy had been jumping in puddles. "Look, Mom," he'd shouted. "My new boots don't leak!"

Dad had straightened up and glanced about him. Then he'd stopped, forcing me to stop, too. "Sarah," he'd said, and I'd turned toward him. "Listen to me because this is important. There will come a day when you feel the weight of the world on your shoulders, and ordinary things—a pair of boots, or a warm meal, or even other people—seem unimportant or unreal. Never give into that feeling. Ordinary things are what life is about. In many ways, what we do is a shadow of what's real. Politics can protect ordinary things and sometimes improve ordinary things, but it's the ordinary things that are important."

I hadn't understood what he was saying. I wasn't sure I understood now, but I attacked my literature paper with new energy.

***

It was Genevieve who headed for the library on Monday. Steph had booked my afternoon completely full. Gen returned well after my supper, struggling under the weight of a giant stack of books, photocopies, and spiral notebooks. She dumped the pile on my desk, shook the hair out of her eyes, and handed over a pink panda zip drive. I hadn't expected half that much material, but what surprised me even more was how old it all was.

"There's nothing modern that's remotely like the problems we're experiencing right now," Gen said.

"What do you mean by modern?"

"The last several hundred years. Since Sarah the First's time, actually."

"Sarah the First? That was—"

"Nearly seven hundred years ago."

I groaned. "Our records that far back stink."

"You're telling me. And they're all mixed up with fairy tales." Gen snagged a cookie from a plate next to my desk phone and munched away. Crumbles fell onto her school cardigan, but she didn't seem to notice.

"Fairy tales?"

"You'll see what I mean. Here's something close to what happened last week in Walksly on—what was the name of that mountain?"

"Copernati Peak."

"Right. Anyway, they've got the same stuff—people dead, terrified, no sign of violence—so they jump to the conclusion ghouls."

"Why ghouls?"

"They needed something to call it, like the newspapers do now."

"OK, but why ghouls and not sorcery or midnight sun or something?"

"If you ask me, they made up the stories of ghouls to fit the case. Here's a description: 'Ghouls can't be seen except when they're within two or three feet of a victim. Then, the creatures appear as elongated shadows. Ghouls move in a shroud of fear, so victims are often conquered even before the creatures make contact, but ghouls also carry weapons that can drive human souls from their bodies.'"

"That's what happened at Copernati Peak! Attacked by ghouls!" I shivered.

Gen shrugged. "Yeah, it's a great story, but I don't see how it helps us."

"Depends. Was there any way to fight ghouls, back when people believed in them?"

"Sure, if you want to get mythological. There's a mythological solution for everything. Are you sick? Get a medicine singer and have them hum the right tunes and voila, you're better. Do you need to fight ghouls, whorls, dhingjacks or dragons? Get yourself a chanter, chant the right chants, and you've got protective barriers or magic arrows, or whatever you need. And hey, if that doesn't work, you can always try to call up the fairies."

Gen was making fun of the stories of magic in the archives, but having sung up healing myself, I wasn't inclined to dismiss songs and chants out of hand. Fairies, on the other hand? "The fairies?"

"Yeah. Apparently Islandia is a thriving fairy kingdom, full of good-natured, industrious fairies who are always popping up in the stories at the moments when people can't handle problems on their own."

"Hmm. That is a bit hard to swallow. Who says Islandia is a fairy kingdom?"

"The chronicles."

"It's in the chronicles but not in our history books?"

"Yeah, well, history is supposed to be real, not fantasy. This stuff is so bogus, it's never going to help us. I wouldn't have kept digging if it hadn't been so interesting."

"How do you know it's all bogus?"

"Sarah, if there were fairies—or whorls and dragons—somebody would have seen them sometime in the past six hundred or so years. We haven't."

"What if we have and didn't realize what we were seeing? Think about Copernati Peak. Even if ghouls exist and caused that disaster, no one will know about them. We don't believe in ghouls anymore, so whether they're real or not, we don't mention them in the papers or even online."

"Well, duh. The whole idea of ghouls is preposterous!"

"A minute ago, you made it sound silly to call in a singer for a medical problem. But I've healed a few medical problems by singing."

"You're joking."

"No."

"I don't know, Sarah. This all sounds crazy."

"Well, I want to keep an open mind. Maybe the myths will help. Thanks for finding them."

"No problem. I doubt it's any use, but it was way more fun than all that hobnobbing. If you ever need a full-time research assistant, I'm your girl. If you don't mind an assistant who disagrees with you three-quarters of the time."

"Dad always says too much of the same perspective is bad for the mind and soul."

Gen nodded soberly. "It's bugging you to disagree with him, isn't it?"

"Yeah. Lately, I haven't talked to him at all. I'm hardly ever home for meals, and when I am here, there are other people around."

"I was in a fight with my mom for a while there—about moving to Bentralia for her job. At first, we screamed at each other a lot. Then, for a couple of weeks, when we first got here, I was miserable, and my mom and I weren't talking to each other. Just 'pass the toast,' and stuff like that. It was awful."

"How did you get over it?"

"I don't know. We took a few walks together and talked—about stuff other than the original problem. And one day I apologized for being rude and stubborn, and she apologized for being angry, and we cried a lot."

"And then it was the same as before?"

"No, it's different now. But we're OK."

"Thanks, Gen, for telling me that. It helps." I stretched. Twisting left, I saw my clock glowing eleven-thirty. "Is that the time? I've still got at least two hours of homework! And a breakfast meeting tomorrow!"

Gen glanced at her phone. "Bother! I've got to get home before Mom's back from her class!" She nearly ran out the door.

***

I felt like I'd just gone to bed when my alarm jangled the next morning. It was pitch black out. I took a second look at my alarm. Did that say four? Why had I set the stupid thing for so early?

I was in the process of changing it when I remembered. Then I dragged myself out of bed and pulled on jeans, a t-shirt, and low-heeled boots. I stuffed my hair into my cap and crept downstairs. The night guard raised a questioning eyebrow but followed me downstairs without asking anything out loud.

There was a light in the stable, as I'd known there would be. "Good morning, Dad. Mind if I join you?"

My father looked up from saddling his huge bay mare. "You're up early."

I rubbed my eyes. "I feel like I haven't seen you in a week. Besides, I figured I could use the exercise."

My father smiled. "Come on, then. We can watch the sunrise over Peace Park."

I shook my head. I was glad Dad wanted me to ride with him, but being up early enough to see a sunrise was not my idea of fun. Still, I saddled my own mare, wishing briefly that the security people would let me have a stallion. But Midnight was a good horse, and I always relaxed when I rode her.

Our pace was leisurely as we let the horses pick their way through the dark. The wind whipped my hair. We didn't talk until after we reached Haybridge Knoll. There we sat, wind in our faces, waiting for the first glimmers of light.

"So," I said, my words falling like drops into a well of silence, "My life's been pretty crazy lately. How's yours?"

Dad chuckled. "Well, my daughter's growing up faster than I expected, and it's taking some getting used to."

"Are you mad at me, Dad?"

"No. A little scared for you. You've been doing things this past week that I didn't try until I was in my twenties, and I worry you might be in over your head. But you're handling yourself well so far. I'm proud of you."

"Thanks, Dad."

He reached over, pulled off my baseball cap, and tousled my hair.

"Dad!" I grabbed at my hat.

He snatched it out of my reach, wheeled his mare around, and galloped down the hill. I followed, urging Midnight forward.

Midnight was younger than the big bay, and I was lighter than Dad, but Dad was a better rider. I didn't catch him until we were nearly back at the palace.

I went back to my room tired and sweaty but more relaxed than I'd been in over a week. The day seemed faceable.

CHAPTER 11

The first Monday in April, Congress voted two-hundred-forty-eight to forty for Walter Cagnew's Camp Defense. It was the biggest vote margin in three hundred years for a bill opposed by one of the country's monarchs. I was elated. I floated through a press conference, barely serious enough for the subject of conversation. I pushed Walter into the limelight as much as possible. I hoped his home county was seeing this.

That evening, after my friends had gone home and the cameras had stopped flashing, I felt empty. I wouldn't miss having two or three business meals and endless meetings every day, but I still felt a sense of loss. Life wouldn't be as interesting with only school and my usual meetings. I sighed and then laughed out loud when I remembered I still had the Royal Tea to keep me busy.

Someone tapped on my door.

"Come in," I said.

"I brought you cocoa and scones," Uncle Malcolm said, stepping into the room. "I thought you might need something to help you wind down."

I grabbed a scone. "How'd you know? I figured I'd fall into bed and sleep a week."

Uncle Malcolm smiled. Deep crinkles formed around his eyes and mouth. "I've known your father since before you were born. He can never sleep after a big vote either."

I nodded. "Sometimes it's hard to believe I'm related to my mom at all, I'm so much like my dad."

"You've got her eyes," Uncle Malcolm said, "and you care about people the way she does—not because you must, but because you like them."

"That's easy. People are so interesting."

Uncle Malcolm smiled his crinkly smile again and tugged on one of his brown-gray curls. "I don't always find it so easy, and unless I'm much mistaken, neither does your father."

Perhaps that was true. Mom was always dashing off quick notes to people she'd met on campaigns or sending flowers to folks she'd heard were sick. She could remember the names of people she'd met once years ago and ask about the dreams or kids they'd talked about in that long ago conversation, while Dad could barely fake it when a staffer put the person's name, picture and dossier on his phone.

It was nice to think I might be like my mother that way. I sipped my cocoa.

"How are things other than politics going?"

I looked up. "OK, I guess. Steph got a soccer scholarship to Perlman. I'm going to miss her next year."

As I spoke, I remembered that Phil was also going to college next year. To Spencer, if the newspapers were right. That was in town. But Andy would almost certainly go to the Dicrandian Military Academy. So, there wouldn't be any more notes in my pocket after baseball games.

"I imagine you'll get out to Perlman pretty often. And she'll come back here. Especially if they pass your staff and funding proposals Saturday."

"Oh, have you seen that?"

"Came out this afternoon. You realize, don't you, that Lord Montressor is going to be livid that you've named his daughter your chief of staff?"

"We were afraid he would be, but he's actually being pretty cool about it."

"Really? Does that mean Steph and Andy can admit they're dating now?"

"Not that cool."

Uncle Malcolm laughed.

"So, you're worried about your friends going to college, and you're getting your hair done. Anything else important going on?"

I think I'm falling in love, I thought. I didn't even know when it had started. Surely not back at the dollhouse? But somewhere before the bleachers. I could feel my face heating and covered my confusion by telling Uncle Malcolm that I'd gotten an A on my Amanda Minkwell paper.

"Good," Uncle Malcolm said, pulling another curl. "Excellent. I was afraid you were going to tell me you'd fallen in love."

I jerked, spilling half my cocoa on my school blouse. Uncle Malcolm laughed again.

"I suppose it will be in the papers tomorrow."

"I'm not telling anyone."

"But you guessed."

"I've known you since you were born. Journalists usually have to see you with someone before they catch on to a love story."

"True."

"So, is the hero being cruel? Or is he unaware of how you feel?"

"It's complicated, Uncle Malcolm."

"Indeed?" He squeezed my shoulder. "I'm afraid that's the story of your life, kiddo. I should get out of your hair. I've made things worse." He stopped by the door and turned. "Sleep if you can." He smiled his crinkly smile and was gone.

I wished I could sleep, but I wasn't at all tired. I tackled a couple of geometry problems. I read the chapters of *Dreamvale* that Mrs. Anderson had assigned. That was all my homework.

I put my books away, straightened a few piles on my desk, and then sat in one of the deep, navy plush chairs I'd put by my balcony. Moments later, I sprang back up, impatient for something to do.

I changed into nightclothes, tossing dirty clothes into the hamper from across the room. I was getting pretty good. I picked up the one sock I'd missed and tried again. Maybe I would make the basketball team next year.

After changing, I brushed my teeth for five minutes, hoping I'd get tired in the process, but I didn't. Back in my main room, I inspected the piles on my desk. The casebooks were still stacked in one corner. I also had a stack of newspapers, a stack of Gen's research, a stack of sample place cards for the Royal Tea, and a stack of papers related to the bill we'd passed.

As long as I was up, I thought I might as well clean the mess. In my filing cabinet, I started a file for Bill #7342, berating myself for not having done so sooner. Into it, I put its casebook, copies of speeches I'd given and materials my friends and I had made, notes from one-on-one meetings and all the personal letters I'd received. I dumped the remainder in the trash.

In a matter of minutes, I'd cleared away nearly my whole life for the past four weeks. How strange. I sat staring at the bare spots on the desk. Then I shook myself and turned to other piles. I skimmed my newspapers and frowned at the Royal Tea place cards. Who cared which they used? I chose one by rolling a die.

Gen's research was another matter. I hadn't had time to read it carefully yet. Now, since I still wasn't tired, I pulled it toward me. It was more like a series of stories than the history at school. In fact, I'd heard some of these stories before, in picture books and from my grandmother.

In the archives, kings consulted with fairies about foreign policy. Heroes knew chants for war and songs for healing. Ghouls and wizards and whorls walked the pages of Gen's notes alongside names I knew from history. King Walter Wildhammer (War) had won his amazing victory in Darrick Harbor with a small fleet of fishing vessels, or so history reported. But in the archive version, a fast fairy vessel captained by a fairy, Darvian, had also been involved, magically decoying some enemy ships onto the rocks of the harbor mouth, and driving others into King Walter's ingenious traps. My history books had failed to mention Darvian or his illusions. They'd also left out the song hospitals that the archives reported as part of the Peace Palace's effective campaign to control the plague six hundred years ago.

Curses and charms, dragon slayings and bewitchings, heroes with magic swords, and chants that kept off evil were sprinkled through the archival accounts. It seemed a different world from the one I knew. And yet, it didn't. Here were some of my healing songs. And there were some explanations of the Northwestern violence that were much more realistic than the *Daily Sun*'s.

If fairies and spells had been real, why weren't they around anymore? And if they hadn't existed back then, what were they doing all through the archives?

My head throbbed. I pushed away from my desk. Maybe it would be better to think about this tomorrow.

My eyes flitted around the room for something to do, but the neatness of the place defeated me. Impatiently, I stalked into the closet, tore off my nightclothes and threw on shorts, a t-shirt, and my baseball cap. Then, grabbing my basketball, I headed out the door.

My night guard, Duke Patterson, jerked upright and mumbled into his radio.

"Sorry," I said. "I need to get out."

In the courtyard, cool night air smacked into me, and I picked up my pace to a jog. I heard Patterson sigh as he also sped up.

On the outside back wall of the stable, I flipped a switch. The overhead spotlight turned on with a click and a hum. Bluish-white light flooded the pavement, etching elongated leaf shadows where gardens edged the pavement.

Someone had given the basketball hoop a fresh coat of paint and hung up a new net since the last time I was out here. I shook my head as I began to dribble. Sometimes I felt too rich. My ball bounced off the rim. I guessed new equipment didn't help me all that much.

I'd been practicing for about ten minutes when a voice behind me said, "Care to play a little one-on-one?"

"Dad! How did you know I was out?"

"Security phoned."

"Sorry. I couldn't sleep. I thought this might wear me out."

"No problem. Exercise won't hurt me either."

"OK. Why don't you start?" I passed him the basketball. He faked right, and then broke out left and went for a lay-up, which I managed to block. Snagging the ball, I slipped one in.

"Hey!"

"Can I help it if you're slow?"

"That does it. I'm not playing nice anymore."

I laughed and stole the ball. This time, Dad got it back before I could score. When he swooshed it in easily over my head, I remembered that he'd played college basketball. Mostly bench warmed, but still, it only took him twenty minutes to leave me exhausted and down by thirty points. I barely had the energy to pretend to block as he whished in one last three-pointer.

"Enough! I give up!"

Dad laughed and made a playful punch at my head. "Hey, I've got to stay better than you at something. How else will we know I'm the dad?"

I hugged him. "You'll still be the dad even when I get good enough to beat you."

"Yeah. You keep on remembering that." He tousled my hair. "Now get to bed. It's late."

It was. I could barely drag my feet across the courtyard. "I don't know if I can make it out riding with you tomorrow, Dad." I yawned as we parted.

"I'm not sure I've got the energy to get up either. See you at breakfast?"

I started to say I'd have to call Steph to check on my schedule, but then I realized the bill had passed. I'd have no breakfast meetings tomorrow. "Yeah. Breakfast."

It felt good to do normal things again. I just wished I could shake the worry that this return to normal was no more than a brief lull in a storm.

CHAPTER 12

I wandered through a fog where friends from school talked nonsense with congresspeople while a persistent alarm rang through the air. Pushing through to wakefulness, I realized the phone was ringing. I shook my head, rushed across the room, fished my phone out of the cushions of one of my new navy chairs, pressed the green button, and mumbled something into it.

"Sarah? I'm so sorry—I thought you'd be up." Steph sounded upset.

"What's wrong?" I glanced at the clock. Five-thirty. I'd missed my ride with my dad.

Then I remembered I wasn't meeting him this morning.

"It's OK. I slept in because I couldn't get to sleep last night, but I need to get up now anyway. What's wrong?"

"Dad found out about me and Andy. I'm grounded from the Spring Fling."

"Sometimes your dad is super messed up."

"Like yours never is."

"I hear you. So, what are we going to do?"

"I don't know. Maybe he'll let me go with someone after all, and you can go with Andy, and—"

"What if I can't go with Andy? Do you think maybe Gen would?"

"What do you mean you can't go with Andy? Are you going with someone else?"

"Well, I kind of have this arrangement…" Or did I? Phil hadn't called the night before. Was the Spring Fling on or not? "Look, Steph, the plans were kind of tentative. It's probably nothing, but I need to make sure before I agree to anything else."

"You're seeing someone without telling me?"

"Not really seeing."

There was silence on the other end of the line.

"Steph, I'm sorry. I've wanted to tell you all about it, but I promised I wouldn't say anything."

"What, you've fallen in love with some thirty-five-year-old married guy?"

"I wish. I swear I'll tell you all about it as soon as we're alone and not on the phone."

"It's that bad? Great. We can both be grounded from the Fling."

"We'll figure something out."

"We always do."

***

At lunch, I stood in line with everyone else for my slab of greasy pizza, ice-cream scoop of creamed corn, and tiny carton of milk. As I walked to my table, the hard soles of my school flats slapping the linoleum briskly the way I'd been taught to walk, I was too tired even to remind myself to get the kitchen to pack me a lunch tomorrow. Gen was already there, poking listlessly at her own creamed corn when I sat at the orange table.

"Are you OK?" Gen asked.

"Do I look that bad?" I set my tray down and maneuvered myself onto the bench.

"Just tired." Gen put her fork down and gave her pizza a dirty look.

"I am tired. I couldn't get to sleep last night. I did all my homework, cleaned up my desk, and even tried to read the stuff you collected. Nothing helped."

"That stinks. What'd you think of it? The stuff I collected, I mean." Gen nibbled at the pizza.

"I'm not sure. It made me wonder if I'm crazy, or if the archives are."

"The archives."

"What about the archives?" Steph asked, mumbling through a cookie that she held between her teeth while balancing two lunch trays, her purse, and a backpack. She set one of the trays down, plopped the bags onto the bench, and mumbled, "Wait. Don't answer yet." Then she took off with the second tray toward another table where a short dark girl on crutches was attempting to maneuver herself onto a bench. Steph delivered the tray to the girl and then returned. "OK. Now, what about the archives?" she said.

Gen looked at me, eyebrows raised.

"Go ahead," I said.

Gen nodded. "If you're sure Krista won't need any more help."

"She's fine," Steph said.

"Well, about a week ago, Sarah asked me to do some research for her on problems like the ones we're seeing up in the Northwest. I did the research, but the history was so chock-full of fairy tales, I didn't see how it could be any use."

"Fairy tales?"

"Literally. Fairies granting wishes. Mythological beasts that fight with invisible weapons. Heroes, dragon hunts—the stuff of bedtime stories."

"My mom and dad always told me those stories were true," Steph said.

Gen raised her eyebrows. "And you believed them?"

Steph shrugged. "They've never lied to me about anything else."

I supposed that was something. But I wasn't sure if it was enough. "Do you believe the stories enough to start building a defense around them?"

"I don't know."

"Aren't there other things we can try?" Gen asked. "We're not desperate yet."

"I don't know that we should wait until we're desperate if magic is our best line of defense against all the crazy in the Northwest. But yes, we should explore other options, too," I said. "Unfortunately, my mind is blank."

"So, we hold a brainstorming session," Steph said.

I nodded. It was a good idea, and we wouldn't even have to wedge it into overfull schedules now that Walter Cagnew's camp bill had passed.

"We should invite War experts and interested Congresspeople," Gen said. "We and our friends don't have the background to brainstorm effectively."

"I don't know, Gen," Steph said. "Could we trust any true War experts or politicians not to hijack the meeting?"

They both had good points. I wasn't sure what to think, and before I could make up my mind, the bell rang for the end of lunch. "Aargh! I haven't even started my pizza! How does this always happen to me?"

The others laughed. I shoved my pizza in my mouth, stuffed napkins in my pocket, slung my backpack over my shoulder, and jostled into line with a dozen other girls to dump my tray.

✳✳✳

That afternoon, in the coatroom of the War Palace after a Royal Tea planning session, Steph and I waited for the staff to locate Steph's umbrella.

"What do you think of Gen's idea," Steph asked me.

"To invite some War Party members to the brainstorming session?"

"I'm all for it," a voice behind me said.

I swirled. "Prince Philip."

"Your Highness. Stephanie Montressor." He lifted Steph's fingers to his lips. I quashed an unreasonable spike of jealousy.

"The staff tells me, Stephanie, that your umbrella was accidentally taken with a load of forgottens to the lost and found. On the other side of the palace. It'll take about fifteen minutes to retrieve if you care to wait." He indicated a doorway off to his left. Though it was Steph he'd spoken to, he stared intently at me.

"Thank you," I said.

Phil signaled his guards to stay behind, so, nervously, I nodded at Clare to do the same. Then Steph and I followed Phil into the waiting room. Though its overstuffed chairs and giant flower arrangement reminded me of home, being closeted in a War Palace waiting room was anything but relaxing.

As the door clicked softly behind us, Phil shrugged off his graceful public demeanor and threw himself onto the floral chair nearest me. "Sarah, I'm so sorry. You will forgive me for not calling last night, won't you? After the vote, Dad lectured me for hours. I didn't get free until dinner. When he finds out I've asked you to the Fling, I don't know what he'll do."

"Sarah?" Steph asked, her voice unnaturally high. "Is he serious?"

Phil turned to her. "As serious as I've ever been about anything."

"And you?"

"I'm serious, too," I said.

"Have you both gone crazy?"

I laughed. "Probably."

"Can either one of you tell me how you intend to tell your parents?"

I sighed. "They're going to throw a fit."

"No kidding," Phil said.

"And what are you going to do when you're passionately opposed on some issue?" Steph asked.

"Argue, of course," I said.

"Sure," Steph said, "but how will you get along, arguing like that?"

"Just because Andy lets you do his serious thinking for him doesn't mean everyone wants a guy like that," I said.

Phil's forehead wrinkled. "Andy who?" Then his face cleared, and he turned toward Steph. "Wait. Are you saying you and Andy Sanderson are going out?"

"So, what if we are?"

"How does your dad feel about that?"

"He didn't find out until last night," Steph admitted.

"He grounded her for life." I giggled.

Phil whistled. "And he's been so reasonable about you helping Sarah, too." He groaned. "We haven't got a chance. What if we keep this secret a while longer?"

"I don't know," I said. "I don't like lying to my parents. And anyway, how can we be secret if we want to be together? It's not like either of us can get around unnoticed."

"That might not be as hard as you think, at least when it comes to the Spring Fling," Steph said. "You go with Andy. Phil can take me. He'll get around my dad somehow. Once we're there, we naturally drift together, and no one's the wiser."

"That's great," Phil said. "It avoids trouble with our parents, and if we do it right, not even the media will know."

"I suppose you're right," I said.

Someone tapped on the door. Phil sprang to his feet and resumed an air of diplomatic poise.

A maid poked her head in. "Miss Montressor? We found your umbrella."

"Oh, right." Steph blushed. "Thanks."

"You'll consider allowing me to be part of your brainstorming session?" Phil asked.

I'd forgotten about the brainstorming session. I had to think before I could answer, "We'll consider it, yes."

"Adieu, then," Phil said, brushing my fingertips lightly with his lips. My spine tingled. Maybe hand kissing wasn't as awful as I'd thought.

Somehow, we got out to the car.

"Sarah Margaret Lithania Seraglio Malcolm Tressarian, you are absolutely nuts," Steph said once the doors shut us in.

"I know, Steph. I know."

CHAPTER 13

If I'd known Lord Montressor would come to our brainstorming session, I'd have reconsidered opening it to whoever wanted to come. I was also regretting having agreed to keep my relationship with Phil secret.

I felt uncomfortable whenever Lord Montressor's sharp glances were directed at Steph, Andy, Phil, or me. It didn't help that Lord Montressor seemed to have come to the meeting mainly to chaperone the young people. His demeanor was polite and businesslike, but I couldn't shake the feeling that he regarded our session as a cover for messing around.

I was frustrated that most of the adults who mattered in the government considered my brainstorming session a juvenile attempt to play at politics rather than a serious effort to solve a genuine problem. Besides Lord Montressor, Walter Cagnew, and another young congressman from the affected area, Uncle Malcolm was the only adult who had come to my meeting. And he'd only come because I'd begged.

I was afraid that with so few people, we wouldn't think of many good ideas, but I needn't have worried. Between what I'd prepared and a nonstop flow of suggestions from Andy, we soon had enough for a lengthy series of recommendations involving everything from improved communications infrastructures and neighborhood watch schedules to relocating some military training to do double duty as extra protection for the affected areas. Arguments between Uncle Malcolm and Lord Montressor pared the list down to practical, passable points.

After a couple of hours, the arguments started to die down. Phil, who had been largely silent, glanced at Gen's notes and said, "I think this is a good legislative agenda for the next couple of months. We've done well."

"Don't sound so surprised," Steph said.

"Honestly, I don't know when I've seen a bipartisan group accomplish so much in so little time."

Was that why he was trying to take over now? I didn't much like it, but I didn't let it bother me. I wasn't done yet. "We still haven't dealt with how to handle conflicts that appear to be magical."

"You're kidding, right?" Walter said.

"No, she's for real," Gen said, sighing. Then she described what she'd found in the archives.

"But that's hogwash," Joe Black, the congressman from Walksly said. "It's got to be."

"I don't know," Lord Montressor said. "I've always believed the archives."

Maybe it wasn't so terrible to have him there after all.

"Come on, have you ever seen any proof of magic?" Walter asked.

"Sarah says she healed Andy's arm with one of those magic songs last week," Gen said, "And that Prince Philip was there."

Phil looked taken aback. "Yes. Yes, that's true."

"How was he hurt—a scrape?" Walter asked.

"No," Phil said. "Andy's arm was seriously injured. I heard a crack when the ball hit it, and he couldn't move it."

"I could too."

Phil rolled his eyes. "Maybe an inch, with obvious pain. After Her Highness sang, you were able to finish the game."

"And none of you said anything about this?" Representative Black asked.

Phil shrugged. "Her Highness and I already get enough publicity. Besides, who would believe it?"

"That's why we can't recommend any magical defense," Uncle Malcolm said. "Even if Her Highness were able to demonstrate, people would think it was some kind of publicity stunt. We'd get laughed out of Congress, and that would undermine the rest of our suggestions, which, as His Highness points out, are worth passing."

I nodded. "I can understand that, but we ought to do something."

"I could set up an informational website," Gen said. "That would get the songs and chants out there for people to try without it reflecting poorly on any of you."

"But you don't believe in the songs and chants," Sarah said.

Gen shrugged. "I don't know what I believe, but I don't think putting the information out there will hurt anyone."

I smiled.

"Sarah, you and Prince Philip could also call in fairy help without legislative approval," Steph said.

"What?"

"Foreign affairs don't have to go through even Joint Council if you've got blood members of both royal houses in agreement on something, right?"

"That's true," Phil said slowly.

"Well, in that packet of stuff Gen dug up, there was a chant for calling up the fairies." Steph pointed out a spot in the sheaf of papers to Philip, who was sitting next to her. "It says that in order for them to return, the royal houses of Dicrandia need to cooperate. Apparently, the Islandian fairies got tired of all the bickering between War and Peace. But since Sarah and Phil are both here, cooperating, calling them up should work, right?"

"If you understand correctly," Lord Montressor said.

"And if the fairies are real, which I doubt," Walter said.

"And still around, listening," Uncle Malcolm said.

"Still, it's worth a try, isn't it?" Steph asked.

I tapped my pencil on the desk. "Extra help couldn't hurt, could it? And if it doesn't come, what difference does it make?"

Phil nodded. "All right. But let's save the funny business until after all the real stuff is nailed down."

So, once we'd finalized our plans for passing the agenda, argued through the order of names on the printed recommendations, and wound up the meeting, Phil and I stuck around to call up legendary help we barely believed in.

"So," Phil said.

"So."

"It says here we clasp hands and repeat this nonsense poem in unison."

I grabbed the sheaf of papers from him. "Let me see that."

Blast. He was right. I put up my hand a bit uncertainly, and Phil grasped it. Anyone looking in would have thought we were about to arm wrestle.

"Ready?" he challenged.

I nodded.

"OK, then. On the count of three."

I heard the numbers, and then my own voice mixing with Phil's:

"Telecran dluxiat sinertifana bly
Anasamerdie sufermentwan
Canellamenthia ply."

A tingling buzz, almost like electricity, swept through me as I said the words. Fairy power? Hormones? Then it was over. I still held Phil's hand. Slowly we released each other.

"Nothing happened," I said.

"Did you expect it to?"

"Yes…No…I don't know. It seemed for a moment like something would."

He raised an eyebrow.

So, he hadn't felt anything? Or was he playing it cool? Perhaps he didn't want himself associated with the magic side of our session's recommendations. I wished I hadn't mentioned my own expectations. "See you later?"

"Looking forward to it." He swept his laptop and papers into a briefcase, brushed my fingertips with his lips, and was gone.

CHAPTER 14

Though Phil had contributed little to our brainstorming session, and his part in implementing the ideas was minimal, I heard several people refer to "the Prince's defense package" at the Royal Tea. I restrained my irritation with difficulty. The important thing, I reminded myself, was that the Northwest got help, not that I got credit.

Besides, our measures weren't working anyway. No matter what laws we passed, news from the Northwest kept getting worse. It was no consolation that the media now hailed me as a minor prophet for recognizing how serious the problem was before the supposedly responsible adults in government did. Andy filed for special permission to graduate early and enlist in the army. He was to report for training Monday, which meant he was sporting a military haircut for the Spring Fling.

The haircut didn't bother me, but getting ready by myself did. Since Steph was going out with the prince, she was persona-non-grata at my house tonight (and I certainly wasn't allowed to get ready at hers.) I'd hoped I could at least spend the time with Gen, but she'd gone back for her hometown's spring dance.

So, I stood alone before my mirror. I thought I looked OK in my long, slim, silver gown, my dark hair held up in a silver tiara, but the only kind of smile I could manage was a political one. I was relieved when Andy's knock came more than half an hour early. Except it wasn't Andy, but Uncle Malcolm.

He whistled long and low. "Wow," he said. "I'm almost afraid to ruin the effect by offering these."

"Offering these what?"

Uncle Malcolm held out two little jewelry boxes. "From me," he said, putting one in my left hand, "and from your dad, who would be here if he hadn't been called out by that infernal Congress. They wanted me too, but he insisted one of us show up to give these in person."

"Oh, Uncle Malcolm, thank you." I hugged him. "They're perfect. I'm sure they are."

They were. Amethysts set in silver hearts—three dangling from each earring, and a large one nestled in the hollow of my throat.

"They're nothing much. Your mom helped us pick them. And there's a price-tag attached. You have to listen to several minutes of avuncular advice."

"Ah, like don't stay out too late, don't talk Andy into doing anything crazy, and keep my heels out of the hem of my skirt?"

Uncle Malcolm laughed. "Excellent tips, but I was thinking more along the lines of, try to forget about politics for a bit. Have a good time, like a girl should at her first big dance. But don't let the atmosphere confuse you. Your life's love is probably not going to step out of the woodwork and declare himself tonight."

"My life's—Uncle Malcolm, I'm going with Andy!"

"Who is not, if I know anything about it, going to be dancing with you."

My face heated.

"Which leads one to deduce that you'll be dancing with other young men."

"And you think I should cloister myself?"

"I said, enjoy yourself. Just guard your heart."

"You're hinting at more than you're saying."

Uncle Malcolm held his hands up, palms out. "Me! Never. I'm a simple man."

I laughed but wondered how much Uncle Malcolm knew or guessed, and what of that he would feel compelled to tell my parents. It would all be for my own good, I was sure. Uncle Malcolm's indiscretions always were. I smoothed wrinkles off my forehead and escaped to Andy, who was far too preoccupied to notice my silence.

The War Palace limo was behind ours at the reception hall. Andy drifted toward it. Amid a barrage of camera flashes, I grabbed his elbow and smiled sweetly while whispering fiercely in his ear, "Wait until we're inside, you dolt."

Andy smiled limply back, and I hoped the pictures would be tolerable. At least my cousin knew better than to try answering the hodgepodge of questions reporters shouted at us. "How are you feeling, Your Highness?" "Don't you think a dance is frivolous with the Northwest in so much trouble?" "Who designed your dress?"

Behind me, I could hear the same questions (minus the one about the dress) being shouted at Phil. Thank goodness journalists weren't allowed at the dance. All the same, I kept my eyes open for kids or staff pointing phones my way. Or I would when I got my sight back. For the moment, Andy and I were halted in what seemed a giant cave, its lights so dim, I could make out nothing. Music pounded.

"Steph," Andy said.

"Andy?"

Bother. They were stopped in the entrance, too.

"You look spectacular," Andy said.

She probably did, but how would he know? He must have been as blind as I was.

"Thank you."

"Do you want to dance?"

"I'd love to." Steph laughed.

By then, I could see her. She'd piled her glossy curls on her head and chosen a flattering dusty green dress, but her true beauty came from the smile she wore as she ran off with Andy. I turned to Phil. He also looked stunning, dressed to the nines, with—could that be an amethyst-colored vest peeking out from under his jacket? But Steph couldn't have told him about my amethysts. I got them tonight. It must have been serendipity. I smiled. "Our dates seem to have deserted us."

"I noticed."

"I'd be crushed if I hadn't expected it."

"Oh?" he said, moving close. His sleeve brushed my arm. "But since you expected it, you feel…"

How did I feel? Like it was suddenly difficult to breathe. I sucked in air and laughed. "I don't know. Exhilarated, I think. You?"

"Lucky," he said, holding out a hand. "Care to dance?"

I glanced about to see who was watching—half the room. What did they suppose was happening? A little royal tiff? I'd better answer fast. "Certainly," I said, putting my hand in his.

He pulled me toward the dance floor so fast, I nearly tripped. Maybe we needed the speed. A few steps into the room, a young man I'd never seen before, shoved forward by his date, approached and said he'd be more than happy…

"Thanks so much," I said. "Perhaps next dance. As you can see, I'm engaged for this one."

Phil smiled, twinkles in his eyes. "Everyone's so eager to save us from ourselves," he murmured in my ear.

I laughed.

The room seemed shocked. Electrified. It was beyond excitement. A strange new energy filled the reception hall. Was this what love felt like? I closed my eyes and smiled my first real smile in days.

Phil's grip on my hand tightened to the point where it hurt, and I opened my eyes in time to see two tall glowing figures appear in the middle of the dance floor. All sound in the room stopped, as if it had been switched off. Everything froze. My classmates and the boys from Regency North formed clusters and pairs of grotesquely contorted statues. Clare posed with her hand on her gun-hip. I bit back a scream and squeezed Phil's hand as hard as he was squeezing mine. As I did so, I noticed, with a touch of surprise, that I could still move.

So could Phil, I realized when he pulled me toward him. "Who are you, and what do you want?" his voice rang out.

"I'm Darvian," one of the brilliant figures came forward. The light pulsing from him was bright, but I could see him if I looked at him sideways. He was taller than most men, and almost too beautiful, as if sculpted out of living marble. His clothes were loose silk and striped with every hue of the rainbow.

"Darvian?" I asked. I'd heard the name. Wasn't Darvian one of the fairies in the old tales? But that was hundreds of years ago. Surely this couldn't be the same guy.

"I've had dealings with your country before, long ago. This is Glenstra. We're from Islandia. We came in answer to your call."

"Our call?" I pulled slightly away from Phil. "That poem thing? We did that over a month ago."

"We had sworn we would not reenter Dicrandia until the two royal houses cooperated," Darvian replied, holding his hands out in supplication.

"We were cooperating," I said.

"Not more than our parties often do," Phil said, grinning.

He had a point. "But if it's so important that we cooperate, what are you doing here now?" I asked.

The other fairy—Glenstra, I reminded myself—laughed a tinkling golden laugh. I turned my attention toward her and saw the most beautiful woman I'd ever seen, tall, with dark, nearly purple, skin, and shiny black hair that rose in a braided circle above her head like a crown. She was more beautiful than Steph, more beautiful even than my mom, and her sunshine yellow evening gown glowed.

"Currently, you two are getting along nicely," she said. Even her words seemed to laugh.

I'm sure I blushed, and I was glad for the darkness of the room.

"And we're running out of time," Darvian added. "To work together, we'll need a more official invitation from your fathers, but your dance was enough cooperation for us to come and discuss our mutual need."

"Running out of time for what?" Phil asked.

I wished I'd asked the question.

"Is there someplace we can talk? Privately?" Glenstra asked.

Now wouldn't that be a headache? It had taken months to line up a private conference with diplomats from Grinlovia, and they at least had diplomatic relations with us. Even if these two were ambassadors from Islandia, there were no treaties or anything in place for this. I glanced at Phil, but his face gave me no clues to what he was thinking. I supposed we could try to get the Joint Council building opened up, but the paperwork would take hours, and all the people we needed to sign it were in the Capitol for that emergency session of Congress. I didn't relish interrupting that. And while Phil and I were getting along reasonably well, we weren't on good enough terms to make either of our houses a great option. The thought of my dollhouse flickered through my mind, but that would hardly be—

My musing was interrupted by an oddly blank sensation. When I came to myself, we stood in my dollhouse—Darvian, Glenstra, Phil, and I. A soft white glow filled the space. I stifled a scream.

"What do you think you're doing?" I said. "We can't disappear like that!"

"You should have warned us!" Phil protested at the same time. "Our guards are going to have a fit. People will worry."

He was still holding my hand. I squeezed, reassuring myself that at least we were together.

"We have arranged things. There will be no trouble," Darvian said. "Privacy is necessary."

"No trouble?" I shouted. How could there not be trouble when Phil and I had both disappeared from the dance? "You all showed up supernaturally and then spirited us out of the Spring Fling. The whole city is probably already looking for us."

"There is no point in getting so alarmed," Darvian said. "We have arranged things. There will be no trouble. Won't you please sit down? We are happy to help you, as you requested, but there is much to discuss."

As he spoke, I felt myself calming, though a nagging worry in the back of my mind wondered how I could be calming so quickly. But the rest of my brain silenced it. We had asked for fairy help, hadn't we? And we could certainly use it. I raised my eyebrows questioningly at Phil. He leaned toward me and murmured, "We may as well listen to them. What choice do we have?"

He was right. In a public place, in front of our guards and half the high-school-age kids in Bentralia, these fairies had essentially kidnapped us. If they wanted to talk, I didn't see any way to prevent them. I nodded at Phil, and we sat down on the bench nearest us. As soon as we settled on it, we held hands again.

Darvian nodded at his companion, and she vanished. "Glenstra will keep guard," he said before sitting on the other bench, arranging his long limbs as gracefully as the tiny trestle allowed. His eyes twinkled. Was he laughing at the table? At us?

As if in response to my mental concern, Darvian became more sober. "As I said before, we are from Islandia, and we come in answer to your call. We know of the trouble you've been having on your northern border with the rebel Stralton's minions, and…"

"Whoa, whoa, whoa," I said. "Back up. The rebel who? I've never heard that name before, even in the old legends."

"Never heard of Darvian before either," Phil muttered.

"Sure, you have," I said back, as softly as I could. "In one of the old stories—something about boats, maybe?"

"Oh, right. Darrick Harbor. I remember the kid version now," Phil said, equally softly. Then, a bit louder, he said to Darvian, "So you're the descendant of Darvian from Darrick Harbor?"

"I am the Darvian from Darrick Harbor."

"Oh, come on," Phil said. "Darrick Harbor was seven-hundred and fifty years ago."

"Seven-hundred-and-fifty-two come this September," Darvian said.

"There's no way," I whispered.

"You doubt me?" Darvian's brow wrinkled, and he glanced around the small cabin. Suddenly, he flicked his wrist, and half the contents of my shelves hurtled toward the table. I yelped and yanked my hand out of Phil's to cover my head, but nothing hit me. Instead, the teapot and cups morphed into miniature versions of the Dragonteeth rocks in Darrick Harbor. I couldn't believe those small and medium lumps of rock had been my tea service. The table itself appeared much less solid, much more a roiling mass of waves. And in Darvian's flying fingers, my paper stash rapidly became a fleet of ships. Two fleets, rather, one low-bodied and deep blue, the other taller and fatter, in shades of green.

Next to me, Phil gasped. "Unbelievable. Exactly like that reconstruction I saw a couple of years ago."

I'd forgotten he'd been there too.

"Silence," Darvian said. "The day was a blustery one." Wind rose on the table-sea, licking at my face when I leaned in.

"The enemy was formidable, but we were ready for him." Low, swift boats skirted the Dragonteeth and engaged the first set of tall, fat invaders. Paper crunched against paper with cracks and groans that no paper ought to have been able to make. It was going badly for the little blues.

Out of nowhere, a great white boat, like a swan, bore down on the front lines of the fighting, turning the tide. As the tall greens fled from the white and the little blues, they found their way blocked by one of the larger Dragonteeth and by another great heap of granite that hadn't been there when the battle began. The enemy vanguard had no choice but to keep fighting until burning or leaking or both, they sank beneath the sea. The little blues then sailed right through the new granite mass to engage another set of tall greens on the other side, while the great white swan engaged a third group, doing enough damage to get them to chase it directly into the largest Dragontooth. The white swan passed straight through, but the greens crashed against the rock.

"I get it now," Phil whispered.

"Get what?" I asked.

"How the Morlans lost so many ships on the rocks that day. It didn't make sense before. So, Darvian, are you saying you can pull this kind of stuff in the Northwest and mop up the mess we've got going on up there?"

"I wish it were that easy," Darvian said. The scene in front of us stopped. The tea service morphed back into its regular china state and flew back to its shelves. The tiny sea stopped roiling and became a rough wooden table again. Hundreds of origami boats littered its surface. The white swan boat skittered off the table into my lap. I picked it up and fingered its delicate folds. I was going crazy. Completely and utterly bonkers.

"You're not crazy," Darvian said. "You are merely dealing with realities you haven't faced before."

"Good to know," Phil said.

I laughed and couldn't stop laughing. I took a deep breath to get myself under control. When that didn't work, I took another. Phil found my hand and squeezed it, nodding at me. That helped. I stopped laughing and tried to think. There was so much in this situation that was totally bizarre, I hardly knew how to navigate it. How did we even start?

I eased my hand back from Phil so I could rub my temples. What was my dad's advice about dealing with situations over my head? That's right. Figure out what I knew and what I needed to know. So, what did I know?

I looked at the man across the table from me. He wasn't glowing anymore, but he still seemed different from a normal man. Bigger. More beautiful. I took a deep breath. "So, you're Darvian," I said, "And you helped with Darrick Harbor." Or he knew enough about it to tell a convincing story. "What makes it so hard to help in the Northwest now?"

"Stralton," Darvian answered. "He may be a rebel, without any honor or respect for life, but he's a powerful, subtle fairy with thousands under his sway. He's behind your trouble in the Northwest, and I'm afraid it'll take more than a few fake rocks to fool him."

CHAPTER 15

“Stralton,” I said. “You’ve mentioned him a couple of times now, but I don’t remember having heard anything about him before.”

“No, I don’t suppose you would have,” Darvian said, flicking his fingers at a few of the paper boats. They danced across the table. “Stralton was yet a youngling when we broke off contact with Dicrandia.”

“And why was that, again?” Phil asked.

“We had warned your royal family that we would not put up with the perpetual bickering in your house.”

“Our house?” Phil asked. “Which royal family do you imagine is the real one?”

“The two houses were one family seven-hundred years ago. Even the regular histories say that, Phil,” I said.

“Regular histories?” Darvian asked.

“The ones without any fairies or magic,” Phil said.

“You have histories without fairies?”

“Most of us think fairies are a myth,” I said.

“But you called us anyway?”

Phil shrugged.

“We thought it was worth a shot,” I said. “There are some things going on in the Northwest that the regular histories don’t explain. If you think you can help us—or even tell us what is causing our problems—we’re willing to listen to what you have to say.”

"We're not desperate or anything," Phil said, "but confronted with enough abnormality, we've become willing to consider unusual alternatives. So, start talking. Why don't you start with this Stralton figure? What makes him a rebel, and what makes you think he's behind the violence in the Northwest?"

Darvian leaned back, as if resting in an easy chair, though he was sitting on a trestle bench, like we were. Then he pressed the tips of his fingers together, tipped his head to one side, and said, "Stralton. Naturally, you need to know about Stralton. Let's see. Perhaps I should say first that we are not generally fighting people. Our government is based on consensus."

"Consensus of whom?" Phil asked.

"All of us," Darvian said.

I shook my head. That would never work with a human society. Nothing would ever get done.

"It does take some time," Darvian admitted. "But we are a patient people. Usually. Stralton, I'm afraid, was never willing to wait. But then, his family never played by the rules." Darvian leaned in and said in a whisper, "His father took a second wife."

"So?" Phil said.

"So, she died when he did—within a decade, anyway. Poor thing, she hardly saw her second century."

I didn't know what to say. "Does that usually happen—dying when a spouse dies, I mean?"

"Always. If we love someone and mate with them, when they die, we soon will as well. They say it is a blessing."

I wasn't sure I agreed, but then again, I knew how miserable my grandma had been for a long time after my grandfather was assassinated. Maybe it was a blessing. "Didn't Stralton's father love his wife?"

"He loved his first wife, right enough. Everyone knew he was dying when he married Stralton's mother. Her family tried to stop her, but she said she'd rather have a few years with him than a lifetime without."

I'm not sure I'd make that choice, but I could sort of understand it. But surely if Stralton's father had loved his mother, the man—fairy—wouldn't have let her sacrifice herself that way. "OK, so his father was unfeeling. What's that got to do with Stralton?"

"Everything. The boy was raised almost from the beginning without parents, by his unorthodox father's family. His great talent made things worse."

"Let me guess," Phil said. "He'd have made us feel like we were sitting in the little paper boats."

Darvian smiled. "He may be nearly as good with illusions as I am, but his real talent, child, is influence. He bends others' minds to his will."

"Mind control? Seriously?" Phil said.

I was impressed by his ability to respond to Darvian's message instead of getting upset at Darvian calling him a child.

Darvian straightened up, and a slight crease between his eyes marred his perfectly molded face. "It is most serious, child. Nearly all our younglings and many older fairies have been affected."

That sounded like a basic generation gap to me. "You're sure they're being controlled—it's not that they agree with Stralton?"

"Quite sure. We've found evidence of the spells. Plus, the changes weren't natural. People who thought one thing their whole lives switched in an instant to the exact opposite—without any apparent reason for doing so."

"That does sound fishy," Phil said, "But how hard can it be to keep your own opinions?"

"For you? Not hard at all. Most humans aren't easily swayed by influence spells, and we believe you in particular, Prince Philip, are immune. But we fairies are weak in that regard. That's part of why we came even though your cooperation is so…fledgling. We need your help."

Wait. The fairies wanted *our* help? What was going on here?

Darvian glanced at me. "Naturally, we are willing to help you as well."

"That's the second or third time you've answered me when I didn't say anything," I said.

Darvian nodded. "It saves time."

"You can hear me thinking?" I shivered.

"If I focus on you, yes."

"Would you please stop? It creeps me out."

"That goes for me, too," Phil said.

"Lad, I don't go any nearer your mind than I have to. If I slipped into even the slightest hint of an influence spell, your natural defenses could kill me."

"My powers? It's Sarah who can do that healing stuff."

"Naturally, she can. She's royal, isn't she? You know the Dicrandian royal families both come from a single line. That line always produces children with powerful magical abilities. Frankly, we Islandians are shocked by how much progress Stralton's advance team has made in your Northwest. None of the old kings would have let a few fairy scouts flummox them the way you have. Why, I once saw Randolph the First cast a word web strong enough to imprison a dragon. And Desmond the Third could sing men back from the edge of death."

I picked up one of the green origami boats and twisted it. "Did you say we're only dealing with a few fairy scouts?"

"Indeed. Though the main part of Stralton's forces will be here in little more than a week if they continue to cut through Islandia at their current rate."

"A week? Nice of you all to give us so much warning." Phil crossed his arms over his chest.

"We assumed you'd detected his army yourself, and that's why you'd called for our aid."

I dropped the little paper boats back onto the table and rubbed my temples again. "If a fairy army is coming this way, like you say, how would we even go about trying to detect it?"

Darvian raised his hands and his eyebrows. "I know little of human magic. There is the underlying ability, which is stronger in some than others, and nonexistent in many. I think there are poems you say or sing.

"What poems?" Phil and I said at the same time.

Darvian shrugged. "I'm afraid I only remember the words to a few of them. Our magic does not work that way—it comes, of itself.

Wonderful. So, maybe some kind of magical army was bearing down on us, and we didn't even remember the skill that would enable us to see it.

"You remember some of your skill if you can heal," Darvian said.

I glared at him. "I thought I told you to stop reading my mind."

"My apologies. It's hard to avoid in such a small space as this."

"Besides, healing is different from seeing and stopping armies. I kind of doubt my songs would be much good for that."

"No. Different songs and chants are for different purposes."

I rolled my eyes.

"We did keep a few," Darvian said.

"Songs or chants?" Phil said. "Let's have one."

Darvian recited a nonsense poem unlike any of the ones I regularly used.

"Do you know what it's for?" I asked.

"Undoing influence spells, it is said. When one with power like Prince Philip's says it in the place where an influence spell has been cast, that spell is broken, and the people affected return to their own minds."

"It won't work from here?" I asked.

"Alas, no. We must ask the prince to accompany us to Islandia proper, to the places where Stralton did magic before retreating into Stralton City. Even without going into his stronghold, this chant could return as much as a legion of our people who've fallen under Stralton's influence."

"He's got his own city?" I asked.

"Five hundred years ago, he carved a country larger than Dicrandia from the western half of Islandia. Have you all been asleep since we left?"

"Apparently," Phil said.

"OK, but that's not the point at the moment," I said. "I understand now why you want Phil's help, but can't it wait? If we're going to be attacked any day now, we need Phil here."

"As much as you need our help defending yourselves? If Phil won't do what he can for us, I don't know if we'll be able to spare the fairies to help you out. We're fighting a war too, you know."

Phil paled. "How long would I have to be gone?"

"About a week if we leave before morning."

Phil nodded grimly.

I bit my lip. "But if what you've told us is true, we'll be under attack by then. We need to get War Powers passed."

"What kind of War Powers?" Phil asked.

"Limited to Silvershire, Walksly, Westerberg, and Livingston. They keep their representation in Congress. Renewable in six-week intervals by a vote of the full Congress."

"Six weeks?"

"Well, maybe three months."

"We've got a war coming on!"

Probably. If Darvian, the self-professed master of illusion was telling us the truth. "So, we've heard. If it comes as predicted, there will be no trouble passing the renewal. I'll vote for it."

"You bargain hard, you know it?"

I shrugged.

"OK. But even with War Powers, my going leaves War weakened."

"Only for a week."

"Assuming nothing happens to me."

I gulped. "You'd better not let anything happen to you."

"Still, nobody in War will go for this."

"If the prince dies, his parents will have another child," Darvian said. "It was provided for in the spell we put on your house—the one that makes every royal child an only child."

"Good to know I'm replaceable," Phil said.

"Don't be ridiculous," I said, grabbing his hand and squeezing. "Maybe your parents could have another child, but they could never have another you."

"Thanks," Phil said, squeezing back.

"Not that it matters. Nobody's going to believe your mom and dad can have another kid. They'll never let you go."

"Perhaps you could come with us, and one of us could remain to help the princess explain to your Council in the morning," Darvian suggested.

"NO!" Phil and I said together.

"Perhaps you could both come. Then War wouldn't be disproportionately weakened," Darvian said.

"No," I said. "We aren't private citizens. We can't run off, even to save the country, without the country's approval. Not to mention without telling our parents."

"Perhaps we could get the Council to agree to our both going," Phil said.

"Maybe. It would be easier if we weren't both only children."

"Can you think of anything better?"

"What about section two-fourteen of the Joint Council Code?" I asked.

"Section what?"

"The part that keeps your grandpa from coming to meetings."

"My grandpa doesn't come to Joint Council because he has dementia and hardly knows who he is anymore."

"That's why War linked his attendance to my grandpa's, but it's the link that legally is keeping him out."

"So, if we link your participation to mine…"

"I can't participate if anything happens to you."

"But the country would need you, eventually."

"Well, could we put a time limit on it—say a couple of years? That should give War plenty of time to get entrenched."

Phil smiled at me. "Better make it five."

I laughed. "Well, could we?"

"I don't know. I don't carry a copy of the code around in my pocket."

"And here I thought you had it memorized."

Darvian obliged with a copy out of thin air. It turned out we could link the attendance of two royal members of Joint Council for any duration if we had a normal eleven count passage and the top four members of each party all agreed to the link.

"That last requirement is going to be a doozy," Phil said.

"No kidding," I agreed. "How much time do we have?"

Phil glanced at his phone. "It's ten-o-clock now."

I nodded. "Council meeting at three?"

"Do you really think we can do this?"

"We're very persuasive people," I said.

CHAPTER 16

At least Darvian warned us before transporting us back to the dance. I came to myself in darkness interrupted by flecks of colored light on fancy-dressed young people frozen in odd, contorted positions.

"What did you do, leave everybody frozen the whole time we were away?" Phil asked.

"I thought you were taking care of things!" I added.

"Children, we couldn't have these young people telling everyone that you'd been whisked away."

"The media has figured out something's up anyway," Phil said. "Can't you see the pile-up by the entrance?"

"But children—"

I wheeled on him. "Don't call us children! And don't call our parents or any congresspeople children, either! You may be immortal and unbelievably powerful, but your political savvy is nonexistent. For the rest of tonight, you're to do exactly as one of us says. No going off on your own. No more magic funny business. Have you got that?"

"But—"

"There is no but. You do it, or you go back where you came from. We can't work with you if you do stupid stuff like this."

Darvian gaped.

"Good. Now that we've got that settled, Phil, do you think you can locate a couple of microphones?"

"With pleasure, Your Highness." He swung toward the DJs table and came back with two.

"Thanks." I made eye contact with Phil, and he nodded. I took a deep breath and said, "Darvian, unfreeze these people."

After a pause, the room came alive. Music pulsed; people moved, and a wave of reporters pushed through the entryway. A chorus of voices added to the cacophony.

"What's going on?"

"Are you all right, Peter?"

"Friends," I bellowed into my microphone. The music cut, and silence fell like a sledgehammer. Uncle Malcolm was right: there were advantages to being a princess. "We are deeply sorry for the trouble you've had this evening."

"You should be," someone called. "Do you have any idea what it's like to stand for hours with your hands over your head?"

"Obviously not," Phil's voice boomed, "but if either Her Highness or I had known what was going on back here, you wouldn't either."

A new kind of electricity permeated the reception hall. I was pretty sure this time it wasn't magic, at least not in the traditional sense.

"We'd love to answer all your questions, but we must contact our parents, who, like many of yours, are worrying," I said. "We have a lot to do tonight, but this much we can tell you. These visitors from Islandia may be able to help us fight against the nameless fears in our Northwest. We are sorry this interruption has disturbed your party, and to try and compensate, we'll see that the dance stays open until two. Enjoy it for us. We've got to go back to work." I turned off my mike and handed it off, preparing to get out fast.

Phil grabbed my hand. "Tonight, friends, is a night of hope! Celebrate it!" He lifted my hand with his, high into the air.

Applause thundered. I smiled as a dozen cameras flashed. The music came up, and Phil passed off his own mike. Everybody started talking again, and in the resulting confusion, we dashed for the back exit, still holding hands.

Steph had preceded us, guessing our course and miraculously calling up both the War and Peace limos.

"Steph! You're a lifesaver." I said. "But what about Andy?"

"He's running interference. He'll meet us back at the palace. Come on, move."

We ducked into my limo, barely making it before the press corps rounded the corner in a fleet of beat-up minis and small maintenance vans.

"Go!" Steph said to the driver, who immediately peeled away from the curb and swung onto a main thoroughfare.

"Call your mom and dad," Clare said, handing over my phone. "They've been calling for the last hour, and I don't think my all-clear text convinced them you're OK."

"I'm sorry I worried them. I didn't mean to. Darvian and Glenstra said they were handling things—that no one would worry about us." Where were those pesky fairies, anyway?

While my call to Dad was still ringing through, Darvian and Glenstra materialized on the seat next to Steph, squashing her between their tall, gorgeous forms.

Steph squeaked.

"You called," Glenstra said.

My mouth dropped open. I clamped it back shut. "I can't get used to the way you appear out of thin air. It's disconcerting. Don't you all ever walk?"

"All the time. In a beautiful wood near my home," Glenstra said.

"I meant to get from one place to another."

"No," Darvian said.

"Never mind. Now, when we get to the palace, follow my lead. Don't patronize my parents. They won't respond well, I promise. And why are you both here? Someone ought to be with Phil."

Glenstra disappeared. I shuddered. Fairy travel was creepy. Steph must have thought so, too, because she unbuckled for long enough to put a seat between herself and Darvian.

It took nearly five minutes to reassure Dad that I was all right, but once he was convinced, he took the news that Darvian was about to visit with remarkable aplomb. He didn't even seem too upset when he heard that Phil and I had given a joint speech at the dance. He merely said we'd talk more when I got home. Then he handed the phone off to my mother.

It took another ten minutes to disentangle myself from that conversation. Then I could set things in motion for a three-o'clock Joint Council meeting. We were twenty minutes into the car ride before I could put down my phone.

Steph finished her own phone conversation quickly. "How did it go with your dad?" she asked as she snapped her own phone shut.

I shrugged. "I don't know. He was worried, and he's not sure what to make of the situation. I don't think he wants to talk about it on the phone."

"He's upset, then?"

"I think he's postponing feeling until he knows more."

We lapsed into silence, the limo whirring along the pavement. It turned abruptly left, then right, into an alley behind a small park.

"We need to head for Peace Palace," I said.

"Yes, Your Highness," the driver said. I could see her grin in the rearview mirror. "I expect I'd be drawn and quartered if I delivered you anywhere else tonight. We're just losing a little tail we've picked up."

The car swung again, this time into an alley littered with dumpsters and old tires. A grey mini with a radio antenna the size of Jasnic Tower swung into the alley behind us.

The limo sped up.

I reassured myself that my seatbelt was fastened.

We were going eighty in the second alley. Then, with a squeal of tires, we turned on Silverstone Boulevard. We whizzed past three intersections, U-turned around the tree-filled median, and headed back the way we'd come, much more slowly. The shadows of leaves on the lighter shadow of the road created a rich, textured carpet beneath the limo's wheels. Seconds later, the mini screamed by, going the other way.

I didn't breathe normally again until we reached the beltway near home, ten minutes after the last sight of our tail. I hated being hassled by the press but wasn't sure I like running from them any better. I leaned back into the firm cushions and closed my eyes. My head hurt, and I wished I could talk more openly with Steph. With Darvian around, I couldn't.

"You are uneasy, child," Darvian said.

"Did I not tell you to stop calling me that?"

Darvian laughed. "But you are a child. Fifteen." He reached out a hand and caressed my cheekbone. The headache at my temple went away completely. I'd forgotten what it felt like to be completely free of the pain. "When was the last time you played?"

"Played?"

"Did something just for fun."

"I do fun things," I said.

"Four weeks ago, last Tuesday," Clare said. "You blew bubbles off your balcony for fifteen minutes when Representative Black cancelled an appointment."

"Come on, Clare. Every day, I…" but I stopped. My four o'clock riding sessions were too early to count as fun.

Darvian shook his head and clucked, like someone's old uncle who'd heard you've been stealing from the cookie jar. The action was incongruous with his youthful face and figure.

I laughed.

"That's better," Darvian said.

I laughed harder, and Darvian joined in. His laughter buoyed up my sense of hilarity. Suddenly everything was funny. The way that press mini passed us in the dark. The strange contortions dancing students had frozen into.

Steph was laughing now, too. "Did you see the reporters stuck in the doorway back at the dance? All cramped together, goggle-eyed and crane-necked?"

Clare snorted and then howled in laughter.

The driver laughed too, at first softly, then harder. In the midst of a guffaw, she pulled the car over to the side of the road. "I can't concentrate," she gasped. "This is all very funny, but I need to keep my mind on the job."

We were just laughing. But it was more than that. It had come on so fast, the same way my headache had disappeared.

"Why are we laughing?" I asked Darvian.

"Everything's so funny," Steph laughed.

"No. That's not it, is it?" I stared at Darvian. "Is that what an influence spell feels like?"

"I was trying to help," Darvian said.

"Well, stop it. Our driver is right. She can't do her job if she can't concentrate. Neither can I. And I'm not fond of artificial feelings, anyway."

"I'm sorry. I didn't mean to offend you."

I supposed he didn't. "I forgive you, but please stop, and don't do that again."

Nothing was funny any longer. We pulled back into traffic. My headache was back with a vengeance, and I was angry, but only partly at Darvian. I had succumbed to the spell so easily.

"Don't be too hard on yourself, child," Darvian said. "You are still young. It is always easier to influence the young."

"You're a slow learner, aren't you?" Steph asked. "Everyone else heard her tell you not to call her a child."

"Yeah, and you're reading my thoughts again. I asked you to stop."

"But how will I know what you're thinking?"

"Same way the rest of us do," Steph said. "She'll tell you."

"You can't keep out fairies in general," Darvian said.

"For the moment, I'm concerned about fairies I can see. If you've dealt with people before, surely you know it's impolite to zip in and out of our minds without permission."

"This crisis seems beyond politeness."

I snorted. "Don't let my parents hear you say that. Politeness is the oil that allows Dicrandian politics to run. The bigger the crisis, the more polite we'll all be—you'll see. Now can I have a few minutes to think—in private?"

"Certainly, Your Highness."

I leaned back and closed my eyes again, but my headache kept me from forming coherent thoughts. I suspected aspirin wouldn't help, either.

CHAPTER 17

At the castle, the limo approached the kitchen gate, which was never used this time of night. Reporters who had been clustering around other gates raced toward us.

The gate was partially open when we got there. Eight of the burliest castle guards manned the winches. As soon as the limo was through, they slammed the gate shut, right in the face of the leading press car. Security surrounded the limo, and we were escorted into the castle amongst a sea of blue and silver uniforms. As we swept past a crowd of castle-attached reporters behind a rope line, cameras flashed, and questions were shouted. I ignored them.

"Twice in one day," Steph muttered when we gained a quiet hallway. "Aren't we lucky?"

I smiled.

Our group was met by my mother's secretary. An interesting choice. I wondered what it meant. Ms. Carter led us to the Blue Conference room, and then told me my father had requested my presence in the Rose Room. I nodded, made sure that Darvian was comfortable and that Steph would try to keep him from doing anything stupid, and headed for the older part of the palace.

The East Wing was down three corridors and up four small flights of stairs. My shoes and Clare's clapped ominously on the marble. When I entered the Rose Room, my parents looked even more upset than they had after the afternoon at the dollhouse. My father was watching the speech

Phil and I had given when we returned to the dance, rewinding and replaying the ending. Mother gazed out the window, pulling on her necklace. Uncle Malcolm sat in a corner, astride a chair. He glanced up when I came in, smiled, and went back to his thoughts.

I cleared my throat.

"Sarah!" My father turned, rushed over, and crushed me in a hug. "You have no idea how scared we were."

"Sorry, Dad. And Mom."

"We're not blaming you." Dad gave me a last squeeze and then held me away from him. When he let go, Mom took his place. He returned to the screen and said, "Now down to work. How long has this been going on?"

"What? The fairies? They just—"

"No. Obviously, our visitors pose some difficult problems. Our security people have been working with the War Palace and other experts since we first lost contact with your guards, and I'll be meeting with key people shortly. At the moment, though, I'm talking about your crush on Philip Castanay."

"I . . ." I could feel myself blushing. "How did you know?"

"It's written all over your face here," Dad gestured toward the screen. "Before tonight, how many people knew?"

"Me. Clare. Steph. Andy. And Phil, I suppose."

"You told him you were falling for him?"

"Sort of. We've talked some."

"Starting when?"

"Around three months ago."

"About the time you started working on Cagnew's proposal?"

"I guess so."

"You should have told me. I need to know when outside influences are compromising you. We could have given the bill watch to someone else."

"And lost the edge we have in the Northwest," Mom said, massaging my shoulders. "War didn't see this violence coming. We didn't see it. Only Sarah did. If they were using Prince Pretty-boy to get her to lean War on key votes, it backfired. Polls show Peace up to a solid majority in all four Northwestern provinces."

Dad shrugged. "As it happens, there's no damage done. But Sarah still should have told me about this before accepting serious work."

"Accepting? Like I had a choice! Anyway, I didn't know then. I'd just met Phil. Really met him, I mean."

A silence fell. The screen hummed.

"You met him the day of your half-vacation and that press nightmare? Interesting that young Castanay should choose that time to gate-crash. Perhaps Stephanie—"

"I don't think he knew I would be there. He certainly wasn't happy to see me."

"Yes, and you never suspect Stephanie Montressor of any political intrigue either."

"No, I don't. Steph's my best friend, and she agrees with me more than she agrees with her dad."

Dad frowned, but he dropped the subject. We'd had arguments about Steph before. I suspected he would like to forbid me from seeing her, but he'd never done it. Maybe he realized that prohibiting the relationship wouldn't work.

After a moment of consideration, Dad asked, "How often have you had contact with the prince?"

I looked helplessly at Clare.

"Other than official business contact, there have been six notes, five phone calls and three meetings before tonight. Sarah mentioned the first meeting. Another was for fifteen minutes under the bleachers at a Regency North baseball game, where Andrew Sanderson was present. The third was for about ten minutes in one of the War Palace waiting rooms after a Royal Tea committee meeting. Ms. Montressor was with them."

"That's all?" Dad asked.

I nodded.

Dad's shoulders relaxed, and he smiled. "But you've told him you like him?"

"Yes. And he says he likes me, too."

Dad rewound to the beginning of that night's speech. He seemed to be concentrating on Phil as he watched this time. "He's lying."

"Or good at hiding his feelings," Mom said.

Dad shrugged off this possibility. "Whatever game young Castanay's playing, it doesn't look like anyone else is in on it yet. We've been lucky. Still, you should have told us. This affects our whole government."

"Oh, Desmond," Mom said. "You can't rationalize love out of existence. You know very well that sometimes the heart sees clearer than the brain."

Dad grunted. "Even so, Sarah needs to be open about her relationships, especially if they're going to be hyper-politically sensitive."

I nodded. This was actually going much better than I'd feared it might. Still, I thought it best to change the subject. After all, we had a lot of ground yet to cover tonight. "Speaking of being open, there's something I ought to tell you."

Dad tensed. I took a deep breath and fumbled through an account of what had happened on the way home in the car. "Anyway," I finished, "I can't guarantee that I'm not being used like some kind of puppet. What the fairies want makes sense to me, but I can't tell if that's because they've been messing with my mind or—"

"Well, what do they want?"

"They want Prince Philip to go with them into Islandia for about a week to say some chants. They think he's got power to undo spells of influence."

Dad snorted.

"In return, they'll help with the Northwest. They think we're about to be invaded by a guy named Stralton, and the violence so far is nothing compared to what's coming."

"Have they given you any proof?"

"No. Their explanations depend on stuff that's not in our history books, so…"

"Rather," said Uncle Malcolm.

Dad smiled at him. "Trust is always an issue, isn't it? Not that I have any objection to sending young Castanay anywhere. But I assume he wouldn't agree to waltzing out of here without some concessions from us."

"He wants my attendance at Joint Council linked to his until he gets back or five years from now, whichever comes first."

"He might be gone that long?" Mom asked.

"He's supposed to be gone a week, but it could be dangerous. And we don't know if this is a trap."

"Does his mother know about this?"

"I assume he's downplaying the danger when he talks to his mother. He's not stupid."

"If that's all he wanted, he is," Dad said.

"No. I also agreed to War Powers for the Northwestern provinces. Renewable at three months by majority vote, and they keep their representation."

Uncle Malcolm whistled. "Somebody's besotted, all right."

"You said you were thinking about it anyway," I protested. "I tried to get six weeks, but—"

Dad laughed. "Malcolm didn't mean you. Our emergency session this evening was about War Powers for the Northwest. War refused to discuss less than six months, auto-renewing."

"Oh," I said. "You didn't want Phil and me there for the negotiations?"

"We figured a night off would be good for you, and that your absence wouldn't make that much difference," Mom said.

Dad laughed again. "Obviously, we were wrong."

"So, you'll do it?"

"If War puts what you've described on the table this morning, I'll sign off on it with pleasure."

"We also want you and King Randolph to jointly issue an invitation for Islandian fairies to help us in our war effort."

"We seem to have gotten along fine without them for a while," Uncle Malcolm said.

"If you say so. I think we're being crushed. And they say what's coming will be a hundred times worse," I said.

"But there's no proof at all?" Dad asked.

I shrugged. "Our problems of the past few months and their obvious ability to do things we can't. That's proof that they're fairies, not that they're telling the truth. It could be an elaborate trick. Though they don't seem that sophisticated."

"All right. We'd better have a chat with them. Malcolm, is the video equipment ready?"

Uncle Malcolm nodded.

"You're not coming in person?"

"Malcolm got someone in archives to do some fast research on fairies for the security people. Apparently, there's some kind of protective wall around this part of the building. If it still works, it would keep your fairy friends from transporting us like they did to you at the dance."

"Well, shouldn't I, at least, go back? It seems rude not to have any royals willing to sit in a room with Darvian."

Dad sighed. "I suppose you should."

"Desmond," Mom protested.

"No, Zelda, she's right. This fairy is a foreign ambassador after all. He deserves some courtesy. And he already knows Sarah."

"Thank you," I said.

***

Steph was explaining soccer to Darvian when I reached the Blue Conference room. Even with Steph's help, it took several minutes to get Darvian to stop talking about sports, and several more minutes to explain video conferencing. Darvian seemed unwilling to use the "magic" until he understood how it worked, but he couldn't understand either my muddled explanation, or Ms. Carter's more cogent one. Finally, Darvian decided the process was unlikely to hurt him, and we were able to proceed.

Ms. Carter was busy at the computer, so I slipped to the back of the room and dimmed the lights. As they softened, the giant screen at the other end of the room flickered and resolved, showing my father before the tapestries of the Rose Room. They looked good for seven-hundred-year-old embroidery.

I barely heard my father introducing himself. I couldn't stop staring at the tapestry. At this distance, the small images formed one larger picture of a face. Darvian's face.

I'd never seen the big picture before. Of course, I'd never been this far back from the tapestry before. The Rose Room was too small.

I jerked my attention away from the tapestry when I heard my father ask Darvian for proof an invasion was coming. Darvian said he could show them Stralton's army, but they wouldn't believe his visions if they didn't trust him already.

Father asked Darvian to show them anyway.

"I'm not sure I can work with this screen," Darvian muttered. He wandered around the room, fingering different objects until he came to a large flower arrangement. He seized it, emptied the flowers onto the table, magicked the water out of the bowl, and upended it on the conference table. He then waved his hand over it. It clouded. Shapes floated across it.

Ms. Carter tinkered with the zoom on the teleconferencing camera, so that it focused mainly on the ball.

The shapes in the glass ball spun and slowed, focusing on a village. Blue-roofed cottages nestled among pines in rolling hills. A craggy peak rose behind them.

"This, I believe," said Darvian, "is Kara."

On the big screen, Dad nodded.

"Stralton's army is west of here. The image in the ball moved rapidly up the mountain, then down the other side so quickly that my stomach lurched, and I had to look away. When I looked back, the ball was racing up a smaller mountain, then slipping along rolling hills, then zipping across a plain toward a dark mass. Soon we were even with it. It was a crowd of monsters and fairies—beautiful and fey. There were huge skeleton-creatures whose flesh hung loose and transparent on their bones. There were twinkling colored globes of light that surrounded flying creatures I couldn't quite see. There were dog-like animals with forked tails and hooves, huge gray wolves, and even a giant flying lizard. A chill ran down my spine. I'd always half-hoped fairies were real, but I'd hoped dragons weren't.

We circled the crowd. I soon gave up counting how many creatures there were. They were certainly headed for battle somewhere. They were well armed and well organized. Unless Darvian's crystal ball show was an illusion rather than a vision of something real.

"Thank you," Dad said. "I get your point."

He paced. The camera followed him. The picture of Darvian in the tapestry shifted in and out of focus.

"Father, I think there's something you ought to see." I knew there was a camera above the door in addition to the one on the conference table, and I asked Ms. Carter to switch the view of the Blue Conference Room to that camera. Ms. Carter nodded, and soon I could see Darvian's face in the tapestry in a window of the laptop as well as on the big screen.

"I don't get it," Uncle Malcolm said.

"I thought you should take a look behind you."

Dad turned.

"From my perspective," I added.

Father turned back and stared intently toward us. "Oh," he said suddenly.

"I see," Uncle Malcolm said.

"See what?" Steph asked.

"If you come to the back of the room, you'll see it," I said.

Steph joined me by the door. "Oh! They must have put it in because of his help in the battle. Just like the archives said."

"You read about this in the archives?" Uncle Malcolm asked.

"Not the tapestry. Darvian being in the battle," Steph said.

"Darrick Harbor?" Darvian asked. "I didn't do much. Made a few illusionary rocks and lighthouses. What is on the tapestry?"

"Your picture," I answered.

"Yes," Darvian said, pointing to a couple of the small scenes. "Here and here. But I don't see how that helps us much."

"No, perhaps you don't," Dad said. "Maybe that's best. You fairies are too good at images, including ones that fool. It is better for us not to explain every way we protect our collective memory."

"Darvian bowed his head briefly. "As you wish, Your Majesty."

Dad had more questions for him, but from that point on he seemed convinced. Soon he ended the conversation. At his request, Darvian vanished, presumably to reappear in the Red Conference Room with Peace's crisis advisors.

Steph turned to me as soon as he'd gone. "What's next?"

"More talk." I sighed. "My whole life is talk."

CHAPTER 18

At three in the morning, the Joint Council Building had a greenish cast from the old fluorescent lights. Shadows flickered in the corners. Faces were strangely wan.

Most of the Council members sat, glumly. The War coffee maker was empty. I filled two cups from the Peace refreshment table and walked toward Lord Montressor. "Steph says you like it black."

"Is this a bribe?"

I shrugged. "She also says you're easier to get along with after you've had some."

He took the cup and sipped. "Do you want to explain why, with a war coming on, we're agreeing to a War Powers act that requires renewal every three months?"

"Because it'll pass," I said, leaning back against the table, "and a six-month auto-renew won't."

"What makes you so sure?"

"More than half these people," I tipped my head around the table, "don't believe there's a war coming on."

"I do not think it's fair for you to be canvassing my people," Phil said from off to my right.

My heart lurched, but I forced myself not to smile too brightly. "Philip," I said.

"Are you sure you want to be calling me that?" He murmured in my ear.

"Excuse me," I said to Lord Montressor. I pulled Phil toward a corner with no people. "We're busted," I whispered.

"What do you mean?"

"My parents figured out I like you."

He smiled.

"What is there to smile about? They're furious I didn't tell them."

Phil stopped smiling, but a corner of his mouth twitched. "Sorry. I know it's not funny. But I like hearing that you like me."

My heart thumped, and I took a deep breath. "Really? My dad said you were using me."

Phil ran a finger gently over my cheek. "I'm taking off for at least a week while we go into battle, you bartered me down to three months of War Powers, and they think I'm the one using you?"

He thought *I* was using *him*?

He laughed. "You could never use me. Not when I can read your face almost as well as Darvian reads your mind."

I gasped and was about to reply when the mediator called us all to order. I gave Phil's hand a quick squeeze and found my seat.

Ponderously, the mediator started on the night's business, reading through the proposals Phil and I had agreed on earlier in the evening. I couldn't believe we'd written that dry, lifeless trash.

"If Your Highness would please come up now and say a few words to open the debate," the mediator said.

I panicked. I thought I'd been tracking, despite the legalese, the mediator's dreadful monotone, and the lateness of the hour, but somehow, I'd missed which highness was meant.

"Which one?" Philip asked.

I breathed easier. Thank goodness it wasn't just me.

"Her Royal Highness Princess Sarah," the mediator said. "Her name is listed first."

King Randolph gave Philip a dirty look as I gathered my papers and went to the front of the table.

With all I'd had to do, I hadn't practiced my introduction. I fumbled through an apology for the lateness of the hour. Then I introduced Darvian. Soon everyone was watching the flower-bowl show, which was the same as the one back at the palace, except it used a larger globe of glass.

By the time it ended, Uncle Maurice was chewing on his knuckles. Lady McGivern looked grey. Lord Montressor said, "We've got that coming at us, and you want us to have to put War Powers up for a vote every three months?"

"Ah," I said, "Are you sure that it is coming at us?" I held up a finger, and the fight scene from *Majestic* came up on the Council video screen. Even though it was older than I was, the special effects were incredible. A horde of demon-monsters bore down on us with such fury that I couldn't help backing up. With the nightmare about to burst from the screen, I clicked off the film and brought up the lights.

"Convincing, isn't it? And by all accounts, fairies have been making believable visual stories far longer than we have."

"Are you saying that army isn't real?" Queen Salome asked.

I shrugged. "Maybe it's real. Maybe it isn't. In which case we have a War Powers act that deals with the current Northwest problem without committing us to years more military involvement than we need."

"And if the army is real?" King Randolph demanded.

"There will be no trouble renewing or even strengthening the War Powers. In the Calconade conflict, such a resolution had to be renewed. That was our last unanimous vote in Congress. During the Pyraket skirmishes, a War Powers renewal passed two-hundred-eighty-five to three. Never has such a measure been even close to defeat in a time of war."

"Why don't we wait and see what happens?" Uncle Maurice said.

"Well, the Northwest is already experiencing violence. And I don't want to be responsible for letting that mess in the back door if it is real," I pointed at the flower bowl. "Do you?"

Uncle Maurice shifted in his seat.

"If we're not sure this is real, what're we doing sending Prince Philip off with these people?" Lord Montressor asked.

"I agree. It's foolish and dangerous," Lady McGivern said.

"Same logic applies," Prince Philip answered. "If an invasion is coming, my trip could seriously improve our odds. If it's not, you deal with the disturbance in the Northwest, pay these guys back, and get on with your lives."

I swallowed, hard.

"As if we could go on without you," Lord Burns said.

"His Highness is irreplaceable," I said. "We've asked the fairies to give us constant visual contact, and we've got people working on back-up plans for rescuing him if it comes to that. Of course, if our visitors are lying, and that isn't good enough…" My voice cracked and my eyes swam. I ducked my head and brought myself back under control. I hadn't lost it in a speech since I was eight. So what, if the thought of losing Phil had me tearing up? Tonight's business was too important to blow. I mastered my voice and finished, "we'll limp along somehow."

Nods and murmurs of assent went around the table. I'd expected to have to fight harder. Maybe my meltdown wasn't such a bad thing.

"Makes sense to me," Lord Montressor said. "I'd be happy to vote for this proposal with a slight modification."

My heart beat faster. "What modification?"

"That while His Highness is gone, you have no political contact at all—not with your parents, not with any Congresspeople, not with my daughter. No reports, no newspapers."

The words hit like a hammer. Almost everyone I knew was in politics. I'd be cut off from everybody. Everything. I schooled my face, and tried to think of what to say, but other people spoke first.

"I don't think that's—" Phil started.

"Excellent idea," King Randolph said. "If this link is to keep things equal, you should have the same disadvantages His Highness does."

My brain whirled. How should I respond to this? My father was giving me no clues. "We do want to be fair," I said slowly, "but would I still be going to school? And could I possibly continue the archival research my friend Gen and I have been doing?"

Lord Montressor raised a finger, but King Randolph snorted. "You and your friend can hang out in the archives all you want, just don't touch anything modern. An approved tutor will keep you caught up on schoolwork. And we'll supply a guard to ensure you follow the other provisions."

I nodded. "I move we put this to a vote, then."

"Seconded," Philip said almost instantly.

The mediator took over. The vote went seventeen to four in favor of both the War Powers and the link, with the top four on each side agreeing. I breathed a sigh of relief. People gathered their belongings.

"If we could impose on your patience a little longer," King Randolph said, "there's one more thing we'd like to do tonight."

Silence fell. King Randolph stood. "Islandia is willing to help us in the Northwest, but only if His Majesty and I issue them a joint invitation. With our obvious need, I'd hate to turn away any help, however unorthodoxly offered, so I want you to know I'm willing to issue the invitation."

"As am I," Dad said. "The instructions on how this is done, please?"

The mediator produced a copy of the poem Phil and I had chanted a few weeks earlier.

"This is it?" King Randolph said, glancing at the poem.

Dad smiled. I'd told him what was coming. "Undoubtedly a jointly-signed resolution would be seemlier, but there's no accounting for taste." His grin broadened into a challenge. "I, at least, am willing to appear a fool for five minutes if it means powerful aid for our current crisis." He held up his hand.

King Randolph slapped his into it. They did not sound foolish chanting the nonsense. I hoped the fairies weren't being picky since it didn't look much like cooperation.

The air sizzled with energy. As the two kings finished, nearly twenty new fairies appeared in the room. Clare had me under the table in seconds. The other guards were nearly as quick in covering the other royals.

"My apologies for frightening you," one fairy said. "We came in answer to your call. We mean no harm. How may we serve you?"

When no one answered, I spoke up. "If you wouldn't mind waiting in the hall until we've finished our meeting, someone will be with you directly to let you know."

As quickly as they had come, the extra fairies were gone. An all-clear was declared on the room, and I got back into my seat. I barely listened to the closing ceremony.

As soon as the meeting ended, King Randolph rose. "Psalting, Montressor, Burns, Let's see what these foreigners can do for us."

My father had also risen. "Your Majesty, not so."

"This is my area, Your Majesty," King Randolph growled.

"Precisely," Dad said. "We agreed to send your son with these folk to the end of the earth. Much as I hate to admit it, we cannot at this moment afford to lose you both."

King Randolph stopped. Then he jerked his head. "You're right. Catastrophe Rules until further notice. Psalting, Montressor and Burns, you'll represent me in talking to these foreigners. His Majesty will accompany you."

Dad nodded and followed the three War lords into the corridor.

"The rest of us will use the other exits," King Randolph said. "Snypes, see to it that Princess Sarah follows the rules we've laid out today."

A large, serious-eyed guard moved from King Randolph's side to mine.

"We should go now," he said to me. I nodded numbly and gathered my files. I wished I remembered what Catastrophe Rules were.

On the way to the east door, I passed Phil.

He caught my eye.

"Be careful," I said. With all these new fairies, I was suddenly less sure of what we'd done. Would Phil be all right? What would I do if he didn't come back? A tear trickled down one cheek.

"I'll be fine." He blew me a kiss. Then he vanished along with his guards, Darvian, and Glenstra.

"I am never going to get used to that," I said as we moved on.

"You and me both," Clare muttered.

The door to the Joint Council room clanged shut behind us.
I couldn't shake the feeling of finality it gave me.

CHAPTER 19

I woke with a start. Late morning daylight streamed through the tower windows. I sat up, threw off the bedclothes, and ran for the shower. Why hadn't my alarm woken me?

"For a girl who's off politics, you're in a hurry," Clare said.

I stared. Then memories of the crazy night crashed in on me. The interrupted dance, the Joint Council meeting. Now Phil was off someplace.

"Oh, right." I dropped into one of my balcony chairs. "Is there anything for breakfast?"

"There's a tray by the door."

I picked out a croissant and an orange from a tray that could have fed twelve and returned to my perch by the balcony doors. Tucking my feet up under me, I munched reflectively. "I'm not sure all this quiet agrees with me."

"You haven't actually tried it yet," Clare said.

I supposed Clare was right. "I could use a ramble in Peace Park."

"A nap afterward might be called for. Last night went late."

Last night and many nights this spring. The archives could wait until Monday. Gen wouldn't be back until then anyway. I crumpled my napkin and shot it into the wastebasket.

After my shower, I donned jeans, a light cotton long-sleeved shirt, and my hiking boots. I pulled my hair back under a baseball cap, dumped extra fruit and rolls from the breakfast tray into my backpack, and filled a couple of water bottles from the tap.

"And where do you think you're going?" the War Palace guard, Snypes, said as we emerged from the room.

"Peace Park," I said. "Of course, you're coming, too."

"Who are you meeting there?"

"Nobody. I'm going for a hike."

Snypes glowered but tramped down the tower stairs behind me.

"There she is," someone shouted as we approached the bottom.

I ducked into a guardroom, so the flash caught only Clare and Snypes. It probably wasn't enough to make the papers, but this would complicate things.

"Our way seems blocked," Snypes said.

"That way," I said.

"You can't run off through some classified tunnel and leave me here."

"So, take the oath of secrecy and come down with us."

"I'm not taking any Peace oath of secrecy."

I shrugged. "Then, meet me in the Park by the bridge after the stable entrance. Sans reporters if possible. I doubt King Randolph wants me giving impromptu press conferences today."

"How long would this take?"

I shrugged. "Forty-five minutes to an hour."

Snypes lowered his eyebrows. "I need to call for instructions."

"Suit yourself," I said. "There's a secure phone on the wall there." I walked to the room's bookshelf and leafed through its calf-bound volumes. *Coredlian: A Short History of the Coastal Provinces. A Short History of Bentralia. Dicrandian Politics: A Short Treatise.* I opened the glass door and picked up the volume. Seven-hundred-sixty-four pages. I shook my head as I replaced it.

Snypes seemed to be waiting for something. Tinned music leaked from the earpiece he held. I bent down to see the bottom shelf. Even inside the glass, the volumes were gathering dust. I wiped off a few titles. *A Trip into Fantasy: The Islandian Waste.* I'd read that once. It had mentioned thirty-five types of fern, but no fairies.

Fairies: Fact or Fable was the next one. I smiled. That had been pretty well settled for me. *A Short History of Islandia* read the next one. I groaned. I should probably read it. I pulled it out, along with its neighbor. That one's cover was blank. I opened it to the title page. In small, irregular print was: *Dragons and Demons: Defending Against the Mythical and Magical.* It was almost uncannily useful. I put the two books into my pack.

The tinny music cut off sharply. Moments later, Snypes said, "Your Highness, His Majesty wants to talk to you."

"OK." I took the phone from him.

"Your Highness," King Randolph's voice boomed. "Couldn't you stay in your tower?"

"I don't remember agreeing to house arrest. Your man can take the oath of secrecy, or he can meet us in the park in forty-five minutes."

"I don't want you alone that long, and you can't require a War employee to take a Peace oath."

I took a deep breath. "No problem. I'll run upstairs, clean up, and head out the front door."

"Your Highness, you're to stay out of politics this week."

"I'll be sure not to mention anything political."

"Don't talk like a fool, child. We both know you're not one. Everything you say is political."

"King Randolph, I want a walk in the woods. I'd rather do it in comfortable clothes and without half the press corps at my heels, but if I can only—"

"Put my man on the line."

I handed the phone back to Snypes. He listened a minute, then hung up. "I'm to take your oath," he said.

I nodded. I pulled a notebook from a box beside the telephone and tossed it to Clare. "Will you do the necessary?"

"You know," Snypes said as Clare flipped to the correct page, "You shouldn't pick fights with King Randolph. He's very powerful."

I turned from lacing up my pack. "As King Randolph guesses, but you apparently haven't figured out yet, so am I."

Clare's mouth twitched, but she didn't smile.

✳✳✳

The tunnels were long passages of square concrete. Metal pipes lined the ceiling and left side. They were colored and clearly marked, "Water" in blue, "Gas—FLAMMABLE," in yellow, "High Voltage Wires—DO NOT TOUCH" in red.

I had touched one once anyway. Nothing had happened. Nothing exciting, that is. My guards had been changed, and I'd earned a spanking and one of my longest lectures. My mom had been nearly hysterical, while my dad explained carefully that the electric wires were insulated, but that didn't make touching them a good idea. And if they ever caught me pulling a trick like that again…I smiled at the memory. It was always like that. With real danger, Mom freaked out, and Dad was calm. With politics, it was the other way.

When I shook myself out of my reverie, we were passing the storage rooms.

"What's in there?" Snypes asked, pointing at one of the doors.

"Grain," I answered.

"Sure," he said.

I stopped, went back, punched in my universal code, opened the door, and flicked on the light. A rat scurried out of sight.

Snypes clomped to one of the huge bags on the reinforced steel shelves. He plumped it and choked on the resultant cloud of dust. "All of these rooms have grain?"

"Mostly," I said. "It's famine prevention. Why? What does War have in theirs? Weapons?"

Snypes tramped back to the doorway without answering. Interesting. Single party caches of weapons were strictly illegal. I made a note to myself to organize an impromptu search of the War storerooms when the violence in the Northwest died down. If the violence in the Northwest ever died down. I sighed as I flicked the lights back off and locked the door behind us.

When we emerged from the tunnels, it was already noon. I dug an apple out of my pack and offered food to Clare and Snypes as well. Clare took a donut and an orange, but Snypes refused anything, claiming he never ate while on the job. I shook my head. It was his loss, though I'd be annoyed if he got dehydrated and couldn't keep up on the trail. I wanted to take the Lake Trail today, and it was no garden path—more of a rough track over the sharp little hills that circled Glasswater Lake.

Last spring, I'd hiked the circuit at least once every two weeks. I'd loved following the progress of duck families and learning the names of trees and bushes from Parker, my favorite guard after Clare. Today I missed his knowledge, but not his complaints that two-and-a-half hours was insufficient time to appreciate an eight-mile hike.

This year, I hadn't even had two-and-a-half hours to spare. The old path was a stranger. The leaning oak at the first turn had finally fallen. Bracken, blown against it in some storm, blocked the way. I wished I'd brought gloves as I cleared it enough to go on.

The steep incline on the other side of the fallen oak was muddy after a recent rain. I had trouble finding purchase and used saplings beside the path to help pull my way up. Clare followed, doing the same, but Snypes had a terrible time. Saying it was undignified to pull oneself along like a monkey, he tried climbing the hill without using his hands but slid backward, smearing himself with mud. On his second attempt, he managed to stay upright as he slid back down.

"Care for a hand?" I asked.

"No, thank you, Your Highness."

I had to give Snypes credit for determination. On the fourth try, he made it up, and we continued. The lake was on our left, glittering in the sun. This year's ducklings, already big and brown, paddled in a line behind their mother.

I had nowhere to be today, so I took the path slowly, adding my own soft hum to the buzz of insect voices and the occasional birdsong. Even under the trees, the day felt warm and sleepy. The breeze rustled softly, breathing a lullaby over the forest. I relaxed, feeling muscles in my shoulders and neck slowly loosen.

It was a wonderful afternoon, and at the end of it, I toiled up my stairs, fell onto my floor cushions, and dropped off to sleep.

✳✳✳

The sun hung low in the sky when I awoke. It took a moment to remember where I was and when it was. Sunday night, which normally meant family supper. Tonight would be the first time I'd missed it. Even when I was sick, my parents had moved the meal to my room and let me eat it in my pajamas.

I smiled, remembering the pajama party we'd had when I contracted the flu last year. I couldn't believe Dad owned anything as old and ragged as the oversized plaid flannel he'd donned that night. It was even funnier next to the purple floor-length gown my mother had sworn was a nightgown, not evening wear.

There were lots more ordinary memories, too. Week after week and year after year of dinners remarkable only because no one besides my parents shared the table with me. Just as I was about to give in to feeling sorry for myself, there was a knock on the door, and Andy threw it open. He'd come to say goodbye before heading to his basic training, and he stayed long enough to trounce me in a game of chess. Without saying much, he managed to cheer me up.

Still, when a dinner tray arrived, I couldn't eat. I tried reading the books I'd picked up downstairs but had no heart for it. Instead, I changed for bed.

CHAPTER 20

Monday morning started late since I wasn't riding with my dad or making the trip to school. It was fun to wear jeans and a t-shirt on a school day. When Estelle came by, I considered sending her away but decided against it. After all, I was going to the archives today, hopefully with Gen, and somebody might shoot pictures.

"Something simple, OK, Estelle?"

Estelle smiled. "Perfect. This is like a vacation for you, no? We will try some braids."

Braids? I couldn't believe my ears. But, as Estelle started to work, I realized that Estelle and I weren't thinking of the same hairstyle. To me, braids were simple plaits parted in the middle and hanging straight. Estelle's were an asymmetrical sculpture, framing my face. They looked relaxed but took an hour to do.

"Thank you," I said as Estelle left. I sighed. What would I have to say to convince her to do something quick?

Not long after Estelle left, Parker walked in with the breakfast tray. "I heard you didn't eat supper," he said.

Nosy guards. "It was family night. I couldn't."

He put the tray on the balcony table. "Well, you ought to be starving by now. Eat up. Your tutor is showing up in half an hour."

Come to think of it, I was hungry. "Have you heard anything about my tutor?" I asked as I attacked the scrambled eggs and pancakes.

"She's some staff person from your school. She has a teaching degree but has been working as a secretary. I've got the name here—Ms. Kramer."

I choked on my pancakes. "Ms. Kramer?"

"What's wrong with Ms. Kramer?"

"Ms. I'll throw the book at any student playing hooky on my time?"

"Sorry, not ringing any bells."

"Oh, right. I was with Clare that day. Let's just say the woman went out of her way to suggest I wasn't trustworthy. I'd say she's War-affiliated, but it sounded like she doesn't trust Prince Philip, either."

"Maybe she's had too much experience with high-school kids to be trusting."

"Maybe, but she's still a pain to be around. You think he's doing it on purpose?"

"Who is doing what on purpose?"

"King Randolph. Sticking me with people I can't stand."

"Ms. Rivers warned me about some hostility between you and Snypes."

I laughed and concentrated on eating. When I came back from brushing my teeth, I found that someone had wiped the table and set out a basket of fresh flowers. It reminded me of my mom.

Ms. Kramer turned out to be less of a pain than I'd feared. She frowned at my jeans and t-shirt and required me to sit ramrod straight in my desk chair, but also made my math and science lessons more interesting than any teacher I could remember. Dicrandian Literature was a lively discussion, and Ms. Kramer's version of history was colorful.

When we broke for lunch, I asked Ms. Kramer how long we'd study.

"Until 2:30. Every day. Just like school."

"OK, but at school, I usually have gym, art, and choir. Besides, I know we covered more than my classes at school."

Secretly, I suspected that my classmates wouldn't catch up with me for several days.

Ms. Kramer pursed her lips. "Art and music, I can teach. For gym, perhaps I can supervise while you do some physical activity. Jump rope, I believe, is good for the cardiovascular system."

"Perhaps I could join a game of basketball outside the stable later this evening."

"That's hardly well-regulated exercise."

"It has rules. It's aerobic. And it's way more fun than doing the same thing over and over."

"I suppose, but that leaves us several hours yet to fill." Ms. Kramer said.

"Well, if you know a foreign language, my parents have been on me to learn one. We just couldn't wedge it into my schedule."

"I only know Fairy."

"Excuse me?"

"Fairy—when I was a girl, all the private schools made us learn some. It was deemed a cultural accomplishment, useful for history and medicine even if the language was long dead."

Hmm. I'd forgotten how old Ms. Kramer was. Hardly any schools offered Fairy anymore. It wasn't practical. Or, until this week, it hadn't seemed so. "I'd love to learn Fairy," I said.

Ms. Kramer sniffed. "Fine. I'll send someone to my house for my old textbooks. I may also have a poetry anthology—*Charm Chants*, I think it's called. Should you like me to have that brought along as well?"

"Please do." Excitement welled in me. Not even Ms. Kramer's beginning lecture on the complicated conjugation of Fairy verbs could dampen my enthusiasm.

That's how I came to spend my afternoons studying Fairy that week. I learned colors, and numbers, and how to say thank you, please, and sorry. I also learned the chants from Ms. Kramer's book. One was for making thoughts private, and another erected a shield that blocked magic weapons. A third rendered other beings temporarily unconscious, and the last warded off ghoul fear.

Gen and I dug up other chants as well.

Late Monday afternoon, we headed for the archives. Press hounded us from the palace to the library, but after watching us scroll through computer databases and thumb through old books for an hour or so, the reporters grew bored and trailed off.

At first, we didn't find much, but finally we located a book that had a song or two and that referenced a slew of potential sources in its bibliography. Those sources pointed us to others, and by Tuesday, we had enough for me to start trying some of them out.

It didn't take me long to figure out that each song and chant took its toll. We had to carefully choose which were worth trying. Ms. Kramer's shield chant made the list, and so did a song to find out what other people had magical ability. Gen had some, we discovered, while Ms. Kramer, Clare, and Snypes had none at all.

We thought a song that enchanted objects to glow when fairies were present might be useful, but the first rock I enchanted glowed constantly. After laboriously translating the song, Gen and I tinkered with the words until we produced a feather that didn't glow immediately but that we hoped would glow if a fairy was within a couple of miles of us. Despite our misgivings about its effectiveness, I attached the feather to the keychain that hung off my backpack.

Gen wanted to find a chant that prevented fairies from whisking people through space the way Darvian and Glenstra had taken Phil and me from the dance, but though we searched hard, we couldn't find one. The only thing that stopped that kind of translation was a protective wall, and even small breaches in these walls allowed some movement.

"Could we at least check the status of our walls?" Gen asked.

"Good idea," I said. We found a chant that could test a wall's defenses and then spent hours consulting maps—laying old ones over new ones to make a modern layout of Bentralia's protective walls. Thursday afternoon, one of our drivers took Gen all around town to chant in alleys, at the backs of grocery stores, in parks, and at street signs. She came back exhausted but with a status report.

"I got to all of them except the ones in the War Palace," Gen said. "I wasn't allowed in there."

I laughed. "You tried to get in?"

"I explained what I was doing."

"Yes, but you're on my staff. It doesn't matter what you say, they won't trust you." Well, if Phil were home, someone might have, but he wasn't there. I hoped he was OK.

I must have let my worry show because Gen asked if I was alright.

"Fine. And this information you got is great." I added it to my growing database while Gen went home to sleep. The data entry took until two in the morning. It was the first time I'd been up late that week.

On Friday, we found a chant that linked people together. If you tried to translate one of the people, the others would come too. If one was behind a protective wall and couldn't be translated, none could be whisked away.

"But none of our protective walls is completely sound except the one around the Gold Room," I said. "There's not even a bathroom in there. We can't make someone stay there so other people don't get translated."

"True, but at least link your guards to you. That way, if you get translated, you still have protection."

"Hear, hear," Clare said.

"OK. I'll try it."

I read through the chant and then said it, slowly.

It was a doozy. I had to lie down, and the world spun for about ten minutes. I needed to discover some way to figure out how much power chants would take before I tried them. Once I'd recovered, I said, "That was the worst one yet. I presume it worked. I wonder how many of you are linked to me now?"

I read the chant more closely. Here was a number—it was probably a range, like the fairy-detecting feather had been. Yes. I was linked to whoever was within ten ilakrein. What on earth was an ilakra? I dove into my fairy textbook.

Gen found the answer first. An ilakra was close to a yard, so ten ilakrein included Clare, Snypes, and Gen for sure, but maybe no one else. We didn't think anyone had been on the tower stairs.

"I did not ask to be part of these ridiculous experiments," Snypes said, stomping off to the balcony.

Gen shrugged, and we got back to work. We wanted to finish our database before Joint Council.

***

Saturday was a terrible day.

Phil didn't come back, and no one would tell me why.

I waited for news of him, pacing my tower room. I didn't feel like going to the park. I couldn't eat.

All morning, I could hear commotion in the courtyards as unusually large numbers of people, many of them in military uniforms, strode in and out of the palace, but my guards claimed not to know what was going on.

In the early afternoon, someone brought me a note. My heart raced. Was Phil OK?

The note didn't mention Phil. It said new security standards had been put in place, and one of my guards, Clare Rivers, didn't make the cut. She wouldn't be allowed back into the palace compound.

It had to be a mistake, but being off politics, I couldn't even ask to see the report. And since Saturday was normally Clare's day off, I didn't have a chance to say goodbye. I choked back a sob. As soon as I was back in business, I would fix this.

I returned to pacing.

Night fell, and still no Phil. I sat in bed, not sleeping. Worry gnawed at my stomach.

Slowly the moon crossed the sky.

CHAPTER 21

The moon was low, and the sky had lightened to purplish-gray when my phone rang. I scrambled across the room to pick it up.

"He's back!" Steph said.

"When? Is he OK?"

"About twenty minutes ago. I haven't seen pictures, but the War Palace is saying he's in great shape."

"If you haven't seen pictures, they're lying," I said. "I wonder how serious it is."

"He's not dead, and he's not permanently lost. He'll be fine. Anyway, we've been invaded, and we need you back. I've got updates for you and a tentative schedule. Your place in thirty minutes?"

"We've been invaded?"

"I know you've been off politics, but surely you heard when the faerie troops rolled in yesterday."

"I didn't. But I'll get working now."

When I checked the official War website to confirm Steph's news, a huge banner hung over the front page with a picture of dark figures silhouetted in fire. *Invasion Facts*, the caption read. Underneath it, the line *What you need to know* linked to a page full of articles and graphs that seemed designed to obfuscate more than clarify.

"What are you doing?" Snypes said, causing me to jerk away from the screen. "You are not allowed to access any political websites."

"Actually, I can access whatever I want, now," I said. "Prince Philip is back."

Snypes didn't believe me at first since he hadn't been informed of the prince's return any more than I had. I showed him the War website, found b-roll of the news Steph had seen, and when he still wasn't convinced to go, I had my guards oust him, though I felt guilty doing it. This couldn't have been an easy assignment for him, and he hadn't been relieved of duty all week.

My compassion for the man didn't stop me from lodging a complaint against the War Party for not informing me immediately of Phil's return. They were busy, but if we'd been invaded, we needed all hands on deck, and that included me. And Phil. Was he seriously hurt? I hesitated a moment before sending the complaint. Was this fair? I thought a moment. Whatever else was on their minds at the War Palace, I shouldn't have had to learn of Phil's return from a friend who'd heard it on the news. But I made the complaint private rather than public.

Urgent business finished, I pelted down the tower stairs. I had to find out what was going on, and the War Palace website was no place to do it.

My father was saddling his bay when I ran up.

"Dad!" I called.

He swung back off his horse. "Sarah! What are you doing here?"

"Phil's back."

He laughed and swept me up in a swinging bear hug. "Are you sure?"

"Saw Joanne Kilmer dishing the news myself, and I checked War's official page to be sure."

Dad shook his head. "I should have checked the news before I headed out this morning."

"You didn't need to. Steph called half an hour ago. I've already lodged a complaint against War and ditched my spy. So, what's going on? We've been invaded?"

Dad squeezed me. "I'm afraid so. Let's go inside." He returned his horse to a stable hand and walked back with me, his guards surrounding us. There were six of them, not the usual three.

"What's with the extra guards?" I asked.

"We've upped security since the invasion."

"It happened yesterday?"

"Yesterday morning."

My brain whirled. Dozens of ideas flitted through. Clare, increased security, the invasion, the fairies, Phil reappearing late, our database of magical chants. So much to talk about. "Did you know they fired Clare yesterday?"

Dad sighed. "Rogers told me she didn't meet the new security requirements."

I frowned. Rogers was our chief of security, and I was sure he hated women. "Did he say what requirements she didn't meet?"

"I didn't have time to get into it, Sarah."

I wasn't satisfied, but I couldn't see a way to get Dad to care. I'd have to deal with Rogers myself. I dragged my mind back to our fairy problems. "How are we doing—with the invasion, I mean?"

Dad frowned. "We've lost most of the Northwest. Without your fairy friends, the rest of the country would be gone by the end of the week. With them, our prospects still aren't great. Their fairies outnumber ours, and when the magic gets going, we humans can't do much."

"Actually, Gen and I have unearthed lots we can do."

Dad laughed. "Excellent. You have won yourself a trip to King Randolph's war commission. I'd come as well, but I think I'm more needed at the new military hospital near the airport."

"You mean I'm going to this commission alone?"

"You can take anyone from your staff, and unless something else comes up, I'll send Malcolm along, too."

"Oh, good. For a second, I thought I was going to be ranking Peace member."

"You are. We voted Tuesday to bump your position in the party to second."

"What?"

"War confirmed almost instantly, probably because it made their loss of young Castanay appear more even."

"But…I thought it took months to make a decision like that. It was almost a year with Phil."

"We've been discussing the move all spring."

"You have? Why doesn't anybody ever tell me anything?"

Dad tousled my hair. "It's tradition, sweetie. A couple of times royal kids have started to show promise and then goofed, and this step got postponed. When that happens, it's less damaging for the young person if they didn't know their party was working on promoting them."

I shook my head. "You are going to tell me well ahead of time when you're thinking of stepping down, aren't you?"

"Trust me. If I have any choice in the matter, I will."

We were at my parents' wing. In the Peony Room, Steph and my mom chit-chatted over a table of fruit and rolls. I rushed over and hugged them both. Then I grabbed a croissant. "So, what's going on?"

"Don't talk with your mouth full, dear. And sit up straight. I was afraid a week of eating alone would ruin your table manners."

"Mo-om."

"Oh, darling. I don't mean to nitpick. I'm sure it was horrible for you. Did you get our flowers?"

I smiled broadly. Big basketfuls filled my room now. "Every day. Bucketfuls."

"I was so afraid you'd be lonely."

"I was, but Gen was around a lot, and Clare, and even Ms. Kramer wasn't so bad."

"Really?" Steph asked.

"Yeah, I'll tell you about that later. For now, what's the news?"

Steph recapped what Dad had said about the invasion, the new hospital, King Randolph's war commission, and my appointment as second-in-command of the Peace Party. She also had details on the upped security: besides extra guards and more stringent requirements, there was also now a rule that no two blood royals of the same house could be in each other's company anywhere other than castle grounds. Holding Joint Council meetings was going to be fun.

Then Steph moved into areas Dad hadn't had time to mention. Dicrandia had imposed a country-wide curfew from sundown to sunrise. People couldn't move around without a permit. I raised an eyebrow. A curfew? Were people going for this?

"Half the Joint Council is doing education on that one today," Dad said.

"Including me," Mom said.

"Sounds like a tough sell."

"We hope not. Queen Salome and I are working together."

"Ah," I said. I couldn't picture them cooperating. Every time they attended the same function, they spent the entire time competing over everything from wardrobe to sound bites. "You're both going for simple old clothes, I hope?"

"Sarah, we can't wear old clothes to important media events."

"I didn't mean ancient. I meant not bought for the purpose. And you agreed on what to wear, so it's not a big issue?"

"I don't think anyone's discussed—"

"But it always makes a difference at Joint Teas."

"She's right, Zelda," Dad said. "A fashion war would detract from the main show. Maybe we should coordinate with the War Palace."

"If you think it's a good idea, dear heart."

I glanced at Steph whose mouth was twitching. We avoided meeting each other's eyes, and Steph plowed on through her notes. A water dispute had sprung up between two boroughs on the northern edge of Bentralia. Both had decided to set up emergency reserves by pulling from the same reservoir. Steph had some inside information that the situation could turn violent before midday, and Dad dispatched Uncle Malcolm to broker a deal. I was surprised but pleased that Dad took Steph seriously.

Steph next outlined a whole crop of legislation that had passed in the week I'd been incommunicado. Most of it related to the invasion, but one education bill had slipped through with far less debate than it deserved. I bet we were all going to regret a few of its riders, especially one that had to do with standardized testing.

Thinking of things that had slipped through Congress and shouldn't have, I wasn't at all sure I liked some of the new resolutions on cooperation with Islandia. Did we really want any Islandian fairy going almost anywhere for almost any reason? We hardly knew these people!

Steph's last two pages of notes were about an online trend: A proliferation of dragon-focused websites and games had cropped up in the last two days.

Dad glanced up from where he'd been scribbling on a yellow notepad. So, he had been paying attention these last ten minutes.

"What do you mean by dragon-focused?" he asked.

Steph shrugged. "Sites about dragons—what they're like, their incredible magic, their other-worldly beauty—that sort of thing. Here, I'll show you one." She whipped out a laptop and showed them a site that featured a gorgeous picture of a red and gold dragon in flight.

"Wow," I said.

Steph nodded. "They're all like that. Beautiful. The games let you fly or pick dragons and have them fight each other. Most sites have shops where you can order posters or crystal figurines."

"Do they mention how dangerous dragons are?" I asked.

Steph laughed. "These sites? Hardly."

"We'll want to watch that. Thank you," Dad said.

"You're welcome. Anyway, that's all I've got."

"Do you have anything else for me, Dad?"

"Your friend's notes are better than the debriefing we'd planned for you."

I smiled at Steph.

"Don't look so smug." Dad said.

I laughed.

❊❊❊

Four hours later, Steph, Gen, and I presented ourselves at the War Palace. Though we used a side entrance, half a dozen reporters battled for microphone placement. I was glad Parker and my other guard, Lewis, were big enough to clear a path for us into the buildings.

War Palace marble echoed as ominously as Peace Palace marble did. Maybe worse. I'd never been ranking Peace member at a meeting that included King Randolph before. I did not want to mess this up.

"Hey, Sarah, calm down. You look like you're gearing up to kill somebody," Gen said.

I laughed, slowed down, and tried to relax. "It's not pretty, is it? But I can't help it. This is going to be a battle. And I'm afraid I've enlisted you on the wrong side."

Gen shrugged. "I don't see why it has to be a battle."

"Two-party meetings always are. And we're outranked and outnumbered, which means we have to know our stuff and present it well to be heard."

Gen tipped her head to one side. "They need the information we've collected. Surely—"

"Sarah's right, Gen," Steph said. "Party politics are fierce. If you don't want to go through with it…"

"No," Gen said. "My mom and I talked about this when Sarah asked me to join her team. We've always been War, and I lean War on most stuff. But I believe in Sarah more."

"I'm not sure I deserve that," I said.

"Sure, you do," Steph said. "Don't go getting soft on us now. We can't afford it."

I laughed.

Then we were there.

The conference room could have been the Blue Conference Room in the Peace Palace except its enormous oval table was mahogany rather than cherry, and ancient weapons rather than tapestries hung on the walls. As I entered, I counted one—no, two—generals, five War Council members, and Glenstra, with a small contingent of unfamiliar fairies. All the congresspeople from the Northwestern provinces were there as well as several influential committee chairs. But where was Prince Philip?

King Randolph rose as we entered, and so, of course, did everyone else. "Your Highness," he said, shaking my hand with an iron grip. "You certainly didn't waste much time getting back into the swing of things."

"The situation seemed to warrant it. I'm surprised Prince Philip is not here. Is he all right?"

"His Highness is fine."

I nodded. I wouldn't get any more about Phil from that source, so I changed the subject, introducing Gen.

King Randolph fixed Gen with a shrewd eye and held out a hand. "So, you're Genevieve Bockert. Pleased to meet you. Tell me, how does a young woman from Coredlian come to be research assistant to the Peace Princess?"

Gen's eyes opened wide. "She's my friend; she asked me; I agreed."

Several people tittered.

King Randolph didn't. "Ah. And how did you get to be friends?"

"I was eating alone in the cafeteria my first week here, and she came over and asked me to join her table."

"You have a good eye for talent," King Randolph said to me.

"Nah," Steph said. "Sarah's always doing stuff like that. If every lonely girl Sarah's asked to join us for lunch were here this morning, you'd need a room twice this big."

"Stephanie!" I said.

"Aren't we getting off topic?" Gen said. "Not that Sarah isn't the best, but haven't we got more important things to deal with this morning?"

Several people giggled again.

I glared at them. "Yes, we seem to be holding up the proceedings." I smiled at Gen and scanned the table.

The opposite end of the table from King Randolph held the only empty seats, so I moved toward them. The one directly opposite His Majesty was marked with my father's name. I nodded to Steph and Gen and sat, hoping I didn't look as uncomfortable as I felt sitting in my father's chair.

As soon as I was seated, King Randolph began the meeting. Reports from the field came first. The news was appalling. Pictures beamed back from cell towers all over the northwest showed fire falling from the sky like rain, in beautiful but deadly hues like purple, green and gold. News reports featured waves upon waves of dark-clothed figures advancing across Silvershire with a semi-transparent shield in front of them that glittered a multitude of colors when it caught the light, and shone silver each time a bullet hit and bounced back toward where it had come from, until one bullet flew directly toward the camera, and the picture stopped abruptly.

Then came the blogs, social media photos, wire reports and testimony of soldiers. Even in the mountains, our enemy moved faster than people could run. They brought choking fogs and a nearly physical sensation of overwhelming fear. They ate ground as if it were a submarine sandwich.

We were out-manned, out-maneuvered, and out-magicked. Though I'd heard much of this before, the details were still shocking.

When the reports were over, King Randolph looked drawn and exhausted. Old, even. His exhaustion deepened as we discussed the pros and cons of a draft and concluded that one wasn't necessary at the moment. We had enough recruits; the trouble was getting them trained and into the field fast enough.

"We need to limp along a while longer with what we've got," King Randolph summed up. "How can we manage that?"

"Records show that the last time we worked with fairies, a mobilization network enabled us to transport army units from one point to another almost effortlessly. That could stretch our manpower farther," I said.

Glenstra raised her head. "You're talking about the Mertinga Maze? That was a stroke of brilliance, but it took a lot of setting up."

"In the books, it seemed like it went up overnight," I said.

Glenstra nodded. "Time's not the issue. It's power. We'd need most of our fairies to work on it solidly for six to eight hours. Then we'd need nearly a quarter of our fairies to run it."

"We can't afford that," one of the generals said, stroking his chin. "We need every fairy we've got for magical protection. We certainly can't spare most of them for eight hours."

"Couldn't we provide our own magical protection for that long?" I asked. "There are chants that ought to do some good, if we've got magic-sensitive people trained to say them."

"That's what these guys keep saying," the other general said, jerking a thumb towards the fairy contingent, "but as they don't use chants themselves, they don't know any."

"Fortunately, our ancestors wrote some down," I said. "We've unearthed a number in our archives and organized them. A full list is on a database we can make accessible to you, but we've also made a field guide with some of the most useful." I nodded at Gen who passed around the green booklets we'd been working on all week.

"We've tried a few of the chants, and they seem to work, though it's hard to tell from our tests how effective they'd be in battle," I went on. "You can tailor them if you know Fairy. Apparently, seven hundred years ago, everybody did. We've included some basic modifications."

The first general flipped through the booklet. "This may give us something to work with, though I'd want to see results for at least a week before I agreed to let fairies turn their attention away from guarding our troops."

The other general asked about getting troops tested for magical ability and trained to use the chants. Then both asked more questions about the maze I'd mentioned.

After that, talk shifted to more standard warfare, and I struggled to keep up. It was nearly an hour before the discussion took a turn that allowed me to be useful again.

"Thank goodness all the fairies we've met are flummoxed by anything electronic," Lord Montressor said.

"How long can we expect that to last?" Lady McGivern asked.

"Until they pay some person with a modicum of skill to betray their country," King Randolph said.

"They don't need to use money," I said. "They can magically influence people."

"I thought humans were immune to that," Lady McGivern said.

"Most adults have strong resistance, but last week Darvian told me that young people are easily influenced," I said.

A few of the fairies in the room nodded.

"Are you saying there's nothing in here to combat this?" King Randolph tapped the green book.

"There are chants that can protect us from influence spells, but they require the agreement of those falling under the protection. You can't just send them over the whole country," Gen said, speaking up for the first time.

"We could try counter-influence spells," said one of the fairies who'd introduced herself at the beginning, but whose name I'd forgotten.

"I don't like the idea of brainwashing people, however good the cause," I said.

"It is morally repellent," King Randolph said. "We will not condone the use of any magic that affects the mind without the consent of those affected."

"But we ought to do something," Lord Montressor said. "Perhaps an education campaign with the opportunity to voluntarily come under these spells would be appropriate."

King Randolph nodded. "That could be done, if we could find the manpower."

"Perhaps Young Peace and Young War clubs could be persuaded to do it. Lots of students are too young for the army and still want to do something," Gen said.

"Good idea," King Randolph said. "Why don't you and Lord Montressor, here, work together to come up with an organizational plan for such a campaign?"

Gen glanced at me, and I nodded. We were supposed to be cooperating. In fact, King Randolph had jobs for us all. He assigned me to train recruits that afternoon using the chants I'd found.

When the meeting finally broke, I was tired, and my head ached. I thought we'd accomplished some good in that meeting, but then again, I'd thought we'd accomplished some good when we'd passed Cagnew's proposal and again when we'd had our brainstorming session. None of those things had helped at all—or at least they hadn't helped much when the invasion came through. Would my little chants and songs make any difference in the war?

Plus, where was Phil?

CHAPTER 22

I didn't see Phil for almost a week. By that time, I had stopped pretending to have any control over my life. I showed up wherever Steph said we were supposed to be and got by with whatever notes were thrust into my hands.

I didn't even remember it was Saturday until we pulled up to the Joint Council building. When I saw Phil step out of the limo ahead of us, I was taken aback. I hadn't known he'd be here—I hadn't even known I'd be here, and the media hadn't mentioned when Phil's first appearance in public would be. I'd given up trying to pry information out of the War Palace days ago. No one over there would return my calls, not even Phil. After our almost dance and then meeting Darvian together, I'd been sure he'd want to talk. When he hadn't called, I'd worried. But here he was, walking into a meeting.

He looked awful, though. He shuffled, and his skin was ashy.

"Are they nuts?" I said. "He shouldn't be seen like that!"

"Well, it's a Joint Council meeting. He has to show up, doesn't he?" Steph said. "He'll be on public cameras whether he's here in person or teleconferencing, and with everyone speculating that he's dead, they probably wanted people to see that he can move."

"Pull over," I said to the driver. "We're getting out now."

"What? The press is having a feeding frenzy!"

"Exactly." When the limos stopped, I stepped into the thickest bunch of reporters.

Half swung to capture my entrance, and Phil's guards wrestled him into the building.

"Your Highness, how do you feel about Prince Philip's return to public duty this morning? Do you think his illness will affect the war?"

"Is he ill?" I asked.

"Please, Your Highness. Surely you saw him as you were pulling up."

"Not clearly. Nobody's changed him into a giant mouse or anything, have they?"

Several reporters laughed, and our party inched our way forward.

"Doesn't his lack of energy concern you?"

"The news I've heard about the western railways concerns me," I said, pushing forward, "but I understand King Randolph has a plan for dealing with it."

Cameras jostled to keep pace with me.

"All in all, we have much better reason for hope this morning than we did a week ago." I turned, smiled brightly, and pressed backward through the last knot of reporters into the entry hall.

"You didn't have to do that," Phil said as I entered the Joint Council room.

I shrugged. "Are you OK?"

"Just tired. Our fairy friends asked me to do too much last week. And they can't cure exhaustion without mind games. No one wanted to try one of those on me."

I checked to see who was watching. Everyone else in the room seemed busy. "I know a rest song, if there's time."

"We've got thirty minutes. We got here early to avoid the press."

I snorted. "Do you want me to try the song?"

"Couldn't hurt."

Humming, I touched Phil's hand. Waves of exhaustion swept over me, but I sang them back to less than a ripple. Then I staggered backward and opened my eyes.

Phil's color was back to normal, and the circles under his eyes had disappeared. A glint of humor had returned to their deep blue.

I smiled. "Not bad. Your parents should have done this before you left the house this morning."

"Not if they were going to wind up looking like you do now," Phil said.

"Really? It doesn't feel as bad as after my training session Tuesday." But I'd had to have my make-up redone after that.

"Excuse me," I said to Phil and headed for the lady's room, calling Steph as I went.

The first ring was cut off by Steph's voice. "What were you thinking? Let *him* look like the walking dead."

"He was feeling like the walking dead, too," I said.

"What are we going to do with you?"

"I figured the usual. Is my mom coming soon?"

"No, she's teleconferencing with your dad. And I can't get in there to help—nobody but security people, members of the Joint Council, and scheduled presenters allowed, remember?"

"Bother." I dumped the contents of my purse onto the bathroom counter. Three months ago, there would have been toys and bubblegum. Now I picked out concealer, foundation, mascara, and hefty compacts of cheek and eye colors. I wished that Clare hadn't been fired. She couldn't do makeup as well as my mom, but she did wear some. "Tell me how to use my make-up."

"You're kidding," Steph said before starting to give me instructions. Five minutes of intense work made things worse, though. Lots worse.

The door to the bathroom opened, and I turned my head away. "Got to go," I said and hung up.

"Can I help?" Queen Salome asked.

I wavered. Now was not the time to be proud, I told myself. I turned to face Phil's mom. "They won't let my friend through, and I'm worse than hopeless with this stuff," I said, gesturing at the mass of make-up.

Queen Salome smiled. "I think we can fix that." She pulled cold cream from her own purse and erased my amateur efforts. Then she reduced my mess of make-up to order and applied it with a firm but gentle hand.

In minutes it was over. I surveyed myself. My exhaustion hardly showed, but I didn't look normal either. The girl in the mirror seemed older and a little bit…seductive. I wondered if Queen Salome saw me that way. Strange. "Thank you. That's way better than I could have done."

"It's I who should be thanking you. You didn't have to help my son."

"It was nothing."

"You've got an odd idea of nothing. You know, I think you might find this useful." She handed over a card with Phil's private telephone number.

"Thank you," I said, searching Queen Salome's face for some sign of what this meant. The queen's visage was inscrutable, however.

Back in the main Council room, I got myself some cookies and wandered toward the head of the table. Second chair. It felt weird.

Uncle Malcolm arrived and said, "Anything new I should know about?"

"Queen Salome slipped me Phil's private number," I said, cursing Uncle Malcolm's ability to read my moods.

He looked at me blankly for a second and then laughed. "I meant on the agenda."

My face grew hot.

"Not that your love affairs aren't important." After a moment, he added, "Queen Salome, did you say?"

I nodded. "Do you think I have to tell Dad?"

"What do you think?"

I grimaced.

"So, is there any news?" Uncle Malcolm said.

I shrugged and handed him the notes Steph had given me in the car.

Uncle Malcolm skimmed and grunted. "Have they softened this youth corps proposal?"

I read it through. "A little, but it's still militarizing kids too young. Dangerous for them and dangerous for the country." I would have gone on, but the mediator started the meeting, and I needed to pay attention. It was harder than usual. Twice I asked for more time to consider things. The second time, on a bill commissioning more helicopters, I almost missed the rider that made the order self-renewing for ten years with preference to a particular company that always funded War campaigns. There was too much new legislation today. If I weren't so tired, I could deal with it better. At least I could do something about the rider on the helicopter bill. I protested, and it was dropped.

On the screen, King Randolph frowned, and he postponed discussion on the youth corps proposal. Why? It was getting late, but we'd had Joint Council meetings go later. Maybe he felt like he'd lost momentum, and he wanted a fresh start.

When the meeting ended, I only saw Phil long enough to shake his hand and wish him a good week. Too bad I'd had to waste so much time before the meeting on make-up.

***

I wanted to call Phil for a real conversation, but I didn't have a free moment until Tuesday night. Then, Phil took so long to answer, I nearly gave up.

"Hello?" he said at last, sounding tired.

"Hi! It's me," I said, kicking myself for sounding squeaky.

"How did you get this number?"

"Your mother gave it to me." Didn't he want me to have his private line?

"What?"

"After she helped me with my make-up on Saturday."

"She's the one who did your make-up Saturday?"

"You didn't know?"

"I've got to talk to her."

"It was nice. I was making a terrible mess."

"I don't think she was doing you any favors."

"I thought it looked OK. Not my usual self, but presentable." I giggled. "Which I was not, left to my own devices. You should have seen me."

Phil laughed. "I wish I had. So, where are you?"

"My tower."

Phil choked.

"Don't hang up. They've promised not to bug it as long as I tell them how long we talk and if we discuss anything political."

"Ahh."

"Please don't be mad at me. I'm not good at hiding things."

Phil laughed. "No, you're not."

"But you'll forgive me?"

"For not lying to your parents?"

"I guess."

"I don't know that you should have to apologize for that." There was a long pause.

"So, how did it go with Darvian and Glenstra?" I said at last.

Phil laughed. "It was weird. We'd go to some field or forest that I couldn't tell apart from any of the other fields and forests, and I'd say the chant, and then sit in a tent drinking a restorative drink for an hour or two, and we'd go do it again. I couldn't even tell if it was working, but they said it was. There wasn't any trouble at all until it was time to come home— they hadn't mentioned the invasion, you see."

"Oh, wow. Why not? You had contact with your parents, right?"

"All they said was that I'd need to take the long route back, and not to worry. I wasn't worried until Dad told me not to."

"I'm glad they finally got you back. How are you now?"

Fine. At least I would be if my parents weren't being so stubborn about the army."

"Your parents are being stubborn about the army? That doesn't sound like them."

"About me joining."

I could see that. "Of course, they don't want you to join! You haven't even finished high school, and with a war coming on, you're needed in the capital."

"That's what my parents said, but it's ridiculous. I'm not doing any good here. I'm going down to the recruiters tomorrow."

"Without your parents' permission?"

"I'm of age. They can't stop me. Neither can Joint Council or Congress. It's level one code."

"Level one?"

"Exactly."

Well, that was unfixable. Changing level one code required a three-quarter vote of Congress and ratification by all the provinces. Nobody was going to open a level one debate in the middle of a war.

I groaned.

"Funny, you and my parents being on the same side."

"It's a sign we're right."

"Nah. None of you is impartial."

"Just because the code can't be changed doesn't mean there aren't other ways."

"Go ahead and try. You've got until tomorrow." A bell rang in the background. "Look, Sarah, I've got to go. Sorry we spent so much time arguing."

"It doesn't matter," I said. "I'd rather be arguing with you than agreeing with half the other people I know."

Phil laughed. "See you around." The phone clicked.

I stared at it a minute before calling Steph and Gen. We had to figure out how to stop Phil from joining the military.

✳✳✳

Hours of poring over code and digging up records left us no closer to preventing Phil from joining up.

"Why not let him go?" Steph finally said. "That's what the rest of us have had to do."

I blinked. My eyes were sore from staring at computer screens. "It's selfish, I know. And I miss Andy, too. Have you heard how he's doing? He hasn't messaged me."

Steph shook her head. "Not since the last phone call. He's allowed one a week. But I think it will be better when he gets out of training."

I shook my head. "Don't you think having Phil restricted that way would be bad for us all? Without Phil, the War Council doesn't fully function."

"Good point," Gen said. "And if we can prove it, maybe we can convince Phil to stay where he is."

"If we find proof, and he still won't give this idea up, maybe we can convince the military to assign him to do his job," I mused.

"He'll be ticked," Steph said.

"I know." I sighed. Phil and I were starting to get along.

Gen squeezed my arm. "Maybe he'll understand."

"We've got to do it whether he understands or not," I said. "We still have a war to win."

"Let's get to work then," Gen said.

✳✳✳

We had a fairly convincing argument by the time I left for my first meeting the next morning. I dropped off a copy for Phil at the War Palace and was assured he'd get it by noon. I hoped he'd be reasonable.

I didn't get back to the palace until nearly dinnertime, having spent a couple of hours with Ms. Kramer in a library conference room after all my meetings were over. The answering machine for my private line was blinking. I turned the volume up, so I could listen while I changed.

Phil's voice came clear and strong from across the room. "Sarah, nice try, but hundred-year-old poll figures are hardly convincing."

I paused with my dress halfway to my shoulders. So, some of our evidence was old. That didn't make it false. And there'd been modern stuff in the packet, too.

"Anyway, I signed up," Phil's voice went on. "I'm due to report for training next Monday. I announce to the press tomorrow. And Mom and Dad have stopped speaking to me. Call me, will you?"

The machine beeped.

I finished pulling up my dress and stepped into strappy sandals. If I skipped having my make-up retouched, I'd have time to call. Barely.

Today he picked up on the second ring.

"Phil?" I said.

"Oh, good," he said. "I was afraid you were going to stop speaking to me, too."

"Never considered it. I'm not mad at you, just sort of exasperated. And I'm considering pulling strings to get you stationed here in Bentralia."

He laughed. "Pull away. I shouldn't think you've got enough influence with military people to make much difference."

"You might be surprised."

"Whatever."

Annoyed, I wished him luck with his press conference and hung up.

Dinner was quiet as dinners lately went. Besides my family, there were only five people: Lord Sanderson, Lord Richter, a man who ran an automobile parts factory, an air force colonel, and a fairy named Warbin. The talk went late, and even the exams I legitimately had to study for weren't a good enough reason to skip out.

When I got back to my room, it was past midnight, and there was a note from Steph saying she had an appointment with General Pinehurst, one of the generals from my first war commission with King Randolph. Good. He'd supervised me for several magical training sessions with troops and been impressed. Still, did I have enough evidence to convince him to keep Phil in town? I sat down at my computer. I needed to strengthen my case. I'd have to wing my exams.

CHAPTER 23

The next day, as Phil held his press conference, I met with General Pinehurst.

The man stroked the smooth dark brown skin of his chin while he read my report. "This looks good, but I know enough not to accept what a royal tells me about their chief rival."

I sat up and tried my best smile. "General Pinehurst, I know the two royal houses are perpetually feuding, but it's a respectful feud. I admire Philip Castanay. I'd hate to see him throwing his life away when he can be doing so much more good here." I teared up. What had gotten into me that I cried in public every time I thought about Phil putting himself at risk?

The general tapped his pen against the desk. "How old are you, again?".

"Sixteen next month." I fought the tears back but was glad for the excuse to look away when my phone vibrated. A fire had broken out in Lower Beckwater, one of the southern suburbs. My dad was busy and had ordered me to see what I could do to help.

I suppressed my frustration as I made my excuses. I didn't feel done here.

As I made it to the door, General Pinehurst said, "Your Highness, Are you all right?"

"I'm fine."

"How many of your friends are already at the front?"

"None yet. A couple go next week. My cousin Andy in four months." Why did he want to know?

The general nodded. "I'll see if I can't arrange something about young Castanay. I suspect we need you both fully functioning here in Bentralia if we're going to win this thing."

"Thank you," I said, surprised. Why would the general say that right after asking about my friends? Was I transparent enough that everyone could see how much I liked Phil?

If so, Dad would be furious, but I couldn't worry about it right now.

***

On the ride over in the limo, I watched an HNC reporter describing fairy flame in Lower Beckwater. Not good. I took out my chant book to study.

The first sign of the fire was a greenish cast in the air. Then came the traffic jam. Cars crawled on all four inbound highway lanes, honking at anyone who tried to merge in. The surface streets were even worse, from what I could see of them. My car was stopped on the exit ramp. The road in front of us was a parking lot with the noses in all four lanes facing north.

"Isn't this usually a two-way street?" I asked.

"Yes," the driver growled.

After fifteen minutes of sitting in the same spot, I overruled my guards' objections, and we walked the last ten blocks. They didn't much like protecting me outside the car in this crowd, but they did it.

At the rope line, green light flickered in the sky ahead of us while a small crowd listened to a tall balding man rant about the inefficiencies of the Dicrandian national government.

"Inefficient we may be," I said, projecting as well as I could without a mic, "but as long as we are the government, we will intervene in catastrophes like this."

The crowd swung. Many had not seen me approach.

"What exactly do you think you can do?" somebody shouted.

"Fight back," I said. "Extra firefighting forces are already on their way. And we have chants for the magic."

"That chanting is folderol," the speaker said.

I studied the green glints. Close enough for the smothering chant I'd learned in the car.

"Oh?" I said and chanted it.

Instantly, the green lights died down. Only the most distant glimmers showed. A silence fell. I gripped Lewis's forearm to keep from falling over. Once I'd steadied myself, I spoke into the silence, forcing myself to sound confident.

"As I said, we come to help. If you are also here to help, get over to the headquarters to get organized. If you are not here to help, kindly get out of the way of those who are.

I maintained eye contact until the crowd broke up.

✳✳✳

Headquarters was a pavilion pitched on a parking lot next to a hardware store. Guys in blue overalls worked on a fire truck, wielding tools I couldn't name. A tall dark man with close-cropped white hair leaned over a map that covered most of a card table. From time to time, he barked orders at a young red-haired man stooped over a tangle of electronic equipment on a second card table.

I approached, picking my feet up just enough to clear the orange extension cords that snaked across the gravel lot. "Chief," I said, "Can I be of help?"

The man with the white hair straightened up. "Could you get me more people and more chemical fire units?"

"There are some on the way, already."

"I need more than Duncan and Central."

"I'll see what I can do." I said. "I could probably also teach a few chants if you've got any people who are magic sensitive."

"I'm sure we've got magic-geniuses hiding all over the place,' The chief said. The red-headed guy messing with the electronics laughed.

"Do you mind if I check with the people who are on break?" I asked.

"Do what you like but get me my reinforcements first."

I made a couple of phone calls to contacts in city emergency response before heading toward a group of soot-covered men and women who were gulping water near a blue cooler on the other side of the pavilion. Several were smoking cigarettes. I shook my head and pulled a white heart-shaped stone from my backpack. Darvian had made me the white stone after noticing how much energy it took for me to test others for magic-sensitivity using songs. Using the stone required less energy and was much faster. I simply held it in my right hand with the point aimed at another person, and it would change color to indicate how magic sensitive they were. Slight sensitivity would turn the stone a light pink. More sensitivity would cause red, yellow, and on up the rainbow. I myself was an inky blue.

Even with the little talisman to reduce my energy output, I was usually exhausted at the end of a day of testing people. I would need to be careful today. I was already having trouble maintaining the dancer-straight posture

~ 141 ~

my mother preferred I use. I straightened my shoulders and advanced on the group of resting firefighters.

"Hello," I said.

A few people nodded. The group seemed weary, defeated.

"I guess it's not going so well," I said.

"It's beating us," a woman with curly black hair said. "It started with the energy plant, and now it's a mile wide and four miles long."

"And it's fast. We couldn't clear the Sunnybrook neighborhood in time," a man said. He looked older than the woman and had a broad face and bristly hair.

"It's magic," a younger man said. "I thought all the talk about magic on the front was an excuse for ineptitude, but now I see it…"

"You know it's real. I've got some chants that should help fight it if any of you are magic sensitive."

"Not likely," the young man said.

"It doesn't usually show unless you try a song or chant. Or you're tested for it."

I placed the heart carefully in my palm, aiming it toward the young man. All twelve firefighters were watching now. The little white stone flushed lemon yellow.

"What does that mean?" asked the second woman in the group.

"That our skeptical friend here can do magic," I said.

"Can anyone else?" the man with the bristle hair asked.

"Let's see." I slowly circled, pointing the heart at each person in turn. One of the smokers, a tall, skeletally thin man, was the only other one who caused any color in the stone. Pointed at him, the stone blushed a light pink. Two hits in a group of twelve. Not a bad ratio, but they'd need more for this fire.

"It's not the same color as T.J.'s," the man said.

"No, you can't do as much." I said.

"What can I do?

"Let's see." I slipped another gift, this time from Glenstra, out of my pack. It looked like a four-inch square of rainbow-colored glass. When I placed it over one of the chants or songs written in my book, a dark curve appeared, graphing a slope that peaked at the light pink edge of the glass and reached a low point somewhere farther along the rainbow. On both the dark purple and light pink edges, numbers counted upward from one. With the numbers and the curve, I could easily see how many people of a given magic sensitivity would be required to safely use that chant or song.

I tried my graph glass on a couple of different chants, and decided it was safe to teach these men the blanket chant for about two square yards.

After that, I chanted with them to make the group's gear fairy-flame retardant. Then the group's break was over, and they were gone.

In the group that replaced them, the only person with magic sensitivity was pink. She and I chanted to protect the group's gear, and I taught her one of my weaker healing songs.

By the time reinforcements showed up, the first group I'd trained had been successful enough that the chief wanted me to train the new people. The stone revealed three more pink flashes, an orange and a green. With this group, I enchanted the chemicals in the firetrucks' tanks before teaching other chants.

I continued training as the chief's original team cycled through. (Another green, four more pinks, and a red.) Then I switched to healing and rest songs.

We made progress with the fire, beating it back bit by bit, block by block. The men and women taking their breaks still looked weary, but they no longer seemed haunted and beaten.

By one, I was exhausted. In fifteen or twenty minutes, the trucks would be back, needing their reservoirs enchanted. I didn't know how much longer I'd be able to do this. I couldn't call on fairy help because every spare fairy was working on the maze that was finally going up. Could my father take over for me?

A call to my dad's work phone got his secretary, who reminded me that both the country's kings were training troops that afternoon.

I slumped. I tried to remember when the fairies would be free again. Was it ten o'clock tonight? Well, with any luck, we'd have this licked by then. I found a folding chair, sat down, deliberately tensed up all my muscles for a moment, and then released them. I breathed deeply. That was a mistake, I realized, as an acidic stink filled my nostrils. The smell wasn't bad enough to keep me from relaxing, though.

Seconds later, someone shook me.

"What? What's happened?"

The firetrucks are back, and they're asking for you," Lewis said.

"Oh. Right." I dragged myself across the pavilion. I no longer cared about maintaining a stately stride.

Enchanting the firefighting foam wasn't nearly as bad as I'd expected. My little nap must have helped. So, when I felt myself drifting off again, I let myself go. They'd wake me when they needed me.

By three o'clock, the fire crews had driven the fire back to the power plant where it had started. It was small enough now that the firefighters could manage a mass blanket chant, which they would follow with a snow of enchanted foam.

I roused myself, and borrowing a telescope, leaned against one of the pavilion's poles to watch. I was unutterably glad the ordeal was nearly finished.

I couldn't see the people chanting, but I saw the green tongues of flame suddenly die down. Smoke rose as foam blanketed the compound. Around me, people cheered wearily.

I smiled. I let the telescope wander over the blackened cement blocks of the power plant.

Suddenly I stopped. Was something moving in the wreckage? It was. Something black and long. I focused in on it, at first not realizing what I saw. Then I shouted, "Chief, get your people out of there!"

Even as he said, "Are you crazy, child?" the black sinuous creature rose on wings of glittering purple and sprouted fresh green flames. One of the fire engines exploded and green flickers lit the sky again. The beast dropped into the fire as if its wings couldn't hold it up any longer.

"What's going on?" the chief said.

"What was that?" someone else shouted.

"A dragon," I said grimly, thrusting the telescope at Parker and stumbling over to where I'd left my chant book. How had a dragon gotten here? An important question, but not one that would help much now. I pushed it aside. What could I remember about dragons?

Not much. They were meat eaters, favoring humans. They were cunning, could talk, and preferred stratagem to force, but were fierce when pushed. They could tear holes in protective walls in less than an hour. Dragons could also fly faster than small aircraft.

Was this one wounded, then?

No, I realized. It was the size of a motorbike. This was a baby. That's why it couldn't fly much and wanted to stay in the fire. It needed the heat to grow.

That thought didn't give me much comfort. Even baby dragons were dangerous, and they grew remarkably fast.

I flipped through my chant book. There was one charm for dragons— a chant for killing them. I wrote in a few words to show that the dragon I wanted to kill was the one up the street, whipped out my rainbow glass, placed it on the page, and gasped.

Killing this dragon would take two of me.

I traced the chart on the glass backward into the other colors. Even if every other magic-sensitive person I'd trained that day helped, we still couldn't do it safely.

For a minute, I stood there, staring.

Then I dialed Phil's number.

He picked up on the third ring. "Who is this?" His voice was cold.

"Sarah," I said. "Phil, I need your help. I've got a dragon down here, and I can't kill it. My graph glass says we can do it if there are two of us. The fairies are you-know-where, and our dads—"

"A dragon?"

"A baby black one. With purple wings." My voice shook. "It exploded one of our firetrucks."

"I'll be there in twenty minutes."

✳✳✳

Around me, people were panicking. I saw a bullhorn by the chief's feet and appropriated it. "Friends, we are NOT defeated yet. Dragons are tricky and dangerous, but this one is a baby. It needs to stay in its fire. We just need to contain that fire for long enough that we can bring in the power we need to kill the dragon. We can do that. We've been containing the fire all day."

"That's right folks," the chief took his bullhorn back and began giving orders. It took some time, but those who had started to leave stopped, and a new shift was sent to re-surround the dragon and its fire.

Once he reestablished calm, the chief came over to me. "What did you mean by 'bring in the power to kill this dragon?'"

"Philip Castanay is on his way. He and I can do it together."

"Have you been smoking something?"

"No."

Just then, a deep red Glory pulled up to the pavilion with much squealing of tires. Phil stepped out of the back seat. "What is it we've got to say?" he asked me.

The chief's jaw dropped.

"Here," I said, handing over the green book.

Phil nodded and counted down.

We chanted together, carefully.

Energy surged from me, and the world went black.

CHAPTER 24

When I opened my eyes, I was staring into someone else's startling blue ones. "Where am I? What happened?" I struggled to sit up.

"It's OK," Philip said, pushing a strand of hair out of my face. "The dragon is dead. The fire's out. Peace Memorial's full up, so I brought you home. To my home, I mean. Your place is half-an-hour farther."

I ought to have been concerned I was in the War Palace, but I wasn't. I sank back into a pile of flowered cushions. "What time is it?"

"Seven o'clock. I'd have revived you sooner, but I was so busy helping the firefighters, I didn't have time. Then I had to work up the energy."

That made sense. I nodded.

"You have a lot of nerve, by the way, calling me to rescue you after that stunt you pulled this morning."

"What stunt?"

"Getting the Army to assign me to my political duties. Oh, don't look so shocked. We've got people all over the military. The palace knew as soon as the order was signed."

"You said I could tell whoever I wanted. It's not my fault you didn't believe it could make any difference."

"You're right. I shouldn't be surprised at you persuading anybody to do anything. But it's ironic that the first thing you do after convincing General Pinehurst that the country needs me alive and whole is run off to fight a dragon."

"I didn't know it was a dragon."

"Would it have stopped you if you had?"

"Probably not."

Philip laughed. "Well, after today, no one can accuse us of avoiding danger."

Was that what his signing up for the military had been about? I hadn't guessed. I decided it was best to change the subject. "Do we know how the dragon got there?"

"I'd guess it was an egg. Apparently baby dragons can't travel without the inferno, which presumably we'd have noticed. But who knows how the egg got there? There aren't any more. We checked."

I nodded again. "Good. Do we know who we lost in that last blast?"

"There were fifteen," Philip said, pulling a folded sheet of notepaper from a pocket and handing it to me.

I unfolded it and found that it was no harder to read Philip's untidy scrawl than my own. We'd lost the driver of the fire engine that exploded, seven of the reserves I'd called in, and most of the first group I'd met by the water cooler.

I groaned and put my head down on my knees. I'd met these people. Talked with them. Some of them wouldn't have even been there if I hadn't called their units in to help. My eyes stung, but I fought the tears back. I didn't want to cry in the War Palace.

"Sarah, are you all right?"

"I will be," I mumbled. But those firefighters wouldn't be. The tears threatened to spill again. I swiped at my eyes with the sleeve of my blazer.

"Here, take this." Phil handed me a handkerchief.

I wiped my eyes and did my best to get myself under control. When I finally thought I could trust myself, I raised my head. "I should go home now."

"Yeah. A few more minutes and the press will be saying I kidnapped you." Phil ran a finger over my cheek. "Take care of yourself, will you?"

"You, too." I struggled to get off the couch, but my legs wouldn't support my weight.

Phil caught me before I completely crumpled. "I'll get a wheelchair and have your car meet you in the courtyard. That is if you're sure you won't stay for dinner."

I laughed. "Right. Like our parents would go for that."

"I don't know. My parents were pretty happy with the way you took care of my military career for them."

"And the dragon?"

Phil shrugged.

In the car, I wondered again how a dragon egg wound up in the power plant, but I had no new ideas. I closed my eyes. Before I knew it, Steph was shaking me awake.

I had her help me into my grandma's apartment since I couldn't manage my tower stairs. The whole way there, Steph kept reassuring me that I didn't have to deal with anything at the moment, not work (was she sure I shouldn't be writing condolence notes?), not school (Drat! My exams!), and certainly not the press. (Tomorrow would be soon enough to convince the world I wasn't dead.)

That last bit roused me from my brain fog. "Who's putting it about that I'm dead?"

"You were on film today. A reporter from Hourly News Central was in with the mob you broke up this morning—great speech, by the way. Anyway, she volunteered to man refreshments for the firefighters and put together snippets in her spare time."

"I didn't even notice."

"I'm not surprised, as busy as you were. Nothing's been playing on HNC for the last three hours but you and Phil firefighting, and you going down in a dead faint is getting a lot of airtime. We're not going to be able to make people believe you're alive until you make a public appearance."

I shook my head and sank into a bamboo armchair under a shell-framed mirror in my grandma's hall. In contrast to the stylish elegance of the rest of the palace, grandma's rooms had always felt like a seaside boutique. The kitschy furnishings made it feel like grandma was still here, even though she'd moved back to the beach ten years ago.

I was glad to rest. I closed my eyes but didn't have time to sleep before my mother clattered down the hall.

"Darling! I wanted to run down there and get you, but your father said I couldn't after you'd promised to fight that thing. And then that boy took you off to his own castle…"

"He had the car stop there on the way home, so he could recover enough energy to do a reviving song. You wouldn't have wanted him to send me home unconscious, would you?"

"Oh, Sarah, I don't know. I want you to promise you'll never do anything like that again."

"Mom, you know I can't promise that."

"I can't get your father to promise either."

"I'm sorry."

"No, I'm sorry. Come on, let's get you showered and into bed. You've got to come to dinner, but you can sleep at least an hour before then."

Shower? I twisted toward a mirror and gaped. My face was grimy and pale, streaked with black and green. I couldn't believe I'd let Phil see me this way. Phil and the whole rest of the country.

I washed my hair four times before the smell of smoke diminished to a tolerable level. My clothes were unsalvageable. But after an hour's nap, I could walk almost steadily down to the dining hall.

Dinner was painfully long, but a night's rest did wonders. In the morning, after breakfast and a press conference, I was able to climb to my tower. My inbox held the missing report on Clare's dismissal. I read through it once, then twice more in disbelief. Was it possible Rogers had fired her for being an inch-and-a-half too short?

I ground my teeth and called him to complain. He refused to reconsider his decision, saying he wouldn't be dictated to by a fifteen-year-old-girl, no matter her title.

I got hot. "That's another thing you might want to reconsider," I said and hung up on the man. I threw the phone across the desk into the wastepaper basket and stamped to my bathroom to splash water on my face. At least I had color now. When I thought I was calm enough, I returned to the main room, fished the phone out of the trash and shot Clare a note with a copy of the report and account of my conversation with Rogers. Maybe she could use the information to file a gender discrimination case. Not that she would sue the government in the middle of a war. I knew I was one of the most powerful kids in the country, and sometimes it felt like I couldn't control anything.

Still, sending the report to Clare got it off my mind, and I was able to work, writing condolence notes, preparing for tomorrow's meetings, checking the news.

I was in the middle of the *Daily Sun* when Ms. Kramer came in with my exams. I had forgotten about them again.

"Do you want to do this another time?" Ms. Kramer asked. "I see you've been sick."

"No, no," I said, taking my cue from her tone rather than her words. "Let me clear my desk."

"Don't bother. You can do these at your conference table. I have an approved laptop, scratch paper and pencils here."

I nodded and moved to the conference area.

Ms. Kramer fired the tests at me one after another—Algebra, Dicrandian History, then Literature. After a brief lunch, I took Biology and a Fairy exam I hadn't been expecting.

Nearly six hours after entering the room, Ms. Kramer packed up the computer and her supplies. "That's it. I'm sure you did well. Come see me in the fall when you're back at school."

"I will." I was surprised by how sad it felt to say goodbye.

Once she left, I thought it strange I hadn't seen or heard from anyone else today. Had I missed any meetings? My schedule had gone curiously blank, and Steph wasn't answering her phone.

I tried the Montressor main line and got Steph's dad. He said Steph and Gen had gone together to the library since my mom had ordered them off the place to let me rest. Apparently, Mom had even told them not to call or answer my calls.

Talking to Mom did not get me phone access to my friends. Instead, as soon as Mom found out about the exam marathon I'd had, she ordered me to rest until dinner and afterward go directly to bed.

"Dad can't have agreed to that, Mom." I cringed at the whine in my voice.

"Your father has agreed not to return you to a full schedule until Monday."

"Can I talk to him?"

"At dinner."

"Can I at least go out to Peace Park?"

"I suppose."

"Can I take a friend?"

"Anyone not on your staff," Mom said, sounding harassed.

"Thanks, Mom." I hung up before she could change her mind.

I was in the mood for company, but Andy was in training, and I wasn't allowed to talk to Steph or Gen. Who else could I call? I thought of several of the girls from school, but I didn't know them all that well.

Then, sure it would never work, I called Phil.

He sounded as surprised to be invited to join me on a hike as I was surprised to be asking, but he said he'd check his schedule. I found myself on hold, listening to the Molten K-wires' *Dragonslayer*. I guessed humility wasn't one of Phil's virtues.

Before the song ended, Phil was back on, saying he'd meet me at the back gate in half an hour. To meet him there, I had to ride Midnight at a pace my mother wouldn't consider relaxing, but I did. Fortunately, neither Parker nor Lewis felt the need to comment.

The wind whistled through my hair and whipped at my cheeks, and I breathed in deep gulps of pure, smoke-free air.

Before Phil arrived, I had enough time to take a quick look in my compact, smooth down my hair, and hand Midnight's lead off to Lewis.

"Gosh, you look good," Phil said.

"Thanks." I unlocked the gate. "Come on in. Have you ever been up to—Oh, how stupid of me. Of course, you haven't."

"Wherever we go is fine."

"I think this walk is pretty. It has lusimatonias all along it. They don't grow anywhere else in Bentralia."

"Lusimatonias?"

"These." I bent down, picked a small red flower from a clump of heart-shaped leaves, and handed it to him. A light fragrance wafted from it. My heart quickened as Phil set the blossom in my hair.

"They're beautiful, like you."

I ducked my head, muttered, "thank you," and walked on, quickly for a moment, then more slowly as the breeze off the trees calmed me again. Our silence felt awkward at first but became more companionable. The lengthening shadows played over us as we walked. When Phil slipped his hand into mine, it felt natural.

My planner alarm made both of us jump.

"What's that?"

"Alarm. I have to go back, or I'll be late for dinner," I said.

"Shocked me. I had forgotten the rest of the world."

"Me too."

"Perhaps I can come another time."

"I'd like that." I meant the words, which surprised me.

We headed back up the path.

"So, when are you taking your exams?" Phil said.

"I took them. Today."

"All of them?"

"Yeah. My mom's furious."

He laughed. "So how did they go?"

We talked school the rest of the way to the gate, and I lingered to watch him get in his car and pull out of sight.

When the last hint of him was gone, I turned resolutely. As I was swinging onto Midnight, though, I caught a glimpse of a figure hiding between two cars up the street. Before I could say anything, Lewis had left my side and slipped out of the gate.

The figure started running. Lewis caught up before the end of the block, collared the person, and marched them back to where I waited. As they drew close, I could see that the person was a girl, younger than me. She was shaking.

"I didn't do anything," she said. "Honest. Let me go."

"Well, you may not have done anything, but it looks like you were stalking a royal, which is a federal offense." I said.

"I wasn't stalking you. I wanted to check on something."

"Check on something? Something on the grounds?"

"That's loitering with intent to trespass," Lewis said.

The girl clamped her mouth shut. I gave Lewis a dirty look. "Miss—what's your name?"

"Andrews. Amy Andrews."

"Miss Andrews. I don't want to detain you any more than you want to be detained. I'm running late for dinner. If you wouldn't mind answering a few questions, we could take care of this quickly."

"I suppose," Amy said, kicking at a pebble.

"This thing you were going to check on. Is it something in the grounds?"

"Yes," the girl muttered.

I thought. If the kid was watching a squirrel nest, I didn't want to bother her.

"Is it something I should know about?" I asked finally.

The girl kicked more at the stone. "You'd kill it," she said at last.

"I'd kill it? How do you know that? Is it dangerous?"

"You killed Maura's," she said.

I blinked. I killed . . . I couldn't remember having killed anything in my whole life except a few mosquitoes and that dragon yesterday.

I opened my eyes wide. "Are you telling me there's a dragon here?"

Amy's eyes widened.

"Don't be ridiculous," Parker said. "If there were a dragon on the grounds, we could hardly miss it."

"Not a dragon," I said, staring at the frightened girl Lewis still held by the wrist. "A dragon egg."

The girl sobbed. "I told the man we shouldn't put it here. You have no sympathy for dragons."

"Well, no, I suppose I don't. The last one we had to deal with destroyed half a district and killed more than forty people."

"Dragons have as much right to live as anybody," Amy said. "They're beautiful creatures. Even the egg was lovely—like a giant green jewel."

"Ah," I said. "Well, that may be. I haven't seen it. But beautiful or not, dragons feed on people. They don't belong in the city. If there's a place where they do belong, I'd be happy to send it there instead of killing it, but I can't allow an egg to sit here on the grounds like a bomb waiting to go off."

The girl sniffed.

"Do you want it to burn up Peace Park and eat everybody within a five-mile radius?"

"No," the girl said. "But the man said it wouldn't cause much trouble."

"Is that what he told Maura, too?" I asked as gently as I could.

The girl cried harder.

"Where is it?" I asked, fighting to keep my rising fear out of my voice.

"In the park's boiler furnace." Amy said.

***

Darvian and Glenstra appeared the moment I called them. I explained about the dragon egg and Amy's aversion to hurting it. They suggested transporting it to Silt Mountain, a volcano in Islandia that housed a number of dragons.

Amy seemed placated by this, so I agreed.

The two fairies flickered, then disappeared. They were gone about twenty seconds.

"Done," Darvian said.

"Just in time, too," Glenstra said. It'll be hatching out any minute now.

I whistled. "I wonder how many more of these we've got to round up?" I had to get more information from Amy, but if I called Dad for help, Mom would take it wrong. Uncle Malcolm was supposed to be at dinner tonight, so that was just as bad. Maybe I could safely slip Dad the hint sometime during supper. Meanwhile, I'd try to reach Steph and Gen again. They'd never done an interrogation, but they might put Amy at ease.

Thankfully, Steph was now answering her phone. I arranged for Steph and Gen to question Amy at Gen's house. Darvian and Glenstra, along with a couple of guards I hadn't even realized were watching the gate, would also accompany Amy there, but they all looked super stern. I made sure someone called the girl's parents to make sure she'd have a guardian taking care of her, and I was working on a plan to get Dad over there as well. It would be a tight fit in Gen's living room, but I didn't want to involve the War Party, so Steph's place was out.

It was eight-thirty. Even at a full gallop, there was no way I'd get home in time to change for dinner. I shook my head as I threw a leg over my horse. Mom was not going to be happy. "I don't suppose there's any way for you to give me a boost?" I said to Glenstra. "I'm really late."

Glenstra smiled. "We'll see what we can do."

As my guards and I took off, Glenstra slapped each of the horses' rumps. I moved into a gallop and then beyond. The woods blurred into an impressionist painting. I let out one laughing scream and then concentrated on keeping Midnight on the path—not an easy task at this speed in the gathering dusk. I was glad my parents weren't watching. They wouldn't even let me get a stallion!

CHAPTER 25

Even though Midnight galloped at the speed of a small aircraft, I got to the palace only fifteen minutes before dinner. I raced to my room, threw on my navy pantsuit, ran a comb through my hair, and concentrated on composing a note to my father.

Dad,

While out in Peace Park, I found a girl who wanted to check on a dragon egg someone had convinced her to put in the Park's boiler furnace. Glenstra and Darvian have relocated the egg to a volcano in Islandia, and the girl is telling Steph and Gen all she knows about the eggs and their handler. They're at Gen's place. I'm assuming you'll want more power involved, but can you please handle it without Mom finding out? I didn't mean to break her rules.

Sarah

I glanced over my work, decided it was good enough, and folded it into a tiny heart. With three minutes to make it to the dining hall, I smoothed my pantsuit and set off at my usual late-for-dinner run.

Getting the note to my father proved easier than I'd feared because before starting the meal, he stopped to put a hand on my shoulder and ask how I was. If she'd been there, Clare would have caught me palming him the note, but I doubt Mom saw.

I knew when he read it because I saw him blanch suddenly and fight to keep his attention in the moment. I couldn't focus on him, though. Tonight, we were meeting with media.

Gerald Green, a senior editor at Daily Sun Telecasts, sat at my right. "So, when will you get back into the swing of things?" he asked.

"Monday, if Mother's willing."

"What are you doing in your free time?" asked a man across the table from me. From HNC? I wasn't sure.

"Resting," I said.

"Do you think that's wise, given yesterday's dragon crisis?" Mr. Green asked.

"I always think it's wise to listen to my mother," I said.

Several people laughed.

"So, you're not dealing with politics at all until Monday?"

"Well, I'm here," I said, "and I'll be at Joint Council tomorrow, but mainly I'm resting. Of course, I could rest a whole lot easier if I knew you all were cooperating fully with the war effort—especially in dealing with young people."

"Dicrandia has a free press, Your Highness," Mr. Green chided.

"It does, and we appreciate that. Our enemies don't recognize freedom of the press though. If you want to keep your freedom, you may want to join the fight against dark fairies and dragons."

"What do you think we can do?"

Good question. Before going to the park, I'd memorized my father's agenda for this dinner, but now I couldn't remember a single item on it. "Well," I said, landing on the first idea that came to mind, "you could offer information about the fairy world. It's not something people have experience with."

"Indeed, Your Highness," Mr. Green said. "I was talking to King Randolph about that very thing this morning. He thought an information segment and talk show might calm tensions. I reminded him of our rules about equal time for royal houses."

I smiled. "Did he recommend Peace do the segment or the talk show?"

"Neither. He recommended co-hosting."

"Co-hosting? Whenever he and Dad get together, fireworks fly. That's hardly reassuring for a troubled nation."

"Not with your father. With you."

"With me?"

"He thought you were good in front of the cameras yesterday."

"I'm flattered, though I can't help thinking his kind offer had more to do with getting around the spirit of your rules than with any talent I have."

"You underestimate yourself, Your Highness."

"You underestimate King Randolph. If he were willing for things to be even, he'd have proposed hosting with my father or having Prince Philip host with me—an even exchange."

Mr. Green rose to his feet. "Are you afraid to publicly face off against King Randolph on your own?"

"No more than he is afraid to face off against my father."

"Who's afraid to face off against me?" Dad came up behind me and put a hand on my shoulder. He'd ended the supper already? No wonder Mr. Green stood up. I should have stood as well. I smiled sheepishly at my dad.

"King Randolph has suggested a splendid plan for encouraging people in these dark days, and your daughter, I'm afraid, is willfully misinterpreting his intentions," Mr. Green said.

"A splendid plan?" Dad said. "By all means, let's hear it."

Hearing Mr. Green pitch the co-hosting plan to Dad made me smile. The editor touted my people skills and brilliance in dealing with the crises of the past few months. Everyone knew Dad had a weakness for hearing me praised.

But he wasn't stupid. As he steered Mr. Green away from the table, he suggested Phil and I could do the talk show together. Relieved to be out of the conversation, I backed up, right into Uncle Malcolm.

"Still a bit off form, hey?"

"Uncle Malcolm, I'm sorry."

"Don't worry about it. I needed to talk to you anyway. I got an SOS from your chief of staff. You wouldn't happen to be able to give me the address of one Genevieve Bockert, would you?"

"Sure. It's in Akonerlie. 12 Builder's Street. Why? What's up?" My heart raced. Had they lost Amy Andrews somehow?

"Can't say. Your mother says you're not to work more than necessary this weekend." He winked so quickly I wasn't sure I saw it. Come to think of it, Steph would never have sent out an SOS without an address. That was the type of thing I did—the type of thing I had, in fact, done in my message to my father. I smiled. Uncle Malcolm thumped my back and headed for the door, saying polite but hurried goodbyes.

I finally moved toward the music room, nearly bumping into my mother on the way.

"Careful, darling. No need to rush. But you look worlds better."

"Thanks. I had my walk in the park."

"Lovely. Did you find someone to go with you?"

"Yes."

"How nice. You must introduce us some time."

I felt heat rise in my cheeks, but Mom didn't seem to notice. She was already in the next room, shaking hands with the head of HNC. I smothered a sigh and followed her in. Thank goodness I was allowed out early tonight on account of not feeling well. Did these things ever do any good?

***

Maybe they did, since Monday, the effects of that particular dinner were evident. At a downtown TV studio, a whole flock of Estelle-like women dabbed at my face and hair, prepping me to co-host a talk show with Phil. King Randolph must have really wanted the airtime. It was a good thing, too. We desperately needed help finding dragon eggs. Amy Andrews claimed there could be a dozen more around Bentralia waiting to be hatched. We'd found three over the weekend, but without more information, we weren't sure we could find the rest in time.

As the TV people brushed powder on my face, I wondered how Phil and I were supposed to turn a talk show into a request for that kind of cooperation. I still wasn't sure when they took me out to the show's set.

The room was like a bowl with seats going up the sides and a round stage in the middle of the bottom. Phil was already there, sitting on the stage on a tiny cream-colored sofa looking fabulous in his army dress black.

He stood when I entered. "Hi. You look great."

"Thanks." I said. "You, too. Pity about the hair, though."

"What, you don't like the buzz cut?" He laughed. I navigated around a glass-topped coffee table to join him, careful not to jostle the towering flower arrangements that stood in giant porcelain urns next to the arms of the sofa. As soon as I sat, cameras wheeled around us, and a dozen people appeared to dab at our make-up, tinker with the microphones, and tell us to sit up straight and smile.

"Just talk naturally," the sound guy said.

Then the people were all gone.

Phil and I both laughed.

"Natural," Phil sniggered. "Like these flowers."

I giggled. "How do they get a carnation to turn this blue?"

"I've no idea, but it can't be any more painful than what they've done to separate you from your ball cap."

"I gave that up voluntarily," I said.

"See, painless."

"I didn't say that."

"And someone told me you two hate each other," the producer said, coming back in to give us last minute instructions before leaving us alone on the stage again.

I only had time to confirm that we were supposed to be getting help with dragon egg hunting before they let the audience in the doors.

"Show time," Phil said.

I nodded, pasting a smile on. Together we walked toward the edge of the stage. We shook hands and signed cards while people told us little bits about themselves. A freckled boy's older sister had cancer. I had tears in my eyes as I signed a poster for the girl. They dried up without any trouble when I tried to pay attention to a whiskered man's complaint about drains in his suburb.

Eventually, an announcement got people in their seats and Phil and me back on the little couch. The room was silent. There was a pregnant pause. Then the intro came on and the questions started.

A middle-aged man with a large moustache said, "We all know it was a dragon that caused such damage in Lower Beckwater last week. How did it get there? Can we be sure there's nothing of the sort in our neighborhood?"

"Good question," I said. "We believe a dragon egg was put there by a teenager who had been tricked into touching it. Dragon eggs bewitch those who touch them."

"Has the kid been punished?" a woman asked.

"We believe she was on hand when the dragon hatched. It ate her."

Amy had pointed them to another girl, Violet, who had been on the phone with Maura when the black dragon hatched. Violet had not made any stipulations about keeping her dragon egg alive.

Phil's eyes widened. Hadn't he heard this before?

Apparently not because he asked, "Seriously?"

"Seriously. That's what the magic is for—to provide the little monsters their first meal."

"How can you call such magnificent creatures monsters?" said a boy from the back of the auditorium.

"Because they eat people, destroy cities, and generally wreak havoc," Phil said.

"But they're so beautiful," a girl down front said.

"If you like enormous, skinny lizards," he shot back.

I shook my head. "I can see her point, Your Highness. They're shiny. Spectacularly radiant, you might say. And those wings—I've never seen anything like them."

"Have you gone crazy?" Phil asked.

"No, but I'm younger than you. More susceptible to its spell. All spells."

"Come again?"

"Dragons give off strong attraction spells. If you come in contact with a dragon, and you're not careful, you'll walk straight into its jaws. The younger you are, the truer that is."

"Are you saying it's not that girl's fault?" someone in the crowd demanded.

Phil rubbed his temples. "Of course, it's her fault. But it was more foolish than evil, and she's paid for her folly. Obviously, others have paid for her folly as well. All we're saying is that if there are people out there who are being foolish about dragons or dragon eggs, we'd like them to come to us before serious damage is done. We're more interested in preventing nightmares than doling out punishment."

"Absolutely," I said. How had he managed to come up with that after being as surprised as he was by my news about dragon magic? I never managed to think on my feet like that. And now, I'd better reinforce what he'd said. "Unhatched dragon eggs are far easier to deal with than baby dragons."

"Are you suggesting there are other dragon eggs out there, waiting to hatch?" a woman in a pink and orange flowered dress asked.

I nodded. "That's exactly what we're saying. We know several more have been placed, and despite our efforts to locate them, we haven't found them all. If you know about one, or know someone who might know something, we'd like to talk to you. Take a drive through Lower Beckwater if you need some convincing."

A man with salt-and-pepper hair and giant round glasses raised his hand. "What do we do if a dragon does hatch in our area?"

"Get out," Phil said.

"It might be a good idea to have a bag with emergency supplies packed, ready to go, just in case," I said.

"Mine has clothes, food, water, a radio, and a solar charger," Phil said.

"Surely you aren't in danger at the War Palace," somebody said.

"We removed a dragon egg from Peace Park's boiler furnace last Friday night," I said.

A deep silence fell.

Finally, a tiny girl put her arm in the air.

"Yes," I said. "Young lady in front." It was quiet enough I could hear the electronic hum of my mike.

"Are you two boyfriend and girlfriend?" the little girl asked.

Laughter burst out all around. The girl's lower lip trembled.

"Well, at least you didn't ask if we're longing to kill each other," I said.

People laughed more, and the conversation moved to other topics. When the half hour was up, there was more hand shaking until finally, the last audience members cleared out, and we could head back to the dressing rooms.

"That was close," Phil said.

"The kid?"

"Yeah."

"Bound to come up with neither of us attached. Unless the rumors I've heard about you and Jennifer Lowell—"

"Forget about that. We've just been thrown together a couple of times. My parents—"

"I understand." His parents wanted him dating a girl from a nice War-leaning family. I still didn't like it much.

"Good to see you, Your Highness," he said as he turned off toward his dressing room.

"Good to see you, too," I replied.

As I watched him disappear down the hallway, I wished we didn't have to pretend to be strangers in public.

✳✳✳

Our show was successful. People seemed to like our frank answers and our chemistry. It even helped us locate dragon eggs. All week, I got phone calls from kids who had seen the show and wanted help with an egg they'd put somewhere. (In a parent's factory, in another power plant, in an incinerator…)

I also fielded calls from worried parents.

"My daughter won't take off her *Pervasive Drumm* T-shirt, and she never responds when I talk to her. I think she might be in contact with these dark fairies," a mom would say.

But when someone, sometimes me, talked with the daughter, nothing at all would be wrong.

For my own amusement, I started a list of "Signs your Kid is Normal." "She's always listening to music I hate," topped the list.

Youth liaising, magic education, and mind-protection took a large chunk of my time. But my youth work blurred with my other work until my days melted into a continuous round of research, meetings, TV spots, chanting sessions in schools, singing sessions in hospitals, and training sessions with troops.

Andy headed for the front. Clare emailed to say she was there too, with her reserve unit. I scheduled times to email them, so it would get done regularly.

The front held at the transportation and protection maze the Islandian fairies made for us. It was better than losing ground, but weeks went by in the stalemate. I found it hard to maintain hope without progress.

I kept up my crazy schedule. I went to meetings, arguing the content with Phil on the phone beforehand. He thought Peace was dragging its feet. I thought War was taking away too many rights and not being careful enough about letting fairies into the country. Our fights were fun. Sometimes they changed my mind. More rarely, they changed his.

My ratings in the polls kept going up, but War Party ratings flew even higher.

Each day, my make-up sessions took longer, as pros had to do more to fake normal energy levels. At least once a week, Mom would say, "No more today."

I'd flee to the park, sometimes alone, sometimes with Gen or Steph or both. Once, when Phil was in the city, with him. We'd argued about Peace's insistence on some kind of customs procedure for fairies entering Dicrandia from Islandia. Phil thought it crippled our defense. I thought it protected us from unscrupulous fairy influence.

Even with the intense debate, I enjoyed our walk. I wished our relationship were public, and we could talk that openly all the time, but Phil thought the extra media attention would detract from Dicrandia's defense.

On a Friday in late August, I attended the dedication of a newly rebuilt middle school in Lower Beckwater. As I sat on a flimsy folding chair with the other speakers, a feather on my backpack started to glow.

"What the heck," I said, pulling the bag toward me. Then I remembered the enchantment I'd put on the feather months ago. "Watch out!" I shouted before the blank sensation of magic transport took over.

CHAPTER 26

I chanted up a shield as soon as I came back into focus, but I hadn't finished when a giant ball of blue flame hit us. It rolled over one figure and hit a small knot of people in front of me. Parker, Lewis, and another man fell to the ground. I fell to my knees from the force of my chant. Green lightning flickered, then was gone.

I wasn't sure I was up to another chant, so I crawled toward the three who'd fallen to see if I could do any good with a few songs.

I got to Parker first. Ignoring shouts and gunfire, I concentrated on him. He was twitching. I sang until the twitching stopped, and Parker opened his eyes. I nodded at him. "Back in a bit," I said.

The man I hadn't recognized at once was that guard from the War Palace, Snypes. He was twitching worse than Parker had been. Singing him back to normal took longer, but eventually, he, too, opened his eyes.

"Back in a bit," I said again and crawled on to Lewis.

Lewis was not twitching. When I concentrated on him, resting my hand over his heart, I began to shake. There was no heartbeat, no breathing, no life.

Once or twice I'd come across newly dead animals in the woods. I'd tried every song I knew, but none had worked.

All the same, I did it again.

It didn't work for people, either.

When I finally gave up, my hands shaking, and tears streaming down my face, the battle had quieted. I surveyed the area, warily. I didn't know where things stood or even how long I'd spent on this hopeless job. Parker knelt on my left, his gun facing the sun. Another guard protected my other side.

"Clare!"

Clare glanced at me and smiled before squinting back into the sun. "I guess you never found a way to undo linkings, huh? I hope they figure out I'm not there soon and send another lookout for the pass I was guarding."

"Have we won or hit a lull?" I asked.

"I think we've got them, but the War Palace crew is making sure."

"The War Palace crew?"

"Yes. Prince Philip and his guards are here. I can't imagine how the fairies thought they'd handle us all with five of them."

"There were five? I didn't see any."

"You probably wouldn't. I could see them because I was enchanted with a vision spell before my lookout duty. Sounded like some of the War guards must have been, too. One of them certainly made contact with the fairy I hadn't hit."

"You killed four of them?"

"Three. The green stuff rebounded on the guy who tossed it. Nasty, snake-like, choking tentacles." Clare shuddered.

I supposed that meant I had technically killed the fifth guy with my shield. I wasn't sure how I felt about that. Since it was his own spell, and he'd been aiming it at my people, I refused to feel guilty.

Patterson, one of my night guards, mentioned that the prince's group had some injuries.

"I'll come," I said, but even with Parker helping, I couldn't walk.

I dragged myself across the ground. Guards surrounded me, doing an odd crouching walk. When I got to the injured, more guards joined them to make a tight ring facing outward. Within were four people: Gen and three War guards.

"Oh, Gen. I'm sorry I brought you in for this."

"Me, too," Gen said.

We laughed.

Her injuries were light—scrapes from where she'd fallen when we first arrived.

"I bet you could take care of this on your own," I said.

"I'll try. I don't really remember…"

I dug through the pack for my dog-eared copy of our green booklet.

"Thanks. If I can't do it, you can help me after the others."

I nodded.

The first guard had a badly burnt arm. Healing him didn't take long, but I was even more tired when I got to the next man whose vision had been seared away. It took fifteen minutes to sing it back. By the time I finished, Gen had already healed herself and the third man.

"Am I ever tired," Gen said.

"Tell me about it."

Thirty minutes later, Phil and his other guards returned.

They hadn't found any fairies in the valley, even using a compass-like fairy detector Darvian had given Phil. Unfortunately, we weren't sure where we were and we had no transportation, no phone service, no magical ways to contact home, and no good places to mount a defense if more hostile fairies came after us. Our best bet was to hike out of the hills in hopes of finding a road or allies—or a sense of our own location, but there was only one path, and anyone who knew we were here would be able to see which way we'd gone.

"We do what we have to," I said, which reminded Clare that we hadn't yet dealt with the dead. Parker and a couple War guards took Lewis's body to a little cave Phil and his men had found, but they cremated the fallen fairies according to fairy battlefield custom. When Parker and the War guards returned, I tried to stand, but couldn't.

My guards decided to carry me. Ransom, another of my night guards, lifted me way too easily and slung me over his shoulder. It wasn't comfortable, but it worked.

The narrow path out of the basin climbed steeply. Ransom stuck to the middle. Gen trudged next to us, carrying my bag, her shoulders sagging. Phil walked ahead of me, leaning on his guard, Percy. I wished I could walk.

Beside me, Gen drooped. "What do you keep in this thing, rocks?"

"Books, papers."

"Same thing."

Even as uncomfortable as I was, I slipped toward sleep.

I'd almost completely lost consciousness when we stopped because Ransom needed a break. Carrying me up a mountain pass couldn't be easy.

I tried and failed to walk, so Patterson took a turn carrying me.

I'd just drifted off again when they switched me to one of my weekend guys, Taylor. About the time I closed my eyes again, we stopped to switch to a fourth carrier.

"How did you come in for this duty?" I asked Snypes groggily after I'd tried once again to walk and once again had failed.

"Volunteered," he said.

"Oh! Thanks."

"Don't mention it."

I drifted off again. When I awoke, he was gasping for air, still carrying me. The sun sat low in the sky, and I was freezing. The cream suit I'd worn for the school dedication, though sweltering in the heat rising from the pavement in Bentralia, was not enough to keep me warm on this mountain pass as day waned.

I asked Snypes to let me try walking. When he put me down, my legs wobbled, but I stayed upright. Gen handed me a knobby but stout length of wood she'd found, and leaning heavily on it, I shuffled along.

We didn't seem to be getting anywhere. We were still going up, and it was nearly five o'clock.

"Has anyone eaten?" I asked Gen.

"There's nothing to eat."

"I think there's a bag of candy bars in my bag."

"I knew I was carrying this thing for a reason. I couldn't have told you what it was, but…"

Today, my candy stash was a Gudya and Peters fifteen pack.

"That's almost one a piece," Phil said. "Do you usually have enough food on you to feed an army?"

I giggled. "Almost always."

We passed candy bars up the line but didn't stop. Everyone wanted to get off the pass as soon as possible.

The day got later. I found it hard to drag my feet along. The pass went higher and higher. Eventually it got too dark to safely move on. Our path still had rock-face on either side, so we halted where we were and tried to get comfortable. We set a watch, but no one let Phil, Gen, or me take part. We argued about this, but even Phil and I together couldn't charm our guards.

In the end, we sat next to each other in the middle of the group, backs against one of the cliff walls. Gen sat on my other side, pressed close for warmth. Her light summer dress was pretty, but even chillier than my suit.

"My poor feet," Gen groaned, slipping off her strappy green sandals and rubbing them.

"What a disaster," I said.

"Yeah, but look on the bright side," Phil said. "You get to spend hours and hours of uninterrupted time with me."

Gen and I both giggled. Then I shivered. Gen's teeth chattered.

"Here," Phil said, taking off his long-sleeved canvas shirt and passing it to Gen. "Put that on." Then he pressed closer to my side and put his arm around my shoulder. I snuggled against the soft warmth of his t-shirt. Despite the day's walk, it smelled of laundry detergent and Phil's cologne.

"Being with you is kind of nice," I said.

"Glad you like it," he said.

I smiled at that. Now that I was both still and almost warm, I drifted toward sleep. "Wake me if anything important happens," I mumbled.

✳✳✳

Apparently, nothing important did because I awoke of my own accord, cold and stiff, as the sky moved from deepest black to dark blue. Myriad stars glowed above. I wished I knew their names.

There was the great dragon whose nose always pointed north. If I read him right, we were heading westward now. Too bad we had no choice in our direction. We'd hardly have chosen to go west, toward Stralton.

Being in the mountains meant we still had to be close to Dicrandia. The only mountains on our continent were near the Islandia-Dicrandia border, unless you counted the small range near the west coast. But those were shorter than this and famous for their red rocks. This peak (I'd certainly seen enough of it to know) was the silver-gray of the Tybernees.

Funny I couldn't remember having heard about this pass. I liked adventure stories and had read many. A pass that climbed like a tunnel through rock was unusual. So was a mountain basin with only one exit. I couldn't remember anything like it from poring over maps. So, where were we? Could fairies hide a whole ring of mountains? Or make them appear where they hadn't been before? Could this be an illusion?

I stood up, trying not to jostle Phil and lowering Gen gently to the ground. Then I put my hand against the rock I'd been leaning against. It felt solid enough. But a fairy illusion would too. I bit my lip. I'd learned a song to tell truth from illusion back when Phil was off on his trip, ages ago. I wasn't sure I could remember it properly, but there wasn't enough light to read my green book.

I tried humming it softly to myself before I put in the words. I was concentrating so hard, I didn't notice Phil sit up.

"What are you doing? You want us to have to—" He shut up suddenly as the mountain melted away to reveal a rolling grassland. The early morning air was chilly, but not frigid. Breeze rustled the grass. We could see nothing in any direction but our people stretched in a thin line.

"You put one protective shield up and can't walk for the rest of the day, but melt a mountain, and you're still standing?"

I'd done a fair amount of healing yesterday, too, but I didn't figure it would help to bring that up. "I didn't melt it," I said. "It was never there."

"Never there? As if we didn't all—" Phil's voice died. "You're saying it was a trick. Stretch us out in a line and pick us off one by one. You'd only need a couple of fairies to do it. We'd never catch on in time if a couple of people disappeared into the rock. And if they took us first—"

"You, Gen, and I are the only ones who have any magical ability, right?"

He nodded.

"I wonder if anyone's coming now?"

Phil cursed, thrust his hand into one pocket, and drew out his fairy detector. "I should have been checking frequently. I don't know how I got so careless."

The disc glowed brightly in his palm. He muttered a few words, and the disc went black except for a pie wedge of faintly glowing light and a single bright line pointing toward me. Numbers flashed near the line and the wedge.

"What does that mean?" I asked.

"That first glow meant there are lots of fairies in every direction if you give the disc enough distance. This nearer view shows a mass of fairies east of us." Phil pointed to the pie wedge. "They're nearly a hundred miles off, heading the other way. But this line shows a couple behind you, about twenty miles away, coming for us. We have to seek cover."

"Everyone up," I shouted.

The guards jumped to their feet.

Gen rubbed her eyes and sat up. "Where'd the mountains go?"

"Mountains? Why they're right here, you ninny," one of Phil's guards said, slapping thin air. He gasped as I stepped into the air he'd slapped and sang my truth song again. As I moved down the line, I heard surprised exclamations and Phil giving orders behind me. Soon the guards were all huddled around Phil, who demanded an immediate retreat to someplace more sheltered.

"Hang on," Clare said. "There's no point in running for the sake of running. If there are fairies after us, they're bigger, stronger, faster, and probably smarter than us. They'll run us down."

"Rivers is right. We need to have a plan," One of Phil's guards said. He was a tall, wiry guy. Percy, I think he was called.

"OK, but there's not much time." Phil said. "These fairies will be here in an hour."

"They're walking?" Snypes asked.

"Yeah," Parker said. "Why don't they transport themselves here? Isn't that the way fairies usually move?"

"The best protective walls stop fairies from traveling instantaneously as well as translating other beings," Gen said. "They stop some of the mind-reading, too."

I had occasionally laughed at Gen's paranoia about fairy translations and her obsession with protective walls, but her knowledge came in handy now. Using it, we realized we couldn't be in Stralton because of the incredible walls on the Stralton-Islandia border. We were probably in the corridor Stralton had built through Islandia for the passage of his armies. We had to be somewhere in the middle part, where translation was possible.

If we were right, we could get out of the corridor and into Islandian space by going either nine miles south or eleven north.

The fairies approaching us were coming from the north, and it wasn't clear whether they were a rescue party from Islandia or more enemies. A couple of Phil's guards were in favor of shooting first and asking questions later, but the rest of us argued them down.

Phil and I thought we could put up a shield and return to our sleeping positions. Rescuers would hail us instead of sneaking up on us.

Our guards were not excited by this plan.

"What if only one of us royals stays in the open with a few guards, and the rest head over to that little hill?" I asked.

"If these guys are enemies, and they're expecting two royals, will they be fooled by that?" Clare asked.

"Are they expecting two royals? You said they only had five fighters there this afternoon. They were prepared for one of us."

"Good point," Phil said, "but which one?"

"Sarah," Gen said. "If they were expecting you, they'd have been stronger. Everyone knows you're in military training and are as likely as not to have heavy-caliber weapons on you."

Several of the guards nodded.

"Fine," Phil said. "I'll head over the hill. But I don't like it."

"Maybe these fairies will be friends," I said.

"We can hope," he said, but he didn't sound hopeful.

Gen, Phil, and his guards headed for the bluff, and I settled into the impression in the grass where I'd been sitting earlier. My guards followed my example. More faced northward than had before, though.

The grass was damp, and the sky was graying. I shivered. I hoped these fairies would hurry. Sitting here with no cliff wall to support my back was uncomfortable and nerve-wracking. I chanted an extra protection chant over us. There weren't as many people, and it was additive, so I figured it wouldn't make me too tired.

Minutes passed slowly. Still as statues, silent in the starlight, we waited.

CHAPTER 27

The fairies sprang suddenly from the deeper gray of the grass, closer than I'd expected. They strode rapidly, silently towards us. I watched them through half-closed eyes. They made directly for me, showing no signs of hailing the group first. A burning panic rose in my throat. I forced myself to close my eyes and stay still, counting to ease my nerves. I'd counted to five hundred when shots rang out, first on my left, then all around. A white light flashed, glowing through my eyelids, and then was gone. The gunfire stopped. I opened my eyes but could see no more than with them closed. I sat in a dense white fog.

Someone grabbed my wrist. "Clare?" I said. The person dragged me to my feet. I screamed, fighting.

Suddenly, a chant came to my mind. I didn't know where I'd heard it, but it was about clear sight. I kicked at whoever was dragging me, shouting the chant as loud as I could. Then, with a hard wrench, I pulled free and dove for the ground, which I could now see.

Above me, a liquid voice laughed. "By all means, let them see."

A sharp pain bit into my shoulder, and I was thrown over. By leaning up, I could see my guards standing frozen, like the people at the dance.

I groaned.

"If you come quietly, I'll refrain from killing them one by one here in front of you."

"Come with you where?"

"Where I tell you to go. Without asking questions."

"Only if you promise to release them when we're far enough away."

"If you cooperate, I imagine some arrangement can be made. Now get up."

"OK," I said. I started, slowly, to get up. When I'd nearly made it to my feet, my knees buckled under me, and I fell back to the ground.

"I am losing patience."

"Sorry," I said. "Maybe if I weren't so hungry…"

With an annoyed snort, the fairy ripped up a clump of grass. "Hungry in a field of honey grass," he muttered. "Eat quickly."

He paced out past the line of my guards, scanning the horizon to the east.

I tried to nibble. I watched the fairy as I ate. He was a more pleasant sight than my frozen guards or the colored mass on the ground near me that I guessed was the remains of the other fairy.

The standing fairy seemed to concentrate. I wondered what he was looking at or who he was talking to.

Crack!

The fairy crumpled. Blood and organ matter sprayed over the grass. My line of guards unfroze.

I vomited the grass I'd eaten as Clare reached my side.

"Way to stall, Sarah."

"I wasn't stalling, I truly couldn't move."

"Well, it worked."

"I felt so helpless. I didn't have a knife or anything."

"Take this one, Your Highness," Snypes said. He'd reached me seconds after Clare had. The knife he handed me was ten inches long and slightly curved. Released from its leather sheath, it shone in the first rays of sunlight that now brightened the soft downs.

"Thank you, Snypes."

"If we can't protect you, at least we can provide some tools for protecting yourself."

I shook my head. I wished I weren't such a burden and that I weren't so tired and hungry. We were going to have a serious hike. I supposed I'd better eat some of the grass.

My guards stopped me, insisting on trying it themselves first. Parker made a salad while my other guards searched the two fallen fairies, coming back with a rucksack full of bread and fruit, two large canteens, and the news that the fairies had been wearing the Islandian military sigil on their inner garments.

"Bizarre," I said through a mouthful of the bread (which my guards had prodded and declared safe.) "I still think we have friends in Islandia and will be safer that side of the wall."

"Yes, Your Highness. We should tell the others."

"I agree," I said. "May I have some of that?" I pointed at the canteen. "This bread is excellent. I feel I could almost stagger along."

Ransom handed over a canteen. I expected water, but a fruity wine burned my throat. It carried energy with it, tingling down to my fingertips. I took a second swallow, and then reluctantly handed the canteen back.

"Good stuff, huh?" Ransom said.

"Amazing," I said, pushing myself to my feet. "I think I can move now. Pity my walking stick disappeared when the mountain did, though."

"One of them had one," Parker said. He retrieved it for me. It was oak and carved over its entire surface in a vertical landscape, full of rivers cascading to lower mountains.

It was too tall for me but would still help. I was trying it out when Phil's group reached us.

"Is that food you found?" Phil asked.

"Are you OK?" Gen asked me as Ransom tossed the knapsack and canteen to Phil.

"Fine. That last chant sort of incapacitated me, but the food helped."

A couple of lines in Phil's forehead deepened, and he scowled like my father did when he was worried but didn't want it to show.

I smiled. "Seriously. I'm fine. Thanks to whoever has the good eye."

"Lincoln," Phil said. "But I don't like the way those guys zipped right through our shields. And how'd you lift that fog? We were flipping through this book searching for anything that might help, and there was nothing."

"I couldn't even remember seeing anything that would help back when we were making our database," Gen said.

"I don't know. It sort of came to me. It seemed like I'd heard it before, but now that you mention it, I don't think I had. I'll write it down for you if you want."

Gen handed me the green book and a pen. "So, you're not just a singer, you're a song-maker. That's rare!"

I shrugged and wrote the vision chant. It was hard work, remembering.

Phil, looking over my shoulder, said, "Maybe you can come up with a new protection chant or two. We need something better."

"I'll try," I said. Then, to change the subject, I told Phil about the Islandian sigils.

Phil shrugged. "I don't know what that means, but we should get moving."

We all agreed, deciding to head south.

I would have enjoyed the walk that followed if I hadn't been so tired and tense. The hills rolled gently in waves of sage and deep blue green. Small, purple, star-shaped flowers studded the hillsides, and bright orange puffs on spindly stems waved about my knees. By lunchtime, I guessed we'd come nine miles.

"It's there, all right," Gen said.

I nodded. I hadn't felt the protective wall at the edge of the corridor until Gen mentioned it, but now I could almost see it as a misty gray line reaching from the ground to the heavens. "So, what now?"

"There's nobody guarding it here," Phil said, checking his compass. The nearest fairies are at least three miles to our east. All day they've been moving up and down a line here that must be inside the wall. They're heading away. I'm guessing they have another seven miles before they turn and head back."

"Now's as good a time as any, then," I said. "I wish there were some way to be less visible, though. I've heard fairies can see for miles."

"We could wait for dark," Percy said.

"No good. They can see almost as well in the dark," Clare said. "And that invisibility spell in your book is next to worthless."

"Well, unless Her Highness can think of a new one, we'll have to risk going across the way we are," Phil said. "But I see some cover between here and the other side. That small hill on the left—and that slightly bigger one on the right that's farther off."

Everyone nodded.

"Good. So, let's split into three groups and cross in stages. While one group runs for the first hill, the other two groups will cover them. After we've all reached the first knoll, we'll repeat the process, heading for the second hill. The third stage should take us across the line to that valley over there."

I looked at Clare and then Parker. They both nodded approval of Phil's plan. "Sounds good," I said.

"OK, then," Phil said. He divided us into three groups.

Then we ate what was left of the fairy food we'd picked up, while Phil, Gen, and I spent several minutes enchanting weapons and strengthening shields. An unreasonable panic gripped me. I couldn't help thinking about that morning, seeing my guards frozen in a line. Right through our shields. My concentration broke, and I stopped in the middle of the chant I was saying over Clare.

"Sorry," I mumbled. I pushed away the fear, but it rose up again. I fought it, holding my head in one hand, touching Clare with the other, and saying the protection chant. I had to sit down afterward.

"That's not what you usually say," Clare said. "Are you sure it worked?"

"Easy to check," Gen said. She was working next to us on Snypes's rifle. She said a chant similar to the one she used for checking protective walls. Then she gave an odd little laugh.

"What is it?" I asked.

"Whatever you said, we want to say it over everybody. Clare's defenses are about ten times stronger than anyone else's."

I was afraid I wouldn't be able to remember what I'd said for Clare, but with some work, I got it. Controlling my fears was more difficult. Thinking they might be caused in part by Stralton's walls, I chanted a mind-protection chant over myself as well. It helped, but I was still jittery. Maybe fear was a natural product of the situation. I would be glad when we made it across the line.

My group went first. One patrol on Phil's fairy detection compass was now about five miles away, the other fifteen.

I was so tired, my run to the first little knoll was wobbly. As soon as we got there, I felt Clare and the other guards tense up around me as they covered Gen's group. For the first time, I realized that if anyone attacked one of the other groups, I had no long-range weapons to use to help them. My chants were nearly all defensive.

Gen's group wasn't attacked, and neither was Phil's. Neither was anyone's on the next stage of the formation.

I still couldn't quell my fears. I was in the open, nearly to the wall, when colored light blasted over me from every direction. Fire cut me off from my guards. Fog descended. I could see nothing, and I choked on noxious fumes.

I hit the ground for cleaner air, chanting all the while. Words to clear the air of smells and fog. Then words to kill the fire.

"Sarah! Thank goodness!" Clare ran to my right side and lifted me, but stronger hands pulled at me from the other side. I whipped the knife Snypes had given me into the opponent I couldn't see. A scream rent the air, and the grip was gone.

Another wave of fire engulfed me, and Clare was pushed away.

"Who's doing this?" Clare shouted. "I can't shoot them if I can't see them!"

Of course. Our opponents were invisible, even to Phil's fairy tracker, while we were visible to everyone. Words rose up in me, and I chanted them in growing anger, ignoring the flames all around me and the fog that threatened to choke off all words.

The force of the chant knocked me to the ground, which was just as well, since a rock whistled through the air where my head had been—a nice, ordinary, non-magical rock. It would have shut me up for a while. I hadn't thought fairies could do anything so practical as throw rocks.

Rifle fire broke out in front of me, so I supposed my chant must have worked, but I was still in an isolation of fog and flame.

I felt too tired to do much, but I could taste that this fog wasn't healthy. I chanted a fire blanket.

For one instant, everything was clear. I lay alone in a field of fairies. One lay dead on the grass in front of me, but more approached from every angle. They came, oblivious to the gunshots, sweeping the ground as if searching for something. The panic I'd been feeling all along increased, paralyzing me.

Clare's voice cut through the panic. "Sarah, you idiot! We don't want to be invisible to each other!"

Of course. I spoke the new words that came to mind while wearily crawling toward the sound of Clare's voice.

The last three words took momentous effort. Somehow, I said them before blackness took me.

CHAPTER 28

"Are they still following?" asked a familiar voice.

"They're coming slower than they were, but they're still gaining on us," said a different, familiar voice.

In the silence that followed, I felt oddly disoriented. Was I upside down? Someone must have been carrying me again.

"I don't think I can go much farther," Gen said, her voice weak.

"We probably won't find a much better place to rest, and we can't pick up the pace without one," the first voice said, clearer this time. Snypes, I realized. He was the one carrying me.

The other voices agreed. Snypes lowered me to the ground. I tried to open my eyes but couldn't. Nor could I move.

"Is there any more food?" the second voice said. Now I recognized who it was—Phil!

"No. I think we ate it all, and anyway, Parker and Ransom were carrying it," Gen said.

What had happened to Parker and Ransom?

"What about that grass?" Phil asked.

"I'm not sure I'd recognize the right kind. Sarah would know." That was Clare. I relaxed.

"Where is she? I'll have a go at waking her again."

"I'm right here," I tried to say, but no sound came out of my mouth.

"Over here, Your Highness."

After a moment, Phil's hands rested on my shoulders and found their way to my face.

My blood quickened.

Phil's singing was low and self-conscious. He'd never be concert quality, but I liked to hear him. I tried to open my eyes again. This time it worked. The world swam into focus—bright, blue sky and silver-green plants, but no Phil. I blinked. Still nothing.

"Where are you?" I tried to ask. An indistinct mutter came out.

"Sarah? Sarah? Did you say something? Talk to me!" Phil's fingers brushed over my lips.

My heart pounded.

"Her eyes are open," Clare said, "but she's still not moving."

I turned toward the voice. At first, I couldn't see anyone. Then I saw some of the grass move where there was no wind. "Clare?"

"I'm right here." A hand touched my arm.

"Clare?" I said again. Tears started in my eyes.

"Don't worry, honey. You're fine. You just can't see me. You made me invisible, remember?"

That was right. I'd made up a chant to make us invisible to the fairies attacking us. But then my spell to make us visible to each other must not have worked. A couple of the tears in my eyes escaped and rolled back into my hair. My lips trembled.

"Are you OK, Sarah?" Phil asked.

"I'm sure she'll be fine. She needs rest. So, do you," Clare said briskly. Phil's hands left my face.

"Rest sounds good, but I could use food more."

"Right. We were going to ask Sarah."

I barely heard the last word. I closed my eyes and drifted back toward sleep. Perhaps I ought to stay awake and help, but I couldn't manage it.

"Sarah," Clare said, shaking me, "Come on, Sarah. Don't go to sleep on us now. Open your eyes."

I dragged my eyes open. "I'm going to show you some grass. If it's honey grass, say, yes."

Some low, broad grass flew up and dangled in front of my eyes.

"No," I mumbled, closing my eyes again.

"OK, don't fall asleep on me. What about this?"

I dragged my eyes open again. This was too thin. "No," I said.

"This?"

"No."

"This?"

I blinked. That was it. "Yes," I said and closed my eyes again. Clare's voice faded into mist.

The next time I woke up was better. I thought I could move. Though I could feel myself dangling at someone's backside, when I opened my eyes, I could see the downs stretching out in front of me, inverted as if in a pool of water. Funny.

Suddenly, I realized I was ravenous. "Is there anything to eat?"

"Glad you're up," Clare said. "We have some honey grass. Here."

I felt pressure in my hand, looked down, and saw grass pressing into it. Grabbing it, I brought it to my mouth and chewed. The light honey taste brought back the image of fairy guts splattering over dew-flecked downs.

I choked back the bile that rose to my throat and forced myself to keep chewing. When I'd finished, Clare gave me more. By the time I'd eaten four or five handfuls, I felt better.

"Mind if I walk?"

"If you can keep up. Those blasted border patrollers are following us." Clare said.

The person carrying me set me down on my feet and pressed something into my hand. Once I'd grasped it, I saw it was the fairy walking stick. With it, I was able to walk, feebly at first, but soon more rapidly.

"Great," Clare said, "But we're heading that way."

"Which way?"

"Toward the slightly bigger hills to your right."

"Really? You were going toward the darker green ones a moment ago."

"No, we weren't," Phil said.

"Please don't tell me you've been walking in circles all morning."

"It's entirely possible," Gen said. "We've been walking forever and never getting anywhere. We're lucky the fairies behind us are moving even slower than we are."

"Why?"

"Nobody knows," said a new voice.

"Who's that?"

"Percy," Phil said. "Anyway, we want to continue going more or less south," Phil said.

"But we don't have a compass," Gen said.

"Nothing's happened to the sun," I said.

"Yeah, well, if you think you can do better, you lead," Phil said. He sounded tired as well as annoyed.

"OK." I glanced toward the sun. "It's afternoon, right?"

"Ever brilliant."

"Shut up with the sarcasm already."

"Typical Peace. Wake up into a situation that's totally under control, criticize everything, and try taking over. I do not have to put up with this."

"Like I—"

A hand grabbed my upper arm, hard.

"Who is that?"

"Who is what?" Phil asked.

"It's me," Clare said. The hand went away. "Clumsy of me. I know being touched by someone you can't see is unnerving."

What was Clare trying to tell me? Probably not to be a baby. Phil and I couldn't afford to bicker. Of course, he'd started it. I bit my lip. That was exactly the attitude I couldn't afford. I closed my eyes for a moment and took a deep breath. "I'm sorry. You're obviously capable. Lead on. I'll concentrate on keeping up."

"You're kidding me, right?" Phil asked.

I clenched my right fist, closed my eyes again, and counted to ten. "No. I'll follow wherever you take us, provided someone gives me a lead cord or something. I can't see anybody."

"You can hang on to Snypes, Rivers, or Percy. They can see me."

"I thought we were all invisible to each other."

"Nah, that last spell cleared up most of the invisibility. Anybody who's not magic can see us."

"But because we're magic sensitive—"

"You got it."

"Oh." I felt stupid for not noticing before that Clare seemed able to see me.

"So, let's get going, shall we?" Phil said.

"Right," I said.

A hand touched my sleeve. "This way, Your Highness," Snypes said.

I stumbled off next to him. We were not going south, more southeast. I wanted to say something but bit my tongue. We couldn't afford the argument. Besides, Stralton's walls blocked a lot of fairy mind games, so staying within their influence would confuse the pursuit.

Not that there would be any doubt about the way we'd gone. The grass along our trail was badly trampled. I started to speak, but remembering Phil's response to my last suggestion, I decided to deal with this myself. At first, I tried prodding the grass upright with my walking stick as we went along, but it didn't work well and took too long. Instead, I worked on composing a song to refresh the grass we passed through. The last new chants I'd made had come to me spontaneously. This was harder. I pieced a few words together, tried them out, and discarded them. Then I tried a few more. After about half an hour, I had a whole song.

I sang it softly and then looked back. The grass had perked up, leaving no sign of our passage. I smiled and kept singing. It was amazing how good I felt. Energy flowed into me, as if the walking stick was a battery, powering me up, and despite my constant grass song, I felt less tired all the time. I had to make an effort not to speed ahead of Snypes. I wouldn't know where to go if I did that. Besides, my grass song would be no good if I were at the front of the line instead of the back.

About an hour later, Clare said, "Gen needs a rest."

I felt a stab of guilt. Concentrating on my song, I'd forgotten Gen was there. Now that I'd stopped singing, I could hear ragged breathing that must have been Gen's.

"I hear you," Phil said, "but they're only about an hour back."

"A couple of minutes won't kill us," I said. "Maybe I can do a refreshment song while we're here."

"I can't believe you're not falling off your feet," Phil snapped. "Did you fake that faint after the fight this morning?"

I gripped the walking stick tighter, reminding myself we did not need a fight. "It's not comfortable being carried like a sack of flour. I prefer my own two feet, trust me."

"I don't," Phil said.

"Don't what?"

"Trust you. You seem half dead for hours, but as soon as you're up, you don't seem harmed at all."

I could feel myself flushing, and I had to blink to hold back an inconvenient impulse to cry. I clamped my lips together until I was sure my voice was under control. "I'm sorry you feel that way. Clare, where's Gen?"

"Over here, Your Highness."

Clare's hand took my left one and led me to where the ragged breathing was. I reached toward Gen. "I'm sorry I didn't notice you were having trouble sooner."

Gen laughed. "You've been wiped out. You didn't need to be thinking about me."

"Hogwash. You're one of my best friends."

I took her hand and dropped the walking stick to let my other hand find Gen's face. Then I sang the refreshment song I'd sung for Phil at the Joint Council meeting. It drained me almost as much now as it had then.

"Wow, I feel so much better," Gen said.

I nodded before remembering Gen couldn't see me. "Good." I fumbled for the walking stick and carefully pushed myself to my feet.

"If we're done with the mushy stuff, we should move on," Phil said. His footfalls fell heavily on the grass ahead.

"I guess wonder boy's miffed he doesn't have your endurance," Gen said softly. I giggled but mostly concentrated on moving. The pace Phil set this time was liable to kill me. And it was hard, suddenly, to sing my grass song. I stumbled forward and sang softly, someone leading me on the left side and Gen walking on my right. I was weary, so weary.

My second time through the grass song, Gen hummed with me, and then sang along. The burden of the song lifted, and it became music to march by, hardly wearing at all.

Energy flowed into me again. It had to be the walking stick. When I used it, walking refreshed me as much as if I'd had a full night's sleep. No wonder I'd been able to bounce back after being knocked out.

Poor Phil. He had worked nearly as hard as I had that morning, and he'd been walking all day without the benefit of a fairy walking stick. Even if he was angry with me now, he'd been worried the first time I'd awakened. He'd sung for me, though he was tired himself. His speed flagged even as I caught a fresh wave of energy. Percy muttered something about slowing down. I couldn't understand Phil's response, but it was terse.

We'd be carrying him soon if he kept this up. But I wasn't sure how to help without making things worse. Maybe I could do the refreshment song for him if it would work from this distance. I'd always needed to touch people for healing and restoration songs to work on them, but Darvian insisted a mind touch would work as well. I closed my eyes and concentrated on Phil. When I could picture him clearly in my mind—the cropped hair, startling eyes, long-legged stride, gray-tinged pallor, and tense scowl—I sang the refreshment song, my voice barely audible.

"Hey! What did you do?" Phil said. The arm that guided me stopped, so I did, too.

"Your Highness," Percy remonstrated.

"Where is Her Highness? No, don't try to stop me!"

I shook loose from the guiding arm that was tugging me backward. "I'm here," I said.

"What did you do to me?"

"Refreshment song. Same as with Gen, earlier."

"How?"

I could feel him near. I closed my eyes and could see him again, bristling with anger. His fist was clenched. I wondered if he was going to hit me. I hoped not. I guessed a fight with him wouldn't go well for me.

I took a step closer so that we were nearly touching. "I've been getting energy from that fairy walking stick we picked up this morning. I'd have loaned it to you, but you seemed unlikely to accept help."

"How did you refresh me? You weren't touching me!"

"Darvian told me that physical touch is one way to create the mind touch required for magic to work, but that you can mentally touch a person without physical contact if you have an accurate enough idea of them in your head."

"You don't know me that well."

"Obviously, that's not true."

He didn't answer.

"I should have asked. I'm sorry," I said.

The Phil in my mind's eye turned away and walked west, toward a low, honey-grass covered dune.

"Please don't be mad at me, Phil," I said, following. "I hate it when you're mad at me. And I'm sorry about earlier."

"Sorry about what?"

"About being such a pain when I first woke up—you know, suggesting we were going in circles and stuff."

The picture of Phil in my mind went fuzzy and faded out. The real Phil said nothing, so I faltered on, "I mean, you've obviously been working hard, and you're worried. I shouldn't have added to the problem. I mean…" I stopped. I hadn't intended to grovel. Why didn't he say something? Do something?

Phil laughed. "The most complete apology anyone from Peace has given a War royal in a couple hundred years, and it's over something not even worth apologizing for. Come on, Sarah, show a little backbone. You were right. We've been going in circles all day. None of us has a clue how to navigate without a compass."

"Parker does."

"Parker's not with us," Phil said. "I thought you knew."

"Did he die? Who else is gone?"

"He wasn't dead when we separated. The only person they got for sure was Patterson. After you made us visible to each other again, the main group put up a firefight to draw off the fairies while we slipped out of the ambush. Snypes, Percy, and Rivers are with us."

I was silent for a moment. I should have realized before that we weren't traveling with our full set of guards. I didn't hear that many people. My head must have been stuffed with wool.

All my guards except Clare. The thought was staggering. I felt numb. "They can't have survived this long."

"No," Phil said.

Suddenly, my mental picture of him was back. He stood before me, lips set, eyes focused in the distance, the way they'd sometimes been during speeches that summer. I reached out and took his hand. "There was nothing you could have done to stop them."

He squeezed my hand, hard.

"After all, we did sign on to protect you." Clare's voice was brisk. "Every last one of them would be furious if they knew we were stopping now to get all maudlin. Where are those fairies who are tailing us?"

Phil dropped my hand, and there was a pause. "They've slowed to a crawl," he said.

"Oh, good! Maybe my grass song is working," I said.

"Your what?"

I explained.

Phil laughed. "Thank goodness you woke up. We are blundering fools in the wilderness. Here—you lead. Gen and I can take turns singing."

"We can take turns with the walking stick, too," I said.

As the sun westered, and shadows deepened, I led our group at my normal walking stride. We zigzagged east and a little south, back-tracking enough to confuse the pursuit, I hoped. Certainly, it had slowed down.

We did not encounter any other fairies.

When dusk fell, we were well to the east of our starting point that morning, and by my calculations, nearly out of the reach of Stralton's wall. We stopped for the night where two of the downs came together in a V. I slept like a stone while Gen and Clare kept watch. Then it was my turn to keep a lookout with Snypes.

The stars glittered above. The wind whipped through the grass. The ground beneath me grew harder, colder, and lumpier. The stars turned in the sky. Otherwise, nothing happened.

At last, Phil and Percy staggered out. I listened anxiously for Phil's report on his fairy compass. Their pursuit was still miles off and had stopped for the night.

Why? Fairies didn't need much sleep. "Strange," I said.

Phil yawned. "I'm glad they're not any closer."

"Me too," Snypes said. I heard his footsteps, heavy and lumbering, back into the V.

I stayed a minute longer, gazing up at the stars.

A dark bird shape blocked some of them. An enormous bird shape. It must have been flying low, searching for prey.

It dove, rapidly becoming even larger. Too much larger. I caught my breath and drew the knife Snypes had given me.

"What is it, Your Highness?" Percy asked.

An overpowering wind and a flapping of great wings kept me from answering. The shadowy form threw me to the ground and then lifted me so rapidly off the downs in a grip of iron that my stomach heaved. My hands were pinned so painfully to my sides that I couldn't use the knife I still grasped, but that was just as well. I didn't want anything happening to this monster of a bird until it put me down.

CHAPTER 29

The bird lifted higher into the sky and flew west at a terrifying speed. The wind numbed me. I could feel my hand stiffening and willed myself to hang onto the knife. I'd need it when we stopped. I gripped it harder, and then slightly relaxed my fist over and over to build up warmth and keep my hand from becoming completely numb. I tried similar muscle contraction and relaxation exercises with my legs and feet. I couldn't tell if it was helping, but knew that if I didn't do anything, I would be unable to move before long.

I'd been keeping it up for what seemed an eternity when I heard a groan.

"What's that?"

This time the groan was clearly a human voice. Another human in the beast's other claw. Phil or Percy?

"Phil?" I shouted, but there was no answer, not even another groan.

"Percy?"

The response was the same.

I didn't like the silence that followed. Whoever he was, the other person was hurt. I wished I could see who it was, so I could try healing him. I thought Phil had been closer to me, but I wasn't sure. If I tipped my head up and back, I could make out the outline of the bird's other claw, but I couldn't see whoever it gripped. This cursed invisibility was getting inconvenient.

It took me almost as long to think of a new chant as it had taken me to make my grass song. I wanted to be careful not to use too much energy, and this time I didn't want inadvertent side-effects. At last, I thought I had a chant that would make me and the person in the bird's other claw visible to each other, but no one else.

I chanted it and was rewarded with a wave of exhaustion and the shadowy outline of a pair of legs in trousers and combat boots poking out of the bird's claw. It could have been anybody.

"Aargh!" I shouted.

I returned to concentrating on muscle exercises. I'd lost feeling in my toes. And my ears. And my nose.

Another groan came from the other person. Good. At least he was still alive.

I tried to see where we were going. The wind beat into my eyes, forcing me to squint. I thought we were still over the downs, though it was hard to tell. The ground below was little more than a blur. Far ahead, the stars showed us still heading mostly westward.

I closed my eyes, counted to one-thousand as slowly as possible, and tried again. Nothing. I repeated the procedure. Again nothing.

The third time, I saw dark jagged shapes below the stars—mountains, maybe? The next time I squinted out, I was sure the shapes were mountains. What's more, I could make out a few lights—a castle, I realized as we rushed toward it. A castle in the midst of a city.

We rushed past the first range of mountains, but then we turned in a great circle, losing altitude. On our second pass, we were so low, we nearly brushed the mountain behind the city. Then we were back in the open, flying even lower. The bird called out like a wheezy locomotive and rushed directly toward the mountainside.

We were going to crash. I closed my eyes even though I knew it wouldn't change anything.

I crashed, all right, but not the way I thought. I fell, just far enough to realize I was falling as I landed, bone-jarringly, on a hard surface.

What was the bird doing? Playing with me? I sang a song for light. It was a feeble song, but it cast a dim glow, enough to show that I'd landed in some kind of opening up near the top of one side of a large egg-shaped cavern.

Directly across from me, on a wide shelf about a third of the way from the roof of the cavern, a barn-sized owl perched on one claw. The other claw dangled Phil by one arm over a nest of four cottage-sized owls. Phil's legs kicked spasmodically. The smaller owls made frustrated whirring noises as they scrabbled against each other, trying to reach him. They bumped blindly. At first, I thought my light had confused them.

Perhaps it had, though it wasn't much more than twilight. Then I realized none of the owls could see Phil, though they could touch him, hear him, and probably smell him.

The big owl must have dealt with invisible food before. Unflustered, it made low encouraging hoots and lowered Phil directly toward one of the small owls' open mouths. Phil kicked the mouth shut, hard. The rebound knocked him enough off center that he wasn't directly over any bird's mouth.

Without thinking, I threw Snypes's knife as hard as I could. It lodged in a bulge of the giant owl's leg. The bird dropped Phil. Its squawk reverberated in the cave.

Now that I knew my companion was Phil, maybe, I could heal. I focused on him. Closing my eyes, I concentrated until I could touch him with my mind and feel where his leg had broken, where the claw had bruised and torn, where one of the talons had ripped his abdomen.

I sang, concentrating so hard that I only noticed the owls when they made contact with Phil, which happened more often than I liked. They had found him and were closing in. I forced myself not to think about it and sang harder.

Rifle fire burst from the nest and echoed off the walls. The great bird hooted so loudly I covered my ears and opened my eyes. The monstrous bird soared toward me.

My song faltered, but I kept singing until the bird swept over me, brushing me backward several yards along the flat, concrete-like floor beneath me. This opening must have been wider than I'd realized, but at some point we'd reach the outside of the mountain, wouldn't we? I glanced backward, and at that moment, the owl kicked me.

I fell, scratching for a handhold on the too-flat surface that had held me before the kick. At the last moment, when I was sure I'd fall right off the mountainside, I managed to grip onto the edge. I hung, my feet swinging loose, as the owl stalked forward, its form outlined in the cave opening. It stood above me, wings outstretched.

If I could have groveled, I would have. Too terrified to speak or move, unable even to reason that a death by falling might be better than what this bird had in mind, I watched, awed, as the rifle fired again. The bird stumbled forward one step, two steps, and then toppled.

It tumbled over me but didn't touch me, only hitting the mountainside much lower down.

It took me a minute to realize it was gone, to feel anything but awed, paralyzing fear.

A shout brought me back. "Sarah? Sarah? Where are you? Tell me you're OK! Tell me I haven't shot you!"

"Phil?"

"Sarah? Where are you?"

Where was I? Hanging. Hanging, with my grip loosening, over the edge of some abyss. There was rock in front of me, but it was flat, like a swimming pool side.

"Sarah? Sarah, do not leave me. You've got to help me get out of here."

"Too tired," I mumbled.

"No! You can't quit. Come on, now. You're the baddest princess Dicrandia has ever seen. You're not going to let a little cold and fright get to you now, are you? I mean, come on, it was just an owl! You've killed a dragon!"

With his help. Like he was helping me now. This time, I didn't have to do any magic, just get back to the cave entrance. A pull up. Like in gym class, with Ms. Debransky shouting I could do it. "Once more: Pull, pull, pull!"

I pulled and pulled. Phil was still shouting, but I didn't know what. The top of my head pulled even with the floor of the opening. I still had found no rest for my feet, but I leaned my toes against the wall, and held hard with my right hand, while the left searched for some better grip farther away from the edge. And found it.

"Sarah? Answer me! Are you OK?"

I grunted. Then, heaving, the way I did at the pool, and ignoring the nasty feeling that I couldn't afford for this not to work on the first try, I pulled myself up until my waist was at the edge. Then, leaning forward, I pulled a bit more. I began to raise my right leg, as I normally would, but pain shot through it, so I brought my left knee up instead.

Pushing with my arms, and later with my left leg, I raised myself the rest of the way up to the entrance and crawled into it.

"Sarah?"

"Here!" I called, panting. "In the cave mouth."

I lay there, assessing the damage. There was something definitely wrong with my right knee and leg. I felt there, concentrating. The patella was shattered, my hip broken. It was miraculous I'd been able to move at all. Could I heal myself?

I tried to sing, but pain broke my concentration. I focused and sang again. This time, I could feel the bones growing back together, the pain lessening. Thank goodness healing songs took less energy than chants, but

I only had enough energy to deal with the biggest problems. My patella knit back together with a series of clicks.

"Sarah? What's going on up there? How hurt are you?"

"It's mainly the hip, now," I said. I could barely carry a tune, but Phil joined in, and my exhaustion eased. I didn't realize it could work that way—me directing the healing, and him providing the power. My hip grew back together, and as that pain disappeared, I became aware of others: bruised arms and ribs, scratched elbows, hands, and knees. Together, we sang them all away. Then I lay exhausted on the floor of the tunnel.

"Sarah? I'm sure you're tired after all that, but neither one of us can afford to be here if that bird's mate decides to check on its nest."

My eyes flew open. Mate? Did humungous owls take care of young together? I didn't even know if regular owls did. There were none in Peace Park.

As if reading my thoughts, Phil said, "I don't know much about owl behavior, but I don't want to sit around and wait if another one is coming. It'll be light soon, and any self-respecting owl will want to get out of the sun."

He was right. Dawn would come soon. With another giant bird? I shuddered. Shaking myself awake, I rose and crawled cautiously to the cave side of the ledge. My light song had worn off. "Phil?"

"Down here. We had light for a while, but it's gone."

"A song," I said. I was exhausted but tried to sing it. Phil seemed to know it once I started. He joined in, singing lustily. The cave blazed with light.

Once my eyes acclimated, I could make out Phil standing in the nest amidst the remains of the behemoth owl babies, looking remarkably fit despite disheveled hair and a torn and bloody uniform. He smiled up at me much more cheerfully than I felt was reasonable.

"Our mothers are going to be furious when they see our clothes," he said.

I laughed aloud.

Phil smiled more widely. "Do you know, if I had to be kidnapped, shot at by fairies, and carried off by a ginormous owl, I can't imagine any better person to do it with than you."

CHAPTER 30

Phil couldn't get up to the entrance except by climbing. He currently stood in the middle of the giant nest of logs, branches, and bloody owl bodies that covered the bottom of the egg cavern, and the entrance was close to the top.

Fortunately, Phil had pursued useful hobbies, like mountain-climbing and marksmanship. I reminded myself that lifesaving and horseback riding would be equally useful—if we were around water or horses instead of a cliff.

Phil found handholds that I could barely see, but he only made it half-way up to the entrance where I sat before he slipped back down.

"This is nuts," he said. Is there anything up there you could tie a rope to?"

"No, and we haven't got a rope."

"I bet this belt I'm wearing would hold my weight. It's Andolan leather."

"I didn't know Andolan leather was standard issue for new recruits."

"Shut up and catch it, OK?" He pulled it loose from his pants and tossed it toward me.

I caught it. "There's still nothing to tie it to."

"Well, buckle it around your arm, lower it over the side, and brace yourself."

Hmm. He was significantly bigger than I was, and there was nothing to brace myself against. "How about an ankle?"

"What?"

"Like this." I looped the belt around my ankle and then sat, feet closest to the cavern, trying to hang on to the flat floor of the entrance. My shoes slipped against the rocky surface and I kicked them off. I'd get better purchase against the stone barefoot.

"Yeah, OK."

"This time, I couldn't see him, but I heard occasional curses as he slipped. Then there was a big slip and a bump.

"I can't get close enough," he said.

"Could we use that strap you've got on your rifle?" I asked, peeking back over the edge.

Phil took the gun off and studied it. "Yeah, maybe. I don't like to throw the weapon, though. Too many things could go wrong." He rummaged through his pockets but came up empty. "But I don't see much other choice." He unloaded the gun. "Here," he said as he tossed it to me.

I caught it by the barrel, fumbling for a moment with its weight.

The strap hooked to the gun with metal clips. Once I figured them out, I unhooked the gun, stretched the strap to its full length, and clipped it to the belt through one of the metal-reinforced notches. I hoped it would hold. Then I returned to my braced position with the improvised rope dangling off the edge.

This time the slipping and cursing was louder. I cautiously crawled toward the edge and looked down. Phil was back at the bottom, nursing scraped fingers.

I concentrated on him and sang again.

"Maybe we could add in my shoelaces," Phil said.

"Your shoelaces?"

"Yeah, they're those round indestructible nylon ones. If we twisted them together—"

"How will we attach them? You know that kind won't hold a knot."

"We've been coating them with pine resin from the trees at camp. I haven't had to retie a shoe in about a week. Of course, my fingers are perpetually sticky."

"OK, but won't you need your boots tied for climbing?"

"I'll take them off. I can do better barefoot anyway." He sat, took the boots off, and stuffed his socks into their toes. Then he tossed them up to me.

He was right. The sticky laces left a resin on my fingers I couldn't remove, but they held a knot. I twisted the two laces together, tied them to the belt-strap contraption, and resumed my blind sitting position.

"Great," Phil called. I heard scrabbling, and then, "I am going to use the rope now."

The belt around my ankle tightened. The soles of my feet dug into the rock in front of me. I pulled hard against the weight.

Then there was no weight, and feeling returned to my foot. I resettled myself, panting, and gripped my handholds harder.

Twice more, Phil called that he was going to use the rope, and I fought against the weight. Then his head appeared above the ledge. A moment later, the rest of him appeared.

I laughed from relief.

For a minute, Phil lay next to me in the entrance. Then he undid our contraption and redressed himself.

I put my own shoes back on. The scrapes on the bottoms of my feet stained the insoles, but I had no more energy for healing songs. Besides, the outfit was ruined anyway.

Together, we crept toward the mountain side of the opening. Phil leaned out over the edge, scanning the mountain in the first gleam of dawn. "Up is impossible. Down to the right is mostly OK. There are about thirty feet of doable ugly, and then a grade we can probably walk, and then what looks like a path."

"That undoubtedly leads to the city down there."

"Hey, we want to find some fairies."

"Not in Stralton, we don't."

"We're in Stralton?"

"Deep in if I read the stars right on that flight."

Phil cursed, long and imaginatively. I wasn't sure I'd ever heard anyone say a couple of the words he used. I widened my eyes.

"Sorry," he said. "Look, wherever we are, we have to go down. We can't go up, and we can't stay here."

I nodded. "At least we're still invisible to others. I think."

"Nice work. I'd be dead if I hadn't been invisible to those birds. Or at least the babies. How do you figure the big one found us?"

"I don't know. It came straight for us like it was sent specifically to get us."

"It went all that way, searching us out, to feed us to its young?"

That didn't make sense, did it? "I don't know."

"Yeah, me neither, but we'd better keep our eyes open and get out of here as soon as we can." He walked about eight paces to the right and swung himself over the edge. "This is going to be tricky at first. Do exactly what I do."

Phil faced the tunnel and lowered himself onto a narrow shelf about five feet down from the owl cave entrance. Then he sidestepped along the cliff face, keeping one hand on the edge of the entrance, until he was about ten feet to my right. There, he stepped down a few more feet to a slightly wider shelf and sidestepped back towards me.

"Don't sit there staring," he said. "Come on."

We were going to kill ourselves.

But it would be better than sitting here waiting for another giant owl.

I went to the spot Phil had started from, closed my eyes, and followed his example, lowering myself down to the next ledge, and stepping left, except my sidesteps were tiny.

"OK," Phil said when I'd gone far enough. "Lower your left foot."

I did, fumbling for the next little shelf. My skirt rode up. Stupid thing. I was never wearing skirts again if I could help it. Yeah, Mom was going to go for that. There. I found the shelf. My foot touched, but my right leg was still high, like I was on a huge step.

I steadied myself with a deep breath before lowering my right leg. My skirt rode up more, but I was not letting go of the upper ledge to fix it.

"Now walk toward me, and be careful. It slopes down. At some point, you're going to have to let go of the ledge and find handholds on the wall."

Fabulous. No self-respecting goat would use these little shelves as a path, but what choice did I have? I sidestepped back to my right, slowly.

The next step down was about three feet, but the shelf was wider—a foot or two. By the time I got down, my skirt had bunched up nearly to my panty line, and I was glad I felt secure enough to let go of the cliff wall with one hand, so I could tug at my hem. "Well?" I demanded when Phil didn't immediately tell me what to do.

"Right," he said, as if calling his mind back from somewhere else. "Step along here about four—no, six of your steps. Then it's down again."

The fourth shelf was two feet down and sloped back toward my left. The fifth continued that way for what seemed an eternity. It was tiny, too. But at the end of it, Phil stepped, twisted, and said, "We're down."

"You're down," I corrected. "How do I get there?"

There was a long pause. Then Phil said, "You know, you've got absolutely spectacular legs."

I flushed and then turned. I was hanging onto a cliff wall here, and he was thinking about my legs? Without stopping to think, I jumped to the ground and yanked my skirt back in place. "I don't think that's funny, Philip Castanay."

"I didn't mean it to be."

I wasn't sure how to answer. I started to stalk off, but he caught my arm.

"Not that way, you'll fall right off the mountain face."

He was right, of course.

"After you, then," I said, embarrassed by my mistake.

"Hey, I'm sorry. I couldn't help noticing."

I glared.

He shut up and picked his way over a steep incline with lots of loose rock. Then he gave me a hand over some enormous boulders.

After about an hour's scrambling, we came down onto a path.

"Which way?" Phil said.

"Away from the city, if possible."

He nodded. "So up."

We turned right and followed the path up the mountain. My flats clanked, so I kicked them off and went barefoot. That was painful but quieter.

Phil nodded his approval and offered to put my shoes in one of the giant pockets in his pants. I gave them to him.

Though the sun had fully risen, the morning was still chilly. I shivered. If I ever got out of this mess, I was going to make sure I always had a sweater and a good pair of shoes on me. That and tinned food for a week—I was starving.

I smiled wryly. I could almost hear what Mom would say if I started regularly toting a duffel bag of supplies. What I wouldn't give to exchange the knot of fear in my stomach for the sound of my mother's lectures.

Our path had risen steadily for ten minutes, but now it descended again. It wound down a curve, back toward the city.

Phil had started down a step or two when I saw the first fairy, barely a football field away, pointing straight at us.

I grabbed Phil's hand and raced back the way we'd come. Phil may not have seen the fairy, but he couldn't very well have missed the blue fireball that billowed over the hill we'd just topped. Phil chanted something. Our new protection spell, I thought.

A red cloud of smoke came at us from the direction we were heading. I couldn't see the fairy who sent it, but I heard a burst of rifle fire and a scream.

I had no weapon, I realized. I picked up a baseball-sized rock, gathered a pile of others, and said a weapons' chant over them, unlikely as it was to do much good. Then I said a brand new chant to clear the smoke.

I almost wished I hadn't. Seeing the fairies who surrounded us made my heart sink. More than a dozen blocked us in, crowding the path both above and below us. Another ball of fire came our way, this one green. Though our shield held, I could feel the heat of it.

"I'll take up, you do down," Phil said.

"OK." I stood with my back to him and pelted my stones. I was lucky with the first two, but then the fairies came too fast for me to hit them.

"They're coming this way!" I shouted.

"Here." He handed me a pocketknife, all the while firing and chanting.

I snapped open the blade and thrust it into the first fairy to approach. He went down, but burning pain erupted in my left arm. I was dimly aware of Phil behind me using his rifle as a club. Something hit me in the head, and I fell.

I grabbed a fairy's leg as I went down, toppling him hard. I wished I could believe it was enough to get Phil out of the fight safely, but I knew it wasn't. Tears filled my eyes as blackness descended on me. At least I wouldn't have to see him die.

CHAPTER 31

Someone warbled a cheerful song. A gentle hand stroked my forehead. I opened my eyes to find myself staring into eyes of clear, startling blue. I smiled and let my eyes drift back shut. "Phil," I murmured.

A warm voice laughed. "There's some good in that lad's unfortunate resemblance to me if it garners me a reception like that."

My eyes shot open again. The person sitting next to me had Phil's eyes, but he wasn't Phil. He wasn't even human. He was a golden-haired fairy with a generous mouth and rippling muscles.

"Where's Phil? Is he all right?" I sat up. A wave of dizziness passed over me.

"Calm yourself. Your friend is fine," the man said.

Peace washed over me, and I lay back down. "Where are we? What's going to happen to us? When can I see Phil?"

"To answer your last question first, as soon as you are well enough. As for where you are, cannot you guess?"

"We're in Stralton…"

"In the Imperial City. It is a great privilege to have you here. In fact, it may enable us to work out our little misunderstanding to everyone's satisfaction."

"Little misunderstanding?" I lifted myself again.

He touched my cheek, causing it to tingle and me to go limp. "Come, come. I can't have you getting up yet. By my calculations, you need at least two more days in bed."

"Are you a doctor?"

The golden laugh rippled like water. "A doctor? No, my dear. I am Stralton."

"Stralton?" Anger flooded me. I had to get out of there. I struggled to stand, realizing as the blankets slipped off me that I'd lost my own clothes and was wearing a soft lavender nightgown. It was hardly appropriate for wandering halls in search of an exit. I also had no idea where Phil was, and, of course, Stralton could chase me, even if now he was choosing to lean back in his chair and watch my efforts, smiling bemusedly.

After a minute of watching me try to stand, he said, "You'll be able to move better in a few days. Then you can prowl about the castle all you like. We'll even provide appropriate clothes."

I grimaced. I'd forgotten about fairies' ability to read minds. The Islandians had avoided doing so for months.

"Don't be silly, my dear. Fairies cannot help reading others' minds. Your allies must have been hiding their deductions. I find all such dissimulation distasteful. Don't you?" He ran a finger over my cheek.

"Don't touch me. Or call me, 'my dear.'"

He laughed. "I will try, but the temptation is nearly irresistible. You are a singularly attractive woman."

I laughed, the sound ripping harshly through the room. Don't insult my intelligence. I'm not that good-looking, even for a human."

Stralton shrugged. "You are more beautiful than you realize, but your attraction is in your uniqueness. The snap in your eyes, even your hostility, is a welcome relief from the tedium of mindless adoration."

"Whatever. I'm sleeping now." I turned away from him, toward the wall, and willed my mind to be blank. I needed strength, and for strength, I needed sleep. I felt strangely aware and assumed it was Stralton's influence. Ignoring him, I counted backwards from ten thousand. The last number I remembered was three-hundred-twenty-seven.

✳✳✳

He was there when I woke. I could feel it even before I opened my eyes. How long had it been? Had he left at all? And he could read my thoughts. Could I make a song to block him?

"I doubt it," he said, coming over and brushing my hair back from my forehead, "but by all means, try. I'm sure it will be most instructive."

"You're laughing at me."

"Not at all. You have created at least one powerful chant if, as the boy indicated, the shield spell the two of you were using was yours."

"He's up? Talking? Can I go see him?" I sat up.

"Come, come. Too much exertion is still not good for you."

"But Phil is up?"

"No, I have been gleaning from his dreams. Now, if you'll lie back down—"

"No, thank you," I said, though I felt dizzy.

"As you like." There was a hint of laughter in Stralton's eyes, but when I scowled at him, it disappeared.

"Have you told our parents what you've done with us?" I demanded after a pause.

"Done with you? My dear, all I've done with you is rescue you from the beasts that live in the Weir cliff and nurse you back to health after an unfortunate misunderstanding with my guards."

A misunderstanding? That was what he'd called his war on Dicrandia too. I got angry thinking about it. I was in no mood to listen to him, but that didn't stop him from prattling on about stupid plans to return us to our parents in two weeks. I might not be able to figure out what he was trying to accomplish, but I knew better than to trust him.

After twenty minutes of sparring conversation, Stralton left me alone, saying I needed to rest and slapping me with an overpowering desire to sleep.

Sleep wouldn't hurt. I yawned and lay down. But as my head touched the pillow, I remembered Stralton saying, "I have been gleaning from his dreams." Mine too, no doubt. I forced myself to sit back up and work on a song to keep Stralton out of my mind whether I was awake or dreaming. I sweated as I pieced together words and snatches of tune.

The sun outside my window had lowered by the time I was ready to try it. Perhaps it had been three hours. I wasn't sure. I sang my song.

The relief of it buoyed me for a moment. Then I was even more tired than before and slumped into sleep.

✳✳✳

The third time I awoke, I felt much better. Sunshine poured in, and birds chirped nearby. I sat up and, feeling well enough, swung my feet over the side of the bed. The stone floor was as cold as the flagstones in the stable mudroom. I suspected this was marble, though.

My room was high and airy. Through tall, thin, arched windows, I could see the castle and the city stretched out below me. People milled in the white streets below, talking. Others blinked in and out before gaily colored stalls that sold fruits, wines, silks, musical instruments, and dozens of other things, many of which I couldn't recognize. It reminded me of a big provincial fair, but cleaner and more beautiful. Flowering bushes and trees in more varieties than I'd ever seen before lined even the smallest avenues. The people wore vivid clothing in reds, purples, pinks, and golds.

"You're up!" a tinkling voice said.

I turned from the window.

A golden-haired slip of a girl in a gold-trimmed white dress stood in the doorway with a basin of water. "I'm Straltia," she said.

"Straltia?"

The girl smiled sadly. "The name became so common after the resistance that His Lordship made rules limiting its use to a select few, so there would be a way to tell us younger fey apart. Are you ready for breakfast?"

I hadn't realized it before, but I was. Not just ready, but ravenous.

Straltia led me out of the room into a connecting chamber with a table and chairs. When I sat, the girl waved her hand over the table, and baskets of luscious fruit appeared. Bread too, light and flaky, and sweet as honey. A goblet of clear liquid burned my throat but left me invigorated.

I ate long and well. As I did so, Straltia padded silently here and there, washing windows and walls, furniture, and the floor. I wondered why all the cleaning was done manually instead of by magic, but Straltia seemed puzzled by questions about it.

"It is the way—we have always cleaned this way," was the best explanation Straltia could come up with.

Straltia was equally vague when I asked how Phil was doing, but she could at least tell me that it had been five days since the fight on the cliff and two since I'd last been up. No wonder I'd been so hungry.

Now that problem was solved, I had another one—how to get out of here? I wasn't going anywhere in a beruffled white nightgown. (And who had changed me out of the lavender one? It creeped me out to wonder.)

"Straltia?"

"Hmm?" the girl said. She paused in her scrubbing the floor.

"Is it possible I could find some clothes?"

"But of course!" The girl laughed, slapped at a corner of the floor, wrung out her cloth, and stood, picking up the basin. "Come this way."

I followed her into yet another high-ceilinged marble room. This one was windowless but full of seemingly natural light. It held two tall, intricately carved wardrobes and a screen embroidered with peonies.

"You'll want a bath, naturally," Straltia said, pulling the screen back to reveal an enormous tub set into the floor. "What do you usually wash in?"

"Excuse me? Do you mean, like a bubble bath?"

"I shouldn't think bubbles would be either comfortable or effective. Should you like Glimmer Lake water? It is extraordinarily cleansing, though it stings a bit.

I blinked. "I don't think I care what water you use."

Straltia smiled. "Then Glimmer Lake water it is." Humming to herself, she opened a tap.

"You don't magic water into tubs, either, I see."

Straltia stopped humming. "One can't 'magic' Glimmer Lake water. It is too real. We pump it up from the lake itself."

"I don't remember seeing any lakes as I flew over."

"It is under the city, very deep. In fact, few of our people go there. The water in that quantity is too potent." Straltia went back to humming.

I wondered what Straltia meant by potent. I hoped the stuff wouldn't eat off my skin.

In a few minutes, the tub was full. Straltia turned off the tap. "Here you are. I'll stay on the other side of the screen to arrange the clothes unless you'd rather—"

"No, no. I'm fine by myself."

The girl smiled and withdrew behind the screen.

I touched one toe into the water. Sting was an understatement. It hurt so much, I hardly noticed how cold it was. And Straltia had suggested bubbles would be uncomfortable?

Still, it probably wouldn't kill me, and I did need a bath. I plunged in all at once, dunking even my head.

"Are you all right?" Straltia called from the other side of the screen.

"Peachy," I gasped as I surfaced.

"Peachy?"

"Fine." I was getting used to the water now. It still stung, but I could tolerate it, and it poured energy into me, massaging my limbs. I felt I could run miles.

And clean! While I watched, my fingernails grew stronger, whiter, and shinier. My skin glowed pink. I ducked my head again, staying under as long as I could bear it.

The stinging grew more intense again. I was about to get out when Straltia asked, "Would you prefer to wear blue or red for your meeting with His Lordship this morning?"

My grip on the tub edge slipped, and I plopped back into the water. "Blue," I spluttered, regaining my balance. Then I sang my shield against mind-reading. To my surprise, I wasn't at all tired by it. It had to be the water. So, while I was immersed up to my neck, I sang an influence blocking song, adding a few impromptu lines to make it stronger.

Unable to stand another second, I jumped out of the tub. My skin tingled, and I shivered. My teeth chattered.

"Oh, my dear," Straltia said, appearing from behind the screen with a thick white towel, big as a blanket. The tub behind us began to drain, though I hadn't seen Straltia do anything to it. Perhaps it was smart enough to know we were done with it. I shivered, though I wasn't cold any longer.

"It's just a tub, you know," Straltia said.

Obviously, the mind-reading shield was not good enough.

Straltia blushed. "I'm sorry. I know you don't like it. I can't help it. I'm terribly good at knowing what other people think. If I weren't, I suppose I'd still be in the kitchen. I'm not good at anything else."

"Cooking is something."

"Oh, I didn't cook. I ran errands for the undercooks and washed up. Everything always has to be washed in the kitchen."

"I suppose it does." Did this mean my song had worked well enough that this girl had been pulled from the kitchens to spy on me?

Straltia fiddled with the wardrobe. "I'm sorry you feel like I'm spying on you. His Lordship wants to make you comfortable. I suppose we make poor hosts. We don't often have humans here, and we didn't know you were coming."

"Stralton's pet owls brought us."

"Those aren't His Lordship's pets! They merely live in the cliffs. The Council has often discussed having them killed—they pose a danger to children. It is only because some are opposed to killing any living thing that they weren't destroyed long ago."

"What do you do if some child gets in to trouble?"

"What we did when the guards reported you flying over—send up a rescue team."

"Oh—those guys who shot fire at us were supposed to be a rescue team?"

"Shot fire at you? I don't know. Maybe you ran into a group of city patrollers, but they are trained not to shoot first."

"Well, *we* sure didn't shoot first."

"It is strange."

"Not so strange. Your country and mine are at war."

"Yes, but that was an accident! Islandia had nearly surrounded one of our armies and forced us to retreat that way."

"Then how do you explain the corridor of protective walls from your border across Islandia into our hills?"

"I know of no such corridor."

"I've seen it running perpendicular to your border for miles."

"We have many walls along that border, parallel and perpendicular. They're useful for our defense. They all end about sixty miles from our border."

I shook my head. This was too much. I couldn't prove Straltia wrong. We hadn't been outside that sixty-mile mark, and I'd never seen the walls near the Dicrandian border, but—

"It's true. I've known about those protective walls since Islandia attacked when I was ten."

"When was that?"

"Seventy-two years ago."

I blinked. How could someone eighty-two years old look younger than I did? Not to mention, seem so naïve? Unless Straltia was an incredible actor, she believed this nonsense.

"Naturally, I believe—"

"Yes, but you'd say that if you were acting, too, wouldn't you?"

The baffled look on Straltia's face as she puzzled that one out was either genuine or frighteningly well done.

I shook my head. "So, did you find something I could wear?"

Straltia produced flowing silk pants of navy blue, a matching silver-studded tunic, and silver slippers that were athletic-shoe comfortable, but gorgeous. Then she took about two minutes to comb and pile up my hair. Although the time was short, the mirror on the back of the wardrobe revealed a more beautiful, older girl than I was used to seeing. I almost wished I could have a fairy lady's maid forever. As I thought it, I saw Straltia smile.

"Are you ready?" Straltia asked.

"I suppose so." I hoped this wouldn't be too painful.

"I'm sure His Lordship would never hurt you."

I laughed. "If you're going to go reading my mind, you ought to learn more idiomatic Dicrandian."

"What?"

"Never mind."

CHAPTER 32

If Straltia was trying to confuse me on the way down to meet Stralton, she was succeeding. The hallways and staircases were all irregular, many-cornered, and walled in pinkish-white marble with thin arched windows and vaulted roofs.

I tried to keep track of the way but soon gave up. I'd have left a trail of breadcrumbs or stones if I'd had any, but it probably didn't matter. We passed so many fairies cleaning the halls that all traces of my passage would undoubtedly have been whisked away moments after I'd gone.

As we passed each laboring maiden, Straltia would nod her head and murmur a name, receiving a nod and murmured "Straltia" in return. At least twice, the fairy we passed was also Straltia. Like my Straltia, these others were slim and golden-haired. Both seemed young, but as I'd learned, age was difficult to tell with fairies.

At the end of a fifteen-minute walk, we turned into yet one more pinkish-white hall, and through an arch at the end into an airy circular room.

Light streamed through arched doorways on all sides. Even the walls between were suffused with light, being lacy scrollwork, though marble. All about, in enormous shapely pots, were flowering trees and shrubs. Green trailed from baskets above as well. I reached up to touch a salmon-colored trumpet flower. "Beautiful," I breathed.

"As are you. I must admit I'm impressed. I expected your song-making efforts to affect you more, but no. Here you are, more gorgeous than ever."

I had neither heard nor felt Stralton come up behind me. I swirled to face him. "Perhaps it's the water," I said, turning back away. "It came highly recommended."

"It may have contributed, but I think your own resilience and inner radiance is chiefly responsible."

Uh, huh. And Stralton was renowned for his circumspection and restraint. "What did you want to talk to me about?"

"Show you, rather. Come this way." He took my arm and pulled me gently but irresistibly through one of the arches into a courtyard even lusher with foliage than the circular room.

I didn't know what I was expecting, but it wasn't this—a giant silver-barked tree with silver-green leaves and fist-sized golden fruit on every bough. The fruit hummed. "What is—"

Stralton pressed a finger against my lips and breathed, "Hush."

A low fruit in front of me vibrated, its hum higher pitched than the others. It began to quake, and then, with a ring like a clear small bell, it burst open, and from it flew a rainbow-winged, sparkly, bird-like creature.

It flew directly at me. I stepped back, startled, into Stralton, who steadied me gently, causing tingles to go up and down my arms. In my confusion, I lost sight of the bird creature, but another fruit was vibrating. Soon, it too released a rainbow-winged bird. A third fruit vibrated.

The birds zipped off into the sky, over my head. I turned, to watch them alight on the wall behind me. There they sat, gently waving their wings like butterflies. The effect was of light sifted through a hundred prisms onto some bejeweled surface.

I stood, stunned.

"Breathe, darling," Stralton murmured after a while, and I did, letting my pent-up breath out slowly, so as not to frighten them. I didn't know how long I stood there transfixed, listening to the ring and hum of the births and watching the celestial quilt pattern of the creatures' wings on the wall.

At some point, Stralton took hold of my arm again. I was afraid he would take me back inside or begin to talk, but he turned me back toward the tree to watch the equally absorbing explosions of the golden fruit. He did not take his hand away after turning me.

He turned me twice more before the chime of birth grew less and less frequent. At last, there were no more rings, only a soft hum, which I thought came from the birds' wings.

Motioning me to be quiet, Stralton stepped softly to the tree and plucked one of the now open fruit. He gave it to me.

It hung together at the stem, but otherwise split and twisted in beautiful curves like a flower. The outside was gold, but the inside pearly. It felt cool in my hand, though the day was now warm.

"Come inside," Stralton murmured in my ear. "They should rest."

He led me back into the circular room, which was now flecked with colored light, and out into a new hallway, around several bends, and down two flights of stairs into a small room with a lavishly set table and two chairs. There was no window, but a vibrant mural on the wall opposite the door.

Stralton seated me and took the chair opposite. "Please," he said, indicating the mounds of food in front of me.

"What were they?"

Stralton smiled, picked up a roll, and spread a dripping piece of honeycomb on it. "The aersyla?"

"The bird things."

Stralton handed the bread to me. I switched my golden fruit to my left hand to take it. The honey was sticky on my fingers.

It must have been sticky on Stralton's as well, for he licked them provocatively before going on. "The aersyla. Beautiful creatures, aren't they? And strange. They live but a few years. Long enough to mate and lay eggs in the ground, some of which grow into aersyla trees. When the trees bear fruit, you see what happens."

"How often do they bear fruit?"

"Once every hundred years, give or take."

I choked on my bread. He was at my side in a moment. Three sharp whacks to my back dislodged it. The places he'd hit would be sore for days.

"I'm so sorry about that, Your Highness." He rubbed the sore places. "I shouldn't surprise you when you're eating. Here, try these dian nuts. They're delicious."

I put down the bread, which now had bits of what I'd coughed up on it and fumbled about for some kind of napkin. Stralton laughed and produced a warm washcloth from nowhere. He wiped my face and hands with it, slowly. His fingers lingered.

I snatched the cloth away. "I can clean myself up, thank you. How old do you think I am? Two?"

Stralton smiled. "You are certainly more than two." He looked me up and down, letting his gaze linger in places people usually didn't.

"Stop that," I said.

"What?"

"Staring at me that way."

"My apologies." He raised his eyes to mine. Their blue was brighter than ever. I was not sure I could look away, even if I wanted to.

"Eat your lunch," he said, "or would you prefer I feed you?"

I wasn't hungry, which was odd since I was almost always hungry, but I certainly didn't want him feeding me. I ate mechanically, eyes still on his. It was good—sweet fruit, salty nuts, flaky bread, and sharp cheese.

"Shall I tell you a story?"

I wasn't sure how I wanted to answer. After a few seconds of silence, he said, "I will just tell it."

I'd heard the story before. A shepherdess in the hills south of Lake Spinoa fell in love with a young fairy. Before, I'd never been impressed, but when Stralton told the story, I lived it. I no longer saw his eyes, but the vibrant green of dew-fresh hills. The smell of hay and sheep and lilac came to me, along with the heart-quickening of that fatal love.

The last words of the story lingered in the air between us. My heart pounded. Silence hung heavily in the room. I felt sure Stralton wanted me to break it, but I didn't know what I felt and didn't want him to figure it out before I did.

I tore my eyes from his and forced myself to eat the apple in my hand.

"You needn't speak if you don't want to."

I kept my eyes on my plate.

"You are remarkably transparent, my dear." He stood up and came toward me. "Refreshingly so." His fingers caressed my cheek, sliding down under my chin and lifting it until my eyes met his.

I didn't know why I didn't stop him.

He smiled. "You know, this is the first time I've shared a story with a human. Delightful." He rested his thumb lightly on my lips for a moment. Not long enough for me to protest, but nearly.

Then, suddenly, he turned away. "My apologies, Your Highness," he said in a brisk, business-like voice. "Something has come up in the lower galleries. Can you get back to your room without my help? No, naturally, you can't."

He produced a map, unrolling it out of nowhere. "The castle and grounds. Perhaps you can explore unless you'd rather rest. You just got up today."

He leaned over and kissed me lightly on the forehead. Then he was gone.

My heart pounded again, and I was confused. He had been so nice, except about reading my mind, which he claimed he couldn't help. But he seemed far more sophisticated than the other fairies I'd met. Was his pleasant demeanor a façade?

Why would he give me a map of his castle? Was it wrong? It would undoubtedly get me to my room, but could any of the rest of it be trusted? And would the map disappear on me without warning?

Well, that last was easy enough to prevent. I could put the contents in my brain. A waste of effort if the map were false, but all I needed to do that afternoon was find Phil and escape. A map might help me do both.

As I started to unroll the map, the table obligingly cleared itself of the remains of lunch.

"Thank you," I said, mostly from habit. Could the table understand me?

The map was huge and marked with miniscule rooms. I sighed. I'd better do as my father always suggested and start at the top. I wished he were here, helping me, throwing in stories of things he'd seen and done, as he had when we'd studied maps of the provinces at home. I could imagine him with me now. "This is the east tower, Sarah. It's mostly used for storage, but if you touch this false bookcase on the third knot on the left side, the case swings out to reveal the staircase to the roof. From there you can see to the sea if you've got fairy eyes. Now down this way…"

Imagining him wasn't as good as having him actually with me, but thinking of what he'd say made the task more interesting and reminded me of things I would have forgotten otherwise.

"These are the servant's quarters, Sarah. Always remember that the state of the servant's quarters directly affects how happy they are with you. And that affects what kind of service you get."

The servant quarters in this castle were tiny. That is to say, the rooms were small, not that they were few. There were hundreds. Perhaps they were enchanted to seem bigger. "I wish I could see them," I said.

Then I could. The map faded away to show a small room. Like the rest of the castle, it was scrubbed white-pink marble, but there were no adornments. Indeed, there was no room for any. Two bunk beds lined each long wall. The mattresses were thin, their covers brightly colored, but patched. A shelf on the wall by each bed held combs, hair ribbons, baskets of fruit, and books. Eight narrow lockers lined the wall opposite the door. One was open, giving me a glimpse of two white dresses similar to the one Straltia wore. Under the beds were basins and soap. Eight round wooden stools crowded the space between the beds.

I felt guilty about my own suite here and my tower room at home. It was a wonder Stralton got anything done for him at all. The best that could be said for the place was that it was clean. And the fairies who lived there probably saw to that themselves.

When I finished with it, the map returned to its normal state. So, it went, from the towers to the storerooms, from the gardens to the gates. Now that I knew it could be done, I zoomed in on whatever struck my fancy. The menagerie held a number of wild animals I didn't recognize. All were beautiful, but some seemed dangerous.

After my morning bath, I was curious about the path down to Glimmer Lake. Straltia was right about it not being much used. It was the first dusty place I'd seen. The map went fuzzy before I could see as much of that path as I'd like, though.

I didn't examine any other rooms for a while, but I could never pass up the chance to peek in a kitchen. The ones here were roaring with fire and bustling noise. While I watched, a young lad slipped on a wet spot and dropped a plate of berries. An older fairy hit him upside the head with a rolling pin and barked at him to be more careful. I shut my eyes to make the kitchens disappear. No wonder Straltia hated working down there.

The map wouldn't let me get close to the armories or the dungeons. I wasn't really surprised. I was surprised, rather, that the map had shown me as much as it had. I wondered how much Stralton had meant for me to see. Surely, he would know what I was doing by now.

Perhaps it was time to move on. I rolled up the map, and carrying it and my aersyla fruit, went out into the corridor.

It had become dark while I was inside. I thought I'd better return to my room. There was some chance of getting supper there. Plus, maybe Straltia could tell me where Phil was. The map hadn't, and I needed Phil. I was worried about him, and he could help me work through my confusion about Stralton. I could be sure magical influences hadn't muddled his brain.

Smiling, I strode toward my room.

CHAPTER 33

I didn't start out to find Phil that night, though. When I got back to my room, Straltia was in a panic.

"Where have you been? Are you all right? Were you lost?"

"Couldn't you tell where I was?"

"You must have been in a part of the castle with walls that block mind-reading. I couldn't sense you at all! If you'd hurt yourself, I'd never have known."

I laughed. So, there were parts of the castle that blocked mind-reading. Too bad that hadn't been marked on the map.

"It's not funny. I was worried about you."

"Slow down. I'm OK. I stayed downstairs for a while, catching my bearings. I got to thinking about my dad, and one thing led to another, and you know…"

"I know what?"

I laughed. "In no time, it was late, and I wanted supper. Is there any to be had?"

Straltia produced an even more plentiful spread than breakfast, and along the same lines.

"Eat with me," I said. "I hate to eat alone."

"I really shouldn't," Straltia said.

"Why not?"

"I'm only a maid."

"So?"

"It's against the rules."

"I won't tell anybody."

Straltia started to back away.

"I'd appreciate it," I said.

Straltia hesitated. "He did say to keep you happy," she said softly.

"It would make me very happy."

Straltia pulled up a seat opposite me, and perched on the edge, as if readying to flee, but as we ate she settled back into the seat and told me stories about growing up in the castle, raiding cupboards, and playing games like Wink and Tadpole, a kind of magical hide-and-seek. Kids could be anything: a tree or a shadow or a glimmer on the water.

"But I was always it." Straltia blinked rapidly, as if holding back tears. "I've never been any good at that kind of trick—doing it or seeing it."

"I'm sorry," I said.

"It doesn't matter," Straltia said brightly.

There was an awkward pause.

I pushed back from the table. "You've been great fun, Straltia, but if you're sure you don't know where Prince Philip is, perhaps I should go to bed for the evening and try finding him tomorrow." I didn't want to wait that long, but I was starting to feel tired.

Straltia's face fell, and I remembered the pathetically crowded dorm I'd seen. "Or maybe I could take another bath," I said. That would wake me up.

Straltia clapped her hands. "Perfect. I know what you need."

This time the bath was warm and scented lightly of lavender. I sank into it, and my tension rolled off. I slipped farther and farther in. I was barely aware of Straltia pulling me out and bundling me into bed.

Then the dream came.

My father walked with more spring in his step and less gray at his temples than he had of late. He came and sat at the bedside. There was sadness in his eyes, but also great joy. "It is going to be hard for you, little one."

"What is?"

"The next few decisions, the next few years. And I can't help you the way I'd like. But remember, I love you. Whatever you do, remember that. You can't kill my love for you."

"I'm so confused, Dad."

"I know, but you're doing very well. I'm proud of you."

He kissed me on the forehead, where Stralton had, and it took away the searing memory of that former kiss. Why had I not noticed it until it was gone?

Dad smiled before fading away. "Remember who loves you," he said.

I had no dreams the rest of the night.

****

I awoke early. It was still dark, though a grayish edge showed on the eastern horizon. Straltia huddled in a corner.

She jumped up and straightened her clothes when I got out of bed. "Your Highness, are you sure you should be up?"

"I feel fine," I said. "I think I'd like breakfast and a bath, and then I'll find Phil."

"With all due respect, Your Highness, he's not ready for visitors yet."

"Perhaps not, but I want to see for myself."

Straltia's forehead puckered, and she dawdled about getting breakfast and the bath. Getting me dressed today (in a deep purple tunic with gold trim) took much longer than it had yesterday. Straltia put the aersyla fruit in my hair, where it gleamed in the room's bright light.

At last Straltia was finished. I got her to locate a bag for the map but went off without consulting it toward a series of guest rooms in the tower next to my own, leaving Straltia wringing her hands and calling warnings not to get lost.

I didn't get lost, but Phil wasn't in the tower. Or the east wing. Or near the kitchens. I found him at last (it must have been nearly ten o'clock) in a room over the gardens.

He was pale and in bed. There were no fairies with him. I went to his side and rested my hand lightly on his forehead. As I concentrated, his condition washed over me. He was feverish and achy. What were these fairies thinking? I sang for him.

The fever abated, his breathing became more regular, and his eyes opened.

"Jennifer? How long have you been here?"

Jennifer? Why would he think I was Jennifer? Was that who he wanted to see? "Sarah," I said firmly.

"Sarah? What do you mean, Sarah? You can't be mad at me for spending time with that kid. I could hardly help it after being dragged off together the way we were."

"You'd only spend time with m-her if you've got no choice?"

"Well, of course. You know the situation with our families."

"Yes, I know." So, that's what he told his other friends about me. I thought he actually liked me.

"Nothing with her could ever go anywhere," Phil added.

My eyes stung. I turned away. "No, I suppose not."

"Come on, Jennifer. Don't leave me. Sing me a song or something."

"I already did."

Tears rolled down my cheeks as I left. Once out of the room, I ran blindly, down some stairs, around a corner, through a passage—

And into Stralton.

CHAPTER 34

"Sorry," I mumbled.

Stralton steadied me. "What's wrong, dearest?" he asked, pulling me close. "Come, tell me about it. Surely it's not as bad as you think."

Part of me knew I shouldn't let him see me like this, but the rest of me was overcome with mingled anger and sadness. I sobbed out my story in a few nearly incoherent gasps. Stralton held me, patting my back, making low, soothing noises. With effort, I brought myself under control and pushed myself out of his arms. I hadn't meant to say this much to him. I certainly didn't want him touching me.

I began to wipe my eyes with the back of my hand, but he forestalled me, producing a lavender silk handkerchief and gently brushing the drops away. Then he led me into a small sitting room nearby.

"I can see why you would be upset," he said, "though the young man's attitude is only to be expected. Your families have warred for years, and that can't change all in a moment."

He was probably right, and it still made me want to cry. "I thought he liked me."

Stralton smiled sadly at me. "You are very naïve, aren't you?"

Annoyance at Stralton flared through my feelings about Phil. "He said he trusts me. He's helped me with passing bills."

"Wouldn't it be more accurate to say *you've* helped *him* with passing bills?"

I opened my mouth but couldn't speak.

"Think about that first proposition you threw yourself behind. Wasn't that originally War legislation?"

"But—"

"And your work to contain problems in the Northwest—it has all increased War power."

"The polls show Peace ahead in the Northwest, even though the army is there."

"Certainly, but with you gone, that's changing. They don't trust your father as much as King Randolph. And the rest of the country has been leaning War all summer. They'll almost certainly have a majority in the next elections."

I wasn't so naïve as to trust Stralton's account of my country's mood. Besides, even if he was right in his analysis, plenty could change. "The next elections are still a year and a half off. Anything could happen between now and then."

"Perhaps. I have not made Dicrandian politics my study, but you must admit that War's numbers have improved, and you've helped with that. You invited Prince Philip to your planning session on defending the Northwest, and he wound up with most of the credit."

Did Stralton know how annoyed I'd been about that? Probably. "He didn't mean for that to happen. And he did work to pass the proposals."

"Minimally. It was you and your people who came up with the ideas, though, and he didn't do much to make that known."

For a man who hadn't made Dicrandian politics his study, he knew an awful lot. As I thought back, though, I had to admit there was something to what he said. But Phil had helped. He at least helped me call the Islandian fairies.

"Naturally, he helped call up the Islandian fairies. It was part of his purpose all along. Islandia had already convinced the War Party that calling them in was necessary for your defense. They were looking for an excuse to introduce themselves to you."

I needed to work on my mind-protection song. Stralton was reading me way too easily. Not that it helped him. His claims were completely bogus. "Islandia hadn't been in our country for hundreds of years! Nobody's seen the smallest hint of them for centuries. They were staying out until our royal families could get along."

"I'm sure that's what they told you, and it is hard not to believe them. Darvian, especially, appears so trustworthy. Everything he says is so plausible. While, I, on the other hand, am often taken for a liar when, in fact, I rarely stretch the truth."

I shook my head. We'd seen Darvian in the tapestry.

"Darvian has also changed in the hundreds of years since that little affair with the boats. Even then he was a show-off and liked to be around humans. They could give him a feeling of superiority, being so easily awed by simple tricks."

"He isn't like that!" Even as I said it, I remembered how he called me a child, how he made illusions with paper and flower bowls, and how he patronized my parents. Maybe he was a bit like that.

"Now he's much more dangerous. His only thought is to defeat me, by whatever means necessary. He thinks it will help him to use humans, so he went about getting your help. He cares nothing for old promises. No oath to stay out until your royal families agreed would keep him out of your country if his treaty with me to leave Dicrandia out of our fight did not. And obviously, it did not."

"You have a treaty with Islandia about leaving Dicrandia alone?"

"I did. You can see it if you like." Stralton clapped his hands, and a young fairy appeared. "Alayin, bring the scroll reader, please."

The young man left. While he was gone, Stralton went to the window and stared out. His shoulders sagged. "It has been a long fight, my battle with Darvian and his like. It never needed to happen. If, instead of kicking me out, they could have adopted some sensible governmental plan—a Council such as we have here, or even your humans' absurd democracy—there would never have been any fight."

"I thought you left."

"Oh, no. I loved Islandia, but I believed government by consensus to be unworkable. They take a hundred years to decide simple problems. Because I voiced my opinion too loudly, they kicked me out. They are lost in the past over there, and do not realize, even now, when nearly every young fairy in their land has left to join me, that times have changed. We younger ones do not feel the old ways are best. Is that such a crime?"

"I don't know."

"Ah. That's the trouble of joining an unfamiliar fight in the middle. How do you know you are on the right side? The side you'd agree with if you took the time to listen?"

At this point, the young fairy came back in, bearing a huge, flat, inch-thick square of crystal. He set it on a table in the center of the room.

"This will show any official scrolls that have been made in my kingdom since its founding. Tell it what you want to see. But you must use fairy."

It sounded like he didn't expect me to know any. "I'll try," I said. I certainly didn't know any word for treaty. But I knew scroll, and Dicrandia, and show. I thought I could remember show. "Show me a scroll with

Dicrandia," I said, paying careful attention to my pronunciation. The crystal glowed a soft rose color, and then a scroll appeared. It was all in fairy, and I couldn't really read it, but I could read enough to see that it was dated 10103, more than five-hundred years ago. It was definitely about Dicrandia, and it was signed by every Islandian fairy I'd met and a whole bunch I hadn't, plus Stralton. I tried to piece together more of the text, but couldn't.

"Would you like a translation?"

"Sure." I couldn't necessarily trust it, but it wouldn't hurt to hear what he wanted me to think it said.

As Stralton translated, I tried to follow along. What he said matched what was written as far as I could tell.

"So, given this, how do you justify having people in our land?"

"I have kept this treaty at great cost to myself and my troops. You notice it says I will not involve you unless you involve yourselves. I did not allow even a pixie belonging to me to touch foot on your land until this spring, when your Prince Philip came out with the Islandians, chanting against me."

"You had werewolves and ghouls in our northwestern villages long before that!"

"Smoke and mirrors, my dear. Smoke and mirrors."

"Those attacks were as real as anything that has ever happened here!"

"I'm sure the attacks were real, but I didn't order them. It was your Islandian friends, I think, trying to provoke you to join the fight."

"That's ridiculous! They're fighting on our side."

"I think it would be more accurate to say you are fighting on their side. They are using you to tie up my northern army while they put their main effort against my border in the south. I have lost battalion after battalion. Good fey, people I've known for years."

A deep sadness hung about him. The room was quiet for a minute. Then he shook himself and continued. "Still, I would have saved you trouble if I could. But with my northern army cut off and pressed hard from the western front, once you joined with Islandia, I had little choice but to allow them to go in and find what cover they could in the Tybernees. I have ordered them to do as little damage as possible."

"As little damage as possible? Villages have been burned to the ground, whole townships wiped out. To say nothing of the dragons in Bentralia!"

"Dragons! I've never had anything to do with dragons!"

"But—"

"Islandian, my dear. Dragons come from the northern Tybernees, the volcanic ones. Dragon tamers never come from anywhere else."

I tried to clear my head but couldn't. "Why on earth would Islandia send dragons against us? We're their allies."

"No. The War Party is their ally. You in Peace are seen as more of a threat, more difficult to control. Think of the ways you've limited which fairies come into Dicrandia. And, around the time of that dragon, weren't you stalling on involving youth clubs in the war effort? Even young Castanay's influence with you hadn't been able to overcome that."

"What do you mean, young Castanay's influence with me?"

"The relationship he's been cultivating to get you to lean War this spring and summer."

"That's hogwash!"

"Is it?"

"Phil hasn't been trying to influence me!"

"No? Hasn't he tried to get you to help change the Northwestern War Powers to auto-renewing when it comes up again?"

"Sure, but that's just talk. He isn't friends with me only to talk politics."

"Oh?" Stralton turned toward a small table by the window which held a crystal ball. He waved his hand, and it came alight with color and then figures. They were King Randolph, Queen Salome, and Phil in a room I'd never seen before.

"Look, Dad, I'm sorry," Phil said.

"No need to apologize," King Randolph said. "So, we've lost ground on a few measures. You've gained a lot of Her Highness's trust. If we use that trust to shift her views in our direction, that will prove more valuable than temporary gains today."

"I didn't set out to—"

"We know you didn't," Queen Salome said, "but it fits in well with our needs and plans. We'd be fools not to use it."

"She's not a fool. She'd find out eventually, and then she'd hate me and try to pay us back."

"I'm not worried about the revenge of a heartbroken fifteen-year-old. Besides, her family is wise enough to hope it dies a natural death," King Randolph said.

"I don't see how you can call betraying her trust a 'natural death.'"

King Randolph looked sheepish. "Well, perhaps not natural. But think, Phil. Our families have hated each other for hundreds of years. One little crush is not going to change that. However far the relationship goes, there's certain to be a break-up eventually. She'll be unhappy with you then, whatever you've done. Being overly honorable—if you want to call it that instead of plain vanity—isn't going to get you anywhere. Our country is in trouble, Phil. We need our best efforts to deal with the current crisis.

Frankly, your performance in the past few weeks has been lackluster. It would go a long way toward setting things right if you cultivate the young lady's acquaintance more purposefully."

"I told you, I'm sorry about these last couple of weeks. I care about our country, and I want to do better, but what you're asking—it's filthy. Her Highness trusts me."

"Then she is a fool," Queen Salome said.

"Politics is a dirty game, Phil," his father added. "There are enough experienced people around the princess to protect her. Let them worry about her. Your first duty is to your country. To us."

There was a long moment of silence. Queen Salome played with her necklace. Phil kicked at the floor. Finally, he raised his head. "Fine," he said. "I'll try to convince her of our ways of thinking."

The crystal ball went black.

"What happened next?" I asked.

"I can't remember exactly. I didn't capture it. I believe the lad and his parents talked strategy for the next few hours. They discussed how they'd introduce the Islandian fairies to you, I believe.

"This was before the dance?"

"Oh, yes. It was after the passage of that camp bill through your Joint Council. It hadn't become law, yet, I believe."

My stomach lurched. This had to be some kind of trick. Phil couldn't have been cultivating a friendship with me all spring for purely political reasons, could he?

It was possible. I'd been half afraid of it all along, and it did make a few things make sense. Like Queen Salome giving me Prince Philip's private line.

"Nasty, I'm afraid," Stralton said, running his finger over my cheek.

I slapped his hand away, but Stralton smiled and went on, "It's a pity the boy didn't have the courage to stick with his first instinct—to protect you. However, as I've said before, your families have warred for years. This kind of deception comes more naturally to him than honest friendship. He doesn't realize, I think, what he has lost. You are such a giving person." Stralton brushed a wisp of hair out of my eyes.

I pushed away from him. Maybe Phil was using me. I felt cold. That didn't mean Stralton wasn't still a jerk.

"If he's using me, what do you think you're doing? You kidnapped me and brought me here."

"No, my dear. It may have appeared that way, and, indeed, I am delighted to have made your acquaintance, but I did not kidnap you. That,

I suspect, was Islandian fairies as well. Didn't you find some signs of that on your trip?"

I thought of the Islandian sigils on the second group of fairies we'd encountered, but the Islandian sigils could be plants as easily as the Stralton ones on the outer garments could be. We weren't fighting Islandia.

"No, you're not fighting Islandia, but the Peace Party is being much less cooperative with Islandia than they had hoped. They have War doing their bidding already, but you are holdouts. Think of the measures you forced King Randolph to add to the fairy invitation bill last week. Without you, any Islandian fairy could go at will anywhere in Dicrandia. Your visa system is troublesome for them, I assure you."

"Kidnapping me wouldn't solve that problem."

"I think, with you gone and your party weakened, War will ride the curve to the top."

"It doesn't work that way. If something happens to me, especially if it happens in the course of me fighting for our country, it is Peace that would become popular."

"A martyr can be made to support all kinds of things she would never have supported if alive my dear."

"My father wouldn't allow it."

"You and your father obviously and openly disagreed politically. He would not be regarded as an accurate depicter of your views."

"He would be more accurate than anyone in the War Party! People aren't as stupid as all that!"

"I suspect it will be Miss Montressor who is chosen as a mouthpiece. After all, she's your best friend and chief of staff. No one would suspect her true loyalties."

"No! Not Steph!"

Then confidence broke through my confusion. Not Steph. Dad had said in my dream, "Remember who loves you." That meant him, of course, but it also meant Steph. I might have been mistaken about Phil's feelings for me. A cold feeling in the pit of my stomach told me I probably was. I might have been mistaken about the Islandians meaning good for Dicrandia. I didn't know them very well. I knew Steph, though, and Steph would never betray me.

"I can understand how you'd have difficulty believing that your best friend is deceiving you," Stralton said, "but you know your parents have never trusted her. They are in some ways wiser than you are."

I turned away from him. That was a surprisingly stupid thing to say if he was privy to my thoughts. He had to have realized I was sure of Steph's loyalty.

But he wasn't stupid. I was sure of that. How was it possible that he didn't realize I knew he was lying about Steph? He'd been picking my brain freely, even today, during this conversation. Though during our meal together, after the aersyla, he hadn't followed along as well. That was the day Straltia showed up, the day after I'd sung my mind-protection song.

Straltia had been so worried she couldn't hear my thoughts. Had I been so successful in throwing Stralton out of my mind that for days now, he'd only been reading me through Straltia? He seemed like he was reading me—but maybe she was reading me, and he was reading her. Straltia read minds well, but she wasn't nearly as good at understanding and manipulating feelings as Stralton. But surely, she'd figured out her mistake by now? Why wouldn't she have told him she'd blown it?

What would Stralton do to Straltia now that she'd messed up? She was so afraid all the time. It couldn't be good.

Of course, if I didn't say something soon, Stralton would figure out that she'd read me wrong—and that wouldn't be good for either Straltia or me.

In the need to think quickly, my confidence from a moment ago was fading, and I could feel Stralton moving closer to me, bringing more confusion with him. I had to do something, but what?

In my mind, I heard my dad's patient voice. "If you're confused and not sure what to do or say, buy time, Sarah."

Buy time. I cleared my throat and turned toward Stralton. He stood inches away.

So very there. Warm. Solid. Better looking than any human I'd ever seen. No wonder some of the earliest human settlers on the Islandian continent thought fairies were gods.

I stared at the floor and gulped. I was supposed to be buying time to think, not drooling over my host. He was old and creepy, anyway. Why couldn't I remember that when I looked at him?

I kept my gaze firmly on the floor, took two deep breaths, and started talking. "I don't know. It's difficult to believe all this at once. Even the part about Phil. Is it possible I could see that scene at the War Palace again?"

Stralton smiled. "Certainly."

It certainly looked like the War Palace. And it sounded like the War Royals. The cold words cut as deeply as before. How could Phil have sold me out like that?

I focused on him, taking in the sharp black outline of his shoulders and the glint of purple inside his jacket.

Glint of purple? If this was real, it was the night of the Fling, not earlier. At least Phil hadn't asked me out—such as it was—for political reasons.

Stralton had confused me—lied to me—about Islandia and the timing. What was he trying to do? Start a civil war? I pressed my lips together. The jerk. Did Stralton think I was too stupid to see through the deception? Too powerless to stop him?

"Then she is a fool," Queen Salome said again.

"Politics is a dirty game, Phil," said King Randolph.

In the pause that followed, I forced myself to keep my senses alert, waiting for Phil's reply.

"Fine," he said. "I'll try to convince her to some of our ways of thinking…"

As the ball went black again, I could hardly believe I'd missed hearing that the sentence went on. Stralton obviously meant for me to imagine he stopped there, but still, I should have heard that Phil wasn't done talking. "What did he say after that?"

"I already told you I don't remember the rest of the conversation."

"I don't mean the rest of the conversation. Just the rest of the sentence."

"My dear, the sentence ended there."

"You have a low opinion of my intelligence, don't you? Anyone can hear he goes on."

Stralton glanced at me sharply, and then smiled softly, sadly, and stroked a jewel on his lapel. His eyes glinted. "Obviously, there is no fooling you. I was hoping to spare you what came next. It was not at all nice."

"I'd like to see it anyway."

Stralton shook his head but turned back to the crystal ball. A few beads of sweat dotted his forehead. The scene flickered back into existence.

"Politics is a dirty game, Phil," King Randolph said.

I held my breath for the pause.

"Fine. I'll try to convince her of some of our ways of thinking, but it'll be a serious pain. She's awfully grubby and has no figure. It's not like there will be any compensation for leading her on."

Although I was sure it was a trick, I felt like I'd been gut-kicked. Did Phil think that way about me?

"I'm sorry you had to see that," Stralton said. He managed to sound sorry. I was impressed. If his comments about Steph hadn't awakened my mind, would I have even noticed how fishy it was? Who talked that way to their parents?

Stralton definitely made it up, but I didn't know what to do about it. Could Phil help me? Slowly, feeling my way, I said, "You know, I think I'd like to hear what Philip has to say. What you've shown me is convincing, but he should have a chance to defend himself." I started for the door.

"He will lie to you for certain. Perhaps I should come along to ensure he tells the truth."

"How would you do that?"

"I can compel people to do things, even things they don't want to do."

To my horror, I found myself turning, stepping toward him, my arms circling up around his neck. I tried to pull away, but the best I could manage was not going any closer—and I wasn't sure whether my ability to pause came from my frantic efforts to put distance between me and Stralton, or if he'd allowed me to stop. I was breathing heavily as if from extreme exertion. His arms circled my waist, pulling me closer to him. I shuddered at the contact—but only internally. My body no longer responded to my mind's commands.

"However, if you don't trust me, my dear—and you are very dear to me—you won't be satisfied hearing the words from his lips either. He could merely be saying what I've forced him to say."

My heart pounded with a claustrophobic panic.

Stralton gently traced my lips with his finger, then let me go.

I gagged, and the force I'd been exerting to free myself sent me staggering backward. I fell on the floor near the door. Pain cleared my mind for a moment, and I knew the truth. Stralton was my enemy, and I hated him for forcing me to his will. Was this how the fairies he'd enchanted felt all the time?

I would end him. And I might even know how to do it. It was time to see if Darvian was right about what could happen if Stralton tried to force Phil to do something.

I rubbed my knee where it had bashed hard against a table and braced myself for his inevitable approach.

"Oh, my dear. That must have hurt. Allow me."

"It's nothing." I allowed him to help me up, forcing myself not to cringe at his touch. I wasn't sure why Straltia hadn't told him yet that I was plotting his demise, but I hoped she'd keep up her silence. "I'd like to talk to Phil."

"Without my help?" Stralton smiled sadly.

"You can come if you'd like. I'd love to hear the truth, but I'm afraid it will be more difficult for you to control Phil than it is for you to control me."

"I'm sure the difficulty can be managed. Shall we go?"

I let him lead me from the room.

From around a corner ahead of us, a figure came running. "Don't, Papa. It's a trick. He's—"

The figure stopped short and writhed as if in pain. With shock, I realized it was Straltia.

My shock must have registered on my face. Stralton dropped my arm and went to the figure. "My child, how many times have I told you not to interrupt important meetings?"

"But, Papa—"

"Enough. One would think from your blubbering that I am incapable of dealing with a couple of human children on my own. You insult me. Stay here. We will talk of this matter later."

Straltia cringed against the wall. "Yes, My Lord." Her eyes drowned in unhappiness too great to be accounted for by Stralton's words. What had he said to her that I couldn't hear? Why had she run to talk to us? Had he cut off his link to her, even though it was the only way he had to read my mind?

Also, she called him Papa! "I didn't realize she was your daughter," I said as Stralton and I continued toward Phil's room.

"My…oh. Her calling me Papa. Many of the younger generation use that title. A term of endearment, you know."

"She usually calls you, His Lordship."

"My more formal title."

"So, you're not actually her father?"

"No, no. I've never married."

"Oh." He was lying, but it wasn't worth pursuing. After a moment, I asked, "What happened to her mother?"

"Whose mother?"

"Straltia's." What had he been thinking about?

"Oh, quite. I'm not sure. I rather think she died. Yes. Not long after Straltia's birth, actually." There was no hint of sadness in his voice.

"What was she like?"

"Straltia's mother? Pretty, but brainless, like Straltia. Not good for much, but I enjoyed her."

That last sentence sent chills up my spine. Stralton thought of women as disposable toys. Enjoy, then discard. And I'd almost trusted him yesterday, after the aersyla and his story. Even this morning, until he'd mentioned Steph, I'd taken his word at more than it was worth. I shivered.

He put his arm around me. I could feel the warmth and a kind of electricity, a force that sped my heart and quickened my breathing. Now, with my distrust of him high and rising, I could feel it happening, but surely it had been happening all along, every time he touched me. I despised myself for how easily I'd been manipulated. It was hard to keep my face impassive as we turned into Phil's room.

Several servants were there—beautiful young women in dresses like Straltia's. One bathed Phil's head with a pungent salve. Another manned a giant tea cart, arranging little cakes and hot tea. A third puttered by the window doing something I couldn't see.

"Your Lordship," the woman with the cart whispered.

"Leave us," he ordered.

The three scrambled from the room, leaving the tools they'd been using behind.

I freed myself from Stralton's arms and went to Phil's bedside. I moved the basin of liquid to a nightstand and sat down where it had been.

"Thank you," Phil said. "I hate that stuff. I'm sure it's keeping me sick. And don't give me that bullshit about Stralton never giving orders that would harm people."

"I wasn't going to," I said.

"Sarah!"

"So, this time you recognize me." A wave of anger swept over me. I suspected it came from Stralton, but I didn't fight it. It would be better if he thought things were going his way.

"This time! You've never been in here before."

"You called me Jennifer," I said.

"Jennifer? No, that couldn't have been you. It looked and sounded exactly like her."

Had Stralton disguised me? "It was me. It was very informative."

Phil stared at my face and paled. "Sarah, I'm really sorry. If I'd had any idea—"

"You'd have lied. And done so convincingly, no doubt," Stralton said.

"Who is this?"

"This is our host."

"I was hoping to make this a pleasant stay for both of you, but I'm afraid, lad, that your deceptive little games with Her Highness have made that impossible."

"My deceptive little games with Her Highness? Tell me this is a joke, Sarah."

"He showed me a conversation you had with your parents where they convinced you to encourage my crush on you for political gain."

Phil blanched. "I told them…anyway, I didn't agree."

"No? It sounded like you did."

"No! I told them I wouldn't do anything sneaky or underhanded, and while I'd try to persuade you, I wasn't making any bargains that involved our relationship."

"Could you show him what I saw, Your Lordship?" I asked sweetly.

"Certainly, Your Highness." Pulling a miniature crystal ball from his pocket, he sat between Phil and me. I watched the scene yet again. It was troubling, no doubt about that. Phil and I would have to chat about it once we'd rid ourselves of Stralton.

When the screen went black, Phil exploded. "I never said that!"

"You can't deny you agreed to use your influence with Her Highness to achieve political ends."

"Well, no, but I never said that junk at the end about—"

"You have never thought Her Highness is grubby and figureless?"

"I've never said any such thing! It's made up!"

"You're disowning one line in a whole conversation. I think you must be forgetting it, lad. The crystal doesn't lie."

"I never…"

I could see him wavering, unsure how to respond. The rest of that conversation must have been legitimate. Definitely troubling.

"Anyway, how can you say the crystal doesn't lie when it left out the other half of the conversation? The conditions I made?"

"The crystal would certainly include them if any had been made, but you know, and I know, that they weren't." Stralton returned the globe to his pocket. "Do make some attempt at telling the truth."

"I am telling the truth. Sarah, you've got to believe me." Phil grabbed my hands. "It's the truth!"

I took my hands out of his and lowered my eyelids. I hated doing this, even if I was mad at him. "I don't know what to believe."

An arm came around my back. Stralton's. "Do you want me to force him to tell the truth?" His voice was all sympathy. I almost felt sorry for him, but remembering Lewis and Patterson, and the dragon, and the look in Straltia's eyes when we'd passed her in the hall, I said, "Yes."

At first, I didn't dare look up, but after a moment, the odd electricity from Stralton's arm died down and I raised my head. Phil and Stralton were both frozen, unmoving except for their nearly identical eyes. Those were blazing. Light connected in two beams from Phil's eyes to Stralton's.

I longed to move from the circle of Stralton's arms but was afraid that if I did, the connection would break and…and what? I didn't know, but I was afraid.

It may have been ten minutes I sat like that, afraid to move, hardly breathing, not knowing how this would end.

It may have been hours.

At last, there was a change. Stralton shuddered. Then, the light between him and Phil exploded in a fountain of flashes.

I was blinded but felt Stralton's arm fall away.

I sang a song to heal my sight.

A fire had started on the bed, near Phil's head.

I screamed and rushed to help Phil. He wasn't moving.

My only comfort was that Stralton sprawled on the floor of the room, equally still.

CHAPTER 35

I doused the fire with the contents of the basin. The flames disappeared, but a horrid, choking steam rose from the bed. Phil was right. The stuff probably was keeping him sick. I dragged his limp form away from the smoke toward the door, but Stralton's body was in the way, and Phil seemed twice my size.

Cursing, I swept the tea things from their cart and manhandled Phil onto it. Dragging Stralton out of the way, I rolled the cart into the hallway, slammed the door shut, and gasped for breath.

I didn't know what to do next. Phil seemed barely alive, and people would search for Stralton eventually. Soon, if he'd been mentally linked with anyone when he went unconscious. Dead? I hoped so.

I whipped out the map Stralton had given me, thinking it might give me inspiration, but it was blank. I shoved it back into its bag and thought. Cover was the first thing. I remembered a small room nearby that opened on three passageways. When I'd done my imaginary tour, it had been empty. I went that way, praying that the map, when it had existed, had been accurate, and that the room was empty today as well.

It was—both there and empty. I wheeled Phil in and sang for him. I couldn't sense any injury, only exhaustion, but that was so intense, I'd never be able to sing him to health, not unless I was standing in Glimmer Lake water.

That was an idea. The map had been fuzzy near Glimmer Lake, but Straltia had suggested it was in a natural cave. Caves nearly always had more than one entrance, which was all to the good, and if Straltia had been telling the truth, the fairies didn't go down that way much, so we were less likely to inadvertently meet people on the way out. Still, I couldn't count on going unnoticed. I chanted our invisibility and shield chants.

Then, tired, but anxious to get away, I cautiously peeked out the western door of the room, which led toward a way with fewer steps. Seeing no one there, I wheeled Phil out. He didn't look comfortable draped over the tea cart, but it couldn't be helped.

By my reckoning, we were three levels above and four long passageways to the east of the entrance to the lake. The first passageway was empty and easily navigated, but I worried about the stairways. I could imagine myself trying to bump the cart from step to step, vainly attempting to keep it from tumbling topsy-turvy to the bottom, but I had to try.

I got in front of the cart and edged it warily over the top step, but even though I was careful, I lost control and slipped backward. I fell two, no three, steps, with Phil and the cart tangled on top of me.

"Stop!" I said, trying to regain my balance. I grabbed the wall. It was good I did, for a wave of exhaustion hit me, and I needed the support to stand. What was going on?

Just above the level of the stairs, the tea cart, with Phil on top, gently levitated. I gasped. I must have spoken Fairy. I hoped I had enough energy left to get the cart down to the lake.

I started down, pulling the cart after me with my left hand while I leaned on the wall with my right. At first, I moved slowly, afraid it would all come crashing down. Soon I gained confidence and moved faster—as fast as I could given how tired I was.

The second passageway was as empty as the first, so I stopped to catch my breath. Fear kept me from lingering long, though.

I navigated the second stairway easily enough, now that the tea cart was enchanted. My heart hummed. Fear? Exertion? Maybe both.

This good fortune couldn't last.

Nor did it. Up ahead, in a curve of the third passageway, stood a young fairy. I sucked in my breath as quietly as possible and shoved the tea cart into an alcove under a window. The figure must have heard us. It was coming toward us. Then I realized it didn't need to hear us. It was Straltia and she could read our thoughts.

Straltia raised her hand. Sparks of light flickered out of it toward us.

The sparks bounced off our shield, around the little alcove and back toward Straltia. They sputtered and fizzled out before reaching her. Seeing this, Straltia crumpled on the floor, crying.

"Straltia," I said.

The girl cried harder. If she kept making this much noise, others were sure to come.

"Straltia," I started again.

"I can't do anything right," Straltia sobbed.

"Come on, now," I said. "You did a good job of—"

"No, It's like he said. I'll never be more than a brainless pretty face."

So, she'd heard that. He must have meant her to hear it, the jerk. What a way for a man to behave—disowning his daughter, insulting her, sending her off to get beat up in the kitchens—

"It's not like that," Straltia said, controlling her sobs.

"You mean he didn't deny you were his daughter?"

"Well, he did, but—"

"Or call you and your mother stupid?"

"But we are—or at least, I am."

"Or keep you in the kitchens even though you hated it?"

"There's nothing wrong with—"

"Hogwash. His behavior has been worse than lousy toward you. It's time you stop making excuses for him."

"But I killed him."

"No, Phil did. You even tried to warn him, and he wouldn't listen to you."

"I should have told him before," she whispered. "I knew you didn't believe him, that you were planning to hurt him, but I didn't tell him. I hid some of what you were thinking, so that he wouldn't find out you'd guessed I was listening to your thoughts for him. I was afraid of what would happen to me if he knew."

"He would punish you for that?"

"Naturally! Incompetence can do more damage than rebellion."

"Where did you get that?"

"It's in our primer. We all have to try our best for the motherland. His Lordship cannot afford to tolerate stupid mistakes."

"His Lordship would be in a lot better shape now if he'd been a bit more tolerant, I'd say."

Straltia sobbed again.

I wasn't sure what to do. The girl needed to cry, but I had to get out of there.

"I can't let you go," Straltia said through her sobs. "They'll kill me anyway, but if I've let you go…"

I chanted to knock her out.

Straltia gaped and then crumpled to the floor. She really wasn't any good at blocking or sending spells.

I wheeled the tea cart back out of the alcove, but when I was even with Straltia, I stopped. The girl was probably right about being killed if she let us go. If she was frightened enough to lie and flub up her job because I'd figured out (after a significant period of time) that she was doing it, who knew what they'd do to her for this kind of disaster?

Hoping I wasn't making a dreadful mistake, I bent down, hoisted the limp fairy up next to Phil, and continued down the corridor.

The final stairs were empty, and I dragged us all down them. Fortunately, the tea cart, even with two passengers, only needed a light touch.

The last passage appeared long disused. I didn't see any fairies but felt the strange panic that had come before the ambush on us at the protective wall. There was nowhere to go but forward, now, though. I'd never manage a fight if I couldn't get to the water.

A great wrought-iron gate at the end of the passage that led down to the lake was locked, but with my fear a palpable thing in my throat, words came to me. It unlocked. Once we were all inside, I shut the gate behind us. The lock clicked, but my fear didn't abate.

Exhaustion set in, but panic made me ignore it. I forced myself down a sloped stone corridor that looked like it would lead to a dungeon, pushing the cart ahead of me. Could this be the right path to the lake? I hoped so.

The cart left thin tracks in the dust, but I had neither the time nor the energy to fix them.

I'd passed the third turn in the slope when the lights suddenly went out. I sang the light song I'd used in the owl cave and went on, pushing myself to run. Too bad I'd never wanted to go out for cross country. I could use the training in getting more out of myself when I was about ready to fall down.

Far behind me, I heard a soft cry, and my fear jumped to a new level. I ran faster.

Then I was there.

The path opened out into such a fantasy world of abstract shapes and clear, clean water, that for a moment I forgot everything else. I'd heard of underground lakes before, but never pictured one like this. The place was huge, glowing with an inner radiance. Pearly mountains and trees grew up from the floor in twists and surreal curves to meet inverted cones from the ceiling. Then there was the lake. It stretched as far as the eye could see, flickering with myriad colors. I hadn't noticed that in my bath.

A sound behind me recalled my wandering mind. I wasn't sure where to go, but I supposed the water was the safest place. About five-hundred yards out from the shore was something that looked like a boat. I didn't know if it was really a boat or just some kind of rock formation, but it was as good a spot to aim for as any. If I remembered this water right, there was no point in dallying. I waded in, pulling the cart behind me and grimacing at the sting on my feet and calves.

I hoped it would float, but it didn't. That meant I'd have to swim out to the boat dragging the cart's passenger's one at a time. I'd get Phil out first. I hoped there'd be time to come back for Straltia.

I pushed the cart back out of the water and unloaded it.

Then, holding Phil under his arms, I dragged him into the water. By the time it was chest deep, I felt sure my skin was being taken off. This was much worse than the bath.

Pulling Phil through the water took almost total concentration. There was no energy leftover to sing with, but perhaps once at the boat I could wake him.

I wasn't even halfway there, though, when Phil started to struggle. I let him go, and he floundered in the water, coming up gasping. "What? Where?"

"Glimmer Lake. Invigorating, isn't it? Can you swim?"

"Yeah," he gasped.

"Make for that boat thing." I pointed out my goal. "I've got to go back for Straltia."

He goggled at me, but ignoring him, I headed for the shore.

Straltia was still unconscious. The feeling of fear was so strong on the shore that I lost no time pulling her into the water. Invigorating was not the word I'd use for it now. More like painful.

Straltia was lighter than Phil, and this time I chanted protection spells as I swam.

Halfway to the boat, I saw fairies in the cave. Even if they couldn't see me, they were bound to know where I was. I'd been making plenty of noise.

Brilliant flashes of blue and green flew out over the water, displaying the cave in gleaming splendor, but doing nothing to Straltia or me. I hoped my chants would work equally well for Phil though he was farther away.

More flashes came. I swam harder.

The fairies reached the shore and yelled at each other. My progress felt interminably slow. The fairies' argument brought them closer and closer to the water's edge. It looked like they were trying to persuade two of the group to come in after us.

I wanted to go faster but couldn't. The water burned into me. I didn't know how I was going to get Straltia over the last two-hundred yards or what we'd do once I had.

I was ready to cry when Phil appeared at Straltia's other side and helped me pull. The extra power sped us up considerably, but we still had a hundred yards to go when two fairies were thrown into the water and kicked away from the shore. The two unencumbered fairies were faster than we were but hadn't caught us before we reached the boat. It was a real boat, smooth and shell purple.

We heaved Straltia in and clambered up behind her. Now if only we could find some way to make it go. The two swimming fairies were within twenty-five yards. Phil played with a bunch of knobs near the boat's font, but I closed my eyes and concentrated. Words came to me, and I sang.

The nearest fairy was five yards off when the boat started noiselessly, smoothly away.

An angry cry rang out behind us but quickly faded into the distance. My fear dropped back to a normal level. I was soaked, my skin burned, and I was cold, but for the time being, we were safe.

CHAPTER 36

Phil was chanting something, I scarcely paid attention to what. I was busy catching my breath. The boat we'd found (much too conveniently if I thought about it) was the size of a small yacht and lined with benches piled with large, firm, purple and white silken cushions. I leaned back in them, causing water marks to form on the silk.

At first, I enjoyed watching the glowing natural structures zipping by. After a while, though, I was too cold to sit comfortably. I sat up and glanced around me. There was a little cupboard built into the bench I was sitting on. It opened easily to my touch to reveal large fluffy white towels and robes.

Phil wasn't looking my way, so I slipped one of the robes on and took off the clothes underneath, hanging them over the side of the boat near the back where it was high enough they wouldn't drag in the water.

Straltia still slept in the bottom of the boat. I tried to arrange her more comfortably and covered her with a couple of the giant towels. I hoped that would keep her warm enough.

"Toss me one of those, would you?" Phil said. He'd finished whatever he was chanting and looked gray about the mouth. I wondered how bad he was feeling. I tossed him a towel and a robe, and then turned while he dried off.

"Thanks," he said after a while. "You can turn if you want to."

I did. We stared at each other for a minute. The silence grew awkward.

"So," Phil said.

"So."

"Is he dead?"

"Straltia seemed to think so."

There was another silence.

"You knew that would happen," he said.

"Yes."

"So, you trusted me."

"No. I knew Stralton was lying, and I could see he was truly our enemy. I didn't—don't—know what to think about you. I wanted him destroyed."

Phil bit his lip. "What did he tell you?"

"That all spring and summer you've been cultivating a relationship with me, so I'd help the War Party. That's the part most likely to be true. He also said your party had some kind of arrangement with Islandia before the dance, and that the Islandian fairies have deceived you—deceived all of us—to get us to join the war against him under false pretenses."

"That's ridiculous!"

"Maybe. There were some facts in there. The way you pushed for me to vote with you on those youth clubs going to fight during vacations. And the visas for Islandian fairies."

"You were pushing pretty hard the other way if I remember correctly. What kind of relationship would we have if we never talked politics? Politics is our lives."

"I'm not saying we should never talk politics, but Stralton made a pretty convincing argument that it's the only thing you want to talk about."

"No, Sarah. I love talking with you about all kinds of things."

"You'd told me you would never spend time with me if you didn't have to. And I'd seen you tell your parents you'd cultivate a relationship with me for political ends."

"But that was taken out of context, even altered!" Phil stopped and sighed. "But I see what you mean. Even the most bizarre fantasy can seem plausible if you're psychologically ripe for it, and this isn't all that strange."

"I guess I was primed."

"Still, he attacked us. He kidnapped us. I'd think you'd naturally mistrust what he said."

"Yes, but he'd been muddling my mind since I woke—magically messing with me, I think. Plus, he showed me some amazing things, and he argued even more smoothly than you do. When he claimed he was forced onto our land by Islandia, and that Islandians had kidnapped us, I wasn't sure at first what was true."

"Were the owls supposed to be Islandian too?"

"Sheer accident. The beast got us in the ordinary course of its hunting. Oh, I know it's weak, but my head was all foggy, and those two guys who overtook us had worn Islandian markings. After all, we don't know Islandia that well. I was confused. I thought we might have made a mistake about them. I don't know, Phil. It sounds lame when I explain it now, but it seemed reasonable in there with him. I couldn't think straight."

"How did you figure out the truth?"

"He said Steph was plotting with the War Party against me."

"Stephanie Montressor?"

"Yeah."

"That girl told me that if I hurt you, she would beat me up herself."

I laughed. "Even my dad doesn't mention doubts about her anymore. I don't know what the man was thinking. Maybe he never had a real friend."

"He didn't deserve one."

"Probably not. Anyway, I knew what he said about Steph couldn't be true, and then I started seeing other holes in his story. When I said I was going to ask you about his accusations, he offered to come along and make you tell the truth. I remembered what Darvian said might happen if he tried to make you do anything—that he might lose power or even die. I figured that would be a great idea, and I didn't think about how it might affect you. I was so scared when you two were locked together in that crazy stare."

"You did the right thing, Sarah. I'm fine."

"But I didn't know that. I should have thought more. Though I was trying not to think too much, so he wouldn't figure out my plan. I'm still not sure why he didn't realize it was a trap, that he couldn't influence you. They were reading our minds pretty freely."

"The Islandian fairies put some special blocking spells on that information, strong ones that Stralton probably couldn't even tell were there. They're good at that sort of thing. They've had a lot of practice protecting their minds from Stralton."

"Ah, well, he didn't seem to know, so I thought it was worth a try."

"Remind me not to get you seriously pissed at me."

"By, say, agreeing to be friends with me so you can talk shop? Or claiming to like me while you tell all your real friends you only hang out with me because you have to?"

Phil looked down. "You're right. I've been a jerk. If I had half your guts, I'd have told my parents where to get off and Jennifer Lowell what I really think, which is that you're intelligent, beautiful, resourceful, incredibly brave, and refreshingly honest. You're loyal to your friends and basically fair to your enemies. I respect you and trust you and am afraid I'm falling in love with you, but if I told Jennifer that, she'd flounce out and tell all her girlfriends, not to mention the press. Then my parents would be furious, and there'd be reporters to deal with. What can I say? I'm a wimp."

Had he actually said he was falling in love with me? My heart lurched. I'd once said that if he ever tried anything like this, I would treat him the way my father treated his father. When I'd first seen the crystal ball, I'd meant to stay mad at him. Now I realized that wasn't what I wanted after all. The relationship we'd had this spring and summer was worth too much for me to throw it overboard even if Phil was using me some. It wasn't as bad as I'd originally thought, anyway. If he was to be believed, he'd told his parents he'd try to persuade me but wouldn't do anything sneaky, and he hadn't. I drew in breath slowly. "I forgive you, and I'm sorry for believing, however briefly, that you are only my friend for political reasons."

Phil laughed. "You apologize for the most stupid stuff, you know it?"

My face grew hot, and I looked down. We were silent again.

For the third time, Phil broke the silence. "Where in the world are we going, and who is this girl we've brought along?"

I'd forgotten about Straltia and the boat. Where was it taking us? It was going awfully fast, but I couldn't slow it down or stop it. I'd come up with words to make it go, but now nothing came to mind even when I tried for it. Phil tried all the knobs and buttons again. We discovered a small compartment with bread and flagons of some gold liquid. Another held dishes, a third held blankets, and a fourth, books—leather bound, gold embossed books, written in fairy. None of the knobs or dials controlled our speed or steered the boat.

"Great," Phil said. "We could be heading for anything."

"And they probably know we're coming."

"I suppose we could jump out."

"Not without hurting ourselves. We're going too fast. Besides, where would we go?"

The lake stretched as far as we could see in every direction.

Straltia was another problem. I wasn't sure how long the knock-out spell would last, but not forever. When Straltia awoke, who knew what she'd do? Try to kill us again, I suspected. I didn't want to keep knocking her out, though. "So, this is Straltia. She's Stralton's daughter, I think. Stralton brought her in to babysit me and report on what I was thinking once one of my songs blocked him from my mind."

"Nice one. The song didn't stop her getting into your head, though?"

"Nope. But she messed up. When I realized Stralton was lying about Steph, she thought it was shock—and he missed my mood shift. That gave me the opening to trick him into challenging you. She was upset about it. Tried to kill us."

"So, why'd you bring her?"

"Well, she's been a friend, and they're going to blame her for what we did and probably torture her before they kill her. Besides, she can't really defend herself. Her spells are pitiful. We won't be in any danger."

"If she's going to try and kill us, we may as well get it over with. Why don't you wake her up? I would, but I'm tuckered out after the chants I did to block Stralton's influence spells. I'm actually surprised I was able to do so much. In Islandia, I was always done for after a lot less than I've done today."

"Is that what you were chanting? What a great idea! I suspect it was the lake water that gave you the power. That's why I brought you down here in the first place. When I had a bath in it, I could do more songs and chants. You were too far gone for me to help in the normal way. Maybe if you splash more water on you, it will make you feel better."

He raised his eyebrows, but leaned over the side of the boat and scooped some water up with a pitcher while I bent over Straltia and sang a healing song.

Straltia came to with a jolt, sitting upright and glancing wildly about. "Where am I?"

"I'm not completely sure," I said. "On Glimmer Lake."

"I haven't been in the water, have I?" Straltia gasped.

"Well…"

"Please tell me I haven't been in the water."

"We had to go in. We were being chased. There was no other way to escape."

Straltia looked around. "You mean you went in voluntarily?" She laughed hollowly. "Of course, you did. I'd told you it was cleansing. He told me to."

"Stralton? Why?"

"It makes you tell the truth," Straltia said, her eyes wide.

I choked back a laugh. What was so wrong with that?

"He could have learned that I didn't like him much, though he was my father. After what he did to my mother…" She covered her mouth with her hand. Her eyes grew wider.

"What did he do to your mother?" I asked as gently as I could.

"He killed her," she said softly. "He showed me after I, after I…"

"Tried to keep him from going with me to see Phil."

"Yes."

"I'm sorry."

"She was in pain and begging him to stop it, and he killed her. He said he'd give me to one of his men who'd do the same to me. Still, I wanted him to live. I tried to avenge him. I would have killed myself for feeling how I feel now. I can't believe I'm not more upset with myself."

At least Phil's chants had done that much good.

"Phil's chants?"

I wished Straltia wouldn't walk in and out of my brain like that. "He said some chants to break Stralton's spells of influence when we first got into the boat."

"I said a bunch in the water while you were going after her, too," Phil said. He had slapped some of the Glimmer Lake water on his face and was looking much better.

"You mean…"

"How else could he have kept you loyal to him while treating you so badly?"

Her eyes filled with tears. "It's my fault. I'm so bad at everything."

"Nonsense," I said. "You're very good at mind reading, and he was quick to use that when it suited him."

"It is his right to make use of whatever small talents his subjects have."

"My father and King Randolph are both kings, and I can't imagine either of them treating an unpromising puppy as badly as your father treated you."

Straltia bowed her head. "I'm still sorry he's gone. Glad and sorry both."

I reached out and held her hand. I didn't know what to say, so we sat in silence. Straltia wept softly. Phil edged back into his cushions as if trying to look inconspicuous.

After some time, Straltia wiped her eyes with one of the large towels, gave us a watery smile and said, "Any idea when we reach Dimthorn Harbor?"

CHAPTER 37

"Dimthorn Harbor?" Phil and I asked at the same time.

"Well, I assume so. That's where the old ferries docked."

Phil and I exchanged a glance. "We're going to another city in Stralton?" Phil asked.

"I don't know of any other exits on the lake, and the ferries are reputedly terribly difficult to stop. In the old days, it prevented people from stopping short without paying."

"So, there'll be a welcome party waiting for us," Phil said.

"A welcome party? I hardly think…" Then Straltia seemed to pick up on his real meaning. "Ooh. And I'm no good in a fight. The fairy my father planned for me will get me after all."

"Not if we can help it," Phil said. "How long does this trip take?"

"It used to take about four hours, I think," Straltia said. "But, no one's done it in hundreds of years. They destroyed all the docks on the Stralton City side of the lake early on since Dimthorn Harbor was an Islandian holdout until a hundred and fifty years ago. Most of the ferries were destroyed too, though the Harbor people kept sending out new ones, I can't think why. The boats stopped farther and farther from the shore until they could no longer be destroyed without someone spending great amounts of time in the lake. No one wanted to do that." Straltia shuddered.

"Unless they were escaping," I said.

"But the water makes you…"

"Tell the truth?" I asked. "If you're in the habit of doing that, it's not much of a sacrifice."

"Let me guess: when you jumped in, you didn't even notice the difference?" Phil asked.

"I noticed that I could say chants all day long without losing energy. If we make a dive for the water once the boat slows and do a couple of chants, maybe we could sneak ashore somewhere away from the city."

"Hmm," Phil said.

"I can't get in that water," Straltia said.

"Come on, Straltia," I said. "You've been thoroughly dunked once, and what have we found out? That your father was a jerk, and you had trouble liking him. It wasn't much of an eye-opener. Even if you repeat the same story to one of your father's lieutenants, he won't learn anything he didn't already know."

"And I couldn't be in much worse trouble than I'm already in."

I smiled. "That's the spirit."

✷✷✷

In the end, we didn't jump because we were asleep. It came on suddenly. By our calculations, we had about half an hour before the trip's end. I'd stopped staring at the cave and rainbow-flecked water long enough to change back into my clothes. They were damp and clammy, but I figured I could live with that since they'd soon be dripping again.

I'd settled back against the cushions when suddenly, for no reason, I was fighting sleep. I started to sing a song to fight the feeling but had no more than half a bar out before I succumbed.

I awoke to the sound of a trumpet fanfare and laughter. A dozen surprisingly gentle hands lifted me from the boat. Phil was being lifted onto the shoulders of a couple of young, brown-haired fairies. "Behold!" someone shouted. "The lad who set us free!" Cheers erupted.

I was about to go after Phil when I heard a couple of voices beside me.

"Who's that with them?"

"One of his children."

"Easily enough dealt with since she still sleeps," said the first voice.

"No!" I shouted, twisting free of an arm that held me and chanting a protection spell as I threw myself on top of Straltia.

The hands lifting me were firmer the second time, but I resisted them, pushing the boat away from the dock and singing new words that came to mind. The boat pulled away from the dock suddenly enough to send five fairies splashing into the water. A sixth landed in the boat with me. I started my knock-out chant but couldn't finish after that fairy caught me by the throat. I choked for breath and became dizzy. Blackness swam before my eyes, but I fought it.

"Don't hurt her," Phil yelled. "Don't hurt either of them."

The fairy choking me waved a hand toward me, and the world went completely black.

When I woke, I was in bed, still wearing the purple tunic, though now it was warm and dry. Phil sat on a chair by the bed, his face uncommonly serious.

"Straltia?"

"In one of the prisons. The Harbor people had intended to kill her but refrained since she's under our protection. They won't let her stay, though. When we go, she has to go."

"Why?"

"Because she's Stralton's child. The Harbor people had some bad experiences with Stralton's children. One betrayed them to give the city over to Stralton."

"Oh."

"Islandia won't take her either, so if you don't want her killed, she'll have to come with us."

"Do you think she'll like Dicrandia?"

"I imagine she'll get along fine if we can convince my dad to let her stay."

"And mine." I closed my eyes. "With all the Islandians advising against it. What a mess."

"Sarah?"

I didn't like the grimness in his voice. I opened my eyes.

"I don't know how to tell you this."

I sat up, fear growing inside me.

He fiddled with the fringe on my blanket.

"Just say it."

"Your father is dead."

I laughed, harshly. "You're joking."

"No. It happened three days ago. There was an attack on Bentralia itself. A dragon. A battalion of fairies. We'd lost a lot of ground."

"No."

"We were running out of chanters fast, and your dad went out to shore them up. Turned the tide. They beat the dragon and were pushing back the fairies when the whole spur of the attack changed. They went for him personally. Materialized around him and beat down his guards."

"No," I said again.

"Our people killed most of them, but it was too late. Your father was already dead."

I got up and pushed him away. I walked to the window. It was a small aperture that opened on the sea. The waves billowed up on rocks, but I hardly saw them.

"I'm so sorry, Sarah," Phil said.

I don't know how long I'd stood there, staring at the sea, when Phil said, "I hate to interrupt your thoughts, but—"

I turned, horror rising in my gut. "There's more?"

"No, no. It's just that we're going home tonight, and there are a few other things you should probably know."

"Oh." I tried to listen to Phil explain how the fairies meant to take us home—out to sea and around the whole continent to avoid walls and Stralton's armies.

"They won't let our parents meet us, something about tightened security, but we'll have other relatives there."

Other relatives. When the only person I wanted to see right now was my mom.

Phil reached out a hand. I put mine into it, and he squeezed. "Is there anything else?" I asked.

"Well, there's some other news, not half bad news, actually." Phil told me about the war—how since my father's death it had been going better for us. Stralton's forces were back to the Northwest. We had hope of ousting them by Yule.

He also knew what had happened to our guards and Gen. A bunch of Islandian fairies had rescued the guards who had formed the diversion, and it was they who'd been pursuing us over the downs, hoping to catch us and take us home.

They'd found Gen, Clare, Snypes, and Percy the day after the owl attack and returned all the humans to Bentralia. They'd even gone back, at some risk, for Lewis's body.

They hadn't known how to rescue Phil and me and distrusted Stralton's plan to return us. If he allowed us to go home, they expected that I would be brainwashed, and they had warned the government to be wary of both Phil and me if Stralton released us.

I listened, but only half heard. I stored the words, but they didn't penetrate. I was empty except for one thought—Phil must be wrong about my dad. There had to be a mistake. Dad couldn't be dead.

At last Phil stopped talking. The room was silent. A gull, far out over the surf, screamed.

"That's it, I think," Phil said.

"I nodded.

He squeezed my hand. "I really am sorry about your dad," he said, his voice a bit broken, sort of pleading. "At least the rest of it is good news."

A detached part of my mind, like a computer, scrolled up the things he had told me, ticking them off one by one—good, good, good. He was right. Apart from my father's death, the news was good. "Yes," I said, my voice sounding far away.

"I don't know what to say, Sarah," he said, his voice cracking. "I'm truly sorry."

"That's kind of you," said the voice I knew was mine. It was an automated response coming from a half-remembered time of black clothes and funeral flowers.

"Do you want to be alone?" Phil asked.

"I don't know."

He stayed, sitting quietly, holding my hand, waiting, perhaps, for me to talk, but I had no words.

The sun flamed red over the sea, and darkness came. Several fairies entered, their clothes bright, and said it was time to go. As we passed into the hall, I could hear snatches of song and the clinking of glasses.

I remembered the moments when my body had left my control to follow Stralton's will, and even in my emptiness, I understood a bit of the intoxicating joy that filled the air around me. It did not enter me, but I understood it.

Phil could easily have been out here, laughing with these people, rather than in a silent room with me. The mechanical, ticking part of me noted that I should feel grateful, but I'd lost the ability to feel.

Straltia was brought out in chains.

"Where do you wish to go?" A fairy in deep purple asked her. "You cannot stay here nor enter Islandia proper."

Straltia stared at her feet. "Anywhere but back to Stralton."

"She shall come with us," Phil said, "at least for now. We will discuss with my father how long she may stay when we get there."

The fairy in purple gave us a thin smile and bowed. "Farewell, then."

There was an odd feeling of nothingness, and then a glimpse of a lush, marshy island, then nothingness again, then a tropical, sweet-smelling place, then nothingness, then a hot, arid place, then nothingness, then a rocky wind-swept shoreline with a crowd of people, Uncle Maurice and Grandma standing in front.

A large man in the uniform of a War Palace guard rushed forward. Phil barely had time to squeeze my fingers one last time before the man threw an arm around Phil's shoulders and whisked him out of my sight.

Uncle Maurice wrapped me in a bear hug and then gave way for my grandma, who held me tightly, tears flowing down her face. My eyes were dry.

I felt only emptiness.

CHAPTER 38

om and Steph were together in my mother's wing when I arrived in the capital. They'd arisen as one when I came into the room. I could barely stand the pain in my mother's eyes, but I went to her and held her. Mom cried.

I told them everything in the far-off voice that didn't seem like mine. I told about Stralton and the aersyla, about the lies, Straltia, and Stralton's contest with Phil.

I told them about the dream visit from Dad, about the emptiness, and about how I couldn't cry.

When I was done, they said nothing, but they hugged me.

Getting back into politics was harder. There were meetings when we first got to town, dozens of meetings. I straightened out tangled problems, made decisions, and answered questions like a machine. With the mechanical, ticking side of my mind, I realized that many of the questions were tests. Was I still the same Princess Sarah who'd left a little more than a week ago?

In my occasional moments of feeling, I felt like yelling, "Of course, I'm not the same, you idiots! My father is dead!" But I couldn't.

A deep empty ache settled in my heart.

I worked later than I needed to, but I hated to be alone at night, staring at the ceiling, unable to sleep, unable to think, unable to cry.

When I did sleep, I dreamed of Stralton, his blue eyes boring into me, burning me. I would wake screaming, knowing that in an apartment across town, Straltia would be awakened.

The fairy wasn't allowed to be with me except for the brief time in the morning when she helped me dress, but it comforted me to know I wasn't alone. Perhaps that was why I didn't insist on immediately building walls that blocked mind-reading. I'd want that eventually, but for now, it was good to be connected.

King Randolph hadn't been happy about Straltia, but I'd argued insistently and well, so Straltia was serving as my lady's maid. She was ridiculously grateful for the job. Perhaps after Stralton's kitchens and horrible little dorms, getting the same wages as Estelle and having a tiny apartment of her own was enough.

Maybe it didn't bother her that King Randolph and others were watching closely for signs that she or other fairies were influencing me.

I saw the traps in questions he asked me at Joint Council. The machine-like ticking part of my mind easily side-stepped them. If I weren't so weary, so empty, I would have enjoyed the game. As it was, the process made me tired.

At least I didn't have to pretend with my mom or Steph.

And they asked me no trick questions.

Mom kept on seeing to it that I ate breakfast and slept occasionally, and Steph went on ordering my days for me. I gave a talk to the staff here. ("Yes, you can rest assured that all will continue, as much as possible, exactly as it has been under my father." Though, I hired Clare back at the first opportunity.) And a press conference there. ("We have every reason to hope that we have turned the corner in our current crisis and will soon be free of the terrible violence of this year.") I went to committee meetings and trainings on how to combat fairy influence spells. I made new songs and chants for the war effort. I worked until I was exhausted, had my nightmares, worked again.

I did not cry.

We'd returned to Dicrandia Saturday night, a week and a day from the time we'd been snatched. My father's funeral was the following Wednesday.

Mother insisted on a new dress for me. It was black velvet and floor length. Straltia piled my hair atop my head, setting in a silver tiara. I wore my dance amethysts.

"You look like a queen," Gen said when she joined us.

"She is a queen," Mom said, her voice low and hoarse.

"It's not supposed to be this way," I said.

***

The body in the box was not my father. It was a lifeless thing, more make-up and chemicals than anything human. I stopped looking at it as soon as I decently could.

There were prayers and a sermon, but I didn't really hear them. I only sat, staring at some goldwork on the altar cloth, wishing I could feel something other than this cold, empty, ache.

The next morning, I woke early. Since I was up anyway, I went to the stables and had the horses saddled. The air was cool. Leaves crunched under the horses' hoofs. The wind stung my cheeks.

On the way back in, I went by the kitchen door. A few voices came from the other side. One was Uncle Malcolm's. I was about to go in when I heard Lord Richter say, "Come on, Malcolm, it's not that far-fetched. You're only fifteen years her senior."

"She thinks me as old as the hills."

"A problem easily overcome. Get a little hair dye. You love the girl, Malcolm. Anyone can see that. And she needs guidance. A strong hand. She can't do this job alone."

I could hardly breathe. Uncle Malcolm? Love me? He was as old…well, over thirty, anyway.

"I'm prepared to give her whatever help she asks for, but I don't want to take her throne from her. And while I do love her, it's not that kind of love."

"Close enough. What are you waiting for? Seriously, Malcolm, you can't let your boyhood ideal of love keep you from your duty to your country."

"What do you know about my boyhood ideal of love? Or my duty to my country?"

"Please. Everyone with eyes knows you've been in love with Desmond's queen since you first came to town. It will never happen, lad. Her husband may be dead, but she still loves him, and while you're mooning over the impossible, our Peace Party needs shoring up. Did you see the way Randolph drubbed the child on Thursday? She barely fought back."

I tiptoed away. Had King Randolph drubbed me on Thursday? Perhaps, but I hadn't really been fighting since I'd felt the measures he wanted were necessary. Of course, I could use more help from Uncle Malcolm. He understood the government better than I did. I didn't want him to do my job for me, though, and I didn't want to marry him.

Especially if—but that was silly. Surely, I'd have noticed if he was in love with my mom.

If I didn't want to be railroaded into a weird relationship with Uncle Malcolm, I'd have to do something. Already, I'd been placed next to him at dinner twice this week. I was scheduled to dance with him at the Harvest Festival in a few weeks, too. The opening dance there was supposed to be with one's consort. People would be watching closely for some clue—after all, since my father was now dead, the law said I had to marry as soon as I turned eighteen. I imagined that people would realize Uncle Malcolm was too old for me, but now it seemed that dancing with him would be tantamount to handing over my crown. I wasn't ready for the responsibility, but it was mine.

"You look worried," Clare said as I came back into the tower bedroom.

"Nothing big." The problem nagged at me as I showered, though. It kept at me as Straltia did my hair and as I sat through my morning round of meetings.

When I called Steph at noon to reconfirm my tutoring sessions—I wouldn't have time in my new schedule to return to high school—I told her that Uncle Malcolm should no longer be seated next to me at meals. "And I need a new dance partner for the Harvest Festival."

"Why? What's Lord Fitch done to you?"

"Nothing, but some influential party members think he should marry me to make sure the government remains in capable hands."

"You're kidding."

"No. I don't want to lend any credence to the rumors."

"OK. I'll see what I can do, but I don't know what we're going to do about the dance. Every suitable guy I know is at the front."

"I can dance with my grandma's friend Daley if necessary. So long as it's not Uncle Malcolm."

"That might work for the dance, but you need to start dating soon if you're going to get comfortable enough with someone to marry within the next two years."

"I'm not much in the mood for romance."

"Still…"

"I know."

✱✱✱

Two weeks later, I holed up in my bedroom scanning carton after carton of files on the kingdom's eligible young men. Somehow, word had leaked out that I was doing this, and every Peace Council member had filled in a few forms on sons, nephews, cousins, and young friends. I couldn't talk about the search but found myself writing it all down in a letter to Phil. I even sealed and addressed the letter, though I wasn't sure I'd send it. Phil could so easily use something like that against me.

Then I went down late to a Peace Council meeting, where I made up for my tardiness by presenting a complete proposal for recovery in the capital and surrounding counties. I'd had to do this from scratch since Dad hadn't known of the problems before he died, and there were none of his notes to guide me. Gen had researched like a maniac, and I'd searched out good advice. I felt good about it, and my Council had been impressed. They'd get my plan passed.

I tossed the letter to Phil. But when Uncle Malcolm shied away from me after the meeting, I decided to attack the boyfriend problem again.

This time I had the cartons of files sent to the dollhouse, thinking it might help me to focus. By canceling a meeting and a couple of classes, I freed a few hours after lunch. When I got to the dollhouse, I told Clare to let friends in, but to keep members of the Peace Council out unless there was a national emergency. Then I settled down to work.

I had sifted through about fifty files, discarding all but three when the door to the dollhouse slammed open.

"Hey, Sarah," someone shouted.

My head jerked up.

Phil stood in the doorway. I'd forgotten I'd given him permission to come here whenever he wanted.

"What are you doing? This is your secret place! I don't care how busy you are, you shouldn't be doing work here."

"I—"

"What is this stuff that's so important anyway?" Phil snatched up one of the files, opened it, and blanched.

"Phil—"

"You're shopping for a boyfriend?"

I laughed nervously.

"Is there one of these with my name on it?"

"Phil…"

"Here, I'll fill one out for you. Name: Phillip Randolph Wellington Davenport Quinlan Castanay. Age 18. Political Experience: Second in command of the War Party, full, voting Joint Council member for six years. Hobbies: Mountain climbing, dragon killing…"

"Phil," I laughed. "this is serious."

"So am I," he said, scooting down onto one of the trestle benches and reaching for my hand. "Don't you want to date?"

I pulled my hand away. "You know I do, Phil, but I haven't got time to just date. They're making me get married within two years."

"You think I don't know that?"

"Phil…"

"What?"

I looked him in the eyes. Such gorgeous blue eyes. I knew they weren't as deceptive as Stralton's, but could I trust them? "Not two months ago, you wouldn't admit to either the media or your friends that we liked each other, and you haven't stood up to your parents on much of anything, ever, Phil, including our relationship."

"That was before Stralton, Sarah. We've been through a lot together."

That was true enough.

"I don't want to throw it all away," he said.

"If we do this, it'll have to be open from the beginning, and I'll want someone along for political conversations, at least at first."

"You think we need a chaperone?"

"Politically, yes."

"You don't trust me."

"Not completely. Not yet. Are you still interested in dating, under those terms?"

"Have I got time to think about it?"

"A couple of weeks, maybe."

✳✳✳

The Saturday of the Harvest Festival broke cool and fresh. The ornamental maple in the courtyard had turned bright red overnight.

That afternoon, I dressed in my silver dance dress. I hadn't wanted to get another new formal. Straltia piled up my hair.

Someone knocked on my door.

"Come in."

It was Uncle Malcolm. "You look stunning," he said.

"Thank you."

"I notice I've been replaced as your dance partner tonight."

I smiled at him. "I accidentally overheard your conversation with Lord Richter a few weeks ago."

Uncle Malcolm smiled his familiar crinkly smile. "You don't fancy marrying your old uncle?"

"I don't fancy being babysat."

"No, and your father wouldn't want you to be. He wouldn't have chosen this for you, but he would want you to find your own way through it."

I nodded, swallowing hard.

"I'm sorry I can't be more help to you."

"It's OK, Uncle Malcolm. Really, it is."

✳✳✳

I was scheduled to dance with old Daley, but when the time came, Phil caught my eye. He rose, and I met him halfway, as if we'd planned it.

"May I have this dance?" he asked.

"You're agreeing to my terms?"

He nodded.

"Then yes," I said. "I'd love to dance with you."

I'd need to see about a chaperone, so I could still do my job and make this work. And there would be a press heyday in a bit. Our parents to deal with. A dozen other worries.

For now, it was home to be in his arms.

I found I could cry.

ACKNOWLEDGEMENT

Books grow slowly, and though writing is often a solitary task, in fact, many people have a hand in giving books life. In the growth of this particular book, I have many, many people to thank.

First of all, thank you, my readers. I deeply appreciate those of you who have stayed with me to this point, and I hope you have enjoyed the journey. I appreciate every reader, but if you left a review (or are about to do so), you have my deepest gratitude. Reviews are a great help to authors, especially ones like me, who are just beginning on their publishing journeys.

I also want to thank the many, many friends and family members who read early drafts of this book. Your encouragement has sustained me, and your insights have made this story better.

My particular thanks go to my critique group, the 93rd Street Irregulars. It is such a pleasure to work with you and to hone our writing skills together.

Of course, I also couldn't have made it this far without the support and indulgence of my husband and children. Thank you for letting me sometimes live almost entirely in the worlds in my mind.

And most of all, I thank Jesus, my God, without whom there would be no stories.

ABOUT THE AUTHOR

R. L. S. Hoff is a writer of mostly young adult sci-fi and fantasy. She lives in a multi-cultural household where she often has to remind one child that he must learn English because it's important for life in the US and the other two children that they must learn Mandarin because it is and always will be their brother's native language.

R. L.S. Hoff and her family live in a just-big-enough house with a messy yard in view of the Rocky Mountains. They keep planning to hike in the hills on weekends, but often get no farther than the park across the street.

When not writing or working at (so far) more profitable gigs, R.L.S. Hoff enjoys reading, gardening, and baking bread.

WANT MORE?

If Anya doesn't marry the guy her parents choose, this generation will be the last with pure-Euros.

She can live with that.

They might not let her.

Leaving Hope by R.L.S. Hoff
Book 1 in the Golden Terrace Colony Series
Available Now

Also, get the latest installment of R.L.S. Hoff's current serial along with occasional book reviews, news about upcoming releases, and bits about R.L.S. Hoff's life, by signing up for her newsletter here:
http://pencilprincessworkshop.com/